EYE FOR AN EYE

EYE FOR AN EYE

ERIKA HOLZER

A Tom Doherty Associates Book
New York

EYE FOR AN EYE

Copyright © 1993 by Erika Holzer

This book is printed on acid-free paper.

A Tor Book
Published by Tom Doherty Associates, Inc.
175 Fifth Avenue
New York, N.Y. 10010

Tor ® is a registered trademark of Tom Doherty Associates, Inc.

Library of Congress Cataloging-in-Publication Data

Holzer, Erika.
    Eye for an eye / Erika Holzer.
    p.   cm.
    "A Tom Doherty Associates book."
    ISBN 0–312–85186–3
    I. Title.
   PS3558.044E96   1993
   813'.54—dc20

                    92–43880
                    CIP

First edition: April 1993

Printed in the United States of America

0 9 8 7 6 5 4 3 2 1

To the victims of crime,
dead or alive.

ACKNOWLEDGMENTS

Thanks are in order:

To Professor Diana de Armas Wilson for this novel's Dante influence. And to my mother, founder, in 1928, of the "Dante Club";

To Clytia Chambers, whose expertise in corporate public relations provided me with indispensable background material;

To my editor, Bob Gleason, who put me through his own version of Dante's Inferno even as he forced me to turn out a much better book;

To Tom and Ralph, who believe in me, and who make the business end of novel writing a real pleasure;

To Maggie Solomon and Stanley and Marie Gray for their loyalty, candor, and unwavering enthusiasm;

To Professor Stephen Cox, whose literary insights—subtle, provocative, wise—have greatly enriched my novel;

To my feline inspirations, Marco and Pola;

And to my first editor and best friend, Hank Holzer.

1

CATALYST

Once the principle of
movement has been
supplied, one thing
follows on after another
without interruption.

—Aristotle,
Generation of Animals

Prologue

Reflections. The diamond at her throat, flashing splinters of orange. The crystal chandelier, out of range of her roaring fire but vibrating with candlelight.

Her tight grip on the telephone? Reflection of a holiday mood gone sour. "Karen, for God's sake," she protested into the phone. "What are you trying to do, scare me to death? Tonight of all nights," she said, willing her voice to turn calm.

"Utter privacy is a mixed blessing. Isn't it?"

"I love it now," she lied. "After three years, even a city dweller gets used to the Westchester woods." But she never had.

"So much crime, these days. It worries me. I was reading—"

"On the West Side of Manhattan, maybe," she cut in, "not out here." But she'd been reading about it, too. Burglars from New York and Jersey heading for the suburbs, looking for bigger game. Burglars with wheels. And what else, guns? Knives?

"Sarah, your alarm system—"

"My security blanket, you mean," she admitted dryly. "We had it upgraded while you were away. It goes off in the police station now. They're on the scene in five minutes, tops. Hold on while I check the roast."

On the way to the kitchen, she glanced in the mirror. The full treatment, she thought, pleased with *this* reflection, at least. Black satin lounging pajamas. Slippers with stiletto-thin heels. Blond hair looking sleek, straight and sexy, just the way Mark liked it.

All's well in the dinner department, she thought, sniffing and prodding, practically sailing back to the living room, her festive mood restored.

"Listen, killjoy," she said, cocking an ear to the phone, "no more raining on my parade, okay? You're supposed to say—"

"Happy anniversary, I know. Don't mind me, dear. Tonight will be very special."

"Starting with my table. Wish you could see it!"

"As exquisite as that? Draw me a picture."

"My centerpiece would knock your socks off—Mark's too, I hope. Masses of tiger lilies, the most glorious shade of orange—"

"In a black vase, of course. What else?"

"Candlelight, crystal, and the good china." She smiled. "Artfully arranged on a lace tablecloth—that wispy, silvery one, remember? Goes with the glasses."

She touched the delicate rim of a smoky, long-stemmed champagne glass. Ran a finger along the intricate pattern of a sterling-silver knife. Picked up the knife just to enjoy the weight of it in her hand. "I even liberated a couple of place settings from the safe-deposit box this morn—"

She could have bitten her tongue.

"Since when do you keep your sterling in the bank? Have there been any burglaries near you? Sarah?"

"Don't be silly. People around here play it safe, that's all." . . . People around here don't want their sterling—not to mention their jewelry—carted off in a pillowcase while they're out to dinner. "What are you sighing about?"

"I just wish Mark didn't take these night classes."

"Mark doesn't *take* them. He's assigned. Besides, I've never minded." Another lie. "Don't start, Karen. You're making me jumpy all over again."

"You're always jumpy on Halloween."

"And you're a big help. Hold on again, okay? I had a hard time getting the fire started and it's looking a bit feeble." Lie number three. She was having a hard time holding her temper.

She took her impatience out on a log that her robust fire didn't need, teetering on the damn high heels as she struggled with the iron tongs, her hair rippling around her shoulders. Like liquid gold, Mark would say. She put the tongs back and gave the radio dial a defiant twist. She said into the phone, "Mood music."

"I can hear the lyrics all the way down here. So could your neighbors if you had any."

"Wise guy. Don't worry, I switch to Brahms the minute Mark walks in the door."

"When *is* he walking in?"

She sighed. "Half an hour, tops. Why don't we play catch-up while we're waiting? Tell me about your presentation. Bet you snared the account."

"Before I even took off my coat."

"They don't pay you enough, you know that? When I think—"

"Boo, Mommy! Boo!"

She whirled around, dropping the phone. Laughed at a small, masked figure in the doorway above. "Only ghosts say boo, darling."

"Oink, oink."

"Thata girl. Now off with Miss Piggy and back to bed."

"Rhyme, rhyme, you owe me a dime!"

"Stop stalling, Susie Woozie. Tell you what. You get *three* dimes for three rhymes. Under the pillow by morning—*if* you're in bed by the count of five. Ready? One . . . two . . . three. . . ."

She retrieved the phone. "Susie's still keyed up. Lots of little trick-or-treaters making house calls earlier."

"Ghost and hobgoblin time. How well I remember."

"You're dating yourself, kiddo. These days, it's characters out of *Star Wars* and the Muppets. Me, I prefer hobgoblins."

"Isn't that your doorbell?"

"What's on the other end of that line, an amplifier?"

"Why would Mark ring? Could he have forgotten his keys?"

"Not likely. Probably some last-minute trick-or-treaters. No home-by-eight in the suburbs. Be right back."

She pressed her face to frosted glass and grinned, feeling like a kid again as she picked out the slightly distorted shapes. Kids draped in sheets, clustering around one little Muppet in green, all of them holding tight to their goody bags.

"Would you believe old-fashioned ghosts outside my door?" she chuckled into the phone. "Takes me all the way back."

"Sarah, maybe you better—"

"One modern touch," she said. "An adorable little Muppet frog. Hang in there while I distribute the loot. Homemade candied apples, this year, if you please!"

She held a silver platter of apples in one hand and, with the other, turned a small key. A chip of light opposite the doorknob went from an unblinking red to bright yellow. She opened the door.

They pushed in on her so that she teetered precariously, almost dropping the platter. "Hey you little roughnecks," she scolded, "I was about to hand you—"

She saw that they weren't so little; only the frog. Seven of them. They fanned out into the foyer, the dining area, the living room. She opened her mouth to yell at them—

She was cut off by a howl. They were howling and whooping! A brown hand flipped the radio dial, turning up the volume.

She took an automatic step backward as a ghost moved in on

her. A denim sleeve shot out from under its sheet and the silver platter shot out of her hand, the candied apples flying.

"What do you think you're doing?" she gasped when she saw where he was headed. He was piling up her silverware! "Don't touch that. Put it back, damn you!"

But he didn't. And then one of them, a ghost like the others but with a black hood, waved the first one away and approached her table, her exquisite table, and she didn't move to stop him because he'd picked up a knife.

A vicious yank of the tablecloth sent her crystal and china to the stone floor with a splintering crash. An overturned vase spilled water, drowning the flame of a candle.

The black hood advanced on her—

And was stopped short by a camera flash. The frog had taken her picture. Black Hood turned away from her, toward the frog. She could almost feel him smiling under his hood—smile for the camera. He stood there holding a knife, waiting for the picture to develop! Instant results from an Instamatic.

Insanity. Her head swayed to the crazy rhythm of it . . . ghosts wearing sneakers and running shoes. Thick denim legs, weaving and bobbing with manic energy. Hands that grabbed, ripped out, piled up, tore through, smashed aside—and stopped, they kept stopping, while a frog took their picture.

She snapped out of it with a jolt. Inching sideways step by invisible step, she moved in the direction of the front door. She was almost there when Black Hood let out a yell. She lunged, her hand snaking out, missing the alarm's panic button by an inch as her heels caught in the doormat.

She went down.

One of them dragged her toward the mess in the dining room.

Water, seeping into black satin. Fabric tearing. And flesh; her thigh, scraping across broken glass.

The howling started up again, turned piercing. It brought her, thrashing, to her feet. Susie! It was less a thought than a silent cry of panic that leapt to her eyes, that sent her glance up three steps to the doorway on the left.

Had he noticed, damn him? He was coming over! She stopped him with her voice. "Jewelry," she said to the one in charge, the one in the black hood. "Up there. The bedroom to the right. My jewels. My husband's. Just open the—"

He cut her off with an imperious wave. Two of them went up without waiting for her to tell them where it was.

But they'd stopped howling. And they'd gone in the opposite direction from Susie.

She listened to the sounds of wanton destruction. Search and destroy. She heard the same sounds behind her, coming from her kitchen. One of them came out of the bedroom with a pillowcase off her bed. She made herself turn away. Another one came out of the kitchen, gnawing on her roast chicken. What turned her legs to rubber was the thought that he had let her see his face. . . .

She backed away slowly as Black Hood came up to her. She knew what he had noticed, this time: the diamond pendant that had been her engagement ring. It rose and fell with her ragged pulse. Too many carats to wear safely in public, she thought with a rush of bitterness as she reached for the clasp and said, "Take it. It's very valuable. Take your loot and get the hell out of my house."

Her hands were still fumbling with the clasp when he ripped her blouse open to the waist.

They came at her like a wolf pack. Her only weapon was a silent litany: Susie, Susie, dear God, let me be quiet for Susie. Her arms were grabbed from behind—Susie. Her legs were yanked up, stripped, pulled apart—Susie, Susie. Her body, slammed against the wet stone floor. A black hood was whipped off.

She stared into utter vacancy. Shuddered at the thin slash of a mouth, at the knowledge that he couldn't be more than sixteen. Gave in to tears because she dared not scream.

The mouth twisted. A hand shot out, knocking her senseless.

Not quite. She felt the tearing pain of forced penetration.

She felt it again. Again. How many more to endure?

"Hey, lookee, a natural blonde!"

They were gloating. Howling. Whooping over her. Someone was protesting, yelling at them to stop—the frog?

She half raised her head in time with a flash of his camera.

Flashing and howling. She was on the verge of howling herself! She was on the brink of unconsciousness. . . .

She was yanked back by a squeal of laughter, an "oink oink."

"Kermit! It's Kermit the Frog!" Then, "Mommy, Mommy!"

Her scream went off like a delayed siren.

When she heard the scream, the telephone clattered to the rug, a strangely muffled sound. She snatched it up again.

"Sarah, in God's name, tell me what's happening!"

No voice to answer her, only the sound of raucous disco and, above it, that weird, repetitive howling. But she'd heard Susie's voice. Babbling about a frog and a—a hermit? She yelled Susie's name into the phone. She yelled for Sarah.

She heard Sarah's voice. She heard her rage.

"No. Don't! Not on my wedding anniversary! You've got the diamond, damn you to hell! What more do you—"

A scream—agonized.

She heard her own scream as she dropped the phone again. Hang up, she told herself. Get help.

But how would she get Sarah back?

She heard the baby crying—so clear, so close to the phone.

"Somebody turn the fuckin' brat off!"

Sobbing—deep-voiced. Sarah? Please God, Sarah?

"We better get outta here!"

"Shut your face and take your fuckin' pictures."

"Hey, anybody want some roast piggy?"

"Put those tongs down! Don't hurt my baby!"

"Leave them alone! Don't hurt them!"

"Shut your face, I tole ya! Wipe those prints, asshole."

"Mommy, Mommy, Mommy!"

"It's all right, darling. Mommy's coming. It's all right."

Sarah. So close she could almost reach through the wire and touch her. "Sarah."

It had come out a whisper.

"Sarahhhhhhhhhhhhhhh!"

"Check the motherfuckin' phone! Hey, man, we got us a snoop!"

"Sonofabitch!"

"—be afraid, Susie darling, it will be all—"

The sound that came through the phone stopped her in midscream. Dry, rasping— She stared at the receiver.

What had she heard?

"You hear that, motherfuckin' snoop? You get yourself a fuckin' earful?"

What she heard then were sharp repetitive cries, a kind of whooping, like Indians on the warpath. Then a click.

She was calm when she got the Bedford police on the line, she would have stayed calm if they hadn't kept badgering her, wasting precious minutes with their questions—who's this calling? where you calling from?—over and over until she had to scream at them to shut them up, she couldn't stop screaming, "I'm her mother!"

Chapter 1

I've never quite approved of the police. They wear their guns too easily on their hips. Show me the regimental blue collar and I see a redneck every time.

That's how I thought of the Bedford police, rednecks. They kept Sarah too long. By the time they released her, it was almost dark. All that time lost. I wanted to drive her into Manhattan, I wanted to be alone with her. Not that Sarah would have regarded her husband and father as intruders, God knows, but I did.

I had the same feeling all morning: their intrusion in the room. Mark, with his ravaged expression, wearing bewilderment like an ill-fitting suit of clothes. Allan, tight-lipped and unwrinkled, determined to be brave. If only I were alone. Alone with my beautiful Sarah.

"It's time, Karen."

I looked up at Allan, looking dignified; impatient. "See what I've done to her gown," I told him stupidly, reaching out to smooth the satin, hating the false look of Sarah's piously folded hands.

Allan grabbed both of mine and pulled me away. "We can't keep people waiting," he said with nervous insistence.

I wanted to hit him. I wanted to pull his tie askew and ruin the part in his neat blond hair. I let him lead me to the door.

My friend Claudia was the first one in; she always manages to be first when you need her. "It's a rotten shame," she said, vehemence in her dark eyes; she'd been crying. "God, what can I say?"

"Don't say anything."

She stood beside me like a sentry while I pressed hands and

nodded gravely at murmured condolences. I felt like a bereaved hostess at a social gathering and, for a moment, I loathed these people, with their muted voices and lowered eyes.

I watched them with Sarah. They looked at her with more than pity and regret. I knew what they were feeling. An embarrassed relief; *their* families were intact. And fear; violence had struck too close to home.

I saw the furtive glances in Claudia's direction. Her puppet-stiff posture told me she'd noticed them, too.

Mark's mother grieved; her eyes were little puff pastries with slits. She kept darting nervous bird-glances at her son as he wandered through the room like the sole survivor of a shipwreck, not so much greeting people as encountering them.

His mother wore unrelieved black—no jewelry, not even her ever-present gold chain. "The city is one thing," I heard her tell an owl-faced man in hushed tones, "but the suburbs?" The man pulled at his earlobe as if he were ringing a bell and muttered something about the inflated value of gold and silver.

Sterling silver . . .

"You going to faint on me?" Claudia sounded alarmed.

"I'm okay," I lied. "I was just remembering something."

Remembering what the homicide detective had told me and Allan: "Your daughter was stabbed from behind. With a table knife. She'd have had a chance if he'd gone for the back or shoulders. See, her bones might have deflected the blade. The killer used a deep forward thrust to penetrate the right side between ribs and flank—"

"I don't know who looks worse, you or poor Mark."

We watched Mark trying to pull the slump out of his shoulders. "He was a bachelor too long," I said softly. "His whole life revolved around Sarah." I frowned, wishing he'd keep his glasses on and stop rubbing the skin between his eyes. It made him seem frail.

Claudia's eyebrow arched. "Here comes Allan's latest."

Blonde in cocktail-party black. I stuck out my hand.

"Hope you don't mind my being here," she said, taking it.

We've been divorced six years. Why on earth would I mind?

I moved on. To friends I hadn't seen since the divorce. Friends I'd seen three days ago. People whose names I couldn't remember. I ran into a fresh round of hushed voices and mumbled condolences, pushing me past the point of endurance—

I fled in the direction of the people I worked with, desperate for the impersonal and the polite, and felt it ease a little, the strain of being a constant object of concern. On any other occasion the presence of my colleagues would have offended my friends—with Claudia at the head of the line. Corporate public-relations people were "damned image makers" who propped up sagging reputations and got people to buy things they didn't need. Not today, though.

I caught her eye. She got the message, mind reader that she was; she went to work on the crowd, coaxing people to the exit.

It hurt me to see the effort it cost her: self-conscious movements as awkward as they were uncharacteristic. She kept running long fingers through her black hair, as if she'd forgotten a comb. This was not an occasion where Claudia cared to stand out.

I stood over the coffin one last time. Lovely, someone had said to me. Peaceful. Nothing so ruthlessly still can be peaceful.

Claudia materialized at my elbow and placed both our hands on top of Sarah's folded ones. She said, "We'll say good-bye together."

The movement disturbed Sarah's hands. Her right hand wasn't folded piously over her left anymore, her left hand wasn't covered up—Behind me, Allan's cry of alarm rose and fell away, merging with Sarah's. . . .

"No. Don't! Not on my wedding anniversary! You've got the diamond, damn you to hell!"

They had cut off her finger. She had tried to save a simple gold band with a sprinkle of diamond chips—her wedding ring—and they had cut off her finger for it.

Allan took my arm and escorted me out of the funeral parlor. We walked through unobstructed space into fresh air, sunshine— flashbulbs in my eyes. I saw a blur of attentive faces.

"They . . . they mutilated my daughter," I told them.

Lowered cameras. Silence. So silent I heard it again, my Sarah's agony. And something more, something worse . . .

What *else* had I heard over the phone?

You hear that, motherfuckin' snoop? You get yourself a fuckin' earful?

"Monsters," I said with a shudder, letting it in for the first time. "They let me hear my daughter's death rattle."

I saw a row of shoulders, stiff with shock. My own were slumped with the small relief of unburdening.

Allan helped me with my coat. His blue eyes were dark with unadmitted pain. Mark looked as if my words, any words, had lost their power to convey meaning.

Someone asked about burial arrangements. "Queens," I choked, starting to cry. "We're going to Queens to bury my daughter."

Allan led me to a waiting limousine. The driver caught my eye, his expression curiously attentive.

I sat between Allan and Mark, fighting claustrophobia and the eerie sensation of being watched by a man in a chauffeur's cap who had eyes in the back of his head.

Whatever was on his mind or in the air didn't affect his driving—fast, but controlled. We lost the funeral procession to traffic. As soon as he pulled up, I went off by myself to wait.

To look into a mocking clear-blue sky—Sarah's eyes. To close my eyes to the rays of the sun . . . and see Sarah's golden hair.

"They'll get away with it."

I turned. The driver held his chauffeur's cap as if it belonged to someone else.

"Monsters, you called them," he said. "We call them savages."

I gave myself time to get a grip on myself. For a moment, I'd felt terror. "We?" I said faintly, keeping my eyes on the cap.

"They'll get away with robbery and gang rape. Mutilation. Even murder. Unless . . . ?" he prompted.

"Unless what?"

"You can fight back. Avenge your daughter. It's up to you."

He was tall, rail-thin, laconic as a cowpoke. Eyes as impenetrable as thick smoke. He had an outdoorsman's bronzed complexion and flat blond hair that was sun-bleached almost to white.

"So you believe in Exodus?" I scoffed. "Eye for an eye, tooth for a tooth—"

"Also Dante. 'O my Leader, the violent death which is as yet unavenged for him by any that is a partner in his shame made him indignant.' We betray the murdered, Ms. Newman, by not taking revenge on the murderer. Keep this," he said, handing me a slip of paper.

With a phone number on it. "Ridiculous!" I snapped.

"Is it?" He stared me down. "Which will win out, I wonder, your sense of the ridiculous . . . or your sense of justice?"

I'd have called a cop if one was within shouting distance.

He showed me his teeth and walked away.

I went looking for Claudia. She stayed with me. Not like a sentry, now; a walking stick. I leaned on her.

Too-erect posture, again. Too stiff-jawed, as if she were ready to ward off blows. A detective investigating Sarah's murder had said to me, "Kids, probably." . . . Black kids, probably. My black friend Claudia—and how many other mourners in the crowd?—would be thinking that.

When they lowered the coffin, my eyes locked with Allan's, willing him to reverse the irreversible, to grab hold of our daughter and pull her out. To make them stop!

In the end I clung to the sight of friendship, to the love and loss standing out on Claudia's face like a bas-relief.

Shovels full of earth. The sound, the crude finality of it, was worse than the sight. My fists clenched in protest. When I opened them, I let go of a crumpled slip of paper . . . and watched as it took its secret to the grave.

I abandoned the limo for a ride back with Claudia. On our way to her car, we passed a jeans and leather jacket crowd: restless, strutting kids with loud mouths and vapid expressions. Just kids, nothing to be afraid of, I told myself, zeroing in on a rugged-looking boy with clean fingernails and curly brown hair.

But, for a moment, I had felt it again. Terror.

I stared out the window, barely aware of trees and houses moving past like the slipped gears of my mind, grateful to be floating above the pain and tension. Except for the clenching and unclenching of my fists. I jammed my hands in my pockets.

And discovered more than the usual. Along with a couple of People Crackers—treats for the inevitable stray cat I'm always running into—I felt something small and square. A business card?

Claudia's eyes strayed from the highway. "What's that about?"

"Haven't the faintest idea," I lied, slipping the card back in my pocket and wondering why I didn't tell her.

Tell her what? That some redneck who looked like a cowboy and talked like a lout had slipped me his . . . calling card?

Some calling card. No name. (He had known mine!) No phone number. Only a two-word message in elegant Gothic lettering. VICTIMS ANONYMOUS.

It had a ring to it.

Chapter 2

Manhattan is full of sirens, an invasion of sounds crisscrossing the sky like searchlights. You learn not to notice.

Unless you're worried about a sleeping child. I got up to check. She hadn't moved, arms wide open to the world, corn-silk hair spread across a pillow shaped like a giant pea pod, with the name "Susie" embroidered in pink. My hands slipped into the automatic motions—tucking in, smoothing down, fluffing up—until I backed away, stung by the cruel trick of a mind slipping into the past. Sarah's baby, not yours. You can't go home again.

Back in the living room, I kept an uneasy eye on the clock. Mark and his night classes. But I was grateful he'd gone back to teaching after putting the country house on the market, that he was staying in New York. His mother's apartment wasn't far from my own. With her away and Mark using the place, it had meant precious time with the baby.

It had meant surviving the last two weeks.

I reached for the papers I'd been pushing aside all evening. What made me look up was the pressure in my head, as if I'd been squeezing words out of a bone-dry part of my brain.

What brought me to my feet were the pictures spread across an entire wall: a family photo gallery. For the last two weeks the wall had drawn me like a magnet. I heard Mark's step in the hall and glanced at a favorite of mine. The camera had captured his characteristic expression of rapturous innocence, a look of happy wonder that rarely goes with a man in his thirties.

It didn't go with the man who walked in the door. Stoop-shouldered, with dark circles like bruises under the eyes, magnified by the wire-rimmed glasses; worse when he took them off.

"I've been thinking about enemies," he said, coming into the living room to take a chair opposite me. "Mine, my little girl's, Sarah's." His eyes roamed the room, sliding off familiar objects—a couch, a painting, a table lamp—as if nothing had the power to hold him more than a few seconds. "Karen, I can't find the enemy, someone to blame. I can't even find a reason. All I have is fear."

"I've been terrified since the funeral."

"Of what?"

I couldn't answer him.

"I'm afraid for Susie. I'm responsible for her." He took off his glasses. "What do I tell her about the world?" he said, trying to hold my glance; failing. "What guarantees can I make?"

His anguish touched off my own. "You have to understand something," I said, shutting out the sight of him. "The moment you give birth to a child, you promise her a contradiction: to give her the whole world, and to protect her from it. Sarah is *my* failed responsibility, Mark. I was forced to break my promise. You won't be."

He crossed the room and cried in my arms.

"New York is Attack City, ladies. Over two hundred violent street crimes a day. It only takes a couple of seconds to lose your life—*or* the life of the person you're with."

Welcome to Angela Russo's Safety in Self-Defense, I thought dourly, arching an eyebrow at our instructor—a retired police-woman of Amazonian proportions. As she launched into the particulars of "hard" versus "soft" martial arts, my attention wandered to a lineup of what looked like sacks of concrete. Punching bags?

I eyed my perspiration-stained leotard in a full-length mirror; a dancer's uniform. And felt like I ought to be wearing camouflaged fatigues, the better to kick, punch and stomp your enemy to death.

I glared at Claudia, across the way. A good workout, she'd assured me—which some of us needed. Low blow, coming from a tall, lithe-limbed ex-dancer when "some of us" barely measure five-foot-three and have to fight borderline-plump all our lives.

The instructor polished off an "attack" demonstration and told us how to knock our assailant off balance by screaming. (The yell of the spirit, they called it.)

I decided to investigate the lineup of "heavy bags." A painfully thin young woman was circling one as if it were human. When she lunged at it, screaming, I grabbed hold of the woman in front of me. "What's the matter with her?"

"Rape victim," she whispered.

As the woman hammered away at a two-hundred-pound bag, she let out a yell: "Kiaiiiiiiiiiiiiiii!" The yell of the spirit?

The bag was still swinging. I marched up to it, my hands balled into fists. I tried to raise my arms. They had turned into two-by-fours, nailed to my sides. I noticed the instructor watching me. And Claudia. I signaled her that I wanted to leave.

Outside, I told Claudia how I'd frozen up. For no reason!

"Maybe you need a shrink," she said, biting her lip.

"Maybe I'm allergic to punching bags."

"Funny. How about lunch? My place or yours."

"How about Mark's? He's home Saturdays with the baby."

We stopped off at a deli for sandwiches, then grabbed a cab. When Mark didn't answer my ring, I used my key. "He likes to nap with the baby," I explained as Claudia headed for the kitchen with the groceries.

I smiled at a familiar sight. Mark sound asleep, the baby cradled in his arms. I picked up a blanket to cover them both and bent to give Susie her "snowflake kiss"—so light it wouldn't wake a sleeping princess.

Her cheek was cold.

I reached out to touch Mark's but my hand shifted toward his mouth. I shouted for Claudia.

"Mark isn't breathing," I said hoarsely when she burst in.

She went to him.

"Susie is cold," I told her, reaching for the baby.

She slapped my hands away.

I slid to the floor and watched Claudia check Susie's pulse, then Mark's. She looked at me and shook her head.

Mark, dead?

"Susie," I whispered, "not Susie. He wouldn't—"

She kept shaking her head.

I stayed on the floor, refusing to be coaxed to a chair or out of the room. I heard every word Claudia said to the police on the

bedroom telephone. I watched her pick some buff-colored enve-
lopes off Mark's bureau. I took the one she handed me.

The doorbell rang. I leaped up, yelling, "Don't answer it!"

Claudia beat me to the front door and the uniforms came
rushing in.

"Don't let them take Susie!" I shouted at her.

"This it?" a voice asked—a cop, holding up a pill bottle.

Claudia nodded and the cop disappeared into the bedroom.

I tried to follow—to stop him—but she held me back, making
soothing noises.

I noticed the buff-colored envelope in my hand. My name was
on it. Mark's forgive-me? I tore it up.

Claudia sat me down. She was crying softly. "They're dead,
Karen. Susie's dead."

I looked at her, my eyes dry. "So am I."

Chapter 3

Three tombstones, now. I stared out the window of a Manhattan
skyscraper as if I were still in Queens; as if I could still see Mark's
coffin being lowered into the ground. And Susie's . . . the obscene
smallness of it.

"It's over," said my boss, Larry, behind me.

I turned. His eyes behind the horn-rims were my favorite color
brown, gold-flecked and warm; wide, now, with concern.

He took gentle hold of my shoulder. "Think you might like to
take some time off?"

A stunning offer from a man devoted to twelve-hour workdays.
He must have heard about my hysterics, guessed about my battle
with depression. I shook my head, backed away a little. "Why
don't you make all these people leave?" He looked hurt. "Sorry,
Larry," I said. It really was sweet of him to turn his apartment into
a postfuneral place of refuge. I, for one, couldn't bear to go home.

I looked around and spotted the only person besides Claudia I
could bear trading a sentence with right now: our friend Roger. He
turned such a gently protective face toward me that I kissed his
bearded woolly cheek—first touching I'd allowed myself all day.

"You've lost weight," he chided. "Look at those circles under
your eyes. Are you getting any sleep?"

"It goes with the dark complexion," I groused. His jacket fell open and I saw the Smith and Wesson on his belt clip. "Your gun is showing, Dr. Stern."

"Thanks," he said with an embarrassed grin.

He was buttoning his jacket when Claudia joined us.

"Couldn't you leave that thing in your car?" she sniffed.

"And have it stolen?" He turned to me, apologetic. "Thursday is gun-club day."

"Maybe I should go with you sometime," I mused.

"Not *my* gun club. You won't see love seats and plush carpets."

"No *haute décor*?" Claudia said caustically.

He grinned. "Let me draw you a picture. Converted basement-warehouse with a garbage smell. A bunch of those macho types who love to stand around and compare scores—" He raised an eyebrow. "You're not thinking of carrying a gun, are you, Karen?"

"She's been threatening to buy a shotgun," Claudia tattled.

"Every unattached female I know keeps a butcher knife in her night table or a can of Mace in her purse," I snapped. "Right, CC?"

She had the good grace to drop her eyes. "We've succumbed to a siege mentality—you, too, Rog," she said. "A gynecologist, packing a pistol?"

"A licensed pistol. Hell, I keep drugs in the office. You know how lawless this city has become," he said, mouth twisting with frustration.

"And you know I don't like guns," I told him. "I just keep thinking I ought to try firing one."

"Better bring some earplugs," he warned. "It gets noisy."

"Very noisy," said a matter-of-fact voice that I recognized.

"I didn't think you'd remember me," he said when I turned.

"Why not?" I parried, looking him over. "It's only been ten years." He was wearing a dark suit under a dust-colored raincoat with an eyeshade-green tie peeking out. I had a flash memory of a whole history of garish ties. "M. McCann, the FBI man," I said—and flushed; it had come out in embarrassing singsong, a ten-year-old office joke. I said quickly, "Meet Claudia Cole, Dr. Roger Stern."

He acknowledged the introductions with a sliver of a smile. "You're wondering what I'm doing here." He reached for my hand.

I was wondering why he took my hand.

"I called Larry when I read about your daughter," he said. "To lose her that way . . . And then, your granddaughter."

He'd had the sensitivity not to mention the son-in-law who had killed her. I said, "Thanks for coming, McCann."

Claudia sensed I was close to tears. "So gun clubs are noisy," she said to him, edging us onto safer ground. "Are they dangerous?"

"Not at all. Beginners are handed the range rules and given hands-on instruction. Horseplay or careless handling of your gun are frowned upon. Dr. Stern is right about the earplugs."

"I think I prefer Mace," Claudia quipped. She and McCann exchanged grins. She bore Roger away with a backward glance at me that said, Interesting man!

I didn't particularly agree, but now that she'd forced the issue, I took a good look at what ten years had done to an old adversary. Not much on the downside, I had to admit. Tall stocky frame with none of the usual concessions to middle-age spread. Straight sandy hair obscuring part of that broad forehead; was he still pushing it away whenever he got into a heated discussion? Narrow blue eyes that squinted, as if they were trained on some vast prairie instead of a tight lineup of smog-tipped skyscrapers. Not your standard G-man image. Didn't he hail from Kokomo or Sioux City or some such?

"If you're serious about a shooting lesson," McCann said, "I'd be happy to oblige. With tree trunks instead of paper targets on motorized pulleys. Friend of mine has some raw land—"

"I don't think so. Aren't you due back in Washington?"

"Tomorrow is Saturday. My soul is my own on weekends."

"I don't know whether to be offended or impressed," I said, on the verge of a smile. "How can you possibly remember a ten-year-old insult?"

His smile was easy. " 'The FBI owns your soul,' you told me."

"You still married, McCann?" I said, trying to remember if he'd had on a wedding band. His hands were in his raincoat pockets.

"Lost my wife four years ago."

"Divorced my husband six years ago." It had slipped out.

He glanced over at Allan. "So Larry said. You look like you could use a dose of the country. Let's see." He went over to the window and leaned out, taking a deep breath of foul Manhattan air. "Rockland County is better. Beats a converted warehouse with a garbage smell any day of the week."

"You win," I said, giving in to a smile. "Need my address?"

"Not unless you've moved in the last twenty-four hours. Noon. Casual dress. Empty stomach. Brevity," he said with mock seriousness, "is the mark of a good FBI man."

He took my hand again. He waved good-bye to Larry.

Allan came over. The chunky, pipe-smoking man with him was familiar. As he stuck out a big paw, the vision of an office-party introduction came back to me in a flash, along with his name. Donahue. Assistant district attorney. Old friend of Allan's.

"We've, ah, confirmed our suspicion that your daughter's killers weren't locals," Donahue said. "Looks like they drove out to Westchester from the Bronx." He went back to his pipe.

"The police have traced Sarah's silverware, a few pieces of jewelry," Allan told me, his normally pale complexion taking on a rosy flush.

"It took you people two weeks to find the knife that killed my daughter?" I said, twisting over the words. "What about the people who used it on her, Mr. Donahue? Do you even have a clue?"

"I know how you must feel," he said lamely.

"The hell you do."

"Karen, please." Allan turned tight-lipped, his eyes slipping from my face to Donahue's.

Donahue caught the glance and cleared his throat. "Allan tells me you've refused to consult my psychiatrist friend," he said, keeping his eyes front and center.

"Allan is a Legal Aid lawyer, not a referring physician."

"My friend is very experienced with traumas of this kind."

"The sick people, Mr. Donahue, are the ones who killed my daughter. As for my psychology—"

"That's your business, of course," he said, catching on fast.

"Yours is to bring Sarah's murderers to justice."

Donahue's pipe must have died on him; he was knocking it against the palm of his hand. I turned away from the two of them, I had to. Allan was no mind reader but who knew about Donahue? I didn't want him to know what I was thinking. . . .

If you two can't do the job, I've met someone who says he can.

Chapter 4

"Coke?"

McCann passed me a can to wash down the hard-boiled eggs.

He was dressed for a picnic: jeans, plaid shirt, electric-blue windbreaker with creases down the front, like he'd just taken it out of the box. No ten-gallon hat, just hair in his eyes; Claudia would be disappointed. He was eyeing my black pants suit as if I hadn't heard him specify "casual dress." Well hell, I was wearing an open-necked red blouse, wasn't I?

"I was telling my friend Claudia how we met," I said. "She couldn't picture the FBI as an old Kemp & Carusone client."

"Old and short-lived. How come you sabotaged the account?"

"Clever of you to have figured that out, McCann," I said.

"Not as clever as our hiring a PR agency."

"Why do you think I resorted to sabotage? I wasn't about to help you people improve your tarnished image after the dark days of your disgrace. Just because you enjoy harassing civil-rights leaders and going in for illegal taps doesn't mean—"

"Bad habit of yours, jumping to conclusions about me. It's ancient history. I'm not proud of it." His tone said, Don't ask me to apologize for it. He leaned back, eyes closed, to catch the sun.

A regular paleface for a Midwesterner—nothing weathered and leathery about him. Smooth skin, big shoulders . . . I looked away when I started picturing him with his plaid shirt off.

"So the new FBI doesn't violate our constitutional rights?" I drawled, letting him hear the skepticism.

He didn't even blink. "We do things strictly by the book."

"M. McCann, the FBI man," I said, not in singsong this time. "What's the 'M' stand for?"

He let me see his electric-blue eyes. "Max. For Maxwell."

"Hiding behind an initial, McCann?"

"You might say that." He stretched all the way out. "Much too literary for an FBI man. Maxwell. Hell, I'm from Minnesota, not the Upper West Side of Manhattan."

"Hell, if it was good enough for Hemingway's editor—"

"We here to spar or shoot?" he said with a lazy, sideways glance at my teasing smile. He got up and reached for his rifle, propped against an oak tree. Handed it to me, along with earplugs. "Down on your belly," he said. "Your first basic position."

The ground was mossy, pungent. Relaxing.

"Fire," he said, and went back to chewing on a blade of grass.

The trigger felt smooth. All I had to do was exert a little pressure. *Pull the trigger, Karen.* I stared at the silver barrel. "I can't," I said finally.

"Try it from a kneeling position. One knee."

"Your second basic position?" I knelt, grinning, feeling like a movie extra in *Gunga Din.*

"Fire."

"Wait till I adjust my earplugs, McCann."

"You're stalling. Here, try this."

He exchanged the rifle for his .38-caliber revolver and told me to stand up and use both hands.

"Brace yourself," he warned.

"For the recoil," I said, not as dumb as I looked.

"Fire," he said for the third time.

I pulled hard. Too hard. I said, "The gun is so light!"

"Three more times. One right after the other."

Snap, crackle, pop—like the old ad for Rice Krispies cereal. "It's so easy to kill," I marveled. "Isn't it?"

"It's why private citizens have no business fooling with guns." He took his back.

I leaned against the oak tree, my posture not as good as the rifle's had been. "Who's fooling?" I said with a shaky laugh. "I think I mortally wounded that little birch tree."

He brushed some dry leaves from the sleeve of my jacket. "I like hearing you laugh," he said.

"Thanks for the lesson, McCann."

"Time to go," he said, getting the message.

On the ride back, he was surprisingly relaxed, even whistled through his teeth (an art I'd picked up on the streets of New York). But the instant we hit Manhattan, he went into alert.

When I told him, he said, "So did you."

"You used to love the city," I said. "Do you still?"

He thought about it. "Guardedly. The way a man might love a wife he suspected of poisoning her first husband. How about you?"

"I've been here too long. I guess you could say I accept this place on its own terms. Like Californians who live with the threat of an earthquake."

"How do you deal with *your* earthquake?"

"Oh, I draw a mental map of danger zones. Which streets to avoid after dark, which ones to avoid, period. Furs are no problem—I don't wear them—and when I'm carrying bagfuls of groceries, I tuck my jewelry out of sight."

"You have all the right locks on your front door?"

"Doesn't everyone? Living in a big city means taking precautions. But you can't afford to think about it all the time."

"You can't afford not to."

"Bad habit of yours, McCann, getting in the last word."

But the last word came at my front door, which he insisted on seeing me to. He found the excuse of a grass stain to lightly touch my jacket again, as if he wanted to memorize the texture. "I'll call you," he said. And waited for me to contradict him.

"I'd like that," I said, surprised to find it was true.

My doorman had handed me a package on the way in. Opening it, I realized it had been hand-delivered; no canceled postage. No return address. It felt like a book I hadn't ordered.

It was Dante's *The Divine Comedy,* gold-leafed, leather-bound. A page from a calendar was stuck inside like a bookmark.

I opened to *Inferno*—to "O my Leader" . . . The entire passage was bracketed in red. Red ink? Finger-pricked blood? I read past the first line: "the violent death which is as yet unavenged"— Someone had crossed out "for him" and written in "for her." And again . . . "by any that is a partner in his[her] shame"—

I closed the book. "Made *her* indignant," I said aloud.

The number 3 was circled in red at the top of the calendar page. I pulled it out of the book. November. Three funerals in the month of November? Three unavenged deaths . . . I could almost hear that insolent drawl. I could see the tombstones.

The phone made me jump. I caught it on the first ring.

"Well?" Claudia demanded.

I held the receiver as if it were a balloon leaking air. "Well what?" I said.

"For heaven's sake, Karen, the Marlboro Man! Your G-man admirer with the gorgeous blue eyes. What's he like?"

"He wore a plaid shirt and chewed on a blade of grass or two. No ten-gallon hat."

"Never mind. He looks great in a battered raincoat. You seeing him again, I hope?"

"I'm calling him back right now," I lied, the only way to get her off the phone like a shot.

I hung up and dialed again before I could change my mind. Before I could let myself forget whose voice I had really wanted to hear just now. When Donahue came on the line I said, "Karen Newman, here. What's your psychiatrist friend's name and number?"

He told me. I rang off before he could ask about my change of heart.

Then I consigned Dante to another inferno—my hallway incinerator shaft. I'm no book burner, but I didn't feel a twinge of guilt.

What I felt was poetic justice.

Chapter 5

He had chosen an English restaurant with a French name for our "informal chat." As I peered through tinted glass, I reflected on Claudia's skepticism about "shrinks." My sentiments exactly.

Still, I didn't see how it could hurt.

I walked in, gave his name to the maître d', and was led past creamy walls featuring tastefully discreet nude drawings.

A man in black pinstripe sat at a curved banquette in the back. He stood up—all six-feet-two of him—and took off his glasses with a gesture that seemed deliberate, almost teasing.

I could see why. Chiseled features, tousled black hair, and honest-to-God silver sideburns. The face was almost too handsome.

"Mrs. Newman?"

"Dr. Coyne. Newman is my maiden name," I said coolly, knowing Donahue must have filled him in on my marital status. I sat down.

"I stand corrected, but so do you. Please call me Jim."

"You don't look like a Jim."

His smile told me I'd said something clever. "Most of the time, I don't feel like one. My childhood name is more to my liking. Jamie," he said—a little tentatively.

"Jamie. It goes with a rogue on horseback," I said with a slow smile. "You know the type. Ruffled shirt open to the waist. Sword swinging at your side."

"Karen Newman. It goes with tailored suits and no-nonsense blouses—or so she wants us to think."

"Truce," I said, smiling in earnest.

I let him order for both of us. Let him casually broach the subject of my work (hoping to relax me?) before I leveled with him. "Look, I'm not sure I should even be here," I said. "Fact is, I had a bad moment last weekend."

"And you prefer to solve your own problems. Fact is, you also distrust psychiatrists."

"Direct, aren't you?" I said, liking him for it. "Let me return the favor. This may be an 'icebreaker' lunch, but talking about my work won't melt any ice. Just the opposite."

"So the world of corporate public relations excites you!"

He had a swashbuckler's smile: ear to ear. I couldn't figure out what I'd said to turn it on. "That's one way of putting it," I said. "It's a highly competitive business."

"It's also a man's world. You're a senior vice president. You must be good."

I shrugged. "These days, I don't feel good at anything."

"Tell me about Kemp & Carusone."

"It's a full-service agency. We offer our clients the gamut of corporate communication techniques. Product publicity, policy structuring, media relations—"

"Your strong suit, media relations."

I stared at him. We media experts in the PR business keep a low profile. He must have gotten the info from his friend Donahue, who'd gotten it from Allan.

"My strong suit," I acknowledged.

"Are you uncomfortable with what you do?" he said slowly. "Guilt feelings about your work?"

"Perceptive, aren't you?" I said, annoyed because he was too damn good at his job. "Let's face it, doctor, K & C is a glorified corporate-image polisher. I spend my time making big business look good even when, sometimes, I don't approve of what I sell. Not exactly a line of work that goes with someone of my liberal leanings. I went into it with misgivings—but at the time I needed the independence. I got used to the salary."

"What else do you like about it?"

I shrugged. "I like the action."

The food arrived. "Care to talk about your problem?" he asked.

I played with the handles of my briefcase-purse. "I called you because I was tempted to act against my better judgment. I didn't. End of problem."

"That's all of it?"

I noticed his eyes—really noticed them. So deep a brown they were almost black. Penetrating. I said, "Not quite all. I've been experiencing an odd sort of fear since my daughter's death." I stared down at my suit for a moment; black. It was all I wore, lately, black. I said, "Ever since her funeral."

For the first time, he looked at me with a psychiatrist's keen appraisal.

"I've tried to deal with it. Just don't ask for details."

He leaned across the table. "You know I have to."

"I took up self-defense," I said, and managed to keep myself from blushing. "Short-lived, as it turned out. I froze up."

"Interesting," he said, sounding like he meant it. "But now you're in control." His smile was comforting. "Aren't you?"

A welcome wrap-up question. I assured him that I was.

As we polished off lunch, the "doctor" disappeared on me and a charmer called "Jamie" took his place. Unsettling, at first. But not unpleasant. There was something almost old-fashioned about the way he saw to my every culinary need, from fresh rolls to refilled wineglass and coffee cup. Naturally, he grabbed the check.

That's when the psychiatrist returned for a parting shot. "If the problem continues, call me," he urged softly. "Therapy isn't a fate worse than death. It actually works if the patient brings two things to it: intelligence and motivation."

"I'm not big in the motivation department," I warned him.

"True. But you don't require much for a single session. If you ever feel you need a sounding board, be my guest."

Not bloody likely. But lunch had served its purpose; I felt reassured. I bade him a noncommittal good-bye.

I stopped off at the ladies' room, one of those soothing lounge-style affairs, all peach and white and dimly lit, and took advantage of a cushy layabout, needing to close my eyes for a minute. It had been a hard morning at the office, topped off by my encounter with the faintly disturbing Dr. James Coyne, aka "Jamie."

When I pried my eyes back open, I saw I was being stared at.

My first reaction—defensive, I admit—was to grab for my briefcase; I'd left it on the floor. I sat up and returned the stare.

The woman was youngish, thin-lipped. Very uptight. Her lipstick, a lurid scarlet, was badly applied. Her small nose twitched.

"Kagan wanted you to know we have proof," she said in the tone of a somnambulist, spacing out each word.

Kagan. The "chauffeur" at the funeral? I leaped to my feet.

She turned around at the door, her eyes like the tiny bulbs in high-intensity lamps. "We know who killed your daughter."

I tried to say something, anything. I watched her leave.

I spent an impossible afternoon at the office, outwardly calm, inwardly fuming. Leaving the damn book with my doorman was one thing. Having me followed to a restaurant and using a zombie to drop that bombshell of a message on me was another. Outrageous.

I was leaving the office when I got another message: M. McCann was heading my way. Was I free for dinner? I told my secretary to say I'd be out of town. "No," I said, reconsidering, "tell him I'm busy." . . . Bad timing, Max. Some other lifetime.

I took a cab home. The moment I set foot in my apartment, I headed for the couch, dropping onto the thick, ultrasuede cushions.

I jumped up, reminded of the cushions in the ladies' room, and went to look out the window at my soothing Central Park view, needing the sense of privacy it always gave me—

Utter privacy is a mixed blessing.

The urge for a double bourbon was overwhelming.

Instead, I headed for the den, briefcase in hand. It was heavy, full of the work I hadn't been able to do all afternoon. I emptied the briefcase onto my desk and reached into its side pouch for a yellow legal pad.

I pulled out more than the pad. A thick envelope.

With my name on it. The woman in the restaurant had slipped me . . . what? It felt like a bunch of photographs.

I slit the envelope open as if it had a bomb inside that might go off. I stacked the photographs neatly on my desk.

The photograph on top was okay, it was bearable, something I might have taken myself. Susie, adorable in her Miss Piggy outfit.

I did a fast count: eleven more to go.

The photograph after Susie was of two ghost-figures with holes cut out for the eyes. One of them held the portable TV set that Sarah had kept in her bedroom. I picked up the next photograph. And the next. More ghosts. They were clutching things. A stereo; a silver platter and matching cigarette box. (A Christmas present; a wedding gift.) I started turning more quickly, the photographs blurring into a montage: ghosts everywhere, leaving a Halloween trail of wreckage. A crystal vase, splintered. A Tiffany floor lamp, overturned. A set of leather-bound books, scattered.

I forced myself to stop. Five photographs to go. The image of a man with flat blond hair and thundercloud eyes told me that "proof" of something besides vandalism was coming right up.

Proof of Sarah being gang-raped?

I felt a stabbing pain. I turned over the next photograph.

Sarah's face, full of fear and revulsion. I kept my eyes on her face, not wanting to move down to the naked backs and buttocks of her rapists—moving down, finally. Having to stop again.

I sobbed until I lost my breath and had to run, choking, to the bathroom.

I came back for number eleven, knowing I needed to see this through to the end. Another ghost. But this one was wearing a black hood. This one held a table knife in his upraised hand.

I turned over the last photograph.

We know who killed your daughter.

And now, so did I.

He stood posing, knife in one hand, black hood in the other. His killer face was a vacant lot. His mouth might have been fashioned by the slit of a razor. He had shoulder-length black hair, a thin black band around his forehead, and a beauty mark under his left eye in the shape of a tear.

I held the phone in my lap for a long time while I thought about the man with the chauffeur's cap. Then I thought about law courts and rules of evidence, judges and juries. I pictured them.

I believed in them.

I do have a sense of justice, Kagan. I will *fight back. But not your way.*

Donahue was working late. I told him there was something new. I told him about the photographs.

The last thing I told him was, "You'd better come and get them."

I hung up, knowing I had stopped lying to myself, knowing I needed to make one more call.

Dr. James Coyne recognized my voice.

He recognized more than my voice. When he named it, I knew I had been right to call him.

Chapter 6

"First, terror," I told him. "Now, rage. What in God's name is happening to me?"

"In a word, displacement. Your daughter is murdered. You feel a kind of suppressed rage. You feel it again when you encounter this chauffeur. His offer is tempting, a prospect that frightens you to the point where your mind won't let it in. That's when it began for you—this process we call displacement. You began to shift the fear of your own rage onto whatever person or object provoked it. Fear of the vigilante because of what the man's offer made you feel. Fear of the punching bag and all those rage-filled women. Fear of the jeans-and-leather-jacket crowd because those kids were vivid reminders of your daughter's killers. You were afraid of what you secretly wanted to do to them."

For the first time in my life, I grasped what my Catholic friends take for granted: the relief of the confessional. I shook my head, not quite believing him. "You're saying they were bogus fears? That all I was really afraid of was . . ."

"Your own vengeance."

"But I abhor violence," I protested. "I always have."

"You're thinking that your rage is abnormal. It isn't—not under these circumstances. Only the sick ones act out a murderous impulse, Ms. Newman."

He had such a gently reassuring voice. I wanted to believe him. I couldn't keep my hands from shaking. He frowned at me.

"Use your common sense. Should a victim of violent crime *not* feel outrage? What's the alternative? Drive it underground?"

"What am I supposed to do with it?" I said, feeling desperate.

"Give in to your rage. Give it room to dissipate. Take comfort from the knowledge that you didn't act out the impulse."

I thought about that. Hadn't I resisted calling this Kagan? Hadn't I turned the photographs over—

The door to the reception room opened and I caught a glimpse of a young boy. Dr. Coyne excused himself. It gave me a chance to check out his office, which I'd barely noticed.

His taste ran to the opulent. An elaborately carved mahogany desk, handsomely fitted with antique brass. Heavy drapes in green and gold brocade. An emerald-green velvet couch that actually looked comfortable—and was. I investigated his bookshelves and discovered, along with the expected technical tomes, the novels of Dumas and Sabatini. A psychiatrist with a taste for adventure and a childhood name to go with it, I thought, smiling.

He came back as I was admiring a sensuous companion to his couch: a coffee table that was a gently curving slab of malachite.

"You're wondering what kind of a practice merits all this."

I took in his gold lion-head cuff links, the mauve Christian Dior tie, the cut of his three-piece suit, and said, "Obviously, a successful one."

"It was. Until I got bored with being the 'in' Manhattan guru for the idle rich."

"The female idle rich?" I blurted out, eyeing his couch.

"You're wondering how I kept it professional. These helped," he said, taking off his glasses and handing them to me.

I looked at them, then through them. "Pure glass?"

"I have twenty-twenty vision. I wore glasses to impose a kind of barrier between me and some of my . . . more persistent patients."

His words had the sound of an involuntary confession. His expression said he wished he could take them back, along with his glasses. "Mr. Donahue tells me you confine your practice, these days, to the criminal-justice field," I said to get us off the subject. "What got you into it?"

"A forensic psychiatrist who succumbed to ptomaine poisoning on the eve of a trial. I covered for him." He sat back, reflective. "Examining the accused gave me my first glimpse of a young killer's psyche. I've been fascinated ever since."

I felt as if I'd been slapped. I stood up. "I'll bet you have a regular rogue's gallery of fascinating patients," I said.

"The bulk of my patients are crime victims. Like yourself."

I sat back down. "You consider me a victim?"

"Not in the same way as your daughter. But still, a victim. In the case of your son-in-law and his little girl—"

"Mark, a victim? He killed that child," I said vehemently.

"Because his perspective was warped beyond repair. Blame Sarah's murderers, not a bereaved husband for whom the world had suddenly turned alien. There's a tragic pattern to these cases. Loving, protective parent—usually overprotective—confronted by a life-shattering event that turns him suicidal and makes the world unsafe for his child, pulling him inexorably toward that final 'protective' act."

"He killed more than his daughter," I said in a low voice. "With Susie alive, needing me, I think I'd have . . . managed. But when I buried her— It was as much my funeral as hers."

It sounded like a confession, which I suppose it was.

He didn't say, "Nonsense!" or "Don't think that way." He said, "In a way, that's true. You've lost so much so quickly."

I looked at him with new respect. "My parents died within a month of each other," I said. "I still remember how it made me feel, a terrible sense of isolation—as if I'd been cut off from my past. Losing my own child, and then hers, is somehow worse. . . ."

"As if you've been cut off from your future."

I could only stare.

"To suffer an irrevocable loss," he said gently, "is to lose something of ourselves, a kind of permanent death."

"You're uncanny," I marveled. "How could you know—"

"I've always known these things." He said it as if it were a curse instead of a blessing. "This sense of loss," he said, his voice sounding a warning, "you may never get over it, Karen."

"Will I get over the rage, at least?"

"In time, if you take my advice and—"

The phone rang. I had no premonition as his professional voice ebbed away and he looked at me. I'd left his telephone number with my secretary in case my boss wanted to track me down.

It wasn't Larry who was looking for me. It was Donahue.

"They've got them," Dr. Coyne told me. "Donahue says—"

I couldn't understand why he hung up and moved toward me, gripping my shoulders. Or how a glass of brandy materialized in my hand. "Easy," he was saying, "take it easy."

He wouldn't say any more until I drank. Then he took the glass away.

"I didn't mean the police had literally arrested them—not yet. They've identified the gang," he said. "By its leader."

"Does he have a name?" . . . *Does he belong to the human race?*

"A street name synonymous with Puerto Rican macho. Indio," he said, pronouncing the word with startling contempt.

Indio. Shoulder-length black hair and a band around his head, like an Indian . . .

"What happens after they arrest him?" I asked.

He led me to the couch, sat me down. "If he's under sixteen, as my friend Donahue suspects . . . a Family Court proceeding."

"A proceeding? Not a trial?"

"Maybe. Maybe not. It's up to the DA in Westchester County. New York allows him to try a juvenile killer as an adult. *If* the case is strong enough to stand up before a grand jury. I'm afraid it's his call, Karen."

"With those photographs?"

"Please. It's too soon to—"

"It's not too soon to talk about a murderer being tried for murder, damn it." I took back my brandy. "Say he's tried as an adult and convicted. Of murder. He'll go to prison, won't he? He'll be sent away for a long time?"

"Technically, nine to life. He wouldn't do more than nine. But . . ."

"But what?"

He reached for my hand. "More likely, he'd pull a reduced charge. He might even end up back in Family Court."

"Dr. Coyne, you haven't said what happens if he's *not* tried as an adult."

"A juvenile proceeding. In Family Court."

"That means 'rehabilitation,' " I said bitterly, "not punishment. Help the kids who never had a chance . . ."

"Some of the most violent offenders are institutionalized."

"What if this . . . Indio ends up in some glorified country club—with bunk beds and tennis courts and unlocked doors?"

He saw what was happening to my face. He took hold of my arm. "Don't be a superwoman. There's nothing weak about needing help. Let me help you."

I pulled away and got to my feet. "Lean on you, you mean? I wouldn't know how."

"Let me be unofficial liaison, at least. Between you and the police, the DA's office."

"You're serious," I said with a rush of gratitude. "But why? I'm not even a patient."

"A friend?"

"I'm sorry," I told him.

"About what? I meant it, Karen. Friend, not lover."

"It's all I'm up to," I admitted. Impulsively, I reached for his hand. "Dr. Coyne, I don't know how to thank you."

"You can start by dropping the formalities."

"Thank you . . . Jamie."

Instant transformation. The infectious smile he'd shown me in the restaurant.

I left his office wearing a phrase like an arm around my shoulders. Friend, not lover. How had he known that I needed precisely that?

I sighed and told myself to let it happen.

Chapter 7

My clock radio jarred me awake with a jazzy rendition of "I'm Dreaming of a White Christmas." I snapped it off, hating the reminder. I took my time dressing, not eager to get where I had to go. But able to face it, thanks to Dr. James Coyne, psychiatrist.

Thanks to my friend, Jamie.

He hadn't wasted any time. Within two days of my office visit, he'd had me feeling useful, distracted from my own pain with the pain of others—a sort of "therapy" called Victims Aid.

A growing phenomenon, apparently. Show up at the scene of a violent crime, armed with sympathy and practical advice.

Therapy. What do you think of as you cradle a blood-spattered man in your arms while the police bear his wife's body away? His pain, not yours. How do you comfort parents—dull the horror of a murdered child? By speaking of your own.

You don't speak of retribution, theirs or yours.

Today, I was free to, even though I had no illusions—Jamie had seen to that. Today was "Indio's" hearing.

Claudia greeted me downstairs in a rented car. She was wearing her fake-jaguar wraparound and a tight smile that spelled confidence. All the way to Westchester, she kept telling me what I'd been telling myself all week: "He won't get away with it."

While she parked, I sized up a modern building with a sun-dappled plaza and tightly manicured grounds, trying to ignore a battalion of fat red bows and holly wreaths. A massive sign over the entrance flashed away in green neon: ONLY 4 MORE DAYS UNTIL XMAS!

Family Court was on the sixth floor. We took a corner bench in the hall and stripped off our coats. Claudia sighed—and read my mind: "Too bad they couldn't indict him as an adult."

Couldn't, or wouldn't? The pipe-smoking Donahue had been as convincing as a ventriloquist's dummy. The Westchester DA's office had been busy. That left a Bedford "youth officer" assigned to the case, who had ground out a half-smoked cigarette, looked at me with a human face, and let me have it right between the eyes.

"The one photograph places him at the scene, knife in hand. But doing what? Rape? Robbery? Getting a glass of water? With that kind of evidence, you get laughed out of court. We figure there was six, seven punks. Which one used the knife? We need an eyewitness,

*Ms. Newman. One punk willing to talk. I'm working on it. Me and
the Bronx. Meanwhile, we get this Indio creep convicted in Family
Court on a lesser charge just so he's off the street. That way, he don't
beat the shit out of his buddies, see, or bribe 'em. That way, we buy
time to build us a case."*

A big man with a cigarette in his mouth and a mournful slope to
his shoulders stepped out of an elevator. The youth officer. I waved
him over and introduced him to Claudia.

"Can I go in with her?" she asked before letting his hand go.

He grinned without losing his cigarette. "Closed to the public,
Ms. Cole. They don't even identify people by name."

"Any feedback on the judge?" I asked him, remembering that
Jamie knew a couple of them by reputation.

"We coulda done worse." He ground out his cigarette. "See you
inside," he said, sounding cheerful. But he walked away like he
had a stone in his size-thirteen shoe.

Claudia tried to distract me. Our words rose like bright balloons.
And sank like dead weights. We retreated into our private
thoughts. I felt my fists clenching . . .

*The charge is juvenile delinquency, the youth officer would be
saying to the judge. Robbery, if done by an adult. Then he'd quote
some law and steer clear, for now, of the murder and the rape—too
much circumstantial garbage. The judge would go for the cut-and-
dried. For robbery. Then afterward—*

They called me in. I had to jam my hands in my pockets.

I walked in on an argument. A flustered kid from the DA's office,
pink-cheeked and hair neatly parted, was on the carpet for daring
to bring up the matter of previous convictions. He hadn't been
able to pry the "juvenile offender's" criminal record out of a sister
Family Court in the Bronx. The Legal Aid lawyer, another
kid—this one wore his long blond hair tied with a red-and-green
ribbon—was being righteous about the "confidentiality" laws that
keep a juvenile's past a secret. . . . Even from a district attorney?

The judge didn't fit the mold, from the look and sound of him.
I'd been expecting bland and irritable, not elegant and restrained.
He was pale and hollow-cheeked, with silver-framed glasses riding
an aquiline nose. His narrow shoulders were squared, his hands on
prominent display so you couldn't miss the long, tapered fingers.
He was issuing pronouncements from his perch like a professor
gently chastising a couple of backward students.

I kept my eyes on the youth officer with the nasty mouth and the
eyes of a minister. Keep your eyes on a focal point and the
"juvenile offender" isn't in the room, he doesn't exist.

Next witness. I walked to the witness stand, telling myself with every step that this poor excuse for a trial was just a way station, that we'd get our murder trial in an adult court.

I avert my eyes from the murderer in this room. One glance and I am lost. I have testimony to give . . . slowly, slowly. I repeat each question. I grip the arms of my chair. It comes easily, what I heard over the telephone fifty-three days ago. . . . Is he serious, this judge? How can I remember in such detail?

How can I not?

Go slower. Bite your lip, if you have to, or look at the floor, but get it right. This is lawyers' territory. This is what "robbery" turns on. Why can't I let go of the witness chair?

Repeat it? Does he know what he's asking? Words are tied to images, Your Honor . . . Sarah, screaming her heart out—

It's when they cut off her finger, Your Honor.

Your Honor is looking pained. That's good because it gets worse, it gets lethal. The taunt at the end. The end of my Sarah. This "juvenile offender" gave me an earful, Your Honor.

Can you hear it? Can you all hear it? Can I stop now?

I swung around, free, now, to look at a murderer. I saw high-top tennis shoes—very lightweight, very "in"—and designer jeans. The black hip-length jacket had leather sleeves, a felt body, and a small yellow crown over the heart. Hero jacket. There would be another crown logo on the back. Every hood a king . . .

I closed my eyes and saw the downturned mouth of a man whose company manufactured the jackets—more popular, these days, with gang members than sports heroes. His company was an unhappy Kemp & Carusone client with a big image problem.

I opened my eyes to the face in Kagan's photograph. Juvenile with long black hair and headband, who played at being an Indian brave. The eyes were as stone-flat as I remembered. I stared at the slit of a mouth. At the oddly disconcerting birthmark . . .

He flashed a sudden smile—something special just for me.

I swung on the judge—the probation officer—the young Legal Aid lawyer. They all saw it: a smile tantamount to a confession. Pride of authorship. Of murder.

It sent me out of the courtroom wrapped in a dignified calm. It made the waiting easy. Nothing human could witness a smile like that, could watch it pass from killer to victim, and not do what was right. In that moment I grasped the essence of justice. It wasn't luck or politics or fine print. It was common decency.

I was able to feel compassion for another mother: the one who still sat hunched over in the courtroom, forced to listen. . . .

The courtroom door opened and the mother came out, dark coat tightly buttoned.

Her son, still smiling, was one step behind her.

I must have leaped to my feet because the mother stopped for a moment to stare. I knew what she was seeing—she had seen it earlier in the courtroom: a face indecent in its agony.

What I saw in hers was blank indifference.

She disappeared into an elevator. With *him*.

A hand closed over my shoulder. "I gambled. You lost." The youth officer's face was bent over mine. "Bad luck, drawing that sonofabitch judge."

Claudia grabbed his arm. "Which son of a bitch?"

"Judge Arthur Younger."

I stood up, fighting off nausea. Jamie had warned me about some judges. Younger was one of them. Judge with a nickname . . .

"—shoulda known he'd buy Legal Aid's 'humanity' pitch," the youth officer was saying. "Who wants to lock up a fifteen-year-old right before Christmas? Not 'Bleedin' Heart Art,'" he muttered, disgust etched in the lines of his mouth.

"They let him go?" Claudia gasped. "I don't under—"

I rushed back into the courtroom.

And got lucky. Judge Arthur Younger—"Bleedin' Heart Art"— was still on his perch.

He saw me coming. It was as if someone had sprinkled red pepper up that imperious nose. "Yes?" he said in a tone designed to put an impertinent student in her place.

"You call that justice?" I said in a voice so low he couldn't hear the effort not to yell in his face.

"Tempered with mercy. My dear Mrs. . . . ah, Noonan, I understand your feelings—"

"Newman. If you did, you'd run screaming out of this room."

Walk, don't run, I told myself, and walked carefully out of the courtroom, past Claudia, still talking to the youth officer. An elevator was closing. It struck me a solid blow as I slid inside. I stood hunched over while a stack of memories—of photographs —paraded by. *I had turned them over to the law.*

I stepped out . . . and got lucky again because it wasn't over. A killer stood in the lobby with his buddies. Raucous sounds of celebration among the hero jackets. Indecent grins on lively young faces. One of them wore a crucifix on a gold chain.

I stared at Indio's back. Then at the back of a policeman who stood a few feet away, blue jacket open to a holster.

I felt the shape even before I saw it, remembered the weight of it in my grip—

"Not this way." I heard the low monotone, felt both arms grabbed from behind, in the same instant.

I collapsed like a house of cards against Kagan's chest.

The policeman, inches away, never even turned around.

"You knew how it would be," I said when we were outside.

"Lucky for you. Shall I show you what even the Bronx Family Court doesn't have a record of? A solid list of Indio's crimes."

I swayed a little, lost in the smoke of his eyes. "You're very organized."

"It's the wave of the future. I'm here to invite you to . . . let's call it a holiday encounter." He was looking past me, his long neck at a calculating angle. "Your friend is almost upon us."

"May I bring her to this . . . encounter?"

"Suit yourself. But there are rules. We'll be in touch."

Claudia came rushing up in time to be introduced to Kagan's mocking smile.

"We'll meet again," he said. "Don't make plans for Christmas Eve."

Chapter 8

"Feel like a damn fool, wearing these on a cold winter night," Claudia grumbled, waving her oversize dark glasses at me.

We were headed crosstown in a cab, me wearing a black scarf that covered most of my short black hair—all you could see were a few stray wisps on my forehead—Claudia decked out in a black velvet turban that stressed her high cheekbones and those slanted eyes—Egyptianesque, her ex-husband liked to call them. Her black pants suit was velvet-trimmed elegance; mine was plain wool.

"The glasses make sense," I said. "Disguise your face and it saves having to disguise your feelings. I gather it can get pretty emotional at these get-togethers. Especially this time of year . . ."

She let my voice trail off, knowing why I hadn't taken off my own dark glasses. I felt like a displaced person. Christmas Eve. I had a destination, but it was the wrong one. I should have been in Westchester. Sarah would be in the kitchen right now, whipping up everyone's favorite sweet-potato soufflé while I sipped my Dom Perignon and brushed pine needles out of Susie's hair—

How will I get through this night?

"What kind of people you figure we'll be meeting—besides faceless?" Claudia said into her compact mirror.

"Crime victims who find it hard to get through a holiday."

"All members of this secret society?" She sounded uneasy.

I shrugged away my own uneasiness. "Kagan was vague about it."

"What else was he vague about?" she said sharply.

"Listen, CC, I appreciate you giving up your Christmas Eve. Don't be my conscience in the bargain. I'm not joining anything."

"Oh, sure, you're just looking. Me, I'm along for the ride. That it?" she pointed, sounding as if she'd been cheated at cards.

The cab had pulled up before an innocuous brick building.

But the frosted windows didn't let you see what you were walking into. A "meeting room." Two flights down, the sign said.

"There must be a couple of hundred people!" Claudia marveled as we hit bottom and rounded a corner.

"More." I took in the PTA atmosphere, puzzled by it. The absence of Christmas decorations was another nice surprise.

"Lot of people violating the dress code," Claudia sniffed.

Kagan had cautioned us to wear a scarf or a hat, dark glasses, dark clothes. Maybe one out of every five people had obliged. I was still puzzling over that one when Claudia steered me to a buffet table—an elaborate spread. I made a stab at eating, then left her with the iced shrimp while I drifted off to eavesdrop.

". . . been three years now and I still can't buy a tree."

"I haven't gotten rid of his clothes yet. I can't bear—"

". . . worst time of the year for the kids. Laura fussed so."

"Insomnia. It's that or the nightmares. All that blood—"

"If only she hadn't suffered. If only they hadn't—"

I had turned into a yellow caution signal: STOP, LOOK, LISTEN. Stories of frustration and despair, but told with a lack of inhibition. Strangers accosting strangers, but not with idle curiosity. It was palpable across the sweep of the room, it was the universal body language: empathy. A common bond.

A Puerto Rican woman wearing dark glasses came up to me and said, "I lost a son." I took the snapshot she handed me.

"So young," I murmured.

"Thirteen. He loved two things, my kid. Radios and bikes."

I studied the photo: inquisitive eyes, an impish grin.

"Spent every spare minute foolin' with junk parts for one or the other," she said. "Then they'd steal it on him—kids his own age, older, some of 'em. He died in the gutter. Chest heavin', gaspin' for breath. They shot my boy for a radio," she said.

"I listened to my daughter die," I said, my voice as honest as hers. "I heard what was happening but I—I couldn't do a thing."

"Like a nightmare where you can't run . . ."

It was easy to become the uninhibited stranger. To talk without reserve. To feel, afterward, a bleak relief.

To realize, only when you'd started to turn away, that you were holding a stranger's hand . . . or she yours.

"Learning anything?"

"That's the idea, isn't it?" I said, turning. "Where are *your* dark glasses, Kagan?"

"Some people don't need them. Either they're not among the committed—family members, friends of the victim—or, like me, they have forgettable faces. No need to alter their appearance."

"Who's committed, damn it?"

"Yes, of course, you're a fence sitter. Care for a drink?"

He propelled me in the direction of the bar. While he was getting my bourbon and his gin and tonic, I was studying his face: even-featured, expressionless. The white-blond hair and the tan notwithstanding, it really was forgettable. Not his figure, though. He was one long stretch of black in denim and open-necked shirt, a sinuous shadow that lurks in nightmares.

"Care for a quick tour?" he asked, and took my arm. We made a slow circle around the room as he singled out individuals with a half-turn of his angular neck, a raised finger or eyebrow. "Office cleaning woman—the one in the olive-drab scarf. Her teenaged daughter was stabbed to death for her lunch money. The big fella with the shades is a security guard. His kid—his son, not his daughter—was gang-raped. The guy in blue pinstripe and fake mustache is a lawyer. Purse-snatcher shoved his wife in front of a subway train a year ago today."

"I get the idea," I said, polishing off my drink. Kagan's remained untasted. We passed by the elaborate buffet just as the shrimp was being replenished. The black stuff in the large crystal bowl was caviar, not lumpfish. "Who pays for this?" I asked him.

"Victims Rehabilitation League. Privately funded and perfectly legitimate. Intrigued?"

"You know I am. What's next?"

"I thought you'd never ask. Come with me."

Into a back room—dark, except for the spotlight over a narrow table and a cane-backed chair. Kagan held out the chair.

"I don't like melodrama," I snapped.

"Better not to see faces. It's for our mutual protection."

I sat down. With the light in my eyes, all I could see around me were shadowy forms.

They let me hear one eerie, monotonous voice at a time. . . .

"The aim of our organization is to avenge the unavenged."

"Like Alcoholics Anonymous, we recruit people with a common problem. Anonymous people."

"Crime victims. Victims Anonymous gives them what they

can't find anywhere else. Moral support. A catharsis. Our motto—"

"Skip the ritual," Kagan said with an impatient gesture. "Just tell her who we go after."

"Savages," an angry voice lashed out in the dark. "The ones who commit violent crime."

"And the ones who let them. Permissives, we call them."

A woman!

"Permissives have to be reeducated," she went on in a sweet, soft voice. "Criminals have to be stopped."

"I mentioned rules," Kagan said to me. "We also have preconditions for membership which—"

The door opened to a sliver of light.

"You don't belong here, Miss Cole," Kagan said flatly as Claudia came in.

"Neither does Karen." Certainty in her voice.

"Wait outside for me," I told her. "Claudia, *please.*"

Kagan stopped her. "Can we trust your discretion?"

"You mean, because my ex-husband is a cop?" she said dryly.

"With a law degree."

"I'm impressed with your snooping service," she snapped.

The door slammed, thickening the silence afterward, so that Kagan's question, spoken in a normal tone, sounded ominously loud.

"Still on the fence, Karen Newman?"

I felt like I had fallen off but I wasn't about to admit it. "I need time," I said. Time to come to my senses?

"A Mission-planning session is coming up. Care to sit in?"

I sensed an exception. Why? I said, "When?"

"In a few days. I'll let you know where."

"May I bring a male friend? Moral support," I said to Kagan's obvious reluctance. "He doesn't have to actually sit in—"

"He'll wait outside, then," he said, capitulating.

I got up. No movement from the shadows, no more disembodied voices. I was tempted to press the light switch by the door.

"Party's over," Kagan said abruptly and escorted me out.

Claudia was staring out of a frosted window. Waiting. "Let's go have that drink we both need," she told me.

"Come meet someone first," Kagan said, pointing the way.

A boy. Very short. Dark curly hair. Somber eyes that shifted into alert when he saw us. He looked vaguely familiar.

To Claudia, too; her eyes narrowed in recognition before she pulled on her sunglasses.

The boy shot her a cool look of appraisal, and her limbs seemed to tighten and grow smaller, like a turtle pulling in its head.

"Meet Tony," Kagan said. "One of our cooptees."

"We supposed to know what that means?" Claudia sniffed.

"A term borrowed from the KGB. Tony cooperates on certain assignments, but he's not a member of the club. Those photographs we planted in your briefcase . . ." Kagan let his voice drift.

"The ones I turned in to the DA?" I said. "What *about* them?"

"Tony risked his life to get them to us."

I had no words. But the kid must have seen what was in my face: gratitude. He turned and ran from it.

Curious about Claudia's turtle-in-the-shell reaction, I asked her where we'd seen him before.

"Beats me. What are you in the mood for besides good booze? Something cozy with patent-leather booths and not much spillover noise from the bar?"

"You know just the place, right?" I said, grinning.

She answered me with a tight smile.

But she didn't get testy until the waitress left us alone with our drinks. "This outfit of Kagan's," she said, swirling her Jim Beam, "it's bad news. And you know it."

"Bad news for whom? If you're about to say it's illegal—"

"Karen, it's racist. You can't tell me these vigilantes don't go after a lot more blacks than whites."

"What's color got to do with it? We're talking robbers and rapists. Damn it, Claudia, we're in the middle of a—"

"Crime wave, I know." She didn't sip her drink; she damn near gulped it down before looking at me. "I just can't turn it off."

"Turn it off?"

"The color of my skin. You know how hard I prayed that Sarah's killer would be white? How relieved I was when he turned out to be Hispanic? It's not reverse racism, if that's what you're thinking," she said quickly. "I'm black."

She said it with a fierce mixture of pride and anguish, making me remember her awkward self-consciousness at Sarah's funeral. Making me want to cry.

"Street crime translates into 'black' in people's minds. Can you blame them? But Karen, you know how that makes me *feel?*"

"Not really," I said with a sigh. "I can't get inside your skin, can I? Sorry if I seemed insensitive. It's just—"

She reached for my hand. "You're the *last* one on my insensitivity list, Whitey." Her smile, this time, was real. "I can't get inside you, either," she said softly, and I knew she was thinking about what had happened to Sarah.

"I'm tempted to join them, CC," I admitted.

Her look of horror was almost comical. "It's a mistake, Karen. Forget racist. It *is* illegal. Cops take a dim view of vigilantes. Stan used to come home steaming—"

"Don't race your motor," I said, not letting her see what was happening to mine. I took a decorous sip of bourbon. "I haven't decided yet," I told her, which was true.

"What's it depend on, a throw of the dice?"

"They're planning something," I said slowly. "I want to check it out. With Jamie."

"So he can maybe talk you out of it?"

. . . So he can hold my hand. "Something like that."

"Okay, I'll get off your case. Keep me informed?"

I smiled. "You'll be the first to know," I lied.

I was thinking she'd be the last. Maybe Kagan could trust her discretion, but I'd known her longer and I wasn't so sure.

"Drink up," she said. "It's past midnight."

Past Christmas Eve. I had gotten through the night.

Thanks to Victims Anonymous.

2

CONVERSION

"O my Leader," I said, "the violent
death which is as yet unavenged for
him by any that is a partner in his
shame made him indignant. . . ."

—*Inferno,*
Canto 29

Chapter 9

A converted basement-warehouse with a garbage smell. What lurked inside, Roger's gun club? A massage parlor?

My hand hesitated over a rusty bell long enough for Jamie to sound a quiet alarm. "You can still change your mind."

"Christmas Eve turned out to be harmless," I reminded him.

"Yes, but this talk of a mission, of planning something—"

"That's why you're here." I pressed the bell. The heavy wooden door opened a crack. "Film club?" I said, turning Kagan's code words into a timid question.

We were admitted into an anteroom. A little old man wearing suspenders that held up baggy trousers put Jamie in his place with a "Wait here, bud," and a gesture in the direction of a folding chair. Jamie took out his newspaper and waved me away.

I found Kagan outside a pair of closed doors. "Welcome to Porno Palace," he said, swinging a door wide to reveal a dark screening room. He led me to a couple of rear seats. "Don't worry," he told me with a dry chuckle, "no pornography tonight."

Just a giant screen. It started flashing headlines . . . and photographs.

—YOUTHS MUG WIDOW. Seventy-Year-Old Woman Opens Door to a Ruse. . . . And has a broken nose to show for it, an ugly gash where a cross was ripped off a neck as fragile as a dead branch.

—MEDICAL STUDENT FATALLY BEATEN. By six "kids" with baseball bats who didn't like his face even after he gave up his wallet.

—RIFLE BARRAGE STRIKES DOWN YOUNG MOTH-ER. . . . On her way to the supermarket. Juvenile Snipers Free on Bail.

Headlines swept by in a blur. ARREST KILLER OF TERRI-FIED GIRL—GANG RAPE ON TENEMENT ROOF—ARSON IN A TOKEN BOOTH—

I got up to leave.

Kagan pulled me back down. "One more. Dramatized," he said.

The film rolled. Disabled station wagon on a country road by a flowing river. Car filled with bags of groceries and a couple of rambunctious preschoolers. Young man in crew cut and corduroy jacket to the rescue? So the mother believed. I shut my eyes fast because she was too blond, too full-figured.

"Rape, first," Kagan said in my ear. "Then murder. He hit her over the head and drowned her in the river. Then the kids."

I was on my feet. Kagan's grip on my shoulder was part barrier, part support. "They got off, all those 'troubled teens,'" he said. "Most of them didn't even serve time in juvenile facilities."

"But the last one murdered three people, two of them kids!"

"He only took credit for the rape. Didn't brag about the rest until he was free and clear. Legally free," he said softly.

". . . But not free from you?"

"From one of our members, you mean? From a grieving husband and father? The bastard died of natural causes—according to the obit, that is. He drowned."

A light flashed on. I saw a half-dozen silhouettes up front.

"That," Kagan said with a wave in their direction, "is an SD Team—self-defense. An integral part of the Mission planning. What you've seen, what you're about to hear, we call Fueling. Sit down and listen to a pro."

A man stood before the others—a shadow with no face.

"—violent crime committed by people under twenty-five? Sixty percent. Six-oh. Our target group, the ones who broke the old lady's nose, are between ten and fifteen years old. They're the ones we think killed the medical student. No kiddie crimes, not *these* kids."

The voice was as matter-of-fact as a bookkeeper's.

"The ten-year-old got his first .45 automatic out of a store he broke into, and his second from his thirteen-year-old brother, who went for a bigger piece. The street price is a bargain—"

"If I had a buck for every punk with a three-hundred-dollar handgun he got for fifty, I'd be rich," Kagan drawled in my ear.

"—crimes of this particular gang are random . . . and pointless-ly brutal, typical of what's going down today—"

"Punks!" someone yelled.

"With oversize macho complexes. Their leader pistol-whips grocers and liquor-store clerks for the fun of it."

"This guy is beginning to sound like a retired cop," I whispered. "What does he—"

"You're half correct."

"Retired? Or—"

We were plunged into total darkness.

"These still photographs, less than a week old, show our target gang on a holiday crime spree." The police-voice had changed; a cord pulled tight.

One by one they flashed on-screen. A viciously beaten young man. A woman so old her face was like a finely stitched lace handkerchief—until they broke her jaw. Broken bones, bloody heads—

"Profile of a gang leader," said the police-voice while the pictures rolled on. "Chronic truant from grade one. Graduated from fistfights to purse-snatcher and cash-register sneak in 19—"

Not retired. He sounded like he was reading from a rap sheet.

"By the age of eight, he'd taught his buddies how to steal. At ten, he had his own gang. Life became a series of assaults, armed robberies, spending sprees, and a street rep that said, Anyone hurts my feelings is dead meat. Dozens of arrests, each one ending the same way: send him back to Mother. Mother lives well on her son's earnings. The juvenile-court judges who keep setting him loose live with their consciences. The most recent offender, the Permissive who set in motion the carnage you saw just now, is Judge Arthur Younger, better known . . ."

"Bleeding Heart Art!" I swung on Kagan.

"—released him right after seeing *these.*"

Ghosts with denim legs.

I bolted and ran, pursued by a relentless voice.

"—free to rape and rob, free to murder. Unless we stop them."

Stop them! I want you to stop them!

"Do you?"

Kagan had followed me out. Had I said it out loud?

"This is *my* Mission," I said. "Isn't it?"

"Tomorrow night. Seven o'clock. Are you with us?"

I jammed my eyes shut. But I saw what he wanted me to see: not just Sarah anymore. The old lady with the broken nose. The medical student. The young mother on her way to the supermarket.

I opened my eyes but I didn't see Kagan, I saw the sanctimonious face of Judge Arthur Younger. After that, all I could see were the broken bones and bloody heads, and I said to Kagan, without really seeing him, "I'm with you."

"Convince your boyfriend otherwise," Kagan said, voice flat. "You've been overwrought. What you saw just now sickened you, brought you back to your senses. He'll believe you. Psychiatrists go for that bullshit."

"You've gone to a lot of trouble over me," I said slowly.

I caught the flicker of an emotion. Annoyance? Resentment?

"Tomorrow?" Kagan pressed.

"Tomorrow."

Chapter 10

I left my building and spotted the car just down the street.

"My own doorman didn't recognize me," I announced, pleased with Kagan's sloping half-smile as I slid in next to him.

I had made a gum-chewing march through the lobby in tight jeans, pea jacket, and a dark wool watch cap over my new gamin haircut. The sunglasses helped, but the coup de grace was a blaring radio held at just the right angle next to my ear.

"You could be Puerto Rican," he said, eyes on the road.

. . . Mother of a boy killed for his radio. I'd thought of her as I sat in front of a mirror, darkening my skin. I said, "It's not just the tanning lotion. I have Sephardic ancestors."

"Nothing like having Portuguese blood in your veins." He glanced at me. "You must have spoiled the boyfriend's plans."

. . . Friend, not boyfriend, and none of your damn business.

"What did you tell him?" he pressed.

"That I was spending New Year's Eve with Claudia."

"What did you tell friend Claudia?"

"A couple of white lies. Why?"

"We don't want curious boy- and girlfriends on our tail."

"That why you keep checking your rearview mirror?"

"You're observant," he said, not looking particularly pleased.

"And you're a damn fool if you think Jamie or Claudia—"

"The man who doesn't post guards is the fool," he said mildly.

"Where are we headed, Kagan?"

"A place you once called home." Dark amusement in his eyes.

"Not the South Bronx!" . . . Where Sarah's silverware had turned up; of course. My destiny, the Bronx. I sat back, waiting for it.

"Quite a change since you left thirty years ago."

"Quite a change since my parents moved here in the twenties," I admitted, looking at what was left of once-sturdy brick and limestone buildings—the Art Deco apartment houses I'd grown up with.

He pulled up to the curb. It took me a minute before I saw what he was up to. "I was born right over there," I said slowly.

He opened my door. We went into what was left of the building. Was there a window that wasn't smashed, a door not gaping open? A sink or a tub that hadn't been ripped out, as if some mad dentist had been let loose on all that porcelain? Everything was either charred or collapsed. "Let's get out of here," I muttered.

In the car, I told him I'd seen signs of occupants.

"Not for long. Best way to rid a place of squatters is set a fire. That brings firemen with axes. Then the strippers, hot on their heels, eager to pick the place clean. They swarm over derelict buildings like this for the metal—pipes, wires, fixtures. Unless the druggies get there first," he said, watching me, "and turn it into a crack house. Pretty soon the city shuts off the water—no more pipes. The ceilings go, then the walls—"

"I get the picture," I said, wondering why he liked me angry.

We drove past piles of debris. Empty lots. Emptier buildings. Postwar East Berlin had come to the Bronx.

Kagan handed me an envelope. "My antidote to cold feet."

A duplicate set of photographs! "Kagan, how in God's name—"

"The Puerto Rican kid stole them for us."

"Tony? But who took them? *Why* would anyone take them?"

"Pedro Luis Morales, alias Indio, is big macho. Man makes a score, he wants mementos. Look at them, Karen," he urged softly.

One last time, I told myself. One by one . . .

Give in to rage, Jamie? That's like giving it a home, a place of refuge in your own body. Do you know how it tastes? Like bile. How it feels? Like blood pounding in your head, ready to burst.

"Ready?" Kagan asked. He had pulled over again.

I picked out six figures in black wearing wraparound glasses. We followed them to a derelict building. Seven of us (where was number eight?) marched up six flights and grouped outside a solid door, locked against intruders.

"Gang headquarters. Nobody home," Kagan told me as a burly black figure smashed through the wooden door—splinters flying —with a four-by-four. People moved around and past me.

I was reduced to staring. Electricity from a rusting generator. An oil painting of the Manhattan skyline on a crumbling wall. An Oriental rug—brilliant crimson—over cracked floorboards. Garment racks of clothes that looked expensive. I edged closer. A couple of Saint Laurent suits . . . an Oscar de la Renta gown . . . a stunning Bill Blass jacket, silk with purple and orange stripes. I had visions of Park Avenue closet raids, of window-shopping jet-setters being whisked out of their furs.

Furs. I gaped at piles of them serving as bedspreads for a couple of sagging mattresses. Broken furniture groaned with the weight of stereos, TV sets, cameras—I spotted a Hasselblad. A gigantic Mitsubishi rear-projection job stood in a corner. I peered into a peeling bathtub: gold and silver right up to its dirty ring. I reached in for a woman's braided-gold chain. For a small man's Rolex. I dropped them, backing away, wiping my hands on my slacks.

"Phase one," Kagan said behind me. "Attack and destroy."

I leaned against a wall and watched. Lithe figures in black, smashing, ripping, battering away. They were ruthlessly efficient. Cracks appeared on television screens. Glass shattered and smoked. Someone took aim and sent a stack of silver sailing through an open window. I picked up a piece that had fallen, a silver platter with an intricate basket-weave pattern . . . a smaller version of Sarah's.

It was like touching a hot stove. I hurled it out the window.

I headed for a fur pile. Stared down at ermine, sable, a glut of mink. Reached for a lush leather-trimmed reddish fur with an extravagant collar. The image of a bright-eyed creature that was smart enough to outwit hound, horse and two-legged creatures in riding clothes only to end up as a coat made my mouth curl.

Kagan stopped me at the window. "That's not what we do with furs," he chided. "Start bagging these!" he called out loudly to the room at large, holding up the fox coat.

He pointed out a safe, almost out of sight behind a large pool table, and said, "Phase two: reparations. Where possible, of course. After that, expenses. Ours are considerable, and the safe of a thief is a real jackpot. Cash, diamond rings—"

"So that's how you finance your operations!"

"Only partly."

I noticed some crack pipes scattered across the floor. "Not just diamond rings," I said. "You people in the drug business?"

"Only when it's easily convertible into hard cash. Care to stick around and see how much coke and angel dust Indio has stashed away?" Even as I shook my head he was steering me out the door.

Someone called out to him. "We'll return after phase three," he yelled back. "Our lookout gave their lookout time to report to his leader," he told me as he hurried me down the steps.

"Then phase three—"

"By now he'll have led our man straight to some ersatz Indians on the warpath," he said with a movement of his lips that was too snide to qualify as a smile.

Our lookout; number eight. "So their headquarters—"

"Weren't deserted?" he said, cutting me off again. "Not entirely. With that much loot, you have to worry about a raid by a rival gang. It's what we want this to look like."

"Our" lookout was already back with the information.

"Big pickings on New Year's Eve," Kagan told me afterward in the car. "People liquored up and careless. All that partying. Indio changes territories tonight. Destination," he said, "Manhattan."

Upper Manhattan. Respectable, middle-class, but with too many side streets. We prowled one after another, looking for prowlers.

"Watch the doorways," Kagan said. "Check out empty lots and subway entrances. Look for broken windows. Tell me what you see."

I saw Indio's brothers in spirit. Shadows in black thermal jackets slouching in threes and fives. Limbs moving in pointless energy with, every once in a while, a streetlight catching the glint of what looked like a Michael Jordan sneaker. I strained to hear, to make sense out of the muttered obscenities and raucous laughter. I tried to see faces but kept seeing pieces of them: nice straight noses, and crooked ones; a sloppy mustache, an occasional beard; chins that hadn't seen their first shave; lots of thick dark hair, but some blonds too; flashing teeth and too many mouth shapes to catalogue except that every one of them was loose.

"Gone," Kagan said finally. "On their way back to defend the fort." He checked his watch. "Time to go."

"We've been marking time, haven't we?" I said slowly. "Why?"

"You don't want to know."

"Your no-questions rule? Not this time. We'll be back after phase three, you said— Kagan, what's wrong with that girl?"

He stopped the car and we got out.

She was bruised and coatless, almost dressless. She led us to her boyfriend. He was barely conscious, bleeding from a knife wound. College kids, home on vacation. Out for a good time.

I called 911 and we sped off to the sound of a wailing siren, like a woman in a fit of hysterics. . . .

"Poor kid," Kagan said. ". . . Ready to hear about phase three?"

The girl we'd just left had been a rape victim. "They raped Sarah," I said slowly. "Kagan, that's not what—phase three— My God, I thought you people preferred Dante to Exodus?"

"Who says they're mutually exclusive?"

"Gang rape." I shivered.

"Happening even as we speak." Kagan sounded cheerful.

"Men raping men," I said bleakly, unable to make it real.

"Courtesy of the C Team, all cooptees—and well paid."

"Not that boy Tony!"

"Relax. We leave that level of retaliation to hired punks. Our backup SD Team—the men we went in with—will keep everyone in line. Good men. You drew the elite."

"Why?" No answer. "Why the special treatment, Kagan?"

"Maybe you're a special person."

"Why do you keep checking your rearview mirror?"

"Jealous boyfriends make me nervous."

"He's not the jealous type," I snapped.

"Is he the worrying type? That could be worse."

I turned away so Kagan wouldn't see what he'd touched off. Jamie, my self-appointed protector. Jamie, definitely the worrying type. Me, worrying about Jamie worrying about me.

Needlessly, as it turned out. We made it back without incident, let alone conversation. This time I crept up the six flights, not wanting to hear what was still going on. Howling and cursing.

"When the word goes out they were buggered, Indio's punks can kiss their tough-guy image good-bye," Kagan said. "After that—"

The sudden silence startled us both. Then, footsteps.

"Everyone's left by the fire escape. The punks back to whatever gutter they crawled out of," Kagan explained. "Almost everyone." He took my hand as if about to lead me onto a dance floor. "It's time."

I pulled away. Sat on the top step like a recalcitrant child.

"We have preconditions, remember?" Kagan snapped. "The one inspired by the Mafia is called 'making your bones.'"

It's called killing someone.

He used the old ploy on me. "Sarah was stabbed to death. Her killer is on the other side of that door."

"I can't go in there," I said hoarsely.

"First Judge Younger, and now you. So he walks again, free to kill someone else's daughter? He will, you know. He has before. Think your Sarah was the first?"

I wanted her to be the last. Desperately. I stood up.

"Phase four—our motto," Kagan said. "Vengeance is mine."

There they stood: my six-man Self-Defense Team in wraparound sunglasses so I couldn't see even a hint of hate or pleasure or fear in their eyes. My backup. I had drawn the elite, Kagan said.

Two of them held a big-chested, narrow-waisted boy-man with skin the color of wet sand and straight black hair that hung to his shoulders and gleamed brighter than his teeth.

Two of them held Sarah's killer.

Was there no justice? Where was the fear in those spaced-out, black-marble eyes? What would it take to wipe the fuck-you expression off his face?

His arms were pinned back, red silk shirt ripped to the waist, open to the garish hues of a tattoo: an Apache brave with a dripping knife in one upraised fist. What made me go closer was the way the tattoo moved—too damn rhythmically.

My own breath was coming in spurts. Blood deserting an artery?

"Murderer," I rasped. "You murdered my daughter. I was on the phone that night. I heard what—"

"Hear her die, motherfuckin' bitch? Get yourself an earful?"

To hear it again—the same voice, almost the same words. To be swamped by the same helpless terror—the sheer horror of not being able to move, to stop it! To see it happening again and again in your imagination . . .

Then to see the face behind the taunt, thrust into yours. Not a face in a photograph. Real, this time. Real eyes, real hair—

The odd-shaped birthmark above his cheek stopped me. Just like last time. It was small and brown, something a child might have drawn to depict a single tear. The Apache began to recede. . . .

The ring in his ear came into focus. Not a ring, an earring. . . . Wasn't it?

It was a gold band, very plain, very wide, with a sprinkle of diamond chips that winked at me, they kept winking—

I took it back, yanking and tugging. I held it on the palm of my hand, my bloody hand, and I could hear Sarah howling—why was she howling? I had her ring back.

I had torn it from his ear. The earring he had made of her wedding band. His earlobe hung like two pieces of limp macaroni, and he was howling.

All I could hear was Sarah.

I saw a knife on the table next to him. I heard a voice. "Hold his hand down, his left hand—" I saw a hand, my hand, pick up the knife, and the voice said, "Not so tight. Spread the fingers. I want his ring finger," I said, "I want—"

A knot of flesh flew at me like a well-aimed baseball.

They caught his fist an inch from my face.

I dropped the knife and backed away, gagging.

"We got company," a voice warned.

"Karen, for the love of God!"

"Hold it right there, Doctor."

I whirled in time to see Kagan's gun hand come whipping out, Jamie in his sights.

"Are you crazy?" I cried, flinging myself between them. I grabbed Jamie's arm. "What are you doing here?"

Jamie bent over me. Kagan, scowling, lay the gun down on the flat arm of a chair.

"You didn't sound right on the phone," Jamie said. "Neither did Claudia—first New Year's Eve you two missed, she told me."

"So you rushed right over to Karen's place in time to see her leave. You followed us. We have business, Doctor." Kagan took rough hold of Jamie's arm, propelling him forward.

The others, good backup team that they were, closed ranks.

I watched six menacing figures in black move off to—

Six?

Every back in the room turned away, a killer forgotten—a killer with a knife in his free hand. The one I had dropped. It was aimed at the nearest pair of shoulder blades—at Jamie!

It came back to me like a shuddering echo an instant before my hand shot out for Kagan's gun—

It only takes a couple of seconds to lose your life—or the life of the person you're with.

I squeezed the trigger. I squeezed it two more times with my ears hurting, white flashes in my eyes.

Kagan took his gun away.

"Better get her out of here fast," he told Jamie. "We'll clean up."

My eyes cleared. "Clean what up?" I whispered.

Jamie grabbed hold of me—too late to block my view.

I looked down at a prone figure in tight-fitting jeans and a red silk shirt.

I looked at Pedro Luis Morales, alias Indio, one sand-brown arm outstretched. Lying in his blood.

On the way to Jamie's place, I let him talk me out of giving myself up. I was not a killer. I had saved his life. Take a life to protect a life. A classic case of self-defense, he kept saying. Look it up if you don't believe me.

I did. It really *was* self-defense. In the eyes of the law, I was not a killer.

What, then?

"You're in shock. It's good for you," Jamie soothed. "Kagan will have Sarah's ring cleaned up. Shall I have it restored?"

"Please. Will Kagan—I don't remember telling you his name."

"You didn't. Just 'cowpoke vigilante,' love."

"I don't understand."

He put a crystal glass in my hand and filled it to the brim with champagne.

"Time for a midnight toast," he said with a glance at the clock. He filled his own glass and raised it.

I looked into the brooding eyes of a stranger.

I refused to raise my glass. Happy New Year?!

"Welcome to Victims Anonymous," Jamie said, banishing the stranger with one of his dazzling smiles. *"Now* do you understand?"

I wanted to toss the champagne in his face. I wanted to give him a medal.

I wanted to close my eyes and disappear.

We touched glasses and I drank.

Chapter 11

"Nervous?" Jamie asked me.

"Numb. You keep saying you people need my help. Why?"

"Later," he said, putting me off again.

"I'd be less nervous if you'd draw me a picture of your so-called inner circle," I groused. A week had gone by and he still hadn't filled me in. I looked at my watch. "There's time."

"Barely," he said, relenting. "You'll like Zack because—"

"No last name?"

"Not for now. He's a working cop. You won't like O'Neal. Hard-hat type. Owns a construction company. Hugh Hunter is a businessman from Queens. The advertising executive is an ex-patient. Earl Bartholemew is a corrections officer. Calls himself Black Bart. Kagan you know. You do and you don't," he said with a sly smile.

The doorbell rang. I watched him turn host, ushering everyone in. A muscular black guy in jeans and a navy wool jacket crossed the room with a no-nonsense stride; Zack the cop, out of uniform?

"Hi," he said casually. But his eyes were grave.

"Say something else," I said. "I'm doing a comparison."

"To see if I was the voice you heard at your Fueling? Damn right." And proud of it! said those velvet-brown eyes.

"Thanks," I said. We shook on it.

The businessman walked over. Everything about him was short and to the point, from his five-foot-four frame and his introduction—"Hugh Hunter, here"—to his carefully groomed salt-and-pepper beard. He wore a three-piece suit that had seen better days, and his look-me-over glance had relief in it, as if he were glad to find one other person in the room as formally dressed as he was.

"O'Neal," said O'Neal with a blatantly perfunctory nod in my direction. The guy had "construction man" written all over him: battering-ram bulk, cigars sticking out of his breast pocket, a surly confidence that boasts its own maleness. Not my type.

Neither was the big fellow decked out in shoulder-to-toe black leather, as if he'd just slid off his trusty Harley Davidson. "Black Bart," he said, sticking out his hand while I tried to keep my eyes off his silver belt buckle—a screaming eagle with talons extended. But he said "Welcome to the club" as if he meant it before sauntering off, a grinning, strutting advertisement for packaged virility.

Kagan gave me an idle wave from across the room.

Missing: one advertising executive.

An animated Jamie seated us around his round table of sturdy oak and served up scrambled eggs on gold-plated china. Watching him pour and repour coffee into crystal mugs, I was struck by his almost boyish eagerness to see to everyone's needs.

"So you're here," Kagan said to me. A real icebreaker.

"I'm not sure why," I told him, nervous again. "You've made exceptions for me from the start. Now it seems you want my—"

"Jamie's idea," he said, cutting me off, his mouth flattening in disapproval. "Which may or may not make sense. Before we get into it, tell me how you feel about what happened last week."

"Scared." . . . Also grateful, I admitted silently. When *I'd* needed help, they'd jumped right in. "I keep wondering," I said slowly, "if I've lost my reason by agreeing to meet with you."

"Maybe you need to know why we're here," said Hugh the businessman, taking pity on me.

Kagan snapped him a make-it-brief glance.

"I had to close my business," Hugh Hunter said, soft grey eyes clouding with the memory. "Twenty years in the same place," he said. "It wasn't the competition that knocked me out of the box. Or bad judgment. Hell, I'd have accepted that. Goes with the territory." He ran two fingers up and down one side of his beard. "But when your people start coming in late all the time, when they stop coming in at all, scared off by the muggers . . . When some of them show up bleeding—" He stood up abruptly. "I'm here," he said, patting his chest, "because *this* is what a businessman ought to wear to the office, not the bulletproof variety I was starting to get used to, God help me."

We both stared at his lightweight silver-grey vest.

Zack stretched in his chair, not in the manner of someone taking his ease, but of a man releasing tension. The wrestler's body didn't go with the face and the face didn't match my preconceptions of a cop: ceaselessly questioning eyes and the perpetual frown of a scholar. "I'm here," he said, "because I got tired of being half combat soldier, half bureaucrat. When the police spend more time filling out forms and cooling their heels in court than they do on the street—" He shrugged. "Don't get me wrong. I don't mind combat. As long as I can trust the generals," he said with a smile. "But with this turn-'em-loose crowd running things, I can't do my job any more than Hugh could do his. Know what really gets to me? The old people. I can't look them in the eye anymore. I can't stand to see the fear," he said, his smile twisting out of sight.

Bart, the corrections officer, hadn't lost his grin. Everything about the guy was dark, from his custom-made shirt and lethal-looking leather suit to his slick hair and hooded eyes. He had the kind of barroom handsomeness that girls in junior high fall madly in love with. But there was something boyishly disarming about that grin. I grinned back. "Our prison system sucks," he said simply.

The door opened and an ethereal blond beauty let herself in.

With a key to Jamie's apartment. Jamie avoided my startled glance.

"Meet Lee Emerson, advertising executive," he said.

She breezed across the room, the slant of her skirt merging with the subtle movement of her hips. Her suit was so pale a beige that her skin flowed into it, her ruffled blouse as light and airy as ocean foam. She had that soft clingy hair men are supposed to want to touch, like the old-fashioned girl in shampoo commercials.

Just when I'd decided that something about her whole floating look was oddly purposeful, not to mention unfair—I was dressed for the office in charcoal-grey severe—she extended a conciliatory hand and said, "Hello, Karen Newman." I shook it, liking her smile.

So did Bart. He fell over himself to serve her breakfast. I liked him for it.

As she eased into the general conversation with an eager rush of words, I noticed her eyes: they were the color of everyone's favorite afternoon sky. But their liveliness seemed forced.

"Have you told Karen?" she asked Jamie. "Has she agreed?"

Kagan picked up the ball. "Jamie thinks your PR expertise could be crucial to us. The name of the game is recruitment."

"Wrong," Jamie bristled. "What we need is more visibility."

Locked horns. I could see it was an old fight.

"Can't we have both?" asked Lee the conciliator.

"A campaign to swell the ranks *and* mold public opinion. Why not?" Jamie mused. "It's time we took credit for the past three years. The public doesn't know we exist."

"Neither does the law," Zack pointed out.

"Visibility as an end in itself?" Kagan said, doling out his words. "A dangerous notion, Jamie."

"Yeah, dangerous," Bart echoed with a fierce frown.

"I don't get it," I said. "If you're talking about some kind of a PR campaign, you'll buy yourself a lot more than increased visibility. What happens to the 'anonymous' in Victims Anonymous?"

"Gone with the wind," said hard hat O'Neal. He lit up a smelly Havana and eyed his bread plate. Jamie got him an ashtray.

"Is it time, then?" Zack was leaning forward.

"I have a better question," Hugh said. "Is it suicide time?"

"Think what a popular image could do for your money-raising efforts, Hugh," Jamie said cheerfully. "You keep saying we're too dependent on my foundation grants."

"We all knew we'd go public one day," Zack said, sounding like he was picking his way across a minefield. "It was just a question of when." He looked to Kagan for confirmation.

Kagan's neck muscles tensed. "Maybe you're right," he said, eyes making a slow survey around the table as if he were taking its pulse; stopping on Jamie. "Maybe it's time to take on the culture."

Bart grinned agreement. "Time we stopped acting like moles."

Lee Emerson was up and pacing. "We'll mobilize people!"

"We'll start slowly." Kagan's tone brought caution back to the room. "Priorities," he said, as if it were a holy word. "I say we ease up on recruiting while we go after mass sympathy." He swung on me. "Can you give it to us, Karen?"

Startling, the sound of my name on his lips. Shocking, that the question didn't shock.

"Your Sarah is avenged," he said, misreading my reaction. "What about all the other Sarahs?"

Crudely put. I said, "You don't have to nail me by my Jewish guilt, Kagan. I'm grateful. To all of you," I said, looking around. Stopping, like Kagan, on the man who had become my life-support system—on Jamie. "But I can't join anything, I won't," I said, holding his glance. "If I were to do this one thing . . ."

"Would you be quits? Sure," Kagan said, as if he grasped what I hadn't even told Jamie. Call it a commitment or a personal code: I pay my debts. I've never been able to fathom people who don't.

Zack refilled my mug. "Before you decide, Karen, make it real—what you'd be doing for us, and why."

"Not just for you."

He smiled. "That's the right answer. I was about to say that none of us in this room, none of the others, feel shame or guilt. We're proud of what we're fighting for, in spite of the way we've been forced to go about it. For now," he added with a glance at Kagan, as if underscoring the words.

"What *are* you fighting for?"

"Justice," Jamie answered me fervently.

"Survival," Kagan said.

"Compassion for the people who need it most," Zack said in the dark tone of a man who'd seen too little of it in his business.

"You're a policeman," I said, "yet you . . ."

"Operate outside the law? Only as long as the law forces the cop to act with one hand tied behind his back. I see what we're doing as temporary. I want to help the police function again."

"Once our message sinks in, once we have widespread support and Victims Anonymous becomes a force to be reckoned with, the politicians and the lawmakers will pay attention. *Then* we'll witness real change," Jamie predicted with a fervor I'd never heard from him. "Karen," he said, squeezing my hand, "the day we all look to is the day we can stop being surrogate lawmen."

"Who needs vengeance once the criminal-justice system starts dispensing justice?" Kagan asked, softly rhetorical.

"It's a terrible thing, force as the solution to anything," I said to no one in particular . . . to all of us. "Yet I can't shake the feeling that what happened last week to my daughter's murderer was . . . right." My eyes sought Jamie's. They were telling me what he'd been saying all week long. *No double standard, Karen. What's right for you is right for us. Right?*

Right. I said, "One PR campaign coming up." . . . And felt, for the first time all morning, that I wasn't Alice in Wonderland. "Question," I said. "What do you mean by 'going public'? Leave your calling card at the scene? 'Victims Anonymous' in elegant Gothic lettering?"

Jamie smiled. "It *is* elegant, isn't it?"

Spoken like the proud designer. I thought of a card slipped into the pocket of my coat. . . .

"What we need now," Jamie mused, "is a new calling card, something symbolic that the public can identify with."

Lee laid a proprietary hand on his arm. "I'm thinking of a certain reckless Englishman who rescued French aristocrats from the guillotine. The emblem of the Scarlet Pimpernel . . ."

"A small red flower? Not bad."

"Or the fleur-de-lis of the Three Musketeers?"

He grinned at her. "Forget Dumas. Give me Sabatini. How about the mask of that consummate swashbuckler—"

"Scaramouche!" Lee's arms went out like a cheerleader.

Like gleeful children, the two of them. Jamie was fingering the silver medallion he always wore around his neck.

It gave me an idea. "I'm thinking of a lovely creature exploited for centuries by man's so-called sporting instinct," I said as the image of a leather-trimmed fur coat came back to me. "What if the target of the fox hunt were to turn the tables and . . . hunt the hunter?"

Jamie's hand remained at his throat, a slow smile softening his features.

I looked to Kagan, reputed animal lover, according to Jamie.

"Forget the hunting nonsense," he said. "The fox is clever, quick-witted. An animal who has learned how to outsmart man."

"To our new symbol," Jamie said gravely. "You've no idea how appropriate it is, Karen." He held his silver fox medallion aloft. "We'll use the same stylized design. Curved body . . . tip of the tail a hairbreadth from the head . . ." He dropped the medallion to slip his arm around my shoulders, bringing a look of resignation to Lee's lovely face, and a look of interest to Kagan's.

I was about to shake his arm loose when O'Neal, of all people, raised his mug of cold coffee in the air and said, "Here's to one foxy lady!"

Everyone but Kagan joined in. He was looking at me with a kind of heightened alertness, as if sizing up an opponent.

"Let's not get sidetracked by details," he said. "Karen asked before what it means to go public. Risk is what it means. New dangers. How do we keep the law from tracing us through the victims we avenge once our calling card, however disguised, is left behind? We could get away with it once. Twice, maybe. But as the incidents pile up, even the cops—no offense, Zack—will begin to grasp a pattern. I figure we can handle the locals. But I'd hate to have the FBI breathing down our necks until we're ready."

"How can you ever be ready for that?" I said, trying to blot out a sudden image and a singsong refrain . . . a face I had put away.

"We'll find a lot of sympathy even in those quarters," Zack reassured me. "I doubt there's a man wearing a badge today who doesn't resent what's going on. Emotionally, we're allies."

"It's no different from your south-of-the-border banana republic. Those people change dictators every few years," O'Neal opined between mouthfuls of scrambled egg—his third helping. "The new revolutionaries stir up the natives. The old order runs scared and starts pulling in its horns. The military smells panic and goes over to the enemy. Viva the revolution." He ground out his cigar in the crystal ashtray.

"Maybe," Kagan said, unconvinced. "But a clever fox is adept at keeping the pursuers off his scent. Suppose we pull back a bit and only target Savages who have no connection to VA members?"

"Avenge perfect strangers?" Zack was frowning. "I see."

"Do the rest of you?" Kagan asked. "Even with a calling card, we won't be traced as long as we stay careful on the job. The cops know we're out there but they can't predict who, how, or where. Not if there's no discernible pattern to our Missions. Then gradually we go back to avenging members—"

"And continue the mix as long as necessary!"

I stared at Jamie. His enthusiasm was untainted by even the slightest hint of fear.

Mine must have been transparent because Zack ambled over as the others were getting ready to leave.

"We really do know what we're doing," he said with convincing calm. "We've built an impressive organization."

"Jamie gets the prize for sheer ingenuity," Kagan drawled. "Ask our leader, sometime, about VA's structure."

"Jamie?" I gasped. "Jamie's your leader?"

"I told you I didn't have the face for it."

I barely noticed when Lee Emerson, with a graceful shrug in my direction, dropped a key onto Jamie's palm and made a dignified exit.

Chapter 12

Jamie eyeballed his watch. "You'll be late for your meeting."

"My boss is getting used to it. Talk to me, Jamie."

"About my role in all this? Forget leaders. Victims Anonymous is only as good as its inner circle."

"Which you organized. Why didn't you tell me?"

"Modesty," he said, looking immodest as hell. "It grew out of an . . . incident. Afterward, I toyed with the idea of victims fighting back. But not alone, not isolated. Organized," he said. "I mapped strategy for a year, ran some tests. I met Kagan. He pushed me over the edge."

"Into what, exactly, these Missions?"

Big grin. "They keep me in shape. I'm forced to practice my karate, lift weights, and go horseback riding in Central Park."

"What else are you 'forced' to do?"

"Join committees," he said, looking bored.

"Like what?"

"Penal reform, victims rights."

"Why, for God's sake?"

"Appearances. My credentials buy me foundation status with

legitimate groups. It's where the bulk of our financing comes from, in case you were wondering."

"Kagan said you raised money by selling off stolen merchandise. When you can't trace the original owner," I added as his eyebrows shot up in protest. "Reparations first, he said."

"It's an ironclad rule. But the money left over is a drop in the bucket compared to what I get in grants. Every year or so I come up with a new anticrime program and give it a sexy title."

"Like Victims Rehabilitation League?" I said, remembering the fancy buffet on Christmas Eve.

"You *are* a foxy lady. Programs like that get us the foundation grants. I turn all the money over to Hugh, who funnels the bulk of it into Victims Anonymous."

"I gather he keeps two sets of books."

"Sure. But the annual Holiday Encounter you attended wasn't as expensive as it looked. We set it up that way so nobody questions where the money goes. Victims Anonymous is mostly where it goes. We're big spenders."

I pulled out a pad and made some notes. "What do you spend it on besides Missions?"

"Oh, travel expenses for our handpicked recruiting units. The start-up costs for each new local cell."

"You were teasing Hugh before about his money-raising efforts. What's that all about?"

"Hugh is a bit of a doomsayer. Worries about the grants drying up on us. He's been hitting some well-heeled business contacts for cash contributions—men of conscience, he calls them."

"He tells them about your crime-fighting activities?"

He laughed. "We're bold, love, not foolhardy. Not to worry. Every one of our businessmen donors is under the impression he's contributing to something civic-minded, like bulletproof vests for cops in patrol cars."

"Been in 'business' long?" I said dryly.

"Officially? Three years. Unofficially, closer to five. It's all on tape. I'm compiling a record for posterity." He leaned back in his chair. "I also like to think out loud."

"You're joking," I said. "All that data—"

"Won't fall into the wrong hands. I've worked out a self-destruct system," he said cheerfully. "What else?"

"Kagan said to ask you about structure."

"It's cellular. It's also national in scope."

"How many cells are we talking about?"

"At last count? At least one in every major city in the country. In big crime centers like Cleveland, Chicago, Atlanta, Detroit—our own New York, of course—we have as many as five or six. The basic idea is to keep every cell a self-motivated unit, but with guidelines from the top. That way, opening new cells across the country requires a minimum of effort. We don't tell the locals who to go after, or how. All they get are the three Ps: principles, prototypes and precautions."

"Four P's now," I said, losing my smile. "Propaganda."

"Is that what they call good PR in your business?" he teased.

"Tell me about Lee Emerson, ad exec and former patient."

"A frustrated romantic living in the wrong century. An aspiring novelist until I helped her realize she wanted to *be* a writer, not do a writer's work. After that she got serious about advertising and turned herself into a superb businesswoman."

"End of doctor-patient relationship," I said. And waited.

"We've been having an affair," he conceded. "But that's not why I brought her in. She came up with a good idea—so good we made her our administrative expert. Over O'Neal's male-chauvinist objections. Bart's, too, until he got a good look at her."

"Bart's still looking."

He turned thoughtful. "Maybe now she'll start to notice."

"Now that you have your key back?"

"With your help, love. Thanks for not giving me away."

"You want everyone to think we're having a torrid affair?"

"Not everyone. Despite my professional efforts, Lee is not without problems. We— She's not good for me."

Something in his face stopped me from asking why.

"You'd be good for me." His grin said: Please don't take me seriously. "Karen Newman. Witty, wonderful . . . wise."

"And about as seducible, these days, as an electric drill," I said, just in case. "I'm so tense that I—"

"Just tense? Or frightened?" His hand was gentle on mine.

"After what I've just agreed to? Something new has been added to my life, Doctor. Feels like a ball in my stomach and it comes from the company I'm starting to keep. Fearball," I said, thinking of cats who get furballs from licking away loose hair.

"I think you just coined a phrase."

"What *really* scares me is the prospect of publicity seekers and crackpots infiltrating the ranks. How do you keep out—"

"Potential whistle-blowers? Same way an airline keeps would-be terrorists and skyjackers off its planes. We supply each cell leader with psychological profiles of people to watch out for."

"Smart," I said, "but not foolproof. Suppose somebody signs on and then has a change of heart?"

"Somebody who's already 'made his bones,' you mean? It happens. But not too often. Happy ending every time," he said with a slow smile. "All it takes is a little reminder . . . Here, take this." He handed me a thick envelope.

"Spare-time reading?"

"Profiles of some recent recruits—on a par with a Stephen King novel, they tell me. No more questions?" he said as I got up.

"Just one. The incident that sparked Victims Anonymous— why haven't you told me about it?"

"Because it's painful. I don't like talking about it."

"Try," I said, sensing that he wanted to.

He looked away. "I was obsessed with the criminal mind . . . with the prospect of retraining it. Here was the key that could unlock the problems of a society caving in on itself. I went after a new kind of patient," he said in the soft tone of a guilty confession. "Inmates of reform schools. Graduates of penal institutions. Karen, I paid them just to show up! I kept tabs on them after office hours while I learned street facts and read up on the literature. Let's go downstairs," he urged, his face pale.

We took an elevator two flights down to his office. He sat me down and put on a tape. The man who liked to think out loud . . .

The culture is swimming in the antisocial personality. Let's call him the amoral psychopath. Personality characteristics? Typically young, male, no conscience development, manipulative and irresponsible, low on frustration tolerance, rejects authority, does not profit from experience, lives in a series of present moments with no sense of the future. Anyone standing in the way of immediate gratification—a grocer defending his cash box, a woman holding on to her gold chain or her virginity—is expendable.

He stopped the tape. "The hostile psychopath is a subcategory," he told me. "You met him on New Year's Eve."

I killed him on New Year's Eve. . . .

"I met him in my office—a patient. After one of our hair-raising sessions, I did something . . . crazy. I followed him, armed with a tape recorder and a miniature amplifier—instead of the licensed .45 I *should* have been carrying," he said, mouth tightening like the pull of a drawstring. He dropped into a chair, eyes half closed. "He murdered a girl that night."

"You blame yourself," I whispered. "Jamie, why?"

"If I hadn't been the detached scientist engrossed in collecting valuable insights . . . who knows? I might have saved her. I'll never forget the girl's family when they found out what happened to her murderer," he said with a bittersweet smile. "There I stood, their White Knight, their instrument of deliverance."

He lost the bitterness, looked at me with a kind of wonder. "It was like snow melting, their despair. They were Puerto Rican poor and I had given them something they couldn't afford to buy."

"Compassion?" I said, bewildered.

"Justice. Seeing it wrenched my perspective."

"Justice? The killer—"

"I disemboweled the bastard."

I got up fast.

"So you think it was gratuitous?"

He had on a loose-fitting brown velour shirt. He started to unbutton it.

"I heard the scream and slid down from my Olympian perch—" He looked sheepish. "I was conducting my 'research' from a construction crane."

I stared at him.

"Shades of the Green Hornet," he said with a shrug. "My patient recognized me. I hit the ground and he lunged."

Jamie's shirt fell open to a six-inch knife scar across his stomach. "I grabbed the loading hook at the end of the rope—"

He stopped to frown at the color draining from my face.

"You're thinking I used excessive force," he said softly.

As he slipped on another tape, something in the set of his mouth made me want to clamp my hands over my ears.

Sunday, the tenth. The Brooklyn waterfront in mid-November. Deserted. Cold. What are they after? Nothing but stick-figures from up here. Find a better perch, then—lower. Move, before you lose the twilight. The crane? Easy, now . . . hand over hand over . . . Test the rope first. Perfect. Fleshed-out silhouettes, now. One living, breathing patient and two moving, grooving buddies—no, three. All that spastic energy.

Who turned off the juice? Look at those arched necks. Noses sniffing the air . . . like predators sensing their prey. Not here. Not at this hour. Who'd be fool enough to—

Two of them. Two damn fools. Arm in arm. Oblivious to the wolf pack, fanning out—

Armed with more than their teeth. Sweet Jesus . . .

Aheeeeeeeeeeeeeeeeeeeeeeeeeeeee!

"The sound that launched Victims Anonymous," Jamie said, killing the tape.

He slipped something flat and cold into my shaking hand.

"A gift from the girl's family," he said. "She wore it the night my patient stabbed her to death."

I looked at his fox medallion, almost weightless in my palm. A symbol, now. A mute cry for help. I gave it back to him.

But not completely.

* * *

My boss came in wearing a three-piece suit and a shine on his pointed shoes, looking more buttoned-down than usual. Larry was in ill humor.

Mine wasn't much better. I'd been making "top priority" piles on my desk and the lineup was depressing. A cosmetics manufacturer with a staid image—"in desperate need of a face-lift," some joker had scrawled across the top sheet. Three CEOs whose speeches needed polishing, not to mention a few original ideas. A small airline about to be plunged into a gargantuan labor dispute. A small Latin American country in desperate need of American aid.

Me, in desperate need of a shot in the arm, a pill to keep my eyes from glazing over. If only I could work on one project at a time, like a problem child you could devote all your energies to.

"The holidays are long gone. You're late," Larry complained—a bit mildly, I had to admit. "You all right?" he asked.

"I'm not up to one of your crack-of-dawn strategy sessions or last-minute travel orders, but I can still function," I snapped. "Sorry," I said as he put a calming hand over mine. I gestured at the desktop. "I think I'm having a concentration problem."

"Maybe you need a little time off?"

The old refrain. My shoulders sagged. "A little, Larry? How about a year or two to get my life back in shape?"

His eyebrows rose a good half-inch, letting me see the mournful look in his eyes. He didn't say, For God's sake, Karen, don't do this to me, I need you! But work for someone long enough and you can read his mind. He sank into the only comfortable chair.

"Make me a counteroffer," I joked, and wondered if ten days and a modest raise might make me feel guilty enough to get the creative juices flowing again.

"Six months," he said, chewing on his horn-rims.

I stared at him. "Six months what?"

"Leave of absence." He was up and pacing. "I don't know how I'll manage, but you look like hell."

He sat down abruptly. "I've been damn worried about you," he admitted with a small frown. "Take some time off, Karen. Meet some people. Fall in love. Get yourself a—"

"Stop it. Wipe that big-brother look off your face," I said, appalled. "Six months." I stared out the window.

And knew, suddenly, that it was what I wanted.

I shook my head a little to make it real. "Starting now?"

He faked a groan, my cue to say, "Don't worry, I'll clean off my desk before we make it official. Thanks, Larry."

We hugged, making it official.

When he left, I thought about the luxury of devoting all my energies in the next six months to a single, mind-blowing project.

I thought of a loose end: Claudia. I called her.

"Why the disappearing act?" Claudia asked. I hadn't seen her since Christmas Eve. She leaned forward, gold-loop earrings swinging. "Having a hot romance with the gorgeous Sir James?"

I had to laugh. "Friends, not lovers."

Our drinks arrived. "He's part of it, isn't he?" she asked when the waitress had left. "His timing was too damn good," she said to the surprise in my face. "He slick-talk you into joining?"

"Don't sneer. If he hadn't picked me up, I'd still be flat on my face," I said, toying with my coaster.

"Don't you think I know that? It's why I can't dislike him."

"It's why I've come to depend on him."

"We never used to sidestep each other's questions."

"Then drink up and don't ask any more."

I reached for my bourbon but she seized my hand before it got there. "Just one question, Karen. Why?"

How do you describe a scream in the night, like an overlay on your thoughts? Replay it often enough and it starts to merge with another scream in the night . . . with Sarah's. How do you explain a phenomenon like Kagan, a man who never lets you forget. . . . *Your Sarah is avenged. What about the other Sarahs?"* Or the gratitude, the driving need to pay off a debt?

I could only tell her part of it. "This is the wrong time in my life for corporate-image polishing," I said—and saw agreement in her eyes because she'd always held my job in mild contempt. "Our streets have turned into nightmare alley," I said. "How can I sit at a desk and write pep talks for top management or make creative contributions to some fat cat's profit-and-loss statement? These people are trying to change things and they need—" I shrugged. "Maybe I can help. But you're wrong about my joining. I've taken a six-month leave, that's all. Claudia, I need to do this."

"Don't say any more," she said, voice turning gentle. "How can I object? I didn't lose a daughter."

"That's why I can't condemn them. Because I did."

3

COMMITMENT

The art of our necessities is strange,
That can make vile things precious.

—Shakespeare, *King Lear*
Act III

Chapter 13

Jane Doe: marriage broke up under emotional stress of multiple rape. Both rapists plea-bargained back to the street.

John Doe: recruited out of prison (by a corrections officer named Bart?) after serving time for voluntary manslaughter—for firing in the dark at a burglar in his bedroom . . . ?

Mr. and Mrs. John Doe: "smash and grab" victims. Smash the display window with a rock or garbage can; grab the loot and run.

I looked up from my synopses of "new recruits" to accept the doughnut someone offered me. I read two more and promptly dubbed them the mad-as-hell joiners. . . .

"You know what the judge asked me before he threw the case out? Did I see the penetration. With a goddamn coat over my face?"

"Thirty years I been driving a cab. When they're not rippin' us off, they're blowin' our brains out. My turn, you bastards!"

I pushed the papers aside to stretch and look around at the ash-grey walls and mismatched furniture of my new office.

I stole a glance at my new officemates. A sweater-and-slacks crowd, all women, all ages, from the college kid in granny glasses to an old lady who peered back at me through pink-tinted oversize frames. Her color scheme was reminiscent of the American flag: red jumpsuit and rouged cheeks, pearls and powder-white skin, blue eyes and hair, both faded. I smiled. She dropped her eyes.

Pity. All the women were polite, but wary. I saw myself as PR consultant but they had me tagged as one of the elite.

It was a game Lee Emerson played to the hilt, I thought, as she swept in, the expensive cut of her clothes underscoring our drab office landscape. Burgundy leather pants suit today, like a gentle coat of armor around her too-thin figure, and a puff of raspberry chiffon at the throat. She pulled up an anemic-looking chair and turned a skeptical eye on my black corduroy jeans and the baggy sweatshirt that spelled CORNELL in faded red letters.

"My alma mater," I said lamely.

Her smile said, How quaint. "Got time for a quick briefing?"

"You're a relief," I admitted. "Two weeks of Jamie's 'horror file' of new recruits and I'm ready to take a swing at somebody."

She looked at me as if I were a bright student in her kindergarten class; it was that kind of smile. "That's the general idea. Why do you think it's called the 'horror file'? Our calculating Jamie brings a psychiatrist's frame of reference to everything he touches."

"So I've noticed," I said acidly. "What does he expect me to do now, come up with a PR plan or volunteer for the bat brigade?"

She laughed. "Not in *this* office. We're all Passives here."

"What's that make Jamie and Zack and the others who—"

"Actives. It's a distinction I came up with," she said with a barely perceptible lift to her chin.

Lee's "good idea" that got her into the club. And it *was* good. I said, "You mean, Moderates versus Bat-swingers, don't you?"

She shrugged. "Have it your way. New recruits, depending on their personal bent, join one group or the other. We Passives are pretty much all women. We do the administrative work."

"Such as?" I pulled out my notepad.

"Keeping records of every VA cell—not to mention every member of every cell. We also keep tabs on Missions and local recruitment through a series of post office boxes."

I must have frowned.

"Don't worry," she said, "it's strictly one-way visibility."

"What else?" I said, annoyed at the way everyone kept urging me not to worry.

"We distribute crime statistics. Pull together data on potential Targets. Permissives, mostly—the soft-on-crime people . . ." She paused while I scribbled away. ". . . as opposed to the criminals."

"Savages," I said, remembering my Christmas Eve briefing.

"Right. Say a local cell wants to publicize the sentencing habits of some criminal-court judge, or how many times a bleeding-heart governor vetoed the death penalty. We provide the figures."

"I'm impressed. You're the administrative head of all this?"

"General Lee Emerson, Bart calls me." Her smile was supposed to be self-deprecating. "My 'troops,'" she said with a casual wave at the women in the room (all within hearing distance) just when I thought I was being too hard on her.

"Any other military allusions I should be aware of?"

"Yes, as a matter of fact," she said gravely, missing the sarcasm. "R and R. That means—"

"Rest and rehabilitation?" I said incredulously, remembering my father's stint in the army.

"Kagan changed it to 'recruiting and revenging'—Actives territory. Nothing that concerns you." What I heard in her tone was *Stick to your files until further orders, Private Newman.* She did a mirror check: blond hair all in place, a quick ruffling of the chiffon. "Well, I'm off," she announced.

I stared at two weeks' worth of Jamie's "horror file"—stage one in my introductory course on Victims Anonymous—and decided I'd had enough for one day. What I needed was something physical, a good workout. I smiled. More than a good workout. Why not a little creative recruitment while I was at it?

I didn't even bother to make my usual semineat piles. "Well, I'm off," I said to the room at large in mock imitation of General Lee, and got smiles all around. Camaraderie at last!

The sign said SAFETY IN SELF-DEFENSE. I had barely walked in the front door when she spotted me and came striding over: retired policewoman Angela Russo, Amazonian instructor of "SIS."

"I like a person who doesn't quit," she smiled, looking down on me from her awesome height—close to six feet, maybe?

The last time she'd looked down on me, I'd been scared off by a punching bag.

I said, "I like a person who likes a person—"

She laughed, a deep, rich sound. "My favorite Sydney Greenstreet line in one of my favorite flicks. What's your pleasure?"

Anyone who liked *The Maltese Falcon* was my kind of woman. This was going to be easier than I thought. I said, "How about a little group instruction on what I wasn't paying much attention to last time—your basic strikes, kicks and escapes?"

"You got it. This way, Ms. . . . ?"

"Karen. Karen Newman."

She said what I hoped she'd say. "Call me Angela."

Group instruction turned individual. Angela Russo was a good teacher. And this time, I was a good pupil.

"You're a quick study," she told me. "Don't be afraid to admit you're enjoying yourself." She went off to help someone else.

I'm not here for enjoyment, Angela Russo, I'm here to pick your brain.

But I had to admit she was right. The scene wasn't offensive anymore.

I told myself I had time to kill until Angela Russo took her lunch break. I spotted a familiar face or two over by the heavy bags. I got in line.

I had wanted to know how it felt. It felt good. More than good. I had wondered how long you could keep punching before your hands got tired or your fists came undone of their own free will, but they didn't—they wouldn't—they had a life of their own.

"Next, please!" The voice of impatience, breaking the spell.

I walked away, my leotard clinging like a damp bathing suit.

"Really got it down pat this time," said one of the old faces.

When I asked her what she was talking about, she gave me a queer look. "Kiai. The yell of the spirit?"

I stared at her. I caught Angela Russo staring at me.

She accepted my invitation to lunch.

Sitting across from her, I almost wished she hadn't. She'd been puffing away at one of those thin cigars through ten minutes of warm-up talk, emitting smoke like a faulty chimney—but with such obvious enjoyment I didn't have the heart to object. She was big and easy in her gestures, a Mother Earth type with deep-set, deep-brown eyes, heavy shoulder-length hair, and the wholesome good looks that inspire trust in men and admiration without envy in women. I steered her in the direction I wanted to go. . . .

"Scared? Turn to the yellow pages and see for yourself. The self-defense business in this town is booming. In a lot of towns."

"A profitable business?"

"It can be," she said, looking chagrined. "If you're not a sucker for hard-luck stories. A lot of my clientele consists of unattached women from lousy neighborhoods with two kids to support."

. . . *What else are you a sucker for?* "Turning the fainthearted into street warriors must be very satisfying," I said. "It's a way to fight back. Tell me more about your clients and how they—"

"Fight who?"

"The crime wave," I said with a vague gesture. "The breakdown in our criminal-justice system."

"Interesting." She put out her cigar. Wiped some ash off the front of her rust-colored sweater. "Your friend told me about your daughter being murdered by a street gang. They ever catch them?"

"The police?" I said, caught short. "No, I don't— They told me he was killed by some rival gang."

Her eyes were on my cheeks; my cheeks were flushed. She turned up the shade to bright red—she said, leaning in on me a little, "Ever hear of a guy named Zack?"

I didn't trust my voice.

"So it's still going on," she said, her deep voice dropping another register. "You one of them, Karen?"

Just a fellow traveler, I wanted to say. What I said sounded pretty lame. "What are you talking about?"

"You. Two months ago you couldn't stomach the idea of self-defense. Today you make mincemeat out of one of my heavy bags. What happened between now and then? Are we going to play games or are you going to tell me why you really asked me out to lunch?"

"So I had an ulterior motive. But who the hell is Zack?"

"Playing games. Okay, Zack is a cop, an old friend. He tried to recruit me once. Had a lot to say about violent crime and the system breaking down. And fighting back. You here to recruit me?"

"Not exactly," I said, matching her grin, "but you're warm. You're not going to believe this, but all my adult life I've thought 'wholesale'—can't help myself. Self-defense is big business, you said. I figured you could fill me in on a lot of details that would impress a friend of mine—"

"Because self-defense courses are breeding grounds for new recruits? Hell, half my students are fighting mad and the other half are mad at how scared they are. Wholesale is right."

"Glad you approve of my idea—mine, Angela. No one sent me, and I am *not* one of them. I'm helping them out with something."

She looked at me with narrowed eyes before lighting up another of her damn cigars. "I chose not to 'help out' a couple of years ago. It was a few months after I'd left the force, and my buddy Zack thought I'd be ripe for the picking. He miscalculated. I'd handed in my badge for two reasons. Zack knew the first."

"Which was?"

"The only man I've ever loved had just been shot to death."

The more matter-of-fact the tone, the more frightening the words. She let them sink in before telling me the second reason.

"When you hand in your badge, your gun goes with it. I knew my gun had to go—fast. I was so raw inside I was ready to shoot the first punk who looked at me cross-eyed. What if I'd found out who shot Joe?"

"You never tried to find out who or how—?"

"The how," she said, "is a Technicolor picture in my head. He was half in, half out of his patrol car, holding a tuna-fish sandwich instead of his .38. Everybody who knew Joe was in shock. I mean, the guy was a walking periscope, the way he could sense danger—a liquor store around the corner, a fire escape two stories up. Every partner he ever had—and I was one—never lost any sleep being on the job with an active cop because Joe didn't just watch his back, he watched yours."

My brows had shot up at the words "active cop."

She said, "That's police parlance for the ones who volunteer for the toughest calls. The guy who knocks his precinct's arrest statistics out of whack by making more good collars in a month than most cops make in a year. That was Joe. Zack, too. They were a team once. What killed Joe was his uniform," she said, eyes turned inward to a Technicolor picture. "Two trigger-happy punks had just shot a druggist. Joe'd been in a deli down the street picking up one for the road. They saw 'cop' and shot him in the back." She sucked in her breath. "Lucky for me they were never identified."

"I don't blame Zack for trying," I said, tight-lipped. "Maybe he ought to try again."

She tilted her head, considering it. "You may not have had recruitment in mind, but your timing is better than his was. Who am I kidding? Helping people defend themselves is a drop in the bucket. You hear things, doing what I do, you see the scars—and not just the physical ones. Guess you know what I'm talking about," she said with such sympathy in those narrowed eyes that it brought tears to mine.

"Yes," I said.

"I'm getting to be as frustrated as the man in the street," she admitted. "When sixty percent of the six million emergency calls in this city are too 'low priority' for cops to respond—"

"But doesn't low priority mean petty stuff?"

"Does it? Burglaries in progress? Thefts under five grand where your only recourse is to notify the insurance company and grease your windowsills? Maybe it *is* time to go wholesale."

The waitress came by with a check. Angela grabbed it. "So you owe me," she said. "I like making important decisions from a position of strength. How's lunch here on Monday? Your treat."

We sealed the bargain with a handshake.

On the way home I thought about what she'd said earlier at SIS. Don't be afraid to admit you're enjoying yourself. Afraid? I was scared all the way up to my teeth.

Which didn't stop a smile from slipping out.

I showed up early, snagged a corner booth and sat down on the "bad" side: it was spilling its white stuffing where somebody had slit the cherry-red vinyl with a razor blade; nice neighborhood.

They came in together. I can't say I was surprised.

"Who invited me to the party, right?" Zack slid in opposite me and Angela pushed in after him.

"Guilty," she said, lighting up a thin cigar. I was beginning to like her particular brand of smoke.

"Congratulations," Zack grinned. "My failure is your success."

"How to succeed in recruitment without really trying," I quipped, feeling a little light-headed about what I'd inadvertently pulled off. We pumped hands. Zack ordered beer all around.

"Angie, Angie," he said, turning those grave eyes on her. "Do you miss us at all?" She touched his cheek. "Do you know what a hole you've left in our lives?" Not just the guys in the precinct, his eyes said. Mine. "Are you happy?" he asked gently.

"Are you?"

"Divorced and lonely. Cath lets me see the kids weekends."

"Just lonely," Angela said.

I tuned out, feeling like a Peeping Tom as their fingers touched and their voices fell into soft reminiscence. I saw him, too—the man they'd both loved—half in, half out of a patrol car with a tuna sandwich in his hand. A cop killed for his uniform.

I studied Zack's, thinking that he wore it well. When he had walked into the coffee shop just now, I'd had a sense of something other than a perfect fit: shoulders erect, chest outthrust—

"I had a gut feeling about you, Karen," he said, returning my stare. "Turns out I was right. Angie told me about your wholesale recruiting idea."

"Zack is a variation on the hero-worshiper," Angela said as if she were telling tales out of school. "He worships brains."

"Any more where that came from?" Zack said, quietly eager.

"Ideas?" I smiled. "One or two. I'm an avid reader of letters to the editor." His face lit up with a Me, too! expression. "Ever notice that with every graphic article on crime, outraged citizens surface like swimmers who've been holding their breath too long?"

"Last week's piece in the *Times* on stabbings in the park," Angela mused. "Some guy wrote in complaining about your standard don't scream, don't resist advice. Appeasement, he called it."

"A woman from Queens said—quote: 'More prison space for murderers? I say, bring back the death penalty!' " I looked at Zack. "Lots of frustration out there, just waiting to be tapped."

"Two potential recruits—and God knows how many others," he agreed. "Easy enough for Lee's people to track them down. Go on."

"Citizen crime patrols are sprouting up like weeds in a vacant lot, but not all of them work. People mad enough to organize—"

"Are halfway there and ripe for the picking. Don't stop now."

"I was cleaning off my desk at Kemp & Carusone yesterday and ran across some interesting figures. Name one of America's newest growth industries. Zack?" He shook his head.

Angela said, "Bulletproof vests, one size fits all."

"No cigar," I said as she waved hers around. "Burglar-alarm companies," I told them. "Over five thousand of them."

Zack whistled through his teeth. And made a hovering waiter wait while he wrote a note to himself: GET AHOLD OF CUSTOMER LISTS.

When the sandwiches arrived, along with a second round of beer, he looked from me to Angela and said, "I wish it were champagne, ladies. Welcome aboard, both of you."

Angela must have spotted what Zack had missed even though I had my beer stein in front of my face: a flash of panic. I wasn't "aboard" anything!

"Tell her what pushed you over, Zack," she urged.

"Frustration, like everybody else." His tone said: I don't want to talk about it. He pushed his beer away, untasted.

"It had to do with a case that cost Zack six months of meticulous police work," Angela said. "Mostly false leads and dead ends. He put in so much overtime the guys at the precinct had him pegged for a distant relative of the deceased." She lit up again.

"Picture a man who grew up to the Harlem night sounds of a different era—Duke Ellington, Cab Calloway, Billy Eckstein, the Apollo Theater," Zack said in a voice so soft you knew the pictures were already there for him. "No education, this guy, just a broad back and a dream, a man who knew how to work and who sweated every nickel until he had enough for the only thing he ever wanted out of life: his own club. Nothing fancy, just a small smart place with good acoustics and the best talent he could afford for a Harlem that had lost track of its musical heritage. Picture the grand opening. Good music, good friends, champagne toasts, and maybe a 'Pinch me, I'm dreaming!' look in his eyes as he sits through his first Saturday-night jam session—a big success, according to the cash-register receipts. Now picture—"

He took his beer back. Drank it without seeing us.

"The only picture I'm left with," he said, wiping his mouth with the back of his hand, "is what the poor bastard looked like later that night after a couple of slugs went through his brain."

Angela mashed out her cigar. I hadn't smoked in years but I almost took the cigarette Zack offered me.

"He put up a big fight for the money?" I asked.

Zack shook his head. "Not even a small one. They killed him for sport. They *felt* like blowing him away. I couldn't let go of it. Even after everyone else did. I found them, eventually. Saw them convicted. Second-degree murder, first-degree robbery. But it didn't stick. An appeals court ordered a new trial because a detective with a hot tip and no time or good sense to get a warrant beat me to the murder weapon in their car."

"The DA's office lost their key witnesses before they could get a new trial date." Angela bit off the words.

"They had to let them go," Zack said. "I didn't."

I opened my mouth—and clamped it shut again.

"We have company," Angela said softly.

I looked up to see a somber little face ringed with dark, defiant curls—and heard Kagan's insinuating voice. *"Those photographs we planted in your briefcase . . . Tony risked his life."*

"Tony Montes," Zack said as the boy edged closer.

Zack was beaming at him. I was wondering what a child of ten or so was doing even on the fringes of this deadly business.

"How the devil long you been standing there?" Zack asked with an affectionate swipe at Tony's shoulder.

A shrug. "I got cold waiting outside."

"How'd you know where to find me, pardner? I never told—"

"I followed you."

"That's not possible," Zack said in slow disbelief even as he was figuring it. ". . . Right from the precinct. How'd you keep up?"

"Bart gave me cab fare but I changed for a Broadway bus. It's easier to see a patrol car from a bus. I saved money on the cab."

"This kid's some piece of work, huh, Angie? A word of advice, my young friend," he said, warmth in his smile. "Next time, get the cabbie to light up his off-duty sign in case the guy you're following should look back. Got a message for me?"

"Bart says to call him," he said, eyeing the remnants of Zack's roast beef on rye.

"Hungry?" I asked him, moving over to make room. But Zack had already signaled our waiter. The boy took the hint and turned away.

He had one of those garish iron-on decals across the back of his denim jacket. A flame-colored, bushy-tailed fox.

"For God's sake, Zack," I said when the kid was out of hearing, "Tony is how old?"

"Older than he looks. Thirteen, I think. But you're right, he's too damn young for us. And if you're thinking of blaming me," he said as if he had a sudden case of lockjaw, "don't. Sometimes our mutual friend shows an appalling lack of judgment."

. . . Jamie?

"Sorry," Zack said to the dismay in my face. "Your reaction was right. Mine was defensive. I worry about that kid. He's the same age as my youngest."

"Thirteen." I shook my head. "Appalling is right."

"A man who makes the kind of judgment that brought you into the fold is entitled to an occasional lapse—hell, maybe a couple of dozen. Friends?" He extended his hand.

"Right from the start." I smiled, taking it.

"Welcome aboard, Karen," Angela said, watching to see if I lost my smile, this time. I didn't.

Chapter 14

"Your strong suit, media relations."

Jamie's words from our first restaurant encounter came back to me. It was why he'd "recruited" me. For the past two feverish months, I had been up to my neck in "media relations"—strategy, in a word—but, instead of my usual half-dozen clients, I was steeped in the affairs of only one.

A PR person's biggest problem, my boss liked to say, is a client that doesn't know how to sell itself to the public. My glance moved in slow motion over a paper-strewn desk . . . Victims Anonymous was no exception.

I glanced at a clock and groaned. "Last one to leave turns out the lights," one of the women had called out in a singsong voice, but with a sympathetic smile in my direction as she walked out the door, headed, no doubt, for a hot dinner. Mine had come out of a paper bag over four—no, five—hours ago. I reached for a cigarette—and sighed; two left in the pack. I lit up, consoling myself with the thought that I was in the homestretch.

You can't "sell" a client without getting to know him inside and out, or, as Larry liked to say, probe, probe, probe. Probing the affairs of a secret organization was a new experience . . . like interviewing monks who'd taken a vow of silence.

Some things I got quick answers to. Victims Anonymous was rife with symbolism and cue words. The enemy was called a Savage, the bleeding-heart judge who set him loose a Permissive. We had Actives, Passives, Fueling, Missions. Why?

"It's designed for mass appeal and a smattering of IQs," Jamie had explained. "Our official motto may be 'Vengeance is mine,' but unofficially, it's 'Keep it simple.'"

But for a long time, I got double-talk on how big we were.

Jamie finally relented with a ballpark figure. "At last count? Let's just say we've passed the five hundred mark."

I consulted my list of the one hundred most populated—correction, most crime-ridden—cities in America. From New York to Hialeah, Victims Anonymous had four hundred–plus operating cells, with maybe another fifty to a hundred scattered throughout smaller towns. My campaign, Jamie kept telling me, would "send those figures through the roof!"

Not likely. Especially since I was starting from behind. A media expert, after all, doesn't just write and research. She holds meetings with company executives to take their measure and pick their brains. My "executives" in this case were hundreds of faceless cell leaders who ran things and kept order. Recruiters who drummed up new members. Armed men who went on crusading Missions. Dedicated women who did the paperwork. Independent little groups of the angry and the frustrated who looked to the parent organization in New York for direction and guidance.

They were all waiting, now, on mine.

I had to smile as I scanned the papers on my desk. It was all such garden-variety Kemp & Carusone material. I mean, if this were a PR campaign for one of my clients—say, a drug company with a new cough medicine—the first rule of thumb would be: Identify the market for your product. For the drug company, it's the consumer; for Victims Anonymous, the victim of violent crime—past, present and future.

The goal of any campaign? Educate the public. How? Get your message across to the media. Our cough medicine kills chest pain and tastes good. Our Missions of vengeance sweep muggers, rapists and killers off the streets—and that's good for the collective soul of America.

Not so easy to get *that* message across. Somebody had asked me if I was going to "plant stories" in newspapers. You plant flowers, I told him. If you want to educate the media, you write "pitches"—fact sheets about what you're selling. A cough cure in three days. Justice in small glances: a mugger mugged, a rapist taken out of circulation, a governor deposed for vetoing the death penalty and letting the killers keep right on killing.

You correct misimpressions. "Breathe Easy" has less—not more—codeine than its competitors. VA is temporary, a stopgap, until the people demand the criminal-justice system they deserve.

Maybe you do a position paper—longer than a pitch—going into a history of the industry as a backdrop for the product you're trying to sell, throwing in anything that might improve the image of the client—like taking a moral stance: Unlike some other drug companies, we don't use animals for research. I hefted a thirty-two-page document in my hand—my position paper on Victims

Anonymous. It was chock-full of moral stances and fortified by a brief, bloody history of what went wrong on our city streets and why the time had come to fight back.

You prepare "backgrounders"—that's PR jargon for heavy research, a lot of it detailed and dull. Until I did a couple for a client named Victims Anonymous. Nothing in here about over-the-counter versus prescription medicine, I thought with a tight smile as I leafed through one of them. Plenty about an anachronism in the law known as the Family Court system . . . and judges who couldn't bring themselves to lock up teenaged killers before Christmas.

My hand shook as I put out the cigarette.

I picked up a backgrounder I had designed for the men who went on Missions—along with instructions to leave copies behind for any members of the public or the press who showed up afterward. It was loaded with statistics. Burglaries: one every ten seconds. A list of a dozen states that gave more jail time to car thieves than convicted rapists. Over nineteen million victims of violent crime or personal theft—annually. More people murdered on American streets in three years than soldiers killed in Vietnam.

I'd tossed in some sobering sci-fi predictions, like: "In view of the epidemic of violence that killed over two thousand people in the Big Apple last year, ten thousand New Yorkers will be shot to death in the next ten years."

And an antistatistic statistic, courtesy of the NCS (National Crime Survey): More than half of all violent crimes are not reported to the police. People figure they can't do anything about it. . . .

I pushed the report aside to light up my last Lucky. To follow the drift of the smoke in an empty grey room that had gone cold on me and think about the most intriguing part of a good PR campaign, at least to me. A company bucking a trend or trying to solve an image problem needs friends, similarly situated, as they say in the business, and part of my job is to find them and form an alliance. People who take the law into their own hands are bucking more than a trend—a whole system!—and the term "vigilante" is about as bad an image as you can get.

Or used to be. Too many people were hurting, now. I had a word for the ones who were hurting the most, I'd coined a phrase—all right, a cue word dear to Jamie's symbol-loving heart. The Vulnerables. VA's potential new allies.

I had written fliers devoted to whole groups of them—to be delivered, some of them, by Actives in every one of our key cities. To be distributed, wholesale, to every state and national organization devoted to a specific class of Vulnerables . . . The elderly, fear-chained to their apartments. Whole neighborhoods of demoralized black citizens, hardest hit by the crime wave. Women all across the country, more and more of them mad enough to be learning self-defense. Frightened enough to be purchasing handguns.

Not me, I vowed, standing up, reaching for my purse. Not yet. All I had inside was a sharp letter opener and a can of Mace.

I was buttoning my coat when I felt it wash over me—the uneasy sense of something important left undone.

Not undone, I realized; things that couldn't be done. No scheduled briefings with the top editors of prestigious newspapers and magazines, where I could stuff their files full of whatever I wanted them to know about whatever I was selling. No face-to-face advice to the client, stressing what to do and not do . . .

It was a poor substitute, my "advice letter" to the leader of every cell. It was full of tips. Research the editorial policy of your local papers. Know your individual reporters. Vary your "pitch" for maximum effect: Horror stories are more likely to persuade the soft-on-crime types than a columnist already sympathetic to the crime victim. Deliver one basic message at a time—much more impact that way. Never forget your top-priority goal: to educate, to raise the consciousness of the man in the street—

My hand reached out—too quickly—to flip off the lights. But even in the dark, I retained an image of what lay on my desk. I felt free, in the dark, to shudder at that morass of facts and figures. At two months of solid immersion in a sewer.

Too many sordid crimes. Too much human suffering. Karen Newman, corporate-public-relations expert, had violated a cardinal rule of the profession: no personal stake in the client's affairs. It was okay to let the client know you cared, but I had gone beyond that. Way beyond.

In my campaign to raise the consciousness of the man in the street, I had succeeded in raising my own.

Chapter 15

I felt odd in my old office, sitting behind an uncluttered desk—a broad expanse of gleaming French walnut. For most of my working life, it had been buried under mounds of paper and yellow legal pads.

I felt odd listening to Larry make small talk.

"Thanks for coming in, Karen," he said with a sweet smile and a surreptitious glance at his watch. "Very sharp, your insights on the Hernstadt matter." He straightened his tie, which wasn't the least bit crooked.

It occurred to me that the Hernstadt matter could just as easily have been handled on the telephone. Why hadn't it occurred to Larry? I smiled back. "You've been missing me."

"Yeah. Don't be a stranger." He squeezed my hand and left.

I stood up and took a slow look around. Only two months into a six-month leave and I was already feeling alienated from the old life. From old friends. From myself, most of all.

I walked out. I thanked my secretary for keeping my desk polished. "See you in four months," I told her.

My spirits sank with the elevator, jammed, now, with the five-o'clock crowd. Even the downstairs lobby struck me as one more old friend I had lost touch with.

It was the last place I'd have expected to run into an old adversary. There stood a slightly frowning Max McCann in his FBI uniform: neat dark suit, dirty-brown raincoat. Waiting for someone.

His smile, when he spotted me, was tentative. I gave him a polite smile back while I put two and two together, while I replayed Larry's voice the day he'd given me my leave . . . *"Take some time off, Karen. Meet some people. Fall in love."* Larry, calling me in for some unnecessary "insights." Larry, breaking it off just in time for me to meet up with his old friend Max. Four, Larry, you matchmaking SOB!

"Hello," McCann said. Not, Fancy running into you like this. "Larry told me about the leave of absence. I was concerned."

"Nice of you. Nice of Larry," I said, letting my annoyance show. "Now what?"

"Dinner?" he said, looking crestfallen but sounding hopeful.

"What if I said I wasn't hungry?"

"You could watch me eat. I'm hungry as a mountain lion."

He was sporting one of his garish ties, that bright shade of orange the Irish-haters wear on Saint Patrick's Day. I said, "It beats taking potshots at tree trunks, I suppose."

He laughed and offered me his arm. Asked me about the leave of absence as we headed out of the building. How was I feeling? What was I doing with my time?

I wasn't about to start spending it with an FBI man!

So I suggested we stop off, first, at my place for a drink and a quick change of clothes.

My devious plan went like clockwork. Fix yourself a drink while I dress, McCann—but first, hang up your coat, McCann.

I caught it in a mirror as I headed for my bedroom: his hand stalling in midair as he reached for a hanger in the hall closet, mouth tightening at the sight of a man's navy slacks and cashmere jacket. Jamie's comfortable change of clothes for the work-filled evenings we'd been spending together lately.

I had intended to slip into a black suit: simple, severe, a little on the dull side. My hand reached instead for a lavender dress I hadn't worn in years: a fuller, softer look with sleeves that spread like wings.

Funny, how clothes can set the mood. I practically floated into the living room—right into my twilight view of the park: a hard glitter of lights softened by the pale silver-blue splash of a lake and the round shapes of trees in miniature.

McCann wasn't taking in the view. Drink in hand, he was engrossed in my bookshelves. He turned at my entrance.

"I've never thought of you in that color," he said.

"Find any interesting books?" I said, the polite hostess.

He reached for my well-thumbed volume of Swinburne. "My favorite poet. Yours, too?"

"From the moment we met in a college library." I turned away. Swinburne and "sensuous" went hand in hand, not what I had in mind for this dinner date. I hoped he would follow my lead and take an easy chair, but he walked around the room too slowly, replying to my small talk in his typical monosyllabic style. Touching things. The ultrasuede cushions of the couch. The nubby texture of the drapes. A paperweight that fit in his hand like a glass ball.

He was helping me on with my coat when he reached out to touch Jamie's jacket. "I envy him," he said, voice as soft as the cashmere, making me ashamed of my male-in-residence ploy.

I took him on a brief detour—an alley where I feed the neighborhood strays—and emptied my ample pockets of People Crackers.

In the cab, he wondered aloud why I didn't have cats of my own.

"The last two died on me. One right after the other. I don't want any more animals to break my heart over," I said, sounding defensive even to my own ears. "I just lost my daughter, and then my granddaughter . . . one right after the other. I'll do my loving long-distance from now on, thank you very—"

I burst into tears.

At least he couldn't see my horrified expression. Not as long as I was sobbing in his arms.

"Happens without warning," I said, coming up for air. "Max, I'm sorry—"

He put a finger to my lips and pushed me gently back against the cushions, as if to say, See how comforting silence can be?

I closed my eyes, afraid to look any longer into his—too much tenderness there, too much let-me-share-the-pain.

The cab pulled up. The sign outside—luminous red and white letters dancing on a bright green background—said CECELIA'S. My favorite kind of restaurant, Italian.

"How's your appetite?" Max asked.

"Hungry as a mountain lion."

He grinned at me.

Cecelia's turned out to be small and elegant, but with a hostess as warm and exuberant as her outdoor sign. I let McCann do the ordering; pasta is pasta. While I cast about for innocuous subjects, he reached across the red marble tabletop for my hand.

"You asked me once if I loved this city," he said. "To a hick from Minnesota, New York has always meant tough, exciting, sophisticated—beautiful. You fit the profile, Karen."

"Come on, Max," I protested. "You want to know the recurring compliment of my life? I have an 'interesting' face."

"It's a matter of style, isn't it?" he said, fixing me in that narrow gaze that almost shut out the cornflower blue of his eyes. "I admire what I totally lack. Your wry sense of humor. The way you give free rein to your feelings. The way you—"

Saved by two steaming plates of pasta. He let go of my hand.

"My wife used to say I buried my emotions in a subterranean vault. Which, in my line of work, has its advantages," he said with a narrow smile. "You were about to tell me my spaghetti is getting cold."

"Pasta, McCann. You're back in New York. Delicious," I said.

So was the wine. And the laughter after he splattered tomato sauce on his orange tie, which we both agreed was an improvement.

I excused myself. When I came back from the ladies' room, there was a vase of yellow roses and red carnations on the table next to the zabaglione. "Flower shop on the corner," he said before I could ask where they'd come from. "Cheerful, aren't they?"

"Thoughtful, aren't you?" I said softly. "I—what's this?"

"Something to keep you smiling."

A little plastic bird, bright yellow. A windup toy? I turned the key. Damned if the thing didn't dart all over the red marble. By the time it keeled over on its side, we were both smiling.

"Keep it with you at all times," he ordered, mock serious.

I slipped it into my purse.

When the cappuccino arrived, he excused himself.

For the men's room, I thought. For the checkroom, it turned out;

he'd come back with his raincoat but without my camel-hair. He pulled a paperback out of the side pocket—my copy of Swinburne?—and started to thumb through it. Tired of watching, I asked what he was looking for. Talk about a leading question!

"A poem appropriate to the occasion. . . . Gotcha." He looked up, finger keeping his place. "I'm about as good at reading poetry as I am at baring my soul, so if I—"

"No apologies, McCann," I said, remembering his finger on my lips. "Read on," I said with a sense of foreboding.

His voice was a steady monotone, touching in its gravity. . . .

> "Before our lives divide for ever,
>   While time is with us and hands are free,
>   (Time swift to fasten and swift to sever
>   Hand from hand, as we stand by the sea)
>   I will say no word that a man might say
>   Whose whole life's love goes down in a day;
>   For this could never have been; and never,
>   Though the gods and the years relent,
>   Shall be."

He closed the book and gave it back to me.

The cab ride home was like gliding through city streets in the hush of slow motion. In the unstrained silence, it didn't occur to either of us not to hold hands.

No strain at my front door, either. We both knew he wouldn't be going inside. But he waited like a bodyguard while I rummaged in my purse for my keys, not daring to look at him, and looking. Afraid to see what I knew he was remembering, and seeing it: me, in his arms. Crying, but in his arms.

I heard a footstep from inside my apartment just as my hand closed over the keys. I got them out just as the door opened.

"Hello," Max said, friendly. Resigned.

Jamie stood there smiling. "Come on in," he said to Max.

"It's late," Max protested while I toyed with the keys and wondered how the hell Jamie had gotten in without any.

"It's never too late," Jamie grinned. "Please," he pressed.

My genial host. *Make some lame excuse, Max,* I urged him silently, remembering what I'd managed to put out of my mind all evening: his line of work.

Max had hesitated too long. Jamie practically had him by the elbow, and he wasn't resisting. I bowed to the inevitable.

Inside, I made introductions, poured the brandy, and sat back like a good Roman citizen waiting for the Circus Maximus to begin.

Which is how it started out: a contest of sorts, each man maneuvering with words while taking the other's measure, trying to get a fix on one another.

If they only knew.

I seized an opening, slipped it in: M. McCann, the FBI man.

The effect on Jamie was as subtle as it was instantaneous. He turned on the charm. Oh, not so Max would notice right away. It was like expensive perfume being dabbed in all the right places. A touch of exuberance here, an ingenuous remark there. A touching anecdote, a sad tale leavened with humor. And questions. Nothing too probing, of course; the kind that a man genuinely interested in another man's work might ask.

A masterly performance. Max sat on my couch with the look of a man who'd been . . . charmed. No way he could have resisted Jamie's special brand of openness.

Jamie sat across from him displaying the eagerness of a boy on a lark. Or a man flirting with danger? Both, maybe. Once again, I had the sense that if I confronted him right now, if I said, "Who *are* you?" Jamie would come up with three very different and equally plausible answers.

They went on talking until I broke it up with a small truth that was becoming more obvious by the minute: utter exhaustion.

At the door Max looked from me to Jamie and said, "I envy you both." That's when I realized Jamie had on his cashmere jacket.

"All right," I said when Max had left, "what's going on?"

"I told your doorman we had an appointment."

"That explains how you got in. It doesn't tell me a thing about why you were wooing that man. Max McCann is out of my life."

"As of when?" he teased.

"Now. Tonight. What's the difference?"

"Pity. I like his style."

"So I noticed. Apparently, it was mutual."

He seemed delighted. "How's the PR campaign going?"

"So that's why you're here. Done by the end of the week," I promised, steering him out the door.

"Wonderful. Get some sleep. We'll talk tomorrow."

He popped his head back in, catching me in midyawn.

"Did I ever tell you what I wanted to be when I grew up?"

"Your childhood dream?" I mumbled, fading fast.

For a moment he looked wistful. Then he turned on his high beams. "An FBI man!"

It was the way he said it that blew the cobwebs away.

Chapter 16

The Ides of March. Fifteenth of the month on the ancient Roman calendar.

I stared at the calendar over my desk, remembering breakfast.

"A fitting day to go public," Jamie had said gleefully, raising a glass of orange juice, officially "launching" my PR campaign.

"The day Julius Caesar got his," Kagan agreed with a faint smile. O'Neal looked confused. "Victims Anonymous is about to declare war on the first half of a biblical maxim. No more rendering unto Caesar," Kagan explained.

"Beware, Caesar!" Bart trumpeted to the accompaniment of rousing cheers while I thought, *Here we go again, more symbolism.*

Now, as I stood looking over the usual paraphernalia of a good public-relations campaign—posters, fliers, stacks of photocopied material—I wondered why I had bothered coming here tonight. A postmortem can be the most satisfying part of a campaign—time to take stock and gloat a little.

Not this time. Not with the sign someone had hung over my desk and the long table next to it, a warning in big red letters: USE GLOVES OR DON'T TOUCH! It suggested the kind of foresight that should have given me a secure feeling.

It made me uneasy. If going public meant increased visibility, it also meant being a more visible target for the police. Scary, when the potential "targets" included people I was beginning to care for.

One of them walked through the door with her characteristic bounce and grinning good humor. We looked at each other. Rosa Ramirez, the most energetic of Lee Emerson's "troops."

The stranger I'd shared a bond with. It was always the same, our first eye contact: a joint memory of Christmas Eve.

I lost a son. I listened to my daughter die.

Tony was with her.

"Told you we'd find her here," Rosa said with an affectionate pat that sent him edging away. The kid who kept his distance.

"Jamie wants you to meet him," Tony informed me.

The little messenger. "Hello yourself," I said.

He looked sheepish for a split second, then made a beeline for the table of posters and fliers. "Use gloves means no fingerprints," he said in case we should think he'd missed the point. "This stuff goes national?"

"All over the country, honey," Rosa said.

"We're lending 'em some of our star recruiters from New York," he announced, dark eyes bright with this special piece of intelligence. "Bet you didn't know we're using eight-hundred numbers with prerecorded messages to all of our cells," he told Rosa, his chest outthrust like a pigeon's. "It's faster than the old system of post office boxes." He looked to me for confirmation.

All he got was a frown. How did he come up with this stuff?

"Your idea?" Rosa asked me.

"Mine. It gives people quick access to useful information."

"Such as?" Tony challenged.

I wanted to send him out of the room like an errant pupil. But he was too good a pupil and he wasn't mine to send. I said, "Such as which Permissive New Jersey judges have been handing out eighteen-month sentences for assault with a deadly weapon while the Garden State suffers from a record-breaking four hundred thousand felonies a year. Good ammo for some future Mission."

"Where's the Action Kit?"

"Not made up yet," I said, glad it wasn't there for him to pore over. But he stood his ground, waiting for me to tell him what was in it. "It's just a lot of dry facts and statistics," I lied. "Sentencing reports, sample press releases—"

"Posters," he said, drawn to one in particular, his eyes rising with each black vertical block up a milk-white expanse. "They look like sticks," he said.

They looked like sinister smokestacks.

"Gun Murders in Washington, D.C.," he read from the top. Then, from the bottom: "Murder rate: more than seven times the national average. Wow!"

"Time to go," I snapped, reaching for my coat.

"The guy downstairs made me sign in. Now I got to sign out," Tony informed me. "How come Rosa didn't have to?"

"Office cleaning ladies don't need to sign in, honey."

"You don't clean offices!" he protested.

"If wearing a scarf and this battered old coat—not to mention my skin color—makes me hired help, who's complaining?" She grinned. "Cleaning ladies get to wander all over with nobody wondering what they're up to, y'know?"

He held his hand next to hers. Matched skins. "What are you up to?" Not one to ignore rhetorical questions, our Tony.

"Just holding the fort." Rosa shrugged off her coat.

I put mine on and we hugged while Tony looked on, appalled.

Which made sharing the backseat of a cab with him a bittersweet experience. He had squeezed his small frame into the opposite corner, sending me a clear signal: Gloves or not, lady, don't touch. As if he sensed how much I wanted to . . .

At least he was eager to talk. "Wanna know what's on Jamie's agenda?"

I had to smile. For a hooky-playing street kid, his vocabulary was impressive. "I'll bite," I said.

"Your first Rouser, right?" he asked with a trace of disdain.

"Not yours, I bet."

"I've seem 'em before," he said in the bored tone of: I've seen it all. He took out a cigarette.

"Don't," I said, ready to snatch it away. "I don't like seeing it, Tony. You're only thirteen."

The look he gave me was ambivalent. He seemed leery of my concern, yet drawn to it.

But he put the cigarette away.

Our cab pulled up to a building that was vaguely familiar. A man directed us to a small room off the lobby where Jamie was waiting, his Rouser not yet under way.

I don't know what I expected—certainly not the sight of Jamie all decked out like Old Hollywood's version of a dashing pirate: black buccaneer shirt, fake black beard, aviator sunglasses.

Tony was looking at him with a skeptical half-smile. I could almost hear him thinking, Funny way for a psychiatrist to dress!

"Well, if it isn't Blackbeard himself," I quipped, tempted to give that unruly beard a tug. "What are you up to?"

Jamie laughed. "You'll see." He aimed a friendly jab at Tony's arm. "Find her a good seat, will you, Tadpole?"

Tony stiffened like a small board. Well, what boy his age likes to be reminded of how short he is?

"Lead on," I told him, following him out of the lobby and into an auditorium. I recognized the place: ex–movie theater turned lecture hall; years ago, Claudia and I used to view our favorite Bogart flicks from tenth-row center. While Tony was busily checking row after worn-red-velvet row, I checked out the audience. Not counting a near-empty balcony, Jamie had himself a full house. I couldn't get a handle on the crowd except that they weren't dressed for the opera and I didn't spot any kids.

With the exception of my personal usher. Tony was beckoning me to the high ground. I almost sent him out to the corner candy store; what's a balcony without buttered popcorn?

I decided it was the ideal spot for a bird's-eye view . . . but of what? As I peered down on four black-clad men in the ubiquitous wraparound sunglasses, I saw them working the aisles with straw baskets. Like dark priests making the weekly collection . . .

"What's going on?" I asked Tony as maybe one person in ten tossed something into a basket. "Who are these people?"

"Cell members from the five boroughs—mostly Brooklyn and Queens. Oh, you mean the guys in black? They're collecting the horror stories."

"Whose stories?" I said as a woman with a floppy hat and the shoulders of a linebacker leaned over to plant a yellow sheet of paper in the nearest basket.

"Whoever has one and wants everybody else to hear it."

"Jamie's giving a public reading of unavenged crimes? He's dramatizing the horror file?" I said just as the lights dimmed.

Tony didn't just nod. He grinned.

I sat back, grateful for the dark. Shades of a revival meeting . . .

Tony touched my arm. "Know why Jamie calls this a Rouser? Lee told me."

A hint of malice in his voice . . . still angry about the Tadpole business?

"She says it's because Jamie needs it right before he goes on a Mission. It replenishes, he told her."

Like a shot in the arm? Packaged melodrama à la Elmer Gantry? I steeled myself for an embarrassing display of breast-beating theatrics.

Jamie appeared, pinned to the stage by a spotlight. He began to read, his voice grave.

"Can you picture it? The night a woman in this audience was made a widow? The night she witnessed her husband's murder? *Give him the money, Ben—please. For God's sake, get away from that cash register!* But Ben, with business bad and getting worse— he needs every dollar—hesitates, clenches his fists . . . steps away, finally. The robber rushes forward, still waving his .357 magnum. *What, a measly five hundred bucks in the till?*"

Silence. Was Jamie milking it? Gritting his teeth? Waiting for the inevitable: a woman's muffled sobs? I couldn't find the sounds in the dark, I couldn't see the intense faces. I felt them.

"A death sentence in nine words!" Jamie lashed out. "A man's brains blown out in a mom-and-pop liquor store by a parolee who has robbed before and, yes, killed before, and—thanks to our system of 'justice'—will live to rob and kill again." He crumpled the paper in his fist. "And again—" He hurled it into the audience.

A hand shot out to catch it. A shout went up. "No!"

"Yes! Unless we stop him! And Savages like him!"

The crowd roared approval.

Jamie reached for another piece of paper. He read it, first, to himself. "Damn . . . damn them," he said, the microphone fling- ing his private mutterings far and wide. He looked at us. "How many times have you heard that it's up to us to make the system work? That we private citizens have a duty to come forward and point the finger so judge and jury can see that justice is done? There is a woman who is *not* in the audience tonight. Her husband is. This woman is doing some late-in-the-day shopping in the back aisles of a grocery store when she hears a loud sound, followed by a scream. What she witnesses, unseen, is a muscled teenager using his hands and feet on a young woman clerk, karate-chopping her almost to death before he hits the cash register. To feed his drug habit. The young criminal gets himself a smart lawyer. And then what happens?"

"He gets out on bail!" A disembodied voice, full of disgust.

"Round one for the defense. Round two: The DA lays out his whole case for the smart lawyer—an eyewitness ready, willing, and brave enough to testify. Round three?"

"The shyster tracks her down!" a hoarse voice called out.

"He tells his client where to find her!" A woman's voice, part horror, part rage.

"Round four," Jamie said in the flat tone of an undertaker. "A campaign of terror, ladies and gentlemen. While the lawyer delays in court, winning postponement after postponement, a six-foot-two-inch drug addict weighing in at close to two hundred pounds stalks a five-foot-three-inch housewife. Phone calls, menacing gestures, graphic threats—she's seen what he can do to a woman. Round five," he said, gripping the podium, "a nervous breakdown."

He held up a straw basket in each hand.

It was a tip-of-the-iceberg gesture. We could see, all of us, that the baskets were full, the horror unending.

When he lowered them and reached for another piece of paper, it was as if a shudder rolled through the length and breadth of the auditorium. The lecture hall had turned back into a theater.

I wanted to leave. I wanted to turn off the sound track and ward off too-graphic images before they became indelible.

I stayed too long, mesmerized by the resonant voice of a poet. . . .

"Who here hasn't been eleven years old?
Who hasn't played marbles after school lets out?
Or turned his face to the sun for a moment, only a moment,
Because even a kid born and bred on these mean streets
Can afford to let down his guard on the schoolyard steps
And enjoy deep breaths of city-fouled air while he
Looks into a rare blue sky for a glimpse of his future—
While that future literally blows up in his face."

Horror begets horror. Anger turns to rage. All around me it accelerated with the sound of Jamie's voice, immersed in a tragedy: a boy at school gunned down by juvenile robbers on bikes. Jamie made it real, the pain of the parents. But the irreparable loss from the dead boy's perspective . . . this, he made palpable.

The false beard and the dark glasses vanished for me. I was seeing instead a face I knew well but with a new dimension, a Jamie I had never even glimpsed, this man with a depth of compassion that took my breath away and who, even as I watched, was losing it to the outrage of a prosecutor addressing the ultimate jury—

"By what right do they spill our blood?
By whose authority do they plunder our lives?
Who told them they could wipe us out of existence—
And go unpunished?
Will we stand by while they rob our homes?
Will we turn the other cheek while they kill our children?
Wring our hands while they wield knives and baseball bats?
While they *casually* take a life?"

I was on my feet with the rest, hands gripping the balcony rail, pirates and preachers forgotten. Tony coughed, breaking the spell, so that I became part observer, part member of the audience, able to appreciate—able to experience—the crescendo: these people gripped by *his* words, *his* will, into an iron fist.

In the moment when I perceived his essence as an avenging angel, I felt suspicion recede like some nocturnal creature fleeing from the sun.

Chapter 17

It was centered on the desk in my den like a fat reproach: Lee Emerson's bulky on-the-spot "report from the provinces," untouched by human hands since it arrived two weeks ago. The attached note was from Jamie, asking for "a report on a report by the time I get back, please!" In time for tonight's dinner meeting.

A quick glance at the top sheet and I knew what I was in for: purple prose. Fortified with a cigarette, I turned the page.

Lee had "opened" in Philadelphia, a has-been town "too dull and dirty to live up to the awesome sight of our Liberty Bell!" I looked in vain for the promised "intelligence" about Mission activity. The only thing that seemed to be happening among the Philly cells was speculation about their mysterious Leader. Was he a Vietnam vet, a disgruntled cop? Better yet, a foreign mercenary? Nothing about a psychiatrist, Lee assured us.

Baltimore was more revealing. Bart was "crazy about" the hotel lobby—"all video games and pinball machines—like being greeted by a roomful of winking, leering ladies of the night," Lee wrote in her breathless prose. Good news: The leader of the Baltimore cell turned out to be a real pro. "We could use this lady's brand of administrative talent in New York!" Lee enthused.

Detroit got short shrift. ("Unsafe at any speed. You don't dare go a city block without taking a cab.")

But it was Denver that earned the purple-prose award. ". . . Low-lying ranch houses humbled before a monolith: the mountain range, vast and brown, like a woman's pleated skirt."

Chicago rang an alarm bell: a vague allusion, buried under amiable chitchat, to a "close call with the police." No details?

No such problem in St. Louis. A close call, this time, with death. VA Target: a defense lawyer who looked the other way while his clients terrorized some motorists out of testifying against the bat-wielding delinquents who had smashed their car windows. That left one stubborn complainant—who lost both in court (the prosecutor had no corroborating testimony), and out (they smashed his head until he was too blind to point the finger at anyone). "The victim's wife 'made her bones' and broke a few in the process before they took her bat away," Lee reported. "She went from smashing the windows of the lawyer's Mercedes to a direct hit on his bald spot. We had to stop her from putting out his eyes!"

Insanity. I made some notes. My headline said: "Permissives Missions Are Supposed to be Nonviolent!"

I moved on to Los Angeles and another Permissives Mission. Object: reeducation of an "ivory-tower pundit" (Bart's phrase). Method: "escort" an appellate judge into a high-crime area. "We came upon a mugging victim," Lee wrote, "a bag lady clutching her pathetic junk as the lifeblood spilled out of her belly."

How had they done it? I wondered, reading on: duping the judge into thinking the woman died with a name on her lips . . . a killer whose conviction he had just overturned. On a technicality.

Lee's next port of call made me gasp. "Targeting a top aide in a DA's office," I wrote in my yellow pad, "means high visibility. Anyone going on such a Mission should be unobtrusive."

How could a stand-out beauty like Lee not stand out?

Not a trace of worry showed in Lee's breezy account, just her usual mix of statistics and melodrama. "With Atlanta the most crime-ridden city in the nation, these days, you'd think the DA's office would do *less* plea bargaining, not more. But our Target keeps putting these—these subhumans back on the street!"

The tour ended in Houston. "The natives call this city the last free country in America!" Lee enthused. "People out here understand what property rights are all about." People who were dropping would-be burglars in their tracks at the rate of a couple of dozen dead bodies a year—Bart's estimate. According to my clipping files, Houston boasted a DA's office that gave out free booklets on handguns, and public officials who'd correct you if you said "gun nut" rather than "self-defense mentality." According to Kagan, the frontier spirit was "alive and well in Houston."

Houston made me skin-deep uneasy; my uneasiness about Kagan went deeper. So when I turned up Lee's little postscript, I decided to keep it out of my report. She had compiled a list of what she'd labeled "real administrative talent": names and addresses of women who would make good Passives material should the need arise. A breach of security that would drive Kagan up the wall, if he knew. A lively Baltimore cell leader ("very chic, very blond"). A savvy lady from Charlotte, North Carolina, with "onyx eyes" (Lee's arch way of saying she was black). The woman who'd produced some "really fantastic intelligence" on the Atlanta ADA. A plucky Detroit housewife. The "superdynamic" founder of our oldest Houston cell, who was "a crack shot" with a pistol.

I stashed the list in the safe I keep in my den.

When Jamie picked me up in a cab, his first words were "What do you think of our Lee?"

"Beautiful and sweet-natured, if a little insensitive when it comes to dealing with underlings. Still, I can't help liking her. I don't think much of her intelligence-gathering efforts."

He looked pleased. "Your leave of absence is up when?"

"Couple of months. Why?" I said, suspicious. "What's this dinner all about, anyway?"

"Business, what else?"

Business in real choice surroundings. I don't like places that are more bar than restaurant—with quaint private rooms laid out like log cabins. This one had lots of dark leather, a couple of dart boards, and man-sized beer mugs on the windowsills.

"Whose choice was this?" I sniffed.

"O'Neal's."

"Figures. Where's Bart?"

"Still out of town with Lee."

Which left O'Neal to play official greeter. He seated the six of us around a massive table with clawed feet. When Hugh pumped Jamie's hand and Zack put on his Dom Perignon smile—a real contrast with Kagan's subdued expression—I knew who was about to be feted even before O'Neal broke open the bottle.

"That successful?" I asked, enjoying the drama of a wordless toast, all big male grins and raised glasses.

"Operation PR is a big hit, Karen." Jamie was beaming.

"We're only a few weeks into the campaign, but I'm cautiously optimistic," Kagan admitted.

"The press is being cautious, period," Zack observed, champagne glass turning slowly in his hand. "Almost as if they're afraid to take us seriously. The police are baffled, of course."

"Even with the clues you've been leaving behind?"

"Don't confuse us with terrorists, eager to take credit for an atrocity," Jamie sniffed. "Instead of some crude, traceable slogan, our symbol—thanks to you, love—is subtler stuff. And definitely baffling," he added, patting his fox medal. (These days, he wore it *under* his shirt—his one concession to caution.)

During dinner, I got caught up in the general excitement. O'Neal had been on the road and couldn't stop crowing (in between puffs on his Havana) about how "things are starting to roll—all those new recruits!" How the country was "with us all the way, by God." Hugh was high on the fund-raising strides he was making. Zack spoke with quiet enthusiasm about police sympathy that bordered on outright support. Jamie was positively gleeful, but not too specific, about his latest Missions. Kagan was quiet.

I asked which aspects of the PR campaign were paying off the most. And got a cornucopia of answers.

Cells were operating more effectively. "Comes from being ideologically armed," Zack said.

Whole groups of Vulnerables, from inner-city middle-class blacks to blue-collar communities in the suburbs to organizations devoted to the elderly, were voicing "loud approval" of VA tactics.

O'Neal claimed my backgrounders were working crowd magic. ("Those stark blowups of crime victims make for powerful ammo, little lady.")

It went on and on.

Until the dessert course, which arrived with more champagne.

That's when I realized no one had asked me about Lee's report.

"Lee's department isn't working," Kagan announced, reading me, as usual. "We'd like you to whip it into shape, take up the slack."

"You mean, help with the administrative work?" I said with a cautious look around at the others.

"Run the whole department," Jamie said. "Unofficially, of

course. No point in pushing Lee's nose out of joint. Don't frown. You're already familiar with the entire operation. It's one reason the PR campaign is working so well. Can you take over . . . just until your leave is up?"

Why not? I thought. The truth was, I'd been feeling useful these last couple of months. . . . I needed to keep feeling it.

I handed my glass to Zack and let him fill it with champagne. Raised glasses all around.

I wasn't too sure this was such a good idea. From the look on Kagan's face, he wasn't too sure, either.

And Kagan was usually right.

Chapter 18

I thought of yesterday's note, dropped off at my building, as I approached Claudia's. "Tomorrow is April Fool's Day," she had written, "an apt occasion for two damn fools to stop keeping a discreet distance. Come to lunch. Just you, me, and my ex. Stan is stopping by to burglarproof my place. Love to see you again, he said. Me, too."

Claudia's apartment was a jewel tucked away in a dirty brown bag. But look past the curbside garbage and crumbling masonry, the artfully garish graffiti, and you could still spot the graceful lines of an old brownstone.

Inside was the house specialty: stale cooking odors from under the doors. The elevator would have made a mole claustrophobic. Also nervous. But it was empty.

So was the hall. The door opened on the first ring. Claudia and I hugged, then sat down to play catch-up: health, diet, movie recommendations—everything except what was really on our minds.

"What happened to your living room?" I asked, noticing. "It has the no-nonsense look of a study."

"Exactly what I was after. Think Stan will go for it?"

"Absolutely." But I was already missing Claudia's lushly over-powering reds, oranges and yellows. Gone were the plump floor cushions and carnivorous-looking plants. "When's he due?" I said.

"Any minute. What do you think?" She did a small, nervous pirouette, her hand sweeping out to a perfectly appointed table and the telltale odors of Stan's all-time-favorite oyster stew.

"Menu and decor, a ten. Ten-plus for the hostess."

She gave my hand a grateful squeeze and hurried off to the kitchen, looking sensational in billowy cocoa-and-cream topped off by an exquisite turban. I wanted to remind her that burglarproofing, not romance, was in the air. It was typical of Stan to worry about "his careless Claudia" and her deteriorating neighborhood, even if she wasn't his anymore—Stan's choice, not hers.

She hadn't given up on him, I realized with a sense of uneasiness. What else but wishful thinking could explain a redecorated living room, the full makeup treatment, and this big fuss of a lunch?

Through a haze of smoke, I contemplated the good old days—old, anyway. How we'd met through our husbands (good cop, good Legal Aid lawyer) at a New Year's Eve party. How our "unlikely friendship" (Stan's "dancer-wife" had been Allan's advance put-down description) had outlasted both our marriages. "Dancer" turned out to be the least relevant thing about her, as I'd discovered that first night. Claudia had looked around at a roomful of assorted Legal Aiders posing for their annual group photograph and railing against the crime statistics that had eroded their public mandate. Then she'd turned to me and said, "Smug." The smugness of people on the defensive. I saw what she meant. "Not my kind of party," said this outspoken, irreverent creature. That's when I knew she was my kind of person.

"Well, look who's smoking. It's been what, six years?"

"Good memory, CC. D day, I quit. Day of divorce."

"What got you going again, as if I didn't—"

"The added stresses of life."

The doorbell rang and we let Stan in.

"Let me look at you," I said, taking his hand. He wore chinos and an aviator jacket. "More grey in the beard, Stan, but still slim and sturdy." Still melancholy in the eyes and tough around the mouth. All cop . . .

Lunch with a detective, old friend or no, produced my first fearball of the day. It melted away with red wine and thick Italian bread dunked in Claudia's delicious stew. It came back in a rush, how much I'd always liked Stan.

How much Claudia still loved him.

"—makes sense after the rash of break-ins," Stan was saying.

"I said yes to an extra lock," Claudia grumbled, "but *bars* on my windows?!"

The butterfly rejecting the net. "Because of the fire escape, Claudia," I reminded her. "It makes you vulnerable."

"No bars then," Stan capitulated. "Would you go for a solidly anchored metal grille? I could install two of them next week."

She went for it; it would mean another lunch. I let her clear the table while I followed Stan to the foyer for a quick education on burglarproofing.

"Claud's rim lock is a deterrent," he pointed out, "but it's not secure against a weak door. Now this barricade lock adds real strength—or will, once I anchor it with a steel rod."

We caught up on the years, which made it easy to pry—to wonder out loud about his wife. "Jan still with Legal Aid?"

"Best damn lawyer on Allan's staff, so he tells me."

Spoken with the pride of a man still in love, Claudia . . .

"What about your own standing offer from Allan?" I asked.

"I'll stick to being a detective with a law degree."

"Seems like a waste."

"The degree?" He looked up and shrugged. "It's my insurance. If I'm ever tempted to become the kind of cop I can't respect, that's the day I'll turn in my badge for a mouthpiece."

"What kind of cop is that?" I said slowly, knowing that "cop on the take" would never tempt him.

"The kind who plays God. There. See what I mean?"

I saw more than an anchored steel rod.

I was thinking, as Claudia called us in for dessert, about the odds of a black cop and a black detective from different precincts running into each other. By the time Claudia's famous lemon meringue pie was quivering on our plates, I had thought of a rejoinder—a defense, of sorts, of my friend Zack.

"Can you blame today's cop for being fed up with the system?" I asked Stan. "You fellas don't control the streets anymore."

"Tell me about it! In the old days you'd spot someone dirty, search him, and nine times out of ten turn up a weapon. Now you're supposed to follow him and wait around until he commits mayhem. How, when we don't have the manpower? Catch him in the act—"

"And the courts don't put him away," I finished.

"Vigilante justice isn't the answer," Claudia sniffed.

"Hell, no," he said. "I was telling Claud the other day about some vigilante action we've run into. . . ."

I half-listened while Claudia's little April Fool's note replayed in my head: *Stan is stopping by . . . love to see you again.* Love to set you up with a good scare and a lecture.

"—all it would do is bring the system crashing down on our heads," Stan was saying.

"Would it?" I said, annoyed at his self-righteous tone until I remembered what Jamie had told me. . . . *"The cop is a victim too, Karen. He's hamstrung by the politicians."*

Stan didn't know much, just what Jamie and Kagan wanted him to. He could find "no rhyme or reason" for the vigilante violence. Why this vicious mugger, but not that one, got his wrist broken. Why an armed robber on one block, but not on the next, was wounded with his own gun. The police had no idea "how organized these people were"—but the propaganda they left behind made clear how far they intended to go. No profile, no real clue to their identity, had emerged. How could it when the would-be victims of the muggers and the robbers couldn't or wouldn't talk? He didn't know the meaning of the group's odd symbol, a fox.

But he said he knew the true meaning of "vigilante."

"A two-headed monster," he told us. "One mouth devours the criminal, the other its own flesh. I'd sooner lose to the criminal," he said, his voice tight.

When he was leaving, I couldn't resist a parting shot. "I'm betting these vigilantes aren't a bunch of crazies, Stan, not all of them. Don't you think they have a right to be frustrated, at least?"

Stan turned to me with a look of such chronic weariness that his features acquired the universal look of "cop"—something I had learned to notice these last few months. "Yeah," he said, "they got a right."

It did something to me, the look on his face.

It did something to Claudia.

"So he'd sooner lose to the criminal," she mused after he'd gone. "Karen, he *is* losing. The poor guy just can't admit it."

"Not yet," I said, thinking, Not ever, I'm afraid.

"You mad at me?" Claudia asked cautiously.

"Because this whole lunch was a setup?"

"I was worried," she said, looking so chastened I forgave her. "Figured you might get religion if Stan let loose on you."

"I haven't joined, CC."

"You haven't gone back to work yet, either. I must say, you seem calmer. Less directionless. Me, I've never felt more like a leaf in the wind." She was twisting the jade-and-gold band she always wore on her right hand: her wedding ring. "Hell, nothing's changed. Has it?" Her eyes begged me to disagree. "He likes me, he loves his wife," she said in the singsong voice of plucking a daisy.

"He still loves you. Not that it does you any good."

"Too little too late," she said with a vehement gesture at the desk end of her redecorated living room. If there'd been a book within reach, she'd have thrown it. "The new studious Claudia won't get him back. Why waste my time getting a college degree?"

"You're almost there. Don't quit now," I said urgently, sensing she was about to. "It's not just about Stan. You enjoy it."

"It's a means to an end—it was. College before law school, remember? What am I trying to prove, that I have as good a mind as that husband-stealing bitch? That I could be a better lawyer?"

"Claudia, don't. You've earned the credits. The good marks. Don't you know your dancing days are over?"

"You could be wrong about that." An ominous tone.

It clashed with her typical way of standing when she was angry: defiantly straight and poised for flight. Indifferent to her own tears. I had the disconcerting image of a young birch tree, tender-looking, surprisingly tough, impossible to know the breaking point. . . .

"You're about to tell me you know how I feel. But you don't," she said. "You didn't lose a husband. You walked out on one."

"Not soon enough," I quipped, pulling a half-grin out of her.

"Good man, Allan. Dedicated to all the good things."

"We weren't a great mix, CC. I don't mind humorless men as long as they appreciate humor. My brand used to irritate him."

"Not Dr. James Coyne, I'll bet."

"No," I said. But I was thinking of McCann.

"Seeing much of Jamie, these days?"

"Enough. Why?"

"Victims Anonymous," she said, as if she were testing the words. "They're starting to make waves. Are they making a difference?"

"Too soon to tell. I think they will. What's on your mind?"

"Maybe I'd like to see for myself what you're all doing."

"What for?" I said, confused by what I heard in her voice: a sense of reluctance and a trace of eagerness together.

"I know, I was against the whole idea. But if it works, if cops like Stan gain control of the streets again . . . Isn't that what you said Victims Anonymous was all about?"

"What *this* conversation is all about falls into the category of Do Something Special for Stan."

"Yeah, I guess," she said, looking contrite. "Karen, whatever happened to Sarah's murderer?"

The question might have been innocent; she was applying a bright red lipstick when she asked it.

"A happy ending, according to Allan's ADA friend," I said with just the right tone of bitter sarcasm. "Seems the whole gang was wiped out by a rival gang—along with their headquarters."

She seemed to buy it. Why not? It was almost word for word what Donahue had told me.

But then she drew her shoulders together like she was cold. "So I'll stick with the books," she said, "but, Jesus, be careful, will you?"

That's when I knew she knew.

Chapter 19

I sat in Jamie's waiting room, wondering at his cryptic telephone message: "I need an hour or so of your time." Nervous (it was Friday the thirteenth), I'd showed up early. He was in with a patient. I spied a pile of back issues on a corner table. I hadn't been able to read a newspaper for weeks. . . .

We'd gotten good coverage. The scandal sheets had been having a field day with VA's calling card—"stylized fox with expressive eyes." Only a few commentators had picked up on the symbolism: victim of the hunt turns hunter. The better papers were good on what facts they had, and every crime reporter worthy of the title was whipping up pieces full of color and high drama.

It was the "human interest" angle that worried me. It was the editorials and the op-ed pages that I started to read with a dry mouth. I knew our PR campaign was working with the general public, thanks to a steady stream of reports coming in on new recruits. Everybody in the office was excited by the figures. As for increased visibility, there wasn't a paper in the country, Jamie said, where we hadn't made the front page.

But the official opinion makers? A mixed reception. To some, Victims Anonymous was the answer to their dreams. To others, we were a nightmare, a local virus that had to be stamped out—

Local?

The more I read, the clearer it got. The press hadn't put it together as a national phenomenon . . . it was "New York's vigilantes" and "Chicago's vigilantes" and no doubt Cleveland's, Detroit's—

The paper I was holding slipped to the floor. Being perceived as "local" meant no FBI interest, no— I closed my eyes.

No Max McCann.

Jamie emerged from his office. "Today's paper," he said, tossing it to me before heading for the bathroom. His patient, a young woman, fastidiously groomed except for runny mascara, nodded in my direction and made a hasty exit. I looked at the newspaper.

A headline leaped out at me. ARE WE ALL POTENTIAL VIGILANTES? *My* words! But in the handout VA had left all over town, I'd made it a declarative statement, not a question. More of my words followed—italicized: the reporter's lead in a long article about the frustrated man in the street.

I had depicted him as a national phenomenon. . . .

> *It's happening all over America:*
> *—A record year for pistol licenses and*
> *instruction in firearms;*
> *—A proliferation of block watchers and*
> *fierce guardians of the local park;*
> *—Cheering while a mugger is punched and kicked;*
> *—Popular match game: burning crack houses*
> *to the ground;*
> *—Subway Mystery: menacing punk with knife*
> *shot by "person or persons unknown."*

Jamie told me I looked a little green around the gills and steered me into his office.

"Better green than smug," I muttered.

"I'm feeling good," he admitted. "Zack called in. The criminal-justice people just had one of their 'coordination' meetings—you know, police, prosecutors, judges, corrections officers."

"Sounds exciting," I said.

Jamie thought I meant it. "There's nothing quite so exhilarating as infiltrating the enemy." He put an eager spin on a glass paperweight and caught it. "One of Bart's people was there. And Zack—strictly as a PD observer. The chief spokesman for the police was a black detective."

"Stan Cole?" I said slowly . . . and groaned. "Stan and Zack."

"They didn't know each other. They do now." Jamie grinned. "We've become a 'specific' crime problem—that's the bad news. A task force has been proposed to deal with us. The good news is that no one can agree on anything. The goal of these meets is coordination—an inside joke, Bart tells me. Especially after his man got through feeding everybody bogus leads."

He was gleeful. "What's the matter with you?" I practically yelled at him. "A task force! The police—"

"They're demoralized. And vastly understaffed, believe me."

I could almost hear Zack grumbling about police strength— barely equal to what it was twenty-five years ago. I said, "You've been breaking the law—flagrantly—and getting away with it. Are the police that inept?"

Jamie looked exasperated. "Karen, Karen," he said, "haven't you of all people grasped the principle? We're *organized.* We—"

Tony walked in the door.

"We'd like you to sit in on Tony's session," Jamie told me. "Tell Karen it's okay, Tadpole."

Tony colored at the hated nickname.

"That's why you need an hour of my time?" I protested.

"It's about his recurring nightmare. I thought it might help if the three of us discussed—"

"Bad idea, Jamie," I said, getting up to leave.

"He has a conflict, Karen. Between you and the person who raised him—a sister he adores."

I sat down.

"Big sister Maria is not exactly what you'd call a nurturing mother. When she's not off somewhere making porno movies—"

"She's a topless dancer," Tony mumbled, working at his scuffed shoes as if he were rubbing firewood. "I followed her to work once."

"Tony has been punishing himself for 'betraying' Maria," Jamie said softly. "For wanting the kind of mother he's never had."

. . . For wanting me.

I spent the next hour sitting in on somebody else's nightmare.

Chapter 20

Saturday morning playing catch-up with a deskful of work is my idea of relaxing. No interruptions or small talk, no well-meaning friends— The doorknob turned in my hand.

I sighed, slipped my key back into my purse and went in.

"Hi, Rosa. You're a surprise."

"So you're killing yourself on weekends now?"

"What about you?" I shot back.

I noticed Lee's closed door. "What brings Lee here of a Saturday morn?"

"Heavy brunch date, maybe?" Rosa sniffed. "The 'troops' get more done when she's off traveling."

"You're too hard on her," I chided. "Lee can be very nice when she's not being standoffish."

"When's that?"

I laughed. "She can't help herself. She really does care. Lee has a finely tuned sense of moral outrage—I've seen it."

"Me, too," Rosa admitted. "So why can't I like her?"

"She's not your type," I said and went to knock on Lee's door.

Bart was parked on the edge of her leather-topped desk. Lee was filling a briefcase. "Did you hear?" she told me, a becoming flush on her cheeks. "We're off tomorrow on another tour!"

I hadn't heard. I couldn't digest it. Kagan, sending standout Lee on another round of Missions? Back on the road with VA visibility at an all-time high?

All I said was "Have a good time and keep a low profile."

Neither of them picked up on it. Lee, demure in pearls and long-sleeved pale pink linen, was busy flirting. Bart, looking more lighthearted than I'd ever seen him—he had abandoned black leather for a light blue sports jacket and loafers—was engrossed in Lee: her coy half-smile, a seductive laugh, the way she'd arch an eyebrow or let a sentence trail off. I liked the way his hand kept returning to the back of her chair.

I didn't like what I suddenly realized about the way Lee dressed and carried on: proper, well-tailored lady just waiting to be dragged from her pedestal by Macho Man. Poor Bart.

Poor Lee. Role-playing might be harmless by itself, but for a high-profile member of a secret organization that had just attracted the attention of a police task force?

I put my hand on her arm. "Lee," I said—and stopped. What was there to say except "Be careful."

She smiled and patted my hand. "Oh, I almost forgot. There's a message for you, a Miss Cole."

Curious. Claudia had never called me here. I went back to my desk to make the call. My phone rang before I could pick it up. It was Angela.

"SOS, Karen. I'm at Tony's place. How fast can you get here?"

"Something's happened to Tony?"

"He's all right."

"I'm on my way." We hung up on each other.

Rosa's "What's wrong?" followed me out the door.

It followed me down to the street.

I wish I knew, Rosa. I wish there were more cabs at this hour. I wish the damn cab would go faster. I wish the South Bronx would stop unfolding its ugliness outside my window. I wish Tony hadn't been born, bred, and unsupervised in the new Bronx tradition, living among the gutted corpses of buildings, having strippers and derelicts for neighbors.

It wasn't bad, his building. Showing its age—crumbling brick around the edges. But a still-sturdy specimen from another era.

I found "Montes." Angela's voice responded to the buzzer. My legs responded to her SOS. Up an elevator, down an alien hall—

Into the reassuring presence of Mother Earth. Angela sensed my relief at the mere sight of her. She reached out a steadying hand and steered me inside to a dining area and black coffee, as if she knew my breakfast was still in a paper bag somewhere.

"Take it easy," she said in her soothing alto. "Zack's in the bedroom with him. He'll be out soon." She wouldn't say any more.

I looked around at bright curtains and scatter rugs, shelf after shelf of knickknacks, lace doilies on an overstuffed couch; his sister Maria's loving touches? I looked closer and saw the dust. I noticed the photographs lining the walls. Stood back to admire their stark black-and-white drama. I was stunned by the photographer's skill. Last summer the sister had picked up an expensive camera on one of her trips abroad. Tony had been ecstatic.

"Either you photograph well or the kid's got real talent." Angela stood before a photograph, alone on a narrow strip of wall.

A candid shot while I was deep in concentration at my desk. Tony was always snapping away. It got so we'd stopped noticing. Alone on a separate wall . . .

Zack came out and closed the door. He was shaking his head.

I grabbed hold of his arm. "Tony's hurt?"

"Not the way you mean. His sister was killed last night."

Zack grabbed *my* arm, stopped me from running to him.

"You better hear it all before you try battering down that wall of resistance in there," he warned. "Friday nights my ex lets the kids sleep over—movie night. I've invited Tony before but last night was the first time in months he accepted—thank God."

"Zack brought Tony home this morning," Angela said. "That's when the call came."

"His sister was . . . killed?"

"Murdered. Must have been a random mugger off the street. Some twisted son of a bitch," Angela muttered.

"Her body was cut up," Zack told me.

"How—"

"Bad. Some yo-yo at the topless joint where she worked must have left a side door unlocked. The other girls had left—it was after the last show. Woman heard the screams and called it in."

"Can you stay with Tony?" Angela asked me.

"I'll stay. Does Jamie know?"

She nodded. "He wants to see Tony this afternoon."

"I'll take him. Zack, how bad is he?"

"All anger and no tears. The doctor left some sedatives. While I was seeing him out, Tony flushed them down the toilet."

We went in to him. Tony was trembling, tight-lipped with rage.

"Tony," Zack said, sitting beside him on the bed, "if you want me to find out more about Maria, you have to do something for me. You have to let Karen take you to Jamie later. What do you say?"

"You'll tell me who killed her?" he asked.

"When I know, you'll know."

"It may take a while," Angela warned.

"I'll find him if you don't!" Tony exploded.

"Listen to me, Antonio," Zack said, taking hold of his small shoulders. "This is not your department so get it out of your head. Now. Okay?"

Nothing.

Angela went over, wanting to hug him. Gently cupping his face instead. It was only a moment, but some of the rigidity seemed to soften under her healing touch.

When they left, I stayed by the bedroom door, sensing that he didn't want me near him. Knowing that he wouldn't cry. His eyes were like the little black buttons you see on stuffed animals . . . pathetic in their glassiness.

I thought about sitting but then everything in me began to slide. Easily. Noiselessly. My body. The memory of funerals. Tony's hopelessness. My tears . . .

I sat on the floor and cried for a long time. It was all I could do for him.

The minute I opened Jamie's waiting room door, he came out of his inner office and took gentle hold of Tony's arm. I repaired to the kitchenette to make us all coffee. On my way in with it I almost collided with Jamie, on his way out to the john. "I'm going upstairs to call Claudia," I said. "Where's the apartment key?"

"On my desk. I'll bring Tony up afterward. I want him to spend the next few nights with me. After that . . ." He shrugged.

Tony handed me Jamie's key in exchange for his coffee.

Both elevators were off somewhere in the higher reaches. I hurried up two flights, uneasy about why Claudia had called me earlier.

She answered on the first ring. "Sorry it took so long," I told her. "We had an emergency. Tony's sister—"

"I know. I need to see you. How's two hours from now?"

"Fine. When and where? And by the way, what's wrong?"

"Later. Take down where we'll meet. Just don't ask me why."

A noisy dive in the seedier environs of Broadway? Don't ask? She didn't give me the chance. I hung up with another bewildering question that would have to wait: How did she know about Tony?

I concocted a makeshift dinner from Jamie's leftovers. When they came up, it was pick-at-your-food time for all three of us.

"Take yourself to the master bedroom, Tony-boy. And take your sedative. He will *not* flush it down the tubes," Jamie assured me.

"Tell her," Tony said, sliding his chair back. Silence. "I'm gonna make my bones. Tell her you promised." He ran off.

"You were humoring him," I said to Jamie's blank expression.

"What do you think? Not that he'll have a killer to make his bones on. Not much chance of turning him up in a case like this."

We brooded over our coffee. "I have to go out," he announced.

"Damn, so do I. I'm meeting Claudia. One of us should—"

"He won't even know we're gone. That sedative works like a sledgehammer. Come see for yourself."

Jamie's elaborate bedchamber was a sea of soothing white satin with a small mound in dead center. I saw a bit of striped pajama and a tangle of dark curls.

"That's that," Jamie said.

I peered inside the entrance of a place called Club 66—Lizard Lounge was more like it. I backed away fast. Even on the street, the heavy metal was earsplitting. Who in their right mind would want to meet here? . . . Unless she didn't want to be heard?

A willowy black gal sporting an outrageously blond wig, a pair of glitter-framed dark glasses and a skintight shell of a dress sauntered past. Her arm shot out—

". . . Claudia?" I said as she pulled me inside.

"Shhhhh. Walk with me."

To a reserved table in an obscure corner of a room the size of a barn. Some of the locals looked me over as I passed, giving my "basic black" attire—my widow's look, Claudia called it—a skeptical eye. The glances that followed Claudia were one step short of attempted rape.

She moved our chairs close and we sat down.

"Why the disguise?" I asked over the so-called music.

"You happen to remember what nights I teach dancing?"

"Thursdays through Sundays. To keep wine and cheese on the table, you said. What are you doing here on a Saturday—"

"Karen, I don't *teach* dancing. That wouldn't even pay for the tablecloth, these days."

"Damn it, CC, why don't you tell me when you need money?"

"Not you, and not Stan," she said, biting off each word. "I won't be in debt to the people I love. I quit my job last night. You know what my job *was?* Karen, I . . ." She couldn't get it out.

I leaned closer, trying to see past the camouflage as she twisted her jade wedding ring or played with a butterfly pin at her throat (Claudia was big on butterflies). "You're in real trouble, aren't you?" I said.

"Let's go next door. Showing may be easier than telling." She was up before I could argue the point, weaving a serpentine path for both of us past a barrier of frantically gyrating bodies.

We went out a side exit, crossed a narrow alley, went through the door of the neighboring building—

And stepped into another universe.

"The job I quit last night," Claudia said, as if she were making a formal introduction.

I stared at an elevated stage, mesmerized by the primitive jungle rhythm of undulating women. Breasts all sizes, colors and shapes. No pasties. A movie screen on stage left competed for customer attention with hardcore porn.

"You wouldn't believe the tips around here." Claudia's mouth matched the bitter twist of her words. "I told you my dancing days weren't over," she said, searching my face for a reaction.

I was searching my memory . . . Tony, in Jamie's office, telling me about his sister. *She's a topless dancer. I followed her to work once.* Tony, when Kagan first introduced us—Claudia had pretended not to recognize him, then had that turtle-in-the-shell reaction when he'd looked her over.

"You and Tony," I sputtered. "His sister Maria—"

"Was a topless dancer." She sighed. "Like me. I can't stay here. Let's go back. We have to talk."

We cut through the alley again while I tried to unscramble my brain. The heavy metal didn't help, but at least Claudia was able to talk without being overheard.

She was able to cry. "Maria was mixed up, but decent, y'know? We were what you'd call arm's-length friends," Claudia said, and laid it all out for me. . . .

A dance lineup of hardened professionals. Two exceptions drawn to each other, trading jokes, problems and dreams over coffee or a drink. Maria, guilt-ridden over her neglect of Tony, determined, now, to "go legit, become an actress or something." Ready, last night, to give her porno equivalent of a pimp the kiss-off, even though she was "in hock to the slimeball," she'd told Claudia. Even though she was about to walk out on a gig in Korea.

"I waited here for her." Claudia's voice had become a whisper. "After twenty minutes, I went looking. The place was deserted but I heard sounds coming from the dressing room, I heard . . .

screams. The door was locked. I yelled for Maria, I yelled for Arnie to unlock the goddamn door! Then I ran like hell."

I couldn't keep my hands still. "So the anonymous caller . . ."

"Me. There wasn't a patrol car in sight. Nobody on the street. I made the call and ducked back into this place looking for help. Too late. The cops were fast but Arnie was faster."

"Claudia, if the dressing room door was locked, then the killer couldn't have seen—"

"He didn't have to. We've met. He knows my voice. He knows the color of my skin. By tomorrow, he'll know all about the black topless dancer who didn't show up for work tonight."

"You need police protection while they look for him," I said.

"And let Stan find out? I'd die first."

Then I knew what she'd had in mind when she called me.

"Remember the Guadeloupe vacation—those lovely French beaches where it's chic to go topless?" she said. "Remember what straitlaced Stan did when I finally gave in to the urge?"

"Pulled you off the beach by your ponytail." I could still see it. Under different circumstances we'd have laughed about it.

"Karen, I can't do it to him. Or to me."

I sighed. "It's Victims Anonymous, then?" She gripped my hand. I glanced at my watch. "We'd better get you moved."

"The hell we will. He can't track me down so fast if he doesn't know my name. You think I used my real one?"

"But when he does, CC, you have no weapon, no—"

"I do now. Stan topped off his burglarproofing efforts by giving me a 'clean piece.' Even showed me how to use it."

"Put those glitter frames back on, at least," I told her, wishing I'd brought my own dark glasses.

We checked out the barn—as much of it as we could see through the thick smoke—and pushed our way to the front door.

On the street we ran into a welcoming committee of one: Tony.

I glared at him. "You didn't take your sedative, damn it. You followed me."

"I didn't! I knew where you were going."

"How?"

But I knew how. *"I'm going upstairs to call Claudia."*

"Eavesdropper," I snapped.

But my anger had no more reality for him than the blare of heavy metal spilling into the street.

He was blocking Claudia's way. "I never told on you," he said, one finger jabbing in the general direction of the topless joint. The unstated implication hung between them: You owe me. He said, "You know who killed Maria."

"Claudia!" I yelled.

But my warning had no reality for her, either.

Sobbing, she reached for him.

No trace of the child in Tony's face as Claudia held him to her. He was looking past her.

He looked capable of anything.

Chapter 21

"What happened?" I said before Jamie was halfway in the door.

"Let's argue over tea," he said, heading for my kitchen.

"Where's Tony?" I demanded.

"Steering clear of you and me. Hanging out with Bart, for the moment."

"Damn Bart," I said, leaving Jamie with the teakettle, too angry to play hostess. Sorry Kagan had called Bart back to New York.

"Don't be mad at Bart," he called after me. "It may be his Mission, but you know who's running the show."

Kagan. "Why is Kagan running so many shows, these days?" I yelled back. "Why not you? I gather you weren't any help at this meeting you people barred me from."

He came into the living room. "In all fairness, I think the Mission planning went well. Turns out our porno producer doesn't take premeditated murder lightly. Arnie won't make his move against Claudia until he's done his own planning, and the man is thorough if nothing—"

"Claudia agreed to play decoy?"

"Oh, yes."

I lit a cigarette. "How safe is she?"

"You're smoking too much. How safe right now, you mean? We have round-the-clock surveillance on her as well as Arnie."

"She never told me!"

"She doesn't know. Once he goes after her, we want him to see a nervous quarry, not someone who knows she's being protected. Arnie's sort smells 'setup' a mile away. At the moment, he's calm, cool, and much too cocky, since the cops have Maria's murderer pegged as some nut case out to carve up 'loose' women."

"What's he like? Swarthy, with greasy hair and custom-made silk suits?"

"Arnie has class. You'll see when you get the photographs."

"Why would Bart send me—"

"Everyone going on the Mission has to be thoroughly familiar with the Target. I had to pull rank to get you on the Team."

"I see," I said, sitting down on the couch while he retreated to the kitchen. "VA has an age limit," I called out to him. "Tony doesn't even come close, damn it!" I mashed out my cigarette.

Jamie came in with the tea. "They're making an exception."

"Which you could have vetoed. Why didn't you?"

"In point of fact," he said, dropping onto the couch beside me, "I agree with Kagan on this one. Tony knows too much about our operation and he's making threats. The only way to neutralize him is to let him have his way. Then he's in no position to blab."

"Have his way. Cute euphemism for letting a thirteen-year-old 'do' Arnie," I snapped. "It's double blackmail. My God, Jamie, you're his therapist. Who's in a better position to know how emotionally unstable he is? Turn him into a triggerman and he'll never be the same."

"I know."

"You know but you don't care?" He looked at me. One of his impenetrable stares. I was learning to see through them, and what I thought I saw was pain. I seized on it. "What kind of future will Tony have after this?"

"The word 'future' isn't part of his vocabulary," he said slowly. "It's the price Tony paid for going it alone instead of falling in with street gangs. You really expect the kid to have a sense of the long-range when he has his hands full with the short—with surviving day by day? He'll survive this, too."

"And Claudia?" I asked. "How's she bearing up?"

"More angry than frightened. She resents being on constant alert. Who wouldn't?"

"When Arnie does make his move—"

"We'll be ready for him. You'll do fine."

"You're not going with us?" I said, dismayed.

He patted my hand. "Only one guardian angel per Mission."

"But what if something should go wrong?"

He stopped me from lighting up again. "What if it should go right? Let me fill you in on a kid named Tony Montes, survivor. . . ."

What if it should go right? A thought to hold on to as I sat in the backseat of Bart's car, a grim-faced Tony a few feet away.

The car pulled over to pick up another passenger.

"Name's Julio," he said, getting in back to sit between Tony and me. He made a playful jab at Tony's shoulder. "How they hanging? You up for it?"

Tony patted his jacket. "I'm up for it."

I took a close look at Julio: a shock of black hair under a dark cap, patched denims, wrists protruding from last year's jacket. . . . A boy too young to be here.

But old enough to have given Tony pointers on using a gun. Bart had ruled out the knife Tony wanted to use—thank God.

I stared at the back of Bart's neck and wished for the hundredth time that it was Zack's. He'd been cut from the Mission, a last-minute switch. At the last minute, he'd been caught reloading Tony's gun—substituting fake bullets for the real ones so that someone other than Tony would be doing the killing.

All Zack had succeeded in killing was the bond growing between them.

When the car slowed for a traffic light, I tapped Bart on the shoulder. "Tell me again why you think this Arnie is about to make his move," I said as he half-turned.

"He's been tailing your friend Claudia by himself, see, only the last coupla days, he let up a little—just followed her to and from the library at night. That tells us where he plans the hit. We figure he'll move on her as soon as she shortcuts through the parking lot to her crosstown bus."

"But why there?"

Bart shot me a glance. "You read about those two college girls who were mugged and garroted?"

"Not far from the library," I said slowly.

"Killer still at large. Arnie's no dope. See, he's setting up Claudia to be victim number three. Looks like a pattern."

"Why tonight, Bart? What makes you so sure—"

He flashed me a grin. "Lee saw it before I did. This guy spends big bucks on his wardrobe, dresses like a Park Avenue lawyer even when he's tailing his mark. But not tonight."

"Jeans and sneakers?"

"Wouldn't be caught dead in 'em. Just off-the-rack stuff so nobody remembers seeing a pinstripe suit in the neighborhood. But the kicker was the scarf. Lee says the well-dressed man-about-town wouldn't be caught dead in a black silk scarf this time of year unless maybe he was on his way to the opera in a tux. We figure he has something special in mind for the scarf—"

"I get the picture."

"Good. Now get loose. Arnie don't know we exist but we know all about Arnie, right down to his lime after-shave and the monogram on his satin boxer shorts."

We pulled in fifteen minutes ahead of schedule—an unattended parking lot. Dark. Deserted at this hour except for half a dozen familiar "overnighters"—cars Arnie would recognize so he wouldn't go into alert. But the snappy blue Ford and the dusty panel truck, parked side by side, were ours. A man in black got out of the Ford, another one out of the truck.

The SD Team joined up in front of Bart's red Subaru wagon, on the opposite side of the lot.

"Synchronize your watches," Bart said. Then, eyes on Tony, "Move into position."

One of the two men headed for the Ford, Julio and Tony for the panel truck. Bart and the other guy stayed with me in the wagon. We ducked out of sight and I went into a deep-breathing routine. Take a deep breath and wait, listen. Take another, wait some more. Breathe, close your eyes, die a little . . .

"Decoy in sight." Bart's harsh whisper was like a voice from the grave.

She had left the library steps behind and was headed our way, following the same diagonal line that would take her through the lot and—more important—between the Subaru on one side, and the Ford and the panel truck on the other. Claudia in full-skirted white, sauntering through a parking lot on a night so full of the soft scent of spring that caution, for once, seemed to have taken a backseat to the weather. *On your mark.*

If Arnie followed his own script, he would move briskly down the same diagonal path. Any minute now.

"Target in sight."

Get set. My eyes flashed to the edge of the lot and picked out a tall figure in loose-fitting raincoat and cap, moving with long graceful strides. The face that took shape went less with baseball caps than ten-gallon hats. . . . *The photographs didn't do you justice, Arnie.* Light eyes—blue? grey?—luxurious silver hair, a well-trimmed mustache over a healthy gleam of teeth. Prosperous-looking Southwestern type in off-the-rack clothes.

Except for the designer scarf. It was black silk. It was long. His hand moved, caressing it, as he closed the distance.

"Cleo!" he called out—the way Bart figured he would.

At the sound of her phony stage name, Claudia turned, passing Arnie's final ID test. She started to run, tripped over something, went sprawling as Arnie sprinted after her—

Go!

Everybody out of the car—three of us on one side, three on the other. Six bodies flanking Arnie like a gauntlet. Six weapons aimed at the Target.

At his stomach, now, as the Target whirled around, backing and filling, *his* target on her feet again and out of reach. Safe.

Tony stepped forward. "You murdered my sister! You killed Maria!" Improvised dialogue. TV melodrama. But a cylinder, like a metal growth, was sticking out of the muzzle end of the gun in Tony's two-handed grip—the silencer his friend Julio had introduced him to.

Julio had put away his own gun. Bart's orders had placed in his awkward grip what would have rested so naturally in Tony's: a camera. Julio raised it like an ax waiting to fall.

I heard the crack—why, with a silencer? I couldn't grasp why Arnie pitched forward instead of back, or why Tony's gun seemed stuck to his hand.

Bart cut the air with a gesture that froze everyone in place. He was peering into the night—the far end of the parking lot, rimmed with low buildings. I saw a figure wave and jump down from his perch, rifle hanging loose as he hurried toward us.

"It's Zack," I said, starting to choke, to laugh, because Tony had made the classic mistake of the good guy who waits too long to savor the moment of the bad guy's comeuppance. The rifle in Zack's hand didn't have a silencer; it had a scope. Zack had shot Maria's killer before Tony could pull the trigger.

"You killed him, you lousy bastard!" Tony screamed at Zack as the realization hit him.

He was holding a gun in his hand but he had never sounded more like a child.

He was no longer holding a gun—Zack had whipped it out of his hand. Tony glared at him. "I quit this lousy organization!"

"Move out, all of you," Zack ordered.

"Jesus," Bart muttered, "when Kagan hears what you—"

"Make sense, Bart," Zack hissed. "Save the recriminations. We're not supposed to leave our calling card on this one, remember? Get your Team out while a cop who just *happened* to be passing by investigates the sound of a gunshot."

That's when I noticed Zack was in uniform.

"Right." Bart hoisted a protesting Tony away. Julio followed, shaking his head. The men in black were racing away. I watched the Ford take off, then the panel truck.

Zack bent over the body.

"I'm making it look like a drug sale gone wrong," he said when he noticed I hadn't moved. "Now what?" he snapped as Claudia came hurrying over, Julio in tow, while Bart sat, scowling, behind the wheel of the Subaru.

"When I say 'action'—you know, like in 'lights, camera, action'?—I want you to take my picture. You never did get Tony's," she told an openmouthed Julio. "I figure a picture must be part of the deal, right?" she said to Zack—and pulled a gun out of her shoulder bag. "My 'just-in-case' piece," she said, her mouth contorted into a skull's-head smile.

"Claudia, for God's sake!" I yelled. I dove at her.

She stepped out of my way as I hit pavement, said, "Action!"— and fired into a dead body.

"That's by way of a formal application . . . Zack, isn't it? Tony quits, I join. Don't worry. It's an unmarked gun, courtesy of my ex. I hear you two have met."

Zack found his tongue before I did. "Okay, okay. Get going."

But Claudia was inching her way across the pavement. One tentative foot came to rest on the edge of a long black scarf. It lay across Arnie's ample shoulders like a limp banner.

"So much for Stan's locks and bolts," she said softly.

She turned to help me up. "You okay?"

"Like you, bloody but unbowed," I said, noticing the reddish brown spots on her white skirt, the bruises on her left arm and leg. Remembering that she had tripped and fallen as Arnie was closing the distance.

"Let's get the hell out of here," she said.

We ran for the Subaru as if someone were in hot pursuit.

Chapter 22

Jamie walked over to my living-room bar and poured a brandy. "I hate seeing you so depressed," he said, offering it to me.

"Who's depressed?" I said, taking it.

"Shall I treat that as one of your wry jokes or ask you to lie down on the couch?"

"How about launching into a description of my symptoms?"

"Better yet," he said, edging me toward a chair, "I'll guide you to the heart of the matter."

"I just got off the phone with Claudia. You know what she said when I tried to talk her out of joining? Quote: 'I feel like a silent partner in Stan's fight.' My God, the man is part of this city's antivigilante task force!"

"Drink your brandy. Claudia's not your real problem, love."

"My gynecologist friend, then? Claudia dragged me to his damn gun club for a practice session with a Smith and Wesson. Roger took one look at her bruises and my skinned knees and practically accused us of joining the vigilantes he's been reading about."

"Pass the brandy," Jamie said, looking alarmed.

"Don't worry about it," I snapped, "we took the Fifth—and anyway, Roger's as frustrated as the rest of us. His parting shot was 'If you need me, call.' So what's my *real* problem, Jamie?"

He refilled my glass. "Ever since you lost your grandchild, you've had a need to lavish affection on everything from stray cats to small homeless boys. You've been resisting it. But Tony got to you. And now, when you're finally ready to take him in, he turns you down flat."

"I've been such a damn coward," I said, starting to cry. "Why didn't I ask him before it was too late?"

"Not too late. Too early." He made me look at him. "Will you take my professional word for it that his latest show of rebellion is only temporary? He needs you, Karen. What I want you to remember is that he knows it."

"You've seen him? He's back in therapy?"

"In body if not in spirit. He's not blaming me for the Mission, but every time he misses an appointment, he's letting me know he blames me for other things. Like keeping him honest."

"This Julio he's living with, is it a decent atmosphere?"

He shrugged. "It's a bed and a place to catch a meal when he feels like it. Think of it as a halfway house. A 'home' is what he'll have with you someday. Weepy tonight, aren't we?"

He didn't comfort me. Just dumped a box of Kleenex in my lap. "How do you always know the right thing to do?" I smiled up at him.

"Long years of practice," he said, heading for the kitchen.

He made omelets and black coffee—strong.

The minute I felt better he switched roles on me. No more psychiatrist. No more perceptive friend. I could tell just from the tone of his voice (playful bordering on merry) that he'd put on another hat—or should I say, cape?

"Your six-month leave is almost up." My eyebrows must have shot up because he said quickly, "I'm not asking you to extend it."

"That's good, because Larry expects me back and I'm going."

"I know," he said. "We need you to do something . . . special. Being back with Kemp & Carusone would provide excellent cover."

Cover. "Jamie, don't you *dare* manipulate me into something else because I won't—"

"Karen," he said, gripping my hands, "the nationwide pattern of our activities has finally dawned on them!"

"Who?" I whispered through a flood of dread.

"The FBI, who else?" He said it as if his wildest dream had come true. "You're familiar with the legend of the Trojan horse?"

I closed my eyes. I was very familiar with it.

He said, "We want you to infiltrate Troy."

Breakfast at Jamie's place. Elegantly served, well attended . . . just like my introduction six months ago to the inner circle. I had been nervous then, but at least I'd been able to eat.

O'Neal, as usual, was stuffing himself. Bart was sharing a private joke with Lee. Zack was out of uniform and Hugh was still in a three-piece suit—seersucker instead of tweed.

Angela was a welcome addition. I sat next to her, drinking black coffee and trying not to look at Kagan, who seemed to be presiding over the rest of us from his vantage point on the windowsill. His body was relaxed but you could feel his glance on the back of your neck.

"Karen?" he said, and the buzz of conversation trailed off.

"I told Jamie I'd do it," I said. It came out defensive.

"I know that. But something else is at stake now."

I said, "The safety of everyone in this room."

"Of the whole organization, maybe," Zack said softly. "Unless you do this, a lot of people could get hurt."

I nodded. "Have to go. I start work today, remember?"

Bart frowned. "Stay on your toes."

"Thanks," I said to the concern in his eyes.

Jamie put on a sober face and handed me my briefcase, along with some encouraging words. "What you're about to do," he said, "is a turning point in our operations, Karen. It's the first real step on the road back to peace."

Peace?

"Just don't forget that we're at war," Kagan told me.

Angela saw me to the door. Even though I had never said two words to her about Max McCann, she got to the heart of the matter.

She said in a voice no one else could hear, "Don't hate yourself too much."

4

CONFLICT

We are dead groups of
matter when we hate; but
when we love, we are as
gods!

—Schiller,
Friendship

Chapter 23

Someone had forgotten that I'm not big on chrysanthemums, but they added a cheerful splash of color and a pungent smell to the dead air in the room. I moved them off my desk onto a windowsill and found the unsigned note underneath: "Welcome back!"

Back to messy labor disputes, reams of statistics, and writing speeches for testy CEOs who tended to trip over their metaphors.

At least my secretary remembered how I took my coffee: black and espresso-strong. She'd even moved my kidney-shaped "guest" ashtray from the coffee table to my desk blotter while, no doubt, frowning with disapproval, bless her.

I lit up and started to roam, taking it one file at a time. "No calls for a couple of hours," I'd told Deanna.

"Need some time to get back to the real world?" She'd grinned.

I'd grinned back, wanting to tell her, "I just left it."

Two hours later I was feeling like a drunken sailor wondering what's happened to his sea legs. It couldn't be this hard to concentrate, I couldn't be this bored.

I made myself a "most pressing business" pile and plunged in.

During the next few weeks, I discovered that everything I was working on was one big yawn. My secretary swore I was turning into a caffeine addict.

"How's it going?" Larry asked from the doorway one morning as I sat contemplating my third cup in as many hours. He had been dropping in—unexpected little "office calls"—ever since I'd come back to work. He looked wide awake in his trim khaki suit and pale blue shirt, matching handkerchief sticking out of his breast pocket at a rakish angle.

"The Wilen communications audit is almost done," I told him, stifling a yawn I didn't have to fake. I had been at my desk since the ungodly hour of seven. "You want a preliminary report, Larry? Management relations are shaky across the board—distributors, dealers, media, et cetera, ad nauseam. An in-depth probe will turn up the usual company strengths and weaknesses with a success factor—"

"Still having trouble, aren't you?"

Along with listlessness, he'd picked up the sound of duty.

"Don't expect a couple of weeks to get you back in the swing of things," he counseled, dropping onto my couch. "Especially when you've got . . . other things on your mind."

Other things. An affair of the heart gone sour, I'd told him. Setting the hook, Kagan had called it.

I didn't have to fake an awkward smile, either, not when I recognized the penetrating look behind the horn-rims: Larry's matchmaking instincts were practically reaching across the room to me.

I joined him on the couch, ready to stretch out like a cat—pretty good trick when you're constrained by a slim shell of a skirt. Two weeks, and I still couldn't get used to the fact that going to work in sweatpants or jeans was a thing of the past.

"You seeing anyone?" he asked with a brow-creasing frown.

I wanted to hug him for his concern. I said, "It's probably too soon."

"Maybe," he said. "Maybe not."

Larry was about to make his move.

I steered him back to the Wilen account.

The next day I stepped out of the elevator and spotted McCann. Same corner of the lobby. Same look of muted anticipation mixed with concern. I let the five-o'clock crowd surge ahead of me while I adjusted my mask . . . while I admitted that seeing Max again— using him—was going to be more painful than I'd thought.

What I let him see as I walked in his direction was surprise on its way to becoming dismay.

"Hello, Max." We were within touching distance.

"You've been letting your hair grow."

"I haven't been to a beauty parlor lately."

"I like it," he said. His eyes said, "I want to touch it."

I backed away automatically. "What do you want?"

"Only to welcome you back."

"To my job? Or back into circulation? Damn Larry for—"

"I thought we might have dinner while I'm in town."

I permitted myself a small smile. "You're persistent."

"It goes with the training."

"What brings you to New York?" I said as we crossed the lobby.

"Special assignment in the offing. I came up a day early."

"After Larry sent you a distress signal?" I asked with a hint of anger.

"I'm grateful to him," he said without apology. "Dinner?"

I was about to accept when I heard Kagan's voice in my ear. . . . *Make contact as soon as you can.*

"Tomorrow night, Max," I said. "If it's convenient."

One day's delay in following orders wasn't much of a rebellion, but it made me feel better. Operation Trojan horse was on hold.

I spent the evening with my waking nightmares. They pop up periodically like malevolent jack-in-the-boxes. Just reaching for the telephone can trigger a memory. . . .

Sarah, tell me what's happening!

This time, it was a less subtle instrument of self-torture: the framed photograph on my night table. Sarah and Susie within breathing distance of my pillow.

Faces are what keep you in the game. Imagined faces from Jamie's horror files. Faces I had seen for myself. Inconsolable loss. The bitterness that eats away like acid. . . . They had left me with a need that burned deeper than acid: to *do* something.

Forgive me the need, Max. Forgive me for fighting back the only way I know how.

Max McCann, dinner date. Odd thought in these surroundings. Arrive early. Get the feel of the place, I'd told myself. Scary.

The tension wasn't mine alone. I saw too many tight-lipped expressions that didn't necessarily go with FBI headquarters in New York. Something to do with McCann's meeting maybe? It would break soon—six sharp, he'd said. McCann is a man of his word.

McCann is a lot of things. Monosyllabic, for one thing. What is he thinking in that intriguing lull between sentences? I had pulled a file and spent part of the morning playing detective. The Bureau account I'd sabotaged over ten years ago had yielded few clues to his character. It had been more revealing about my own: The lady doth protest too much. My attraction to him had been apparent even then, and I'd resented it. Given my liberal sentiments, FBI men were off limits. Besides, we were both married. McCann had had my number right from the start, I realized. Why else bait me with all that soft-spoken good humor? I had remembered him as smug; it was close enough.

Only once he'd lashed out in anger, the incident marked in my notes. The notes had struck a memory chord. . . . *G-man McCann, is it? You think in stereotypes, Karen. Macho, trigger-*

happy redneck. Subpoena in hand. Wiretap in the pocket. Midnight knock at the door. Have I covered the field? Every FBI man a chump.

Not this FBI man. This one loves Swinburne and owns up to being "a hick from Minnesota." This one has a love/hate attachment to my city. He says things like "You're letting your hair grow" and "I've never thought of you in that color."

And during the lull in between?

I've never thought of you in that color but I think of you. I've never kissed you but I've held you in my arms. I've never possessed you but I've made you cry. I've never envied a man until the man who opened your door. I've never been in your bedroom . . . except when I close my eyes.

Dangerous business, to play at reading a man's mind. He's liable to sneak up on you and maybe read yours.

All he said to me was "Shall we go?"

We were sharing a platter of steamed clams at the Italian restaurant of our first dinner date when one of his refused to open. I decided that McCann was a clam when it came to opening up about the Bureau; all my innocent questions got short, dull answers. But I detected an undercurrent of excitement when he said that, aside from me, he couldn't wait to return to Washington.

I tried again with the pasta course. "Pretty ordinary-looking, your New York headquarters. I was expecting something more stately on the outside and sinister on the in."

He laughed. "You'd find Washington more to your liking."

Don't count on it! "Did you get the assignment you wanted?"

"Hard to tell. It would mean more time here."

Remembering Kagan's instructions about letting Max "get personal, but not too personal," I led him into a guarded conversation about Jamie. In the process, I let him know I was still feeling "bruised" even though Jamie and I had "remained friends."

Max took me home. And asked for herbal tea. "I could use less caffeine in my life right now."

"How's cinnamon grab you?" I said while I crossed fingers that I could dig some up. Black coffee had aced tea out of my life.

I left him in the den. When I came back with the tea, he was so engrossed in a wall of photographs that he didn't even hear me.

"You'll have to settle for chamomile," I said.

He turned and something happened to his eyes—a slight widening: the small shock of comparing my picture, taken nine months ago, with the woman who had just walked in the door.

Before and after.

I looked in a mirror. What leaped out made my heart shrink.

Innocence isn't the dominant trait in a forty-six-year-old face.

Yet how else can I describe what the camera had captured in my birthday portrait of last September? What had replaced it? I groped for a phrase that went far beyond the tough-mindedness some people see in my features.

I found it. Cynic.

"Karen, what's the matter?"

"I think you should go."

Hard, not tough—my voice was *hard.*

"I think we should talk."

"Sorry, Max," I said. "Drink your tea, please." Don't say any more, please.

He burned his tongue on the first sip. It broke the tension, at least. I rattled on about always having energy to burn and how the old on-the-job excitement had dissolved on me like a soft tablet in hot water. Which makes for a short temper and an exhausting day. I let him assure me it was natural, not to worry.

We had a nightcap in the living room. "What's happened to your green thumb?" he asked, frowning over an untidy row of drooping plants that had dropped half their leaves on the windowsill.

How could I tell him that I hadn't even noticed?

I said, "We could use a shot in the arm, my plants and me."

"Karen, let me—"

"Next time you're in town," I said, and led him to the door.

I spent the night on my living-room couch, watching the plants on my windowsill. . . . *What's happened to your green thumb, Karen?*

Chapter 24

"What happened to your living room?"

Claudia decorously lowered herself onto a plump red cushion with her favorite butterfly motif. "I got bored with straight-backed chairs."

I looked around, happy to see the old arrangement. Gone was the dignified-office look: trim, tight furniture in grays and tans; indirect lighting and shelves of unread books. Back were all the knock-your-socks-off colors, the exotic plants, the cushiony chairs that forced you into a reclining position. Her lighting scheme was new and there was nothing indirect about it: the pulsating blues, pinks and ambers of a disco or a fireworks display.

I pulled up a burnt-orange cushion and joined her on the floor.

"Okay, CC," I said, accepting a glass of Chardonnay, "why the summons? I take it Kagan wants you to be my official contact."

"Makes sense, don't you think? Now that you and your FBI man have gotten together, he wants you to steer clear of everybody but old friend Claudia."

"So what does he want?"

"A report on McCann, what else?"

I gave it to her, taking a dim satisfaction in the fact that my "report" took all of ten minutes. Blame it on a clam, Kagan.

Claudia's report from the front took much longer. Spontaneous vigilante episodes were breaking out all over; Kagan's prediction coming true. I thought of his newest slogan. *Today, shared values. Tomorrow, a meeting of the minds.*

Tomorrow was already here for Hugh. His fund-raising efforts were setting new records. Jamie and O'Neal were Mission-hopping all over the place . . . breaking heads? Lee was busy letting Rosa pick up wherever she'd left off. We had valuable pipelines into the police—

"Thanks to Zack and Angela?" I said, not liking the look on Claudia's face.

"Come off it. Who better to pump the new head of the police task force than yours truly?"

"Claudia, it's Stan we're talking about! How can you—"

"The pot calling the kettle black? You don't like what you're doing. Neither do I. Given the stepped-up FBI interest, your intelligence-gathering efforts could prove vital. Mine keeps us a step ahead of the local law."

"How can you be so calm?" I marveled.

"Look past the makeup job."

I saw it then: signs of stress like the faint cracks in old plaster. "Are you being careful, at least?"

"Not just careful, dah-ling," she said, slipping into her Tallulah Bankhead routine. "Clev-ah." She hugged my fears away. "And very tactful—honest. I have a question, Doctor, and don't you dare laugh at me. What the hell is a Trojan horse?"

We both laughed. I told her how the ancient Greeks had schemed their way inside the walled city of their enemy by leaving a hollow wooden horse full of soldiers outside the gates of Troy.

"Ah-so! Beware of Greeks bearing gifts." She pulled a dictionary off a shelf and went hunting. "Any subversive device," she read, "insinuated within enemy ranks . . ."

She looked at me, put the book back, and refilled our wine glasses. "Sorry," she said.

"Me, too." We drank deeply.

"Kemp & Carusone will be getting a call from the National Corrections Association," she told me.

"Bart's outfit? What on earth for?"

"You're in the image-polishing business, aren't you? Gives you an excuse to meet with Bart."

"And discuss what?"

"Tactics, I gather. We're swimming in FBI waters, now."

"I ought to be talking to Kagan," I protested. "Bart's more of a human being but he doesn't exactly inspire confidence. Not after what Jamie—"

"Don't sweat it. I figure Kagan's calling the shots. Bart's just the detail man."

"You're probably right." I lit a cigarette.

Claudia finger-traced the butterfly pattern on her cushion. "According to my Chinese-mythology professor," she mused, "the butterfly, also known as *l'angelica farfella,* is a symbol of longevity. Dante's symbol for our immortal soul, he said."

"How about the Greek language? They use the same word— psyche—for butterflies *and* souls. Beats me why an insect that's lucky to live out the summer should stand for longevity."

The quip turned sour in my mouth. Something about it scared me. The way Claudia identified with butterflies, maybe . . . or the increasing danger of our situation as we headed into our own risk-filled summer.

"Bart's not a bad guy," Claudia said in that same musing tone.

"Because he headed the get-Arnie Mission?"

"Because he helped keep me alive."

She had said it so softly that I knew she was feeling it, too, the exquisite fragility of life.

Bart and I met in the East Village—cocktail hour, or I'd never have set foot in the neighborhood, let alone a bar with an overflow crowd that smelled of sweat and leather and cheap beer. On the way to a booth in the back, Bart led me past a lot of tattoos, well-oiled muscles, and "old buddies."

"What's up?" I asked as soon as he'd ordered drinks, wanting to get the hell out of the place while it was still light.

"A big power struggle is what's up. Between Washington and New York. Will FBI agent McCann get to head a certain vigilante investigation?" He lowered his voice. "We're with Washington on this, we want McCann. You give him the edge he needs, see—"

"Help Max get the assignment? But that's crazy!"

Not crazy. Scary, maybe. As Bart explained what Kagan had in mind, I had to admit it made sense.

"—so McCann is in like Flynn. Then you pull out the stops."

"Meaning?" I said, on instant alert.

"Kagan wants you to play Mata Hari."

"Kagan can go to hell."

Big grin. "I told him you'd say that. Always figured you for a one-man woman."

"You figured right," I said, more than willing to cash in on the fiction of my torrid romance with Jamie.

We were finishing our drinks when some heavy action broke out at the bar. A loudmouthed shoving contest had degenerated into armed warfare—two big bruisers, one menacing the other with a broken beer bottle.

"Jesus, Harry!" Bart jumped into the fray, even as the other guy pulled a knife. "Break it up!" Bart yelled, with a backward glance at me, even as I shrank from it, averting my eyes.

For God's sake, Bart, you don't have to prove anything!

But he did. "The bravado is an act," Jamie had told me when I'd remarked about Bart's fearlessness. "Man's a PK—Principal Keeper—responsible for hundreds of cons doing hard time in a Staten Island penitentiary. He's in big trouble if the animals in his jungle catch the slightest scent of fear. But it's there."

I wasn't so sure, judging by the man's cool in the aftermath of victory—especially when I'd gotten a good look, on our way out, at the size of the knife.

Bart flagged a cab for me and went back inside.

I made the cabbie wait while I went back inside myself—no way I was going to abandon a very expensive pair of sunglasses.

I found Bart sitting in our back booth with a glass of whiskey in his hand. His hand was shaking.

Chapter 25

Some orders go down easier than others. *"Be wined and dined, if that's his pleasure. No more prying until you get the word."*

My pleasure, Kagan. Your move.

A week, and nothing from Kagan. A whole week of Max in town and me in his arms. Max, it turned out, loved to dance. Every time we went to dinner, he seemed to have an ear cocked, waiting for the music to begin. I never wanted it to end.

"Penny?" Max asked, not one to read my thoughts like Jamie.

"Just enjoying the moment. I like it here."

A slick little combo swung into melody, danceable tunes with the kind of lyrics you want to croon in your partner's ear. Max gave me the let's-dance high sign and stood up.

A beefy fellow with a shock of wavy blond hair, standing at the bar, spotted Max and signaled him.

"Be right back," Max said with an apologetic half-smile.

He was back ten minutes later with a newspaper under his arm and preoccupation in his eyes.

"Dance?" I prodded.

"Sure."

But his mind wasn't on the dance floor. "Who was that?" I asked with a glance in the direction of the bar.

"Just a barhop with a big pair of ears. An informant."

. . . *Yours or Kagan's?* I wondered, remembering the newspaper. When the music stopped I said, "I'm ready for a cappuccino."

While we were waiting for it, I reached idly for the newspaper. It fell open to a headline: THE FOX STRIKES AGAIN.

The beefy fellow at the bar had given Max the paper.

Kagan had made his move, giving me my gambit.

I looked through the article while Max sipped his coffee and I pretended mine was too hot. I looked up with a troubled frown.

"What's the matter?" he said, noticing.

"This news story . . . the vigilantes. I thought it was some aberration limited to Manhattan, but there's a reference here to Chicago, Detroit, LA . . ."

"I know," he said with a frown of his own.

"You know? My God, Max, you're not . . . involved in this vigilante business?"

"I may be. Karen, what's the *matter?*"

"This is the assignment you've been after?"

"Yes," he said, puzzled.

I stared at him. Pushed my coffee away. Lit a cigarette. "Max, if I'd thought these people—these vigilantes—had anything to do with you, I'd have mentioned them sooner. Not that I'm eager to talk about the whole thing, it's just . . ."

I let him interrupt my nervous rambling, let him guide me back to the beginning—to Kagan at Sarah's funeral. *I had been approached by these people.* When they'd tried again after the funeral of my grandchild, sending me photographs of the gang that had attacked Sarah—including a photograph of her killer—I'd been tempted to join them, God help me!

Instead, I had called in the assistant district attorney.

I didn't want to see what was happening to Max's face. I was thinking of Kagan's rule of thumb, glad he wasn't here to gloat over the results. . . . *"Build as much truth into a cover story as you can get away with, Karen."* Max was rigid with shock. Then came a slow, soft smile . . . a man who could hardly believe his good fortune.

I had passed my first real test in deceit.

"I have to call Washington." He motioned for a check.

I stole a glance at the dance floor. They were playing a waltz.

"The guessing game is over," Max explained as we emerged from Dulles Airport into the steam bath that is Washington, D.C. in July. "This gives us a modus operandi on how these vigilantes recruit."

"One version, at least," I said, as nervous as I sounded.

"It's a start. It could lead anywhere."

It had led me to FBI headquarters in Washington; score one.

"The card they gave you helps," he said, hailing a cab.

"How?"

"We have a name." He pulled it out of his pocket and we both stared at it: VICTIMS ANONYMOUS, in elegant Gothic lettering. "Up to now, we weren't sure. Our information has been sketchy."

Score two. Kagan wanted to know how much they knew.

In the cab he took my hand, a total departure for M. McCann when he had business on his mind, and proceeded to point out the sights. Washington was his adopted city now. Its clean straight lines and stark white monuments suited him. I told him I preferred the chaos of New York.

Our cab rolled into an ample courtyard ringed with columns, like a circular row of guardians. There were statues everywhere. We got out of the car, and I mentally compared a forty-story skyscraper—FBI headquarters in Manhattan—with the Bureau's "home" quarters: a squat stone building with sledgehammer solidity.

"I told you you'd find Washington more to your liking," Max said with a grin as I halted before an enormous bronze flag, the backdrop for a cluster of three figures.

"Fidelity, Bravery, Integrity," I read out loud.

"How do you like J. Edgar's pride and joy?"

"Sexist, since you asked. Bravery stands tall—a man of action. Brother Integrity sits in thoughtful contemplation. Will you look at Fidelity? She's kneeling in abject adoration!"

Joined laughter. It tore a hole in the tension I was feeling.

Inside, a somber guard checked Max's badge, an impressive bit of heraldry and gold stars. Max slipped a visitor's badge-on-a-chain around my neck.

He grew away from me with each floor we passed on the

elevator, routine setting into the lines of his face. With almost brisk formality, he led the way to his office on the fourth floor.

It was what I'd pictured: no frills. Books, portrait of "J. Edgar," the American flag and not much else. A spartan home away from home for a company man. He even had a gold key.

"On the occasion of my tenth anniversary with the Bureau. This year I pass the twenty-five-year mark." He said it with a matter-of-factness that went beyond pride.

He seated me on a couch that might have come his way via a garage sale and put in a call "to see if he's ready for us"—"he" being Section Chief of the Criminal Investigation Division. Max's immediate superior—at the moment, a busy man. A reprieve of sorts.

Max offered me a welcome distraction. Would I care for a private tour? "We run them all day long," he said. "Top-drawer image-polishing—right up your alley." He rang for an escort.

He forgot about me while I waited. He tried not to but he couldn't help himself. When his phone wasn't interrupting us, his secretary was. The paperwork on his desk was as daunting as anything I'd seen at Kemp & Carusone. His deskside manner was crisp.

I was almost relieved when the escort, a pretty young woman, arrived. Max barely acknowledged our exit.

We didn't bother with an elevator. Down a few flights, the inevitable video waited: a rousing welcome by the FBI Director (soft-sell, conservative banker type). Let the tour begin.

Ten minutes into it and I was issuing silent congratulations to the Bureau's PR staff; very slick. A stark photograph is worth a thousand words, especially when accompanied by an artful arrangement of startling facts and figures. (Hadn't I introduced the same format to Victims Anonymous?) The FBI labs were a marvel, exploring everything from the obvious (fingerprints, blood, urine) to the not so obvious. (We can be identified by the sweat of our brow? Our tear ducts?) I saw firearms by the thousands on display (labeled the "Gangster Era"). A documents section that looks into fraudulent checks, anonymous letters, and stolen art. A "Crime Clock" Jamie would have killed for: one murder—rape—burglary—robbery every x minutes.

I was cheered by the Bureau's four "priorities": organized crime, foreign counterintelligence, white-collar crime, terrorism. (Nothing about vigilante justice, thank God.)

I was chilled by the statistics my guide reeled off. She put the total number of FBI agents at "well over eight thousand." They operated out of sixty field offices. A lot of manpower. Of the hundreds of criminals on the FBI's ten-most-wanted list, she told me, the Bureau had caught all but twenty-five.

That efficient? They'd only been at it forty years!

When my guide launched into a description of the Bureau's Washington-based computer network—they called it the National Crime Information Center—I smiled and looked interested.

"Talk about instant information!" she said.

Talk about instant fear.

Max showed up while she was trying to talk me into their firearms demo. "Has she discovered our Achilles heel?" he asked. My guide looked blank. Max showed us a statistic we had missed, all right. No female FBI agents until 1972. The year Hoover died?

"Oh, we had three women in the early twenties, but two of them resigned right after Mr. Hoover took office. The third one lasted a couple of years," said the girl with impish good humor.

On the trip back upstairs to the executive suite, I went on and on about the tour, using idle chatter to cover up my fear.

We entered a wood-paneled office.

"Karen, this is Bernard Rees."

The "how do you do"s went well. Then the "won't you sit down, have some coffee" business. My fearball really started to roll the minute Rees slipped into the "I know you've been over all this, sorry to put you through it again" routine.

It took a few questions before I began to appreciate how adroit this man was . . . a debriefing that never for an instant left the comfortable arena of an informal chat. Hard, after a while, not to go with the flow, even to the point of doodling on a yellow pad.

It gave Max an idea. "Think you could do a quick sketch of the man at the funeral?"

"I don't draw," I lied. Actually, I do a fair likeness, but even if I'd attempted it, they would have been disappointed. Kagan would have emerged a lean-faced Everyman with not much in the way of distinguishing characteristics.

"I'm interested in the assumption you and the police made initially," Rees said, leaning forward to show how interested he really was. "Tell me again why you assumed these vigilantes were a strictly local New York operation."

"I guess because *I'm* local," I said. "I live in Manhattan. I buried my daughter in Queens. Her attackers were from the Bronx. All New York City territory. I just assumed it was *their* territory. God knows, there's enough crime there to keep them busy."

"A national pattern has been emerging," he told me, and began to describe it.

Kagan had figured they didn't know much, and he was right.

"What do you think of us, Ms. Newman?" he asked as he lit my cigarette.

"What do I think of the FBI?" I forced a laugh. "Max has been telling tales out of school. Besides, we're talking about the old FBI. From what Max tells me, things have changed."

He smiled. "Would it surprise you to learn Max and I share your views about the 'old FBI'? Illegal wiretaps, harrassment of civil-rights leaders—deplorable business. Some of us still refer to it as 'the dark days.' But you see, Ms. Newman . . ."

He seemed such a reasonable man, had such a reasonable face. Big, cow-brown eyes. Lots of friendly wrinkles, the ones that betray how often a man laughs. He chewed placidly on an unlit pipe. I kept waiting for him to light it.

He lit a fuse instead. That's my feeling whenever someone in my business tells you they're going to let you in on an in-house secret. Max looked unhappy, which told me the two of them hadn't worked out this part of the scenario in advance.

Rees launched into a loving description of the "new FBI," one that was leery of trampling on constitutional rights. He mentioned a faction within the Bureau that "shall we say, sees things in a totally different light?"

"Is this wise, making Karen privy to information—"

"Why, I think we must, Max. Hold your reservations in check, will you? I understand you've taken our tour, Ms. Newman. Gives you a fair idea of our jurisdiction—kidnapping, terrorism and the like. *Federal* crimes. But what sort of crimes are making headlines today?"

"Street crimes," I said, wondering at his direction.

"Fast becoming *the* social issue of our times," he agreed. "One no savvy politician can afford to ignore. A matter, not for the FBI, but for our local police forces, wouldn't you say?"

"It ought to be."

"Exactly. Yet in the next presidential election two years hence, I can tell you with assurance that some politicians will be tempted to translate the public's growing impatience with escalating vio-lence in their cities into legislation of, shall we say, dubious validity? Some of us worry, not unduly I think, about the role that the Bureau might be forced to play."

"I read something about a presidential task force . . .?"

"On violent crime—quite so," he said, looking pleased. "A trial balloon to test public reaction. It is headed by a former attorney general whose task is to discover, and I quote, 'what the federal government can do about what traditionally has been the respon-sibility of the states.' "

"What they can do is federalize crime," Max said tightly.

"There's talk of resurrecting an old idea in FBI circles," Rees said, telegraphing his distaste by the angle of his nose. "Create a national criminal-history system—computerized, of course. A dangerous precedent, in my view. Another trial ballooon is floating about—those 'career criminal' bills being introduced by ambitious congressmen. We have anticrime rhetoric emanating from the White House that, quite frankly, I find ominous."

"They won't be happy until they've turned the FBI into a national police force. To concentrate that much power into a single government agency!" Max snapped, spilling his coffee. "What do we use for a model, a Latin American dictatorship?"

"Max is quite the fanatic on this," Rees said with delicacy. "What he means is, it's safer to disperse the power. Roughly ninety percent of our crime is handled locally. Always has been."

"That can change."

"What he means, Ms. Newman," Rees said softly, "is that this vigilante outfit could be the catalyst for such a change."

"But why?" I asked with genuine alarm.

"Timing," Max said. "The apparent scope of the organization."

"We appear to have a nationwide conspiracy on our hands. Individuals committing crimes to avenge crimes. Once their criminal activity crosses state borders, it means FBI jurisdiction."

Rees finally lit his pipe.

"It's also an excuse," he went on, "for a certain faction in the Bureau to point to a breakdown in the system that our local police aren't equipped to handle." Rees paused. "Or so they'll claim."

"If those eager beavers get to step in and mop up—" Max broke off with a harsh laugh. "They'll make a federal case out of it."

Rees laughed in real appreciation. "It would dovetail with a president's desire to get people aboard his 'federalize crime' bandwagon, Ms. Newman. Worse, it would give the FBI the kind of hero publicity we could do without right now. Because you see," he said gravely, "if we drag the case out just to keep making headlines—and, in the process, political capital—if we bring down this Victims Anonymous with a series of big splashes, I'm afraid it could spawn that national police force we have every reason to be afraid of."

"Unless?" I said, naming what he'd left unspoken.

"I like this woman," he told Max. "Unless a very different faction in the Bureau were calling the shots. Unless Max, here, were to take charge of this investigation."

"Big power struggle. Between Washington and New York. We're with Washington on this, we want McCann."

I said, "What difference would Max make?"

"I'd wrap it up fast."

My skepticism must have leaped out at them. Max was looking slightly offended.

Rees said, "It can be done. You've played follow-the-leader? Very effective when you want to defuse a widespread operation. Ignore the little people and take out the leaders."

I said, "Cut off the head of the snake and the body will die."

"I remember the film. A hard one to forget." Rees was smiling at the memory. *"Viva Zapata!,* was it? Very apt."

I had to ask. "What if all there are is little people?"

"No," he said, "no, it's too well organized. There are clever brains at work here. It's they who must be pursued and stopped."

Score three for Kagan. He had wanted to know their strategy. I was desperate to know more. "But where do you start?"

"New York, of course," Max said.

Had I sounded too bewildered?

"You read that article," he said.

The Fox strikes again.

"Evidence points to Manhattan as their base."

"And as you yourself pointed out," Rees chimed in, "it's where they tried to recruit you."

Did Max know where this was leading? Did Kagan have to be right *all* the time?

"Given encouragement, they might try again," Rees said gently.

Max was on his feet. "No, Bernie. Karen, I swear—"

He didn't have to. I said, "It's all right, Max."

"Just the same," Rees said quickly, "it must have occurred to you, Max. The logic is inescapable." He turned to me. "You see, our director is on the fence about this, never mind why. In his heart of hearts, he knows Max, here, has the perfect background for the job, and quite apart from sheer experience, Max works well with local law enforcement. But more important, I trust Max. Give me what I need to convince a fence sitter, Ms. Newman. Permit me to tell my director that if your good friend Max were to be in charge, you would agree to reestablish contact with the vigilante outfit. I gather from Max that you know how."

"I don't know what to say." *Vacillate,* Kagan had told me.

"I daresay Max is eager to talk you out of it so, in fairness, let's not try to resolve the matter in one sitting. Decide soon, will you, Karen?"

Karen. He might as well have said, "Welcome aboard!"

Max and I had planned to stop off for a drink at his place, but he wasn't in the mood to play host and I'd lost my taste for lovely views of the Potomac. We were silent on the way to the airport. But as soon as we boarded, he took my hand.

"No," he said.

"No what?"

"It's too risky, Karen. I don't want you to do it."

I couldn't tell him that I had to.

We had planned dinner in the city, but he took me straight home and saw me to the door.

"Stop torturing yourself," I told him. "I have no choice and you know it." *None at all, Max dear.* I dug out my keys.

He looked like he wanted to shove his fist through the door. "I'll call you," he said and walked away.

"Come back here," I said, "and kiss me good night."

He came back down the hallway like a sleepwalker, as if giving himself time to believe it.

He didn't give me a chance to take it back.

I never wanted it to end. Until I remembered Kagan's Mata Hari plans . . . and knew it never should have begun.

I pulled away. His eyes devoured my front door like a hungry man. I unlocked it, knowing he wouldn't push it open without an invitation. Max didn't push.

I went in, not trusting my voice even to say good night.

Minutes later, the phone rang. I answered, surprised that my voice should sound so normal.

Kagan sounded smug. "Congratulations," he said.

"If that's a joke, I'm not in the mood."

"It's no joke. I wanted to mark the occasion. The role you've just undertaken—"

"What role?" I snapped.

"Karen Newman, double agent."

I hung up and repeated the words but they had no reality. . . .

Chapter 26

Max was five minutes late. I wondered if it was because of the heat or the excessive security precautions. Thanks to the remote possibility that my vigilante contacts might have put a "tail" on me, Max was making "damn certain" nobody connected him with me. *(What if they should trace me to FBI headquarters?)*

I was eyeing the meat-loaf-and-potatoes menu and bemoaning

the demise of our elegant dining-and-dancing days ("too risky to be seen at the old places") when Max came in, looking wilted.

"August in New York," he groused, as if Washington had never heard of heat waves. "You know this place?"

He was looking around with suspicion at pseudobrick walls and a fake stucco ceiling. The marigolds on every other table were real.

"My once-favorite diner," I said, handing him the menu. "Let's hope the cook hasn't gone the way of the decor. Used to be comfortable red leather booths instead of these tight little tables. And chrome all over the place—mirrors, counter, bar stools."

"No more counter," he observed. "Food's good, you said?"

"Used to be. Try the egg-lemon soup and the stuffed grape leaves. You like moussaka? I'm getting the meatless version."

The service was still fast. "Real down-home cooking," Max admitted as he savored his meatless moussaka—for about five minutes. "Three weeks," he said, putting his fork aside. "God, I hate the waiting."

"It's worth waiting for if I get to meet a leader or two," I said, wishing I could reassure him.

"But to risk your going on some vigilante mission—"

"Max," I said, wishing I could tell him it wasn't my first, "there's no danger—not when they want something from me."

"Beats me what they want with you when they're putting out stuff of *this* caliber," he said, producing a familiar-looking sheet of paper—bright orange. He handed it to me.

"'So It's Come to This . . .'" I read out loud, marveling at the steadiness of my voice. "'Teenagers who sweep through our subways, relieving us of our watches, wallets and chains. Teenagers who rove in bands. Who teach us to send our kids to school with stickup money in their lunch bags and—' Not bad," I said, handing it back; picturing the day and the hour I had written it.

"So why the special interest in you?" he persisted.

. . . *Good question, Max.* "Obviously, they think I can improve on this sort of thing," I said with a shrug. "Frankly, I think they're right."

He couldn't help smiling. I had to bite my lip to keep from joining him.

It changed abruptly, the quality of his smile.

When I saw who was responsible—who was headed our way—I dropped my fork, which is not too far off the mark, I suppose, for a heartsick lady at the unexpected sight of her great lost love. Unexpected is right.

"What have they done to our oasis of chrome and neon?" Jamie exclaimed with a sweeping lord-of-the-manor gesture. "An architectural lobotomy, by God! Curtains and tablecloths and cheap carpeting on top of that glorious black-and-white tiled floor. A glitzy coffee shop pretending to be a restaurant."

I managed a wan smile of acquiescence.

"So you're partial to old diners," Max said, offering a chair.

"They're going the way of the dinosaurs, I'm afraid," Jamie said, accepting it. "How are you, Max?"

Max was fine. I was getting over the shock of hearing Jamie call him by his first name.

Small talk until the waitress left and returned with Jamie's order. When she was gone, Jamie looked from Max to me and dropped his bomb.

"This meeting is not accidental," he said to Max. "Karen confided in me about what she's planning to do."

Max slid his chair back, eyes narrowed, as if to get a better view of us both.

I didn't even have the luxury of digging four inches of heel into Jamie's patent-leather boot.

"Are you upset by this . . . breach of security, I think you'd call it? You won't be," Jamie assured him, "when I explain."

"I'm listening."

I listened, on a different level, to an artful blend of truth and fiction—Kagan's cover-story rule. How I'd come unglued over the incriminating photographs and consulted Jamie professionally. How we'd talked about the irrationality—and the dangers— inherent in vigilante solutions to injustice (ha!). How *he'd* persuaded *me* to turn the photos over to an ADA friend of his. How, during the course of helping me over the guilt of my short-lived temptation and the trauma of a tragic loss, we had become . . . good friends (read lovers). How it was hardly surprising, Max, that even after our personal relationship (read affair) had altered, Karen would confide in her friend and former psychiatrist when, once again, she found herself in the unsettling position of taking up with these vigilantes—albeit for a good cause. Did Max blame him for being worried about me? For wanting reassurance?

Max didn't blame him. Or me. "You should have told me how frightened you really were," he said, reaching for my hand. Holding it on the tabletop for all the world—for Jamie—to see.

"Karen has fewer reservations than I do, frankly."

"If you came here for reassurance," Max said slowly, accepting Jamie's offer of a cigarette, "all you'll get is a good supper."

"Can we talk, at least? It would clear the air."

"If you don't mind doing it in the night air. Security."

They exchanged smiles; it was getting to be a habit.

"Bringing tension to the table is bad manners, my mother used to say. Forgive me," Jamie said, and proceeded to engage us in a merry round of entertainment while we finished our meal.

I watched it happen all over again: Max, being pulled into the vortex of Jamie's charm. The small pleasure of discovering some shared experience, a common ground. A hearty laugh, sparked by an exquisitely antimetaphysical joke.

As lonely as all that, Max? I wondered. I had barely been able to pull a smile out of him since our Washington trip.

When the check came I grabbed it. First sense of control I'd had all evening.

It didn't last five minutes on the street. Jamie, asking Max questions he damn well knew the answers to. Max, responding as far as he could while a bond cemented before my eyes.

It was a bond constructed on the fraudulent foundation of mutual concern. I didn't appreciate being a pawn in whatever new game Jamie was playing. I liked even less what I sensed in his manner: a man flirting with danger.

"I have to admit these vigilantes have a sharp point to their dagger, Max. Just last week I was browsing through a mail-order catalogue and four items jumped out at me. A doorknob alarm that goes off at a touch. A key ring with a gas-propelled shriek canister—I'm not kidding. A woman's belt with a knife disguised as a buckle . . . oh, and Italy's latest fashion accessory—a leather antimugging pouch."

"The Department tells me we have a greater chance of getting mugged than of getting a divorce," Max said with a grin.

The switch to jocular good humor over the sad state of our criminal-justice system was a cool breeze in the midst of a heat wave. It blew the tensions away. Jamie was leaning against a lamppost when Max announced that we'd earned ourselves dessert—something sinful—and for one wild moment, Jamie seemed about to swing round the pole like a kid who'd been told he can stay up late.

I walked on eggshells after that, sensing more truth than fiction in Jamie's behavior.

As we left the ice cream parlor, Max said, "To be continued."

Jamie grinned and I saw "When?" in his eyes. (He lets you read them when he wants to.)

"Next Sunday?" Max asked me.

Next Sunday we'd scheduled a defiant picnic in Central Park just to prove it still belonged to the good guys.

"What is this, a remake of *Jules and Jim?*" I quipped. But Max, not being a movie buff, let alone a connoisseur of French film classics, missed the sarcasm, and a laughing Jamie had to spell out its ménage à trois theme.

In the end I went along, of course. Did I have a choice?

We let Jamie have the first cab and spent twenty minutes talking about him before a second one came along. Max kept ours waiting while he delivered me to my doorman. In unspoken agreement, we'd been avoiding my apartment door since the good-night kiss.

Tonight, we avoided more than that. I walked in on Jamie, enjoying a sherry on my couch. My glass waited on the coffee table.

"Angry with me? Or just confused, I hope?"

"How about both?" I said, annoyed because I needed the sherry.

"Kagan was expecting a personal slant on Max. That's not what you delivered to Claudia, is it? What's more, he knows you don't intend to. Missed my calling," he said, pouring himself another sherry. "I should have been an actor, don't you think?"

"Were you acting, Jamie?"

"Missed yours, too, love. You should have been a therapist."

"You're glazing over," I said, looking closer. "Are you four ahead of me, or five? What the hell is happening?"

He went to stand before a mirror. "Should've been an actor. Should've been *something."* He picked up the bottle of sherry and raised it like a flag. "To my mother," he said, still looking in the mirror. A lethargic toast. He refilled both our glasses.

"What's wrong, Jamie? Are you ill?"

"Mother is what's wrong."

"I thought she was dead," I said, frowning with the memory of the only other time he'd had too much to drink. He had pointed out the portrait of a beautiful young woman. And told me what?

"Oh no," he said with a grim smile, "she's very much alive."

And told me he was fifteen when she'd died.

"Go home," I said gently, "while you're still able to."

"See you on Sunday," he said.

He got as far as the door before it dawned on me. It must have dawned on him at the same time because he reached in his pocket and placed a key on my foyer table. "I lied to you before about the doorman letting me in," he said. "Sorry."

A duplicate key, surreptitiously made. Naive of me not to have realized what I'd forfeited along with my peace of mind. What else, besides my privacy? Surveillance? A tap on my telephone?

I let it go because Jamie was in no condition to give an accounting of anything. And because the problem I was wrestling with was far graver than duplicate keys to my apartment.

* * *

Sunday in the park was a revelation. Jamie's picnic conversation was riddled with provocative asides about some thorny issues confronting the people in criminal justice. Why? To get telling admissions out of Max?

Max, it turned out, despised light sentences for rapists and murderers, was one of us on the parole issue, and had less of a problem with capital punishment than I did!

The talk made me uncomfortable, so Jamie's suggestion of a movie was a welcome relief . . . until I heard what we were going to see: the latest in a series of vigilante-style melodramas. That's when I suspected that Jamie was after much more than a personal slant on FBI agent McCann. That's when I got scared.

I'm getting good at a new game called how to hide your fears. Besides, I lose sight of everything when I go to the movies. Seeing one in the Big Apple is an experience. What you get for the price of admission is a group encounter with a lot of irreverent sidewalk philosophers. This particular theaterful of critics expressed themselves periodically in jeers and cheers, howls and whistles, thumbs down and rallies round the flag.

They were mostly rallying on this one. Lots of frenzied applause every time the hero—a tough-talking, gun-toting Vietnam vet—mouthed such non sequiturs as "By God, I didn't fight for my country just to come back home and watch some foulmouthed punks take over the greatest city in the world. No way!"

We retired to my place for cold beer and pizza.

"Admit it, Max, you enjoyed the film as much as we did," Jamie teased. "You can't witness some trigger-happy psycho getting away with the slaughter of innocents without rooting for the good guy to blow his so-called brains out. Saw it in your eyes, lawman."

"Saw what, Doctor?"

"The same dark satisfaction as the rest of us."

"Guilty." Max was regarding Jamie with squint-eyed amusement. "I thought only fortune-tellers read minds?"

"Therapists too," Jamie retorted, looking delighted with himself. "Keep the admissions flowing, Max. I've barely begun. The rapist who buried his victims alive, you wanted him to go down."

"Makes me human, does it?"

"It makes you one of us, all right. How about the scene—"

It makes you one of us. Are you trying to recruit him, Jamie?

I watched Jamie steer the conversation back to reality. Saw a deeply troubled Max grope for solutions to the crime problem.

Heard him concede failure. "I don't have the answers," he said with a sigh. "But neither do they."

"No more vigilante talk," Jamie announced. He took out my

best brandy with a proprietary air that was not lost on Max. "A piece of my personal history, Max," he said, pouring with a flourish, "in exchange for a chunk of yours."

Brandy mellows. Was that it? Or the impression Jamie gave of a fellow loner? Whatever the magic numbers, it was as if he'd found the hidden combination that opened the door to the secret room. Max's usual reticence gave way without a shudder of resistance. What came through was a man who loved the Bureau without ever losing sight of its flaws and who, over the years, had paid the price. Losing plum assignments because of disputes over tacky surveillance tactics. Making enemies for putting the quality of an investigation ahead of its goal. Pursuing a career riddled with "political" reassignments.

"Been shifted all over the lot, haven't you?" Jamie said.

Max's smile was more resigned than bitter.

"That's what you get for being a hero-worshiper, my friend."

"Who me? Not likely," Max scoffed.

"Not lately, you mean. I'll wager it was different growing up in the cornfields, longing to be an FBI man—"

"No cigar, Jamie. I was going to be a New York cop on horseback. Saw two mounted police in a movie, once, and that was that."

"Cop on horseback. What an adventurous notion!"

"I'd have made tracks after high school, but my old man had his own obsession. First man the family could afford to educate goes for the brass ring—a profession. We struck a deal: midwest college, followed by law school in Manhattan. Then if I still wanted to be a cop, well, I was in the right city for it. If not, I could use my law degree to become another kind of cop. My dad was the Hoover fan, not me."

"But when things began to sour, you didn't cut and run," Jamie pointed out. "Admirable perseverance, Max."

"That what you shrinks call it?"

"Loyalty, then. How else could you stomach the Hoover personality cult? The power lust of a man who kept secret files to—"

"Shut up, Jamie."

"Since when is the truth off limits?"

"It isn't. Just don't rub my nose in it. I've fought my battles. Even won a few. But I don't bad-mouth an employer."

"Come off it, Max, the Bureau's no employer. It's home."

"Am I supposed to apologize for that?"

"Don't ever apologize for love and loyalty."

In the deafening silence which followed that ironic remark, I cursed Jamie, glad Max wasn't in the mind-reading business.

"Have much in common, these days, with your fellow agents?"

Max dropped his eyes from Jamie's and stared into his brandy. "About as much as I ever did," he admitted.

"Odd man out," Jamie mused. "What is it one's colleagues are supposed to represent? A camaraderie born of similar interests and shared values? When I was young and foolish, I joined the American Psychiatric Association. Instead of camaraderie, I found that most disappointing of substitutes—the functional relationship."

"It didn't stop you. Or me. I'm still what I'll always be."

An FBI agent, do or die, Jamie. Still bent on recruitment?

Still playing in a danger zone. Jamie brought us back to vigilante talk. It was only a matter of time before Max thought to ask him the obvious. . . .

"I'd like the benefit of your insights on victim psychology, Jamie. Do you mind?"

Jamie didn't mind. Jamie acted as if he were flattered. He waxed eloquent about displacement and loss of control. Then, covering himself with a disclaimer ("All I know about Victims Anonymous is what I read in the papers"), he switched over to "armchair psychologizing" about the sort of people who would join a vigilante organization.

Max's idle curiosity turned to fascination.

Jamie dropped some minor revelations. Eagerly. I couldn't see any harm in them. I couldn't see the point, either.

More brandy, Max? More insights and shared confidences?

Next on Jamie's hidden agenda was a host of general-interest questions about the FBI, the kind that a man who loves his work is only too eager to answer. . . .

"The preinvestigation stage, you mean? Call it an FBI probe.

"What makes it federal? When two or more persons conspire— key word—to deprive you of your constitutional rights—say, by killing you. Our catchall conspiracy laws make me a little uneasy.

"Very controversial law, RICO. Pick any two crimes in the book, from pushing drugs to mail fraud, link them up to 'interstate enterprise,' and the FBI has a 'racketeer' to crack down on.

"RICO against the vigilantes? Going after a bunch of frustrated citizens with a law intended to net mobsters, you mean? Theoretically, yes. But you'd be risking a huge public outcry."

I tuned out of the question-and-answer period, intent on maintaining a blank-faced calm while I asked a few silent questions of my own—like whether I could be part of a "catchall conspiracy" if I wasn't an official member of the "interstate" conspirators. Like, could anyone in his right mind consider me a—a racketeer?

When I rejoined the party, Jamie was answering the questions. "—seeing too much public sympathy for the victims, Max."

"So how would *you* break the back of a massive conspiracy?"

"Go after the leaders, of course."

Max kept his face impassive. So, by God, did Jamie.

"Just don't lose sight of what you're up against, Max," Jamie warned. "Savvy individuals. Probably ruthless, some of them."

Dr. James Coyne, unofficial adviser to the FBI.

"—mean it, Max. I'd bet my psychiatrist's license on it."

"Don't risk it. Not with those impressive credentials."

"Not as impressive as yours."

Jamie wasn't joking.

"May I?" he asked Max.

Max dug in his pocket and came up with something resembling an oversized wallet. "Not much to look at." He handed it over.

I'd seen it before: just Max's picture and the FBI director's signature, attesting to Max's status as an agent.

Jamie slipped the thing into his own pocket and pulled it out again. "Agent James Coyne at your service," he said, flashing his credentials, smile on high beam.

Max grinned at the joke and took it back.

Something went out of Jamie's face. Something pathetically wistful and boyish took its place.

"Guess what I wanted to be when I grew up? An FBI man!"

They left together. I counted ten minutes on the clock, picked up the phone, dialed—

Hung up fast.

I tried again, but it was as if the dial mechanism were stuck in molasses. I told myself it wasn't a matter of being disloyal to Jamie, of not loving him. It was a matter of security.

I dialed and let it ring, this time. When Claudia answered, I said the magic words: "Love to see you, CC. Are you free?"

Chapter 27

Claudia was ten minutes late. But then, so was I. I hadn't let her hear a thing in my voice last night; the code words carried their own cryptic message. I was about to go back inside for a nostalgic cup of coffee—this was where I first broke bread with Angela and Zack—when I spotted Tony getting off a motorbike.

Tony, who had slunk back to the organization like a chastened animal returning to the feed bowl, Jamie had told me. Where else could he go for the kind of sustenance he needed?

"Claudia's not coming," he said, walking over. "Bart needed her to do something."

"No 'hello, how are you?'" I chided.

"Hi." Very soft.

"I've missed you," I said, my voice tuned to his.

"I came in Claudia's place." He was playing with his belt buckle.

"You know where I'm supposed to meet Kagan?" He nodded. "Coffee?" I offered, pretending to be all business. Another nod.

We went inside. Tony marched over to a booth, his sturdy little frame lean and tough as a wire hanger. His black eyes were solemn, trying not to show what was in the air like energy: how glad he was to see me. I wanted to crush him to my chest. I ordered two coffees, black.

He told me where to go, and when, insisting that we synchronize our watches. He took me through a step-by-step procedure to make sure I wasn't followed "without making it obvious you're trying to shake a tail." Tony, showing off his street smarts.

Business concluded, he allowed himself the small luxury of a hot dog. "Claudia quit school," he announced after the first bite. "She won't be going back in the fall, either. She won't like my telling you."

"Thanks," I said faintly, accepting the inevitable with a sigh.

"Kagan thinks you've changed," he blurted out. "That's why he wants you to honcho your own Mission planning. Said you needed a Rouser. He doesn't know I heard," Tony said, making wet rings on the table with his mug, uneasy with telling tales out of school.

He doesn't know you came here to warn me.

"I'll take care of it," he said as the waiter left our check. The easy part was letting him. The hard part was saying good-bye.

As I watched a small boy drive off on a man's machine, I wondered if Jamie was making any progress—Tony was keeping regular appointments again. My own appointment with Kagan wasn't until late afternoon. I hailed a cab. Jamie's place was off limits to me now, but the hell with it. Maybe he could fill in some blanks.

If he'd been in, he could have.

"Looks as if Jamie's corner cutting is rubbing off on you," Kagan said from the doorway of Jamie's office. "Come in for a moment, if you wish. I was just leaving."

"Where's Jamie?"

"Upstairs, nursing a headache."

I went in because I sensed Kagan didn't want me to. The door to Jamie's inner office was open, a scatter of tapes on Jamie's desk. "Destroying evidence, Kagan?" I said lightly.

"Too soon for that. Just taking inventory."

"I won't keep you. Four-thirty?"

"Four-thirty," he confirmed. "Unless we get rained out."

No such luck. Just an overcast sky as my cab pulled up at the designated entrance to Central Park. Kagan's impeccable directions led me right to the appointed bench, empty except for a dented diet-soda can. Off in the near-distance I spotted a boy, a dog and a man. I recognized the casual slouch, the angle of the neck. I walked over. A lazy wave of acknowledgment put me on hold. I shrugged, knowing I was fifteen minutes early.

It was fifteen minutes of grist for my what-makes-Kagan-tick mill. It wasn't just the fascinating sight of Kagan putting a large German shepherd through its obedience-training paces. It was the odd chemistry of the situation. The boy, afraid of his own dog; the dog, afraid of Kagan. Kagan, intent on the dog's increasingly eager responses as he learned how to distinguish friend from foe; the boy, increasingly awed by Kagan's success. But if Kagan recognized wide-eyed hero worship in the boy's glance, he was indifferent to it.

I decided that Kagan was utterly incapable of relating to another human being. The "why" eluded me.

He related well to the German shepherd—"the next best thing to a burglar alarm in a high-risk neighborhood," he'd told me once.

His voice was firm now, his gestures authoritative, his smile easy. Any warmth in it? Anything personal for the dog, at least? I wasn't close enough to see.

While Kagan dismissed his charges, I went back to the bench, ready to catch him off balance. When he ambled over, loose-limbed in khaki shirt and slacks, I said, "Kagan, the mystery man. No home, no woman, no discernible pleasures. What do you live for?"

"Victims Anonymous," he said easily.

"And before that? After that?"

"Don't you know there's always a Victims Anonymous? Nice dog."

Boy and dog were almost out of sight. "What's nice about him?"

"He's predictable. It's why I like animals. Press the right buttons and you get results, not surprises. Can you say the same for our unpredictable Jamie?"

"How did you know I wanted to talk about him and not McCann?"

"Because I leave nothing to chance. Mind telling me what the hell your little threesome is all about?"

So he knew. "I'm not sure," I said, because I wasn't. I laid it all out for him—in the best possible light, I admit. Nothing about FBI worship; it was only a theory. "In fairness," I concluded, "even if Jamie had some crazy notion about trying to recruit McCann, he got off it as soon as it began to look hopeless."

"He should have known it was hopeless from the start. I fear Jamie is getting bored with the action—or lack of it." He lit a cigarette, forgetting to offer me one. "Nothing a few good Missions won't cure," he said with a thin coating of contempt. "I trust the strain of separation won't weigh too heavily on the big romance?"

"No sacrifice too great for the cause."

He smiled. Kagan liked his humor dry. He said, "The price of conviction runs high."

"A noble sentiment," I retorted, thinking that in Kagan's mouth, the words lost their nobility and acquired a neuter sound, like "potatoes" or "dry-cell batteries."

"Are we really being noble? Or just self-serving? McCann is smitten. My sources tell me the attraction looks mutual."

"If your sources are so good, why ask *me* about Jamie's surprises?" I shot back, stalling for time. I knew what was coming.

"Just wanted to see if you'd blow the whistle on your lover."

He had given me a good transition. "I passed your damn test, Kagan," I said. "Now let's see if you can pass mine. What do you do if your lover is taking risks that can explode in his face—his and maybe ours?"

"You tell *me* so I can defuse the situation."

"A-plus. So 'blowing the whistle' doesn't mean I'm about to trade one lover for another, does it? Don't ask me to do what—"

"The closer you get to McCann, the safer we'll all be. Bed him down, Karen. You might even like it."

My hand didn't even get close to his face—that's how good his reflexes are.

"Not your style, sleeping with two men?" he said with that insolent smile that presses *my* buttons. "Your loyalty is touching, Karen, though I'm not sure Jamie deserves it. Not after setting you up on your Mission in the Bronx. He could cite mitigating circumstances, I suppose. He did risk his life. On the other hand, a man who walks around like he has nine lives and is eager to throw half of them away doesn't deserve too much credit for deliberately turning his back on a punk with a knife. Does he?"

"Indio?" I said, choking on the name.

"Well, why not? You weren't about to make your bones on your own—no stomach for it, as I recall. Jamie was counting on you to use my gun in a self-defense situation. Lucky for him you came through. Lucky for all of us. In the clamor and confusion, we got our photograph. Nobody joins the organization without it."

My ears hurting. White flashes in my eyes.

"Blackmail," I said bitterly, remembering Jamie's guarded explanation for how VA kept troublemakers in line: all it took was a little reminder.... All it took was an incriminating photograph. "So I'm in your little black box," I said slowly.

"Why would you be an exception?"

"Because I'm not a member. I didn't join a damn thing!"

His smile was patronizing. "A nice distinction."

Twilight in the park. I calmed myself in its tranquillity while I asked myself astute questions. Like: What was Kagan's game right now and how did I keep from playing it? Was he trying to throw cold water on the "big romance" so Max could catch me on the rebound? Or letting me know I was in no position to cut and run, even if I were ready to? Did he think I was ready? Could he have sensed what I wasn't fully aware of myself?

"Truce, Kagan," I said with a smile that had surrender in it. "I take it I won't be breaching security anymore by seeing Jamie occasionally—with or without McCann?"

"By all means, expand your social circle by one," he said. What I saw in *his* smile was: Give him hell!

My very thought. But I said with a shrug, "Don't get your hopes up. Jamie can be a manipulative SOB but that doesn't mean we won't kiss and make up."

Did he believe me? He looked as if he was pretending to.

The thought of Kagan's eerie perceptiveness returned abruptly as we left the park together and he gave me an update on VA activities. He seemed to know exactly what—and who—I wanted to hear about. Not surprising if you move through life on constant alert.

Alert and oblivious at the same time. As Kagan finished the update and we continued walking, conversation died. The streets were congested with summer tourists and people who'd worked late, but for Kagan they didn't exist . . . they did and they didn't. He was like a computer making rapid calculations—not of individuals, but of functions. The man in the blue blazer, I could almost hear him thinking—how would he react under combat stress? At what point would the woman wearing the saucy red beret hit the panic button? Had he even noticed the exuberant swing of her shoulder bag or her possessive hold on the arm of her male companion? It was as if he lacked the antennae to tune in to the whole of human behavior, let alone respond to its subtleties.

I was so engrossed in the spectacle of his detachment that I missed what Kagan did not: a hungry cat lurking behind an empty garbage can. In a flash, he had dipped into my jacket pocket (everyone knew about my ongoing supply of People Crackers) and had that kitty eating out of his hand. His features were relaxed.

It hit me—the contrast between this unguarded moment and Kagan's laconic cowpoke image: his soft-drawled conversation and easygoing way of moving through a room with an untasted drink in his hand. A pose.

I confirmed it in the split second when he stood up and I saw what was already happening to his face: behind the thick grey smoke of his eyes—impenetrable, I'd once called them—was a controlled tension that was like a light bulb with an infinite source of energy. It never burned itself out. It was the tension that made me acutely aware of his presence in a room, that made me breathe a little freer after he'd left it. It was his studied casualness that had made me miss it altogether.

He waved a cab over. "Yours or mine?" I got in. His hand lingered for a moment on the door. "No more corner cutting, Karen."

The remark brought Jamie to mind. I went home to shed my office uniform for jeans and an old shirt. To toss "a change of clothes"—one pair of navy slacks, one cashmere jacket—into a paper bag. I called Jamie to say I was on my way over.

Pasta puttanesca—my favorite—waited for me on a candlelit table set for two. Jamie was disarming in a white apron.

"I'm in no mood to break bread with you," I said, tossing the paper bag in his Judas face. I told him what Kagan had told me.

"But I did you a favor," he protested.

"This ought to be good," I said, taking the nearest chair.

"I won't deny I was out to protect the organization and get you aboard. But I had another purpose. I wanted to give you the killing experience."

"But that's horrible!" I said, believing him. "Look how much therapy you had to put me through before I got over it. I'm not over it yet!"

"Everything has a price tag." He steered me to the table. "Whatever else Victims Anonymous stands for, it breeds violence. Using a gun for the *second* time—should the need arise—is easier than the first. It could save your life."

"I won't eat your damn pasta," I said, not looking at it, trying not to breathe it in. It smelled wonderful.

"Don't go," he pleaded. "I want to talk. About Max."

That got my attention, especially since the concern in his voice was real. I gave in—and not just to pasta puttanesca. I sensed a new alliance: Max, Jamie and me.

Jamie was troubled. "Nothing specific, you understand. I'm relying on instinct. Twice Kagan has alluded to Max as a worrier. What would Kagan's devious mind expect a worrier to do?"

Dissect. Analyze. Probe. "Jamie," I couldn't help asking after twenty minutes of it, "have you switched sides? Are you in league with the FBI or what?"

"Whatever else you may have told Kagan, I hope you didn't wave *that* red flag under his nose," he said with a lopsided smile. "I could never be disloyal to my own creation. VA was my idea."

"You've lost control of the leadership," I told him gently.

His smile collapsed. "All the more reason not to lose sight of what it stands for. We're the good outlaws, Karen—that's what Victims Anonymous is all about. Justice for the crime victim was my goal," he said slowly. "What is Kagan's?"

"Better question," I said. *"Who* is Kagan? I vote for Power-luster. A man who dislikes people but likes ordering them around."

"He's much more complex than that," Jamie reflected, tracing the rim of his wineglass. "Now *there's* a man I'd like to strap to my psychiatrist's couch."

"What would you find? Man with a cause, dedicated—"

"Consumed. Kagan has the soul of a revolutionary. His is a darker need. . . ."

I refilled our glasses and brooded over mine. "He always has a drink in his hand but I've never seen him touch it. What's that all about, Doctor?"

"Makes him look like he's hanging loose with the rest of us," Jamie said without hesitation. "We drop our guard while Kagan never misses a beat. Incidentally, he's very impressed with you. A good field officer, he says. You anticipate trouble and you figure the odds."

"I do? And here I sit feeling hollow, wooden and treacherous. A bad case of Trojan horse-itis, wouldn't you say?"

"And here you sit, meeting anxiety and regret with your incomparable sense of humor," he said with a soft smile.

"Tell me the truth, Jamie. Were you trying to recruit Max?"

"Let's just say I was testing the waters," he said, looking sheepish. "Max may think the way we do on a lot of issues—he hates what's happening on the street—but he won't cut corners to stop it." His eyes narrowed in sympathy. "Not even for you."

I sighed. "The company man."

"Have you ever asked yourself why a man doesn't pursue a ten-year-old attraction? I have."

"Max was married. Unhappily, I'm beginning to suspect."

"Exactly. He couldn't forget you, yet he never looked you up until after his wife died. Max toes the line."

"You're just full of happy insights tonight," I said. "Jamie, if he ever finds out—"

He put a comforting arm around me. "We'll see he doesn't. It's late and we're both exhausted. Why not stay the night and spare me the effort of putting you in a cab? No," he said as I started to protest, "I won't let you go downstairs alone. You take the bed. Tony loves it, by the way. My couch, I've discovered, is quite comfortable."

"Sure you have no romantic intentions?" I teased.

He planted a chaste kiss on my forehead. "The moment has passed us by, love."

Were Kagan's "sources" on the job, waiting for the lights to go out? The thought of bolstering my kiss-and-make-up fairy tale, coupled with bone-weary fatigue, made the invitation irresistible.

Jamie's bedroom was richly colored and heavily draped. The feel of fresh satin sheets put out my lights almost at once.

I woke up in the middle of the night. Whatever it was—strange bed, lustful thoughts of Max—I couldn't get back to sleep. I slipped into the ivory-colored robe Jamie had left on a chair and padded out to the kitchen for a glass of juice to go with my cigarette. On the way back I glanced at Jamie on the couch. Patchwork quilt askew. Arms and legs in a jumble. Tousle-haired and deeply asleep. A boy who kicked off his bedcovers.

Not asleep. Pretending to be.

"What's the matter, Jamie?" I said, walking over.

He sat up. "Dissecting Kagan's psyche tonight . . . put me in mind of my own. What's a psychiatrist's strong suit?" he said as if we were playing Twenty Questions. But he kept biting his lip.

"Empathy?"

He sighed. "Sensitive in the extreme, the best of us—even as children. Easy targets for an emotionally insecure parent."

"Your mother?" I said, remembering his bitter, drunken toast.

"I was five when my father left her. For the next ten years, I played the substitute: confidante, constant escort, worshipful little man of the house. Karen, don't you see? I was so busy tuning in to her neurotic needs that it whizzed right by me—those formative years when a child must discover his 'self' or risk growing up without one!" He looked away. "Narcissistically deprived, they call it. . . . Do you see what Victims Anonymous gave back to me? My aborted childhood. Who needs Batman and the G-man who always gets his man when, waiting in the wings, is King Arthur and the Scarlet Pimpernel?"

And the Green Hornet, I thought. The characters out of Dumas and Sabatini—you and Lee. The perceptive psychiatrist who shifts without warning into gleeful child or man with a cape. The avenging angel who needs the artificial stimulant of a Rouser or a Mission . . .

"Shall I tell you my personal definition of terror?" Jamie whispered. "To search for yourself in the mirror and know that what stares back is someone else's unlived dreams. To go through life knowing that your mother has stolen your identity."

I shivered; I couldn't stop shivering in the August heat.

I spent the rest of the night holding him in my arms.

Chapter 28

At the sound of my voice in the foyer, they filed out of Claudia's bedroom: a faintly expectant Kagan; Bart, wearing a this-better-be-good expression; Lee, looking eager and gorgeous in an off-white silk jumpsuit with a purple scarf at her throat. At least Kagan had taken my SOS seriously.

"Getting cold feet?" Bart asked. My Mission was a week off.

"It's about Lee," I said and saw his jaw tighten.

I didn't know much, only that reports had come in about "a tall blonde" who had been spotted on two different occasions during vigilante activity that "might or might not" tie in with the FBI investigation of Victims Anonymous.

"Someone saw you in Atlanta," I told Lee. But the reproach in my voice was really for Kagan, who should have known better.

"Ah yes," Kagan said, "that high-visibility Mission against an assistant district attorney you were so up in arms about. Don't worry about it."

Bart was worried. Lee, looking uncertain, tried to calm him. Kagan was uncharacteristically reassuring, calling it a "near-impossibility" that Lee would ever be identified in New York.

"But to be on the safe side, no more Missions," he told her.

"How is Operation Feeder coming along?" Lee asked brightly.

Coy label for what I was doing. "Ask me again next week," I

said, wanting to choke her with her deep-purple scarf. "You have to let me in the club before I have anything to feed him."

Bart was still frowning with worry. "Tell us about the original game plan, Karen. The FBI won't break us up cell by cell?"

"And indict a lot of 'sorely misguided' people as co-conspirators? No way," I said. "The latest bulletin out of the Bureau's Congressional and Public Affairs office says they're looking into different groups of vigilantes—so-called extremists—but with no solid evidence, so far, of a national conspiracy."

"What does that mean?" Lee asked breathlessly.

"They're stalling while they try to run down the leaders," Bart told her. "I hear good things about the man in charge," he said, his mouth relaxing into a grin. "McCann headed an experimental task force of New York cops and Federal agents a few years back. Over a hundred career criminals arrested in ten weeks, Zack says. Too bad McCann's on the wrong side of the ledger."

I didn't blink, not with Kagan watching.

"How about a progress report while you're here?" he asked me.

"You can tell Hugh he's not the only one with budget problems. Drug enforcement being top priority, the FBI has, and I quote, 'limited resources for investigating a bunch of vigilantes.'"

Everybody laughed. Everybody got ready to leave.

Lee had to give me a personal update first. "Our fox symbol is turning up all over, Karen. Written on walls. Spray-painted in the subways. People are on the offensive. *We* did that."

. . . Isn't it a thrill and a half, Karen? Aren't *we* important? Isn't my life significant?

I wanted to tell her that with every thrill comes a danger. I wanted to say, "Go back to advertising." I smiled at her and said, "That's nice."

Kagan saw through my straight face. His expression—alert, wary—reminded me of when I'd had the brainstorm about the fox.

"Good luck next week," he said, sounding as if I'd need it.

I sat in a darkened screening room, packed with recent recruits, strangers whose features I couldn't see clearly. What struck me was their body language: not just alert, but eager.

A little too eager. The whole purpose of a Mission planning is to get the SD Team primed for action. These guys were on the prod before I'd even opened my mouth.

I didn't bother with my notes, just signaled the projectionist and waited for the anonymity of total darkness.

"A fifteen-year-old who violates the child labor laws," I said as a muscled figure with a mop of dark hair appeared on the screen. "He works nights. I'll let him tell you at what."

"I look for the creeps with briefcases, y'know? And watches, good ones. Broads with gold chains. Hey, I got expenses!"

"As for *how* he does business, let's just say he likes waving his Magnum around. After ten arrests and two convictions, does he look worried? Look at him." . . . *Look at him laugh in your face.*

"Next," I said.

We looked at a new face. An old story . . .

"You kiddin' me, man? I go for drunks, old ladies, anything that moves. I dig some sucker's running shoes? I take 'em."

They all "took 'em"—one smug teenaged face after another.

I turned up the pace, film images tumbling one after the other while I felt a small hard deposit pressing into my breastbone, like the residue of minerals that hard water leaves behind. By the time I got to the punch line, it had become a solid, painful lump.

"The object of tomorrow's Permissives Mission," I said, "the man responsible for turning these young Savages loose on the rest of the world"—*the man responsible for Indio, for giving me the killing experience*— "is Judge Arthur Younger. The conviction record of this Family Court judge is a sick joke," I said. "His dismissal rate is an abomination."

For twenty minutes I spelled it all out: a sort of "rap sheet" on Judge Arthur Younger. How many young hoodlums he had released to their mothers, sisters, or big brothers, with a single admonition: Go to school and keep your nose clean. How many of those he had released who'd gone on to bigger and better—more violent—crimes. A graphic picture—documented, in a few cases, on film—of some of the true "beneficiaries" of Judge Younger's charitable outlook on law and order: a body count of crime victims that numbered in the hundreds and ran the gamut from the very young to the very old—maimed, fractured, scarred. Dead, some of them, or as good as dead.

I said his name for the last time—"Judge Arthur Younger"— and it was like three knife thrusts plunged into the blackness.

The lights went on. I'd spotted Kagan earlier, but he was gone now. Jamie had waited, a dignified presence in the back of the room.

"Very effective," he complimented me. "How did it feel?"

"Dirty."

"Take you home?" he offered.

I had to stop myself from taking his arm; we were becoming a mutual support society.

After a while, I couldn't stop myself from asking him a

disturbing question. "Jamie, why do I hate Judge Younger even more than the criminals he releases?"

"Because you know where the real control center of evil is: in his courtroom. When the judges abdicate responsibility, the criminals multiply into big numbers. How's Max holding up?"

"He took me to lunch and tried to make me back out."

"Interesting," Jamie said. He didn't talk the rest of the way, just held my hand.

When I got home, I took a Valium instead of a sleeping pill.

I woke up in a stupor. All day at work I avoided mirrors.

I didn't look in one until I got to Claudia's. I started to giggle; the onset of hysteria?

"Good thing you decided to dress at my place," Claudia observed with a wicked grin. "No way you'd have made it past your doorman, Whitey."

Not in my black leather miniskirt and five-inch heels.

"My rouge is redder than your lipstick," I said with a frown.

"My skirt is shorter and my beret is metallic gold."

Mine was black. I tugged it down on one side, struck a pose, then eyed my long-legged friend Claudia as she slowly swung a thin-strapped gold shoulder bag to some invisible beat. "You win the vamp prize, CC," I said, grabbing my own shoulder bag. "Let's go."

"Plenty of time. We'll just zip up the West Side."

"What if we get stuck in traffic?" I said, sorry that we were driving. "It's that time of day."

"Night," she corrected, adjusting the blinds over her window.

We moved out.

We got stuck in the elevator. Me, Claudia, and a man who had joined us on the second floor. He kept hitting the button, a furious jabbing motion, while my heart kept pace and I kept my panic to myself. *Stuck in an elevator on the way to my Mission?*

Claudia pressed the red emergency button. Nothing. I asked her if the building superintendent would be out at this hour.

"Out to lunch, more likely. We could be here all night."

"Don't say that!" The man was portly and past sixty, with a face getting redder by the minute.

I don't recommend a solid half hour of banging and shouting in a steel cage. That's how long it took for help to arrive in the form of a super with rum on his breath and a marijuana look in his eye. Our companion in claustrophobia chose that moment to slip, groaning, to the floor. I yelled for a doctor as Claudia bent to loosen his collar.

The super returned with a cop. He was nice enough to us,

considering his lightning evaluation: a couple of savvy, civic-minded hookers. What with seeing the man to an ambulance (his color was good and he had a pulse) and giving particulars to the man in blue, it was another hour before we were on our way.

"Where to?" Claudia wondered out loud. "Show's well under way by now. They won't be——"

"Wait, let me think. Kagan said something about a slam-bang climax. Wouldn't tell me what and spoil the surprise. But Tony, bless him, had the foresight to tell me where."

"The kid's a first-class eavesdropper," Claudia drawled as she braked for a traffic light. "How 'bout telling *me* where?"

"Twenty-sixth and the Hudson River."

"Nice neighborhood. We'll make it," she promised, hitting the gas. "I'm a whiz at timed lights."

She was good, all right, even if she did cheat a little by going through two stop signs and the last red light.

"Bingo," she said as we slowed on Twenty-fifth Street and drove right past an untidy little procession. We went around the next corner, pulled into an empty lot, and jumped out.

It was them, all right, half a block away and headed in our direction: my eight-man Self-Defense Team moving four abreast, with the judge in the middle. They looked like juveniles on a late-night mugging spree, and they had a cover story to match. (In their "drug-crazed" euphoria, they'd intercepted a Family Court judge on his way home—just wanted to take him on a motherfuckin' trip, man!)

"Here come de judge," Claudia muttered.

He was sandwiched between a weight lifter and a guy Jamie had pointed out as Kagan's new protégé—a slim-hipped, fair-haired fellow who looked as if he ought to be herding cattle on the range instead of working the dark side of New York in sneakers and hero jacket. He looked surprised as hell to see us.

We walked up like a rear guard behind eight black hero jackets and a torn navy suit—no way the judge could get a look at us.

But I'd gotten a look at *him*. Judge Arthur Younger was blinking rapidly—somewhere along the way he had lost his silver-framed glasses—and a blood smear had dried on his upper lip, a sort of half-mustache under that aquiline nose. There was nothing imperious about the rest of him: eyes glazing over, pinched mouth, hunched shoulders. His hands were shaking.

I kept seeing those tapered fingers.

I had waited a long time. Dreamed savage dreams in my waking hours. A soul-satisfying sight. Wasn't it?

As we neared Twenty-sixth, I noticed the couple coming down the sidewalk toward us: a shapely young girl in a short skirt swaying from one drink too many, her male companion in a suit and tie, too smitten with his date to think of crossing to the other side of the deserted street. Nobody did anything, exactly. What tipped me off was body language, especially coming from the head of the line: Kagan's protégé had half-turned, head tilted, one hand slipping into his pocket. For a knife?

"Don't you dare," I hissed, before he could give the order to spin a Permissives Mission into a real mugging. He glared at me, brown eyes glinting in the lamplight, but he took his hand out of his pocket just as the couple sailed blithely through our midst like a small boat through a mined harbor.

Twenty-sixth and the Hudson River. We slowed, turned a sharp corner—

And practically walked into a police car, parked at the curb!

The judge broke free, made a run for the car—

I heard gunshots and spun around to see a pistol in the hands of the leader.

Claudia slammed me against the wall of a building.

I looked up to see a cop slumped over the wheel of the police car and his partner leaning into a blood-spattered windshield. The judge lay on the sidewalk in a dead faint.

"Oh . . . my . . . God," Claudia breathed.

I staggered forward on my high heels.

The cop who'd been slumped over the wheel—a black cop—sat up. . . . Zack? Up off the windshield snapped the "bloodied" head of his partner, a few strands of long dark hair escaping from under her cap. *Her* cap? Angela?

Kagan's slam-bang climax, complete with fake blood and blanks. Before I could speak, let alone bring my muscles back to life, the scene lit up like a movie set.

"What the hell? Turn that goddamn thing off!" Zack yelled.

Angela, one arm in front of her face, was blinking like an animal transfixed by the headlights of a car.

The "goddamn thing" was a spotlight that Kagan's man seemed in no hurry to put out. "Sorry about that," he muttered as everything went dark again.

Sorry? If the judge hadn't fainted on us, the damn spotlight might have given him a good look at his would-be rescuers—at Zack and Angela. Was Kagan's man crazy? Was Kagan?

"Better check out Hizzoner," he told Zack. "The man don't look so good to me."

Zack was out of the car and on his knees, Angela right behind him. "Cardiac arrest," he told her, his fingers on a limp wrist. "Party's over. Everybody move out," he ordered, not looking up.

The SD Team scattered, just like they had at Tony's Mission.

Claudia and I stayed put. We watched. Five compressions to every lungful of air. Dusky complexion—much worse than the man in the elevator. Time beating in my temples.

"I've got a pulse." Zack's voice was matter-of-fact.

"He's coming around," Angela agreed, breathing for herself, now.

"Beat it, all of you," Zack said. "I'll get him to a hospital. Get rid of the uniform, Angie."

We followed her around the corner while she took it off.

Claudia and I slipped out of our heels. The three of us made a mad dash for the car.

We were on the highway, well within the speed limit for a change, when Angela said, "It's not as if I didn't anticipate something like this. Damn." She lit up one of her thin cigars. "You know what we flirted with tonight? Felony murder."

Claudia went through her second red light of the evening. "That judge isn't about to die on us, is he?"

"He'll be all right."

"But if he'd died," I said, "we'd have been . . ."

"Murderers, in the eyes of the law."

We drove the rest of the way in silence.

Claudia pulled over two blocks from the rental garage so Angela and I could get out. Security meant taking separate cabs.

Before Angela got into hers, I said, "We have to talk. You, me, Zack, Jamie—"

"Claudia?"

"Why do you say it like that?"

"She's not ready to get out, and you know it. We'll talk," she said with a shrug.

I rode home thinking about what she'd left unsaid, even though I'd seen it in her face: It's easier getting in than getting out.

I was wiping off what was left of the red lipstick (I'd chewed off most of it during the judge's artificial respiration) when I noticed the light under my door. I went in, more glad than mad.

"Another duplicate key?" I asked Jamie, not really surprised.

"Your mascara is caked. Sit down. We have things to discuss."

"My very thought. When I tell you what happened tonight—"

"Claudia just did. I picked up when she called a few minutes ago. She'd just checked in with a couple of hospitals. The man you two encountered in the elevator checked out ten minutes after he'd checked in. Looks like the only genuine cardiac arrest patient was Judge Arthur Younger, and he's doing fine."

I lowered myself into a chair. "Jamie, what's going on?"

"A first-class game of chess, the better to checkmate you."

It had clicked for Jamie when I'd told him Max wanted me to back out of the Mission at the last minute. Why, with so much at stake? Why, over a Permissives Mission where I was in no particular danger and no one was likely to get hurt?

"Kagan sees Max as 'McCann the worrier,' right?" Jamie said. "I figured Max must have been approached by one of Kagan's informants with a last-minute tip: Your Mission might turn ugly, even violent. Easy to figure what Max would do with *that* information."

"What?" I said, accepting a glass of my own brandy.

"Jump into the fray in order to protect you. Plan on being there for Kagan's climax, just in case—out of sight, but armed."

"But how would he know when and where—"

"Twenty-sixth Street and the Hudson River? He knew all right. Kagan made sure of that. Max knew, and he would have been there tonight if I hadn't tricked him."

"You called him?"

"And said you had just called *me* when you couldn't get ahold of him. VA didn't trust you enough to give you the Mission's true location, you told me. The one on Twenty-sixth was a phony, to be switched at the last minute. You gave me some vague directions in Brooklyn, where the real thing was going down, and hung up."

"He bought it? Jamie, how do you *know* he bought it?"

"I know because I went with him on his wild-goose chase to Brooklyn. I'm exhausted. More brandy?"

"Ludicrous!" I said, on the verge of laughter, just as he was. "Then that portly man in the elevator . . ."

"A setup to keep you—and, more important, Claudia—away from that Mission without your suspecting anything. If Max had taken the bait and showed up, as Kagan expected him to do—"

"He'd have recognized Claudia," I said slowly. "He's met her a few times. He's knows we're close friends."

"Precisely. There's more. When Max and I took off for Brooklyn, he brought a camera—standard operating procedure for stakeouts. Claudia said the police car was lit up by a spotlight."

"It seemed deliberate. What was Kagan after?"

"Pictures. They'd have given him real bargaining power, don't you see? A way to keep you in line. He wanted to *control* you through Angela and Zack. Cross him and he'd have supplied the FBI with names to go with the faces he wanted Max to photograph."

"He'd expose Zack and Angela just to keep me from quitting?"

"And to keep you from becoming a turncoat. He knows you and Max are falling in love."

"*You're* the one I'm supposed to be mad about," I protested.

"Kagan got the truth out of me," Jamie said, not meeting my eye. "I'd been drinking too much one night—"

"You still are," I said. "You've got to put a lid on it. I need you. Some of us want out, Jamie. I want it without telling Max and I want it fast but I . . . I know I have to take it slow."

"Very slow," he said. "Max was tipped about a mysterious woman at the top of VA's administrative heap. He's assuming it's the statuesque blonde who was spotted in Atlanta."

"Poor Lee," I said.

"She deflects suspicion from you." He took my hand. "I want Max to keep right on thinking you don't know a thing about our PR efforts. I don't want you crossing swords with Kagan until I've made sure he can't point the finger back at you." He checked his watch. "Better call the worrier."

"My God," I said, leaping up. "Max will wonder—"

"Wait. Think first. You have to back up my story and add a few details of your own. You have to be convincing on why you couldn't reach him and how you finally managed to get through to me with your SOS."

"I'll say I always know where my shrink is—emergency number, et cetera. Max, on the other hand, isn't easy to find, especially when there's no time to leave a trail of messages."

"Sounds good. Ironic, isn't it," Jamie mused, "Kagan knowing we're not lovers, Max thinking we are. . . ."

"Thinking we *were*."

He frowned. "I sensed something in his attitude tonight."

"Jamie," I whispered, "what's going to happen to us?"

"Nothing a guardian angel can't protect you from."

He flashed me a faded smile and let himself out.

Chapter 29

A damp Friday in the country that turned rainy. Picnic with Max in a parked car. Not exactly a duplicate of our first date. An improvement, if I took into consideration not having to fool around with guns. Max handed me my egg salad on rye.

"You look better already. Less strung out."

I felt worse already, knowing he was leaving for Washington.

"Are you free Monday night for dinner?" he asked me.

"Back so soon? Why don't I make dinner, for a change?"

"Suits me." He started the car.

I couldn't get used to the formality. Did he really think Jamie and I were back on track? Why, when I'd given him no reason?

"Dirt roads," he grumbled, rolling us out of a pothole.

"This is horse country. They keep them unpaved to—"

We stopped with a jolt. "Wait here." He got out of the car.

I saw him bend over a mound of fur; grey. I sighed, hands slipping into my pockets, empty for the moment of People Crackers.

"A squirrel?" I asked, getting out.

"A cat. Whoever struck him kept right on going. Don't look. Give me a minute."

He had his windbreaker off—a bright blue stretcher for a dead pile of fur. I watched him carry it to the side of the road and roll it, gently, onto the ground.

When he came back, his windbreaker had a crescent-shaped smear across the front. "Karen, I'm sorry," he said at my expression.

"I'm so sick of the sight of death!"

He held me, dry-eyed, against his chest.

"You won't be alone while I'm away?" he asked when we were back in the car. "Jamie will be around?" Concern in his voice.

I shrugged. He started the engine. We weren't back on the old footing, but the drive back to Manhattan was filled with companionable silence.

I didn't have to drift into the Monday-morning blues; I had lived them all weekend. Kemp & Carusone had become the discarded lover who made you wonder afterward what you ever saw in him. I still enjoyed attacking a thorny problem with Larry, but he was too discerning not to notice my general lack of enthusiasm for corporate public relations. I put on a good face and smoked a lot; Larry walked around, tight-lipped, as if waiting for me to hand in my resignation.

My spirits picked up as the dinner hour approached. I stopped off for sourdough bread and ice cream. My tenuously upbeat mood must have communicated itself to my doorman—old stoneface, as a rule. The silly grin on his face was out of character.

One foot into the foyer of my apartment and I knew someone had been here and gone. The louver doors to the kitchen were open, the door to my guest bathroom closed. It should have been in reverse. I yanked an umbrella from its stand and tiptoed over.

The noise from inside the bathroom was peculiar. Bread and ice cream hit the rug while I raised my improvised weapon with one hand and reached for the doorknob with the other. Now!

I had a sense of color and shape—two balls of energy, streaking out of prison. Two little cats. The image in a mirror—me, wielding my big bad umbrella—bent me over double. A few choice curse words floated through my mind. I found a box full of kitty litter in my bathtub and a message in lipstick across my medicine cabinet, a message that made me cry.

"Loving long-distance can be a lonely business."

I half-expected what I'd find in my kitchen. I was half right. Not a case of cat food, an entire shelf! I saw that my supply of People Crackers had been replenished, and there were a couple of lemon-yellow bowls that spelled out FEED THE CAT. A note told me my new roommates were brother and sister strays threatened with eviction from a Greek coffee shop whose lease was running out. The last line said, "They need you."

I can't afford to be needed, Max. Not by a couple of strays and not by you. Not now.

I went looking for them, guided by dead-giveaway sounds under and behind my living-room furniture. I caught a glimpse, finally, of amber eyes and an adorable split-personality face: dark grey on one side, orange and white on the other. Tantalized by the swinging tassels of a chair cushion, she came out to let me admire the split pattern in reverse that ran the length of her body.

A flash of grey and white took to the air. Her brother, exploring the top of a china cabinet with long white legs that would have made him top cat in a feline basketball game. He looked down at me with inquisitive eyes—they might have been outlined in mascara—and licked his lips. Message received.

I emerged from the kitchen bearing yellow bowls—and erupted into laughter. The boy cat looked up from the mess on my rug, as if to say, Who wants cat food when they're serving melted ice cream?

By the time Max arrived with a semiguilty grin and red roses, I was ready with the introductions. "Meet a couple of nonstop explorers," I said, a cat in each arm. "This is Marco and his sister Pola—that's feminine for Polo. Fellas, meet a matchmaker named McCann."

"In love already?"

"Trying not to be. Max, they can't stay."

"Why not?" he said, following me into the kitchen while I took dinner out of the oven. "They need a home. You need—"

"Don't say it. Look, I'll find them a—a more stable environment. I mean it," I said as he burst out laughing.

I burst out crying.

Max pulled me into his arms. "Karen," he whispered, "Karen, Karen," as soothing as the rain. He held me away from him—a fraction of a second—and it changed for both of us. His hand on my cheek was a resting place. I leaned into it. His eyes were stretched too thin and his finger slipped to touch the corner of my mouth. "Oh my love," he said, and I swayed.

He caught me, his arm a clamp around my waist, his mouth a greedy seeker of barriers . . . of hidden places.

He broke them down, one by one. He found them all.

I lay naked on a bed I hadn't shared for a long, long time. I thought I should feel awkward, the usual aftermath of a first intimacy. What I felt was a sense of coming home. I moved to get up but Max pulled me down against him, almost as if he were tucking me under his wing.

"Close your eyes," he murmured, his own half open. "Stay with me. Sleep with me."

I stayed until the rhythm of his breathing let me go.

I slipped into a robe and fled to the den—to smoke furiously and cry silently and curse the day I had accepted an invitation on Christmas Eve. Woman on a chessboard, with no way to get off.

No way . . . ?

"Think you could do a quick sketch of the man at the funeral?"

I took a folder from a locked desk drawer: sketches of Kagan— caricatures, really. I'd been playing with them on and off since that day in Washington. I'd have settled for a reasonable likeness, but all I'd captured was the peculiar angle of the neck. The man with the forgettable face. No distinguishing features, Bernard Rees would say.

But Kagan wasn't the only game in town.

I reached for my sketch pad, hesitated—then penciled in hooded eyes, heavy black hair, a toothpaste-commercial smile. Earl Bartholemew alias Black Bart. Had he replaced Jamie in Kagan's mind? Was there a circle within the inner circle that reflected the latest nucleus of power? O'Neal would be in it, I thought, and tackled him full-figure—piece of cake when your subject resembles a battering ram.

Max walked in. As I made a methodical pile, slipped it into the folder, dropped it into a drawer, I was thinking that Jamie was right again; what we do automatically, as opposed to what we say or think, is a true indication of where we're at. Sorry, Max. . . .

"Follow me to my microwave," I told him, smiling. "Unless you're not in the mood for reconstituted broccoli quiche?"

"Zabar's or homemade?" he wanted to know.

"You tell me."

"Homemade," he said with a grin after the first couple of bites. "A businesswoman who can cook."

The grin faded as we drifted into the meeting that was coming up. He asked if I was nervous about it. Only marginally, I told him;

September seemed light-years away. I could see that he wasn't convinced. I thought I knew what was bothering him. . . .

"So Rees thinks they'll ask me to join?" I said.

His frown was troubled, all right. "It may be too soon. But if we get lucky, you'll meet someone important. The quicker it happens, the sooner you're out of this."

"Stop worrying, Max."

He reached for my hand. "Jamie worry about you the way I do?" The question sounded involuntary.

So was my answer. "I doubt it."

"I don't blame you," he said slowly, "now that I know him."

"Don't blame me for what, Max?"

"For . . . getting back together. What happened just now—"

"Don't you dare apologize for it."

"Look," he said, letting my hand go, "I know you're still in love with him."

"You couldn't be more wrong," I said.

"Then why are you still sleeping with him?"

If it hadn't been for his anguish, I'd have slapped his face.

I listened to Max confirm what I hadn't wanted to believe even though Kagan had already primed me for it: FBI surveillance. How Rees had insisted. How Max had gone along, finally, because of the potential violence they had exposed me to. How I had made a dull and sometimes elusive subject.

Until the evening I had gone home and gone right out again *(. . . the evening when anger with the manipulative Jamie had made me careless)*. The evening I'd gone to Jamie's apartment for a showdown, stayed for supper—and left the next morning. *(The lights had gone out for more than Kagan's sources.)*

They had pulled their men off the job on the hectic night Claudia and I had played hookers and Jamie had lured Max to Brooklyn (thank God!), not daring to compromise my Mission.

"Wasn't using my doorman out of character?" I said, my voice in deep freeze. "What's next, a telephone tap?"

"I'd never approve it," he said, looking as if he'd just been kicked in the stomach.

Talk about a quick thaw! Karen Newman, dealer in double-talk and deceit, on her high horse. I climbed down fast.

"Forget it, Max," I said. "You did what you had to. But you're wrong about the night I spent with Jamie. We're good friends, not lovers."

"Then tonight was . . . ours?"

The tears in his eyes brought tears to mine.

I walked into his arms.

There was no dam-breaking urgency in our embrace. What

threatened to overwhelm me, this time, was the tenderness. The slow, piercing sweetness of his hands. The way he moaned when I touched him. The confessions, half-spoken, as if saying the words out loud made them irrevocable. The words left unsaid, as if to name what we were feeling would be to lose it forever.

In the end, I said it to myself: You are the first, the only, the best-loved . . . the inexorable climax to much more than this night.

He held me with a new kind of strength. A man without doubts or inner conflict.

I stared at the ceiling, knowing that someday I would give him both.

5

CAUSALITY

Bethink thee, how much more
grievous are the consequences
of our anger than the acts
which arouse it.

—Marcus Aurelius,
Meditations, Book II

Chapter 30

Claudia greeted me at the door with a look of sharp appraisal. "What's going on? You haven't looked this good in years."

I went inside and checked myself in a mirror. It was true.

"How about me?" she said, preening.

"What have you done to your hair?" The smooth straight look had become a wild and woolly tangle cascading down her back.

"Back to basics. Stan used to say I looked like a black stand-in for Sheena, Queen of the Jungle. What do you think?"

"Wild and woolly," I said. "I like it. Seeing much of Stan?"

"Still pumping him about the special task force, you mean? Bits and pieces are all I'm getting lately. Kagan says that means something's going down. How goes it with M. McCann?" She grinned. "He the reason for the natural blush in your cheeks?"

"You don't expect me to answer that. How about you and Stan?"

"I'd take him back in a minute, and he knows it."

"Pretty good trick with him all cop and you a vigilante," I said, seizing the opportunity. "You prepared to quit, CC?"

She took too long to answer, a bad sign. "Guess I'd have to."

We sat down to a Claudia special: spinach lasagna and garlic bread. The Beaujolais nouveau flowed. I told her I was sorry she'd quit school. She told me it was only temporary.

"Sure," I said, "like rent control in New York City."

"What are you here for besides the food and the company?"

"I'm setting up a meet. You, me, Angela and Rosa, Zack. Jamie, maybe. It's time we talked about our options."

"We got any?"

"Only one way to find out. I want you to be there."

"Why not? Just don't make it before Labor Day."

Before the next Mission. Something—a touch of vehemence?—made me ask why.

"In three words? Black crime victims. While we clean out the gutters in the ghetto, New York's sacred cow fills them up again."

"Our Target is Legal Aid?" I said, surprised.

"A Mission to end all Permissives Missions, if I have anything to say about it." She leaned back in her chair. "And I do."

Full circle. I was thinking of the night we'd met. "Smug" had been Claudia's preliminary verdict at a New Year's Eve party. But Stan had taken her behind the scenes and she'd come to see some of the lawyers, the younger ones mostly, as members of a universal fraternity. The Great Defenders, she'd called it. I reminded her.

"So I've changed. My current attitude, in case anyone should ask, is decidedly Shakespearean. Let's kill all the lawyers."

"You could form a club, judging from the op-ed pages."

"Who do you think's responsible? Legal Aid took a big dip in the popularity polls, thanks to us, and they're working their collective butt off to climb back up. We'll finish them off at this Labor Day rally of theirs," she said with a dark satisfaction that was totally out of character. "Wouldn't miss it if I were you."

"What do I do about being recognized by an ex-husband?"

"You'll think of something. More lasagna?"

"Won't you have the same problem?" I asked, remembering.

"Stan's wife? She'll be there, all right."

Venom in her voice. "Black crime victims," I scoffed, "or a personal vendetta? Claudia, this isn't you."

"Don't be silly," she said, voice back to normal. "The lady lawyer is frosting on the cake. More wine?" I held out my glass. "You could be right about this vigilante business," she said, staring into the flame of a candle. "We used to have a lot to talk about besides the crime wave."

"Why don't we start right now?"

We touched glasses in a wordless toast.

Then it was gone: tension, venom, wistfulness. What replaced it was the shared knowledge that some things sailed above life's practical issues, even its dangers, and we were fools to let this or any business make us lose sight of what we meant to each other.

I left, convinced we had already achieved the impossible. We were back in control of our destiny.

By the morning of the rally I wasn't so sure. I wanted to be on hand for what promised to be high drama (I'd gotten Allan to invite me) but had second thoughts about not spending Labor

Day weekend with Max. I started to flip through an old back-grounder. . . .

Question: What is the favorite activity of Legal Aid lawyers? Keeping score. Toting up a "win" each time an overworked judge buys their standard cop-out lingo ("no known criminal record, Your Honor"). Each time a mugger or an armed robber walks.

. . . Each time a juvenile like my daughter's murderer is released in the custody of his mother.

"Too many Legal Aid lawyers," I had written, "develop on-the-job skills, and the greatest of them is called 'rationalization.' Armed with it, they see themselves as defenders of the system." Without it, I thought, they'd turn into insomniacs.

I put the file away. You lose, Max. . . .

By high noon I was heading for a site in Central Park more accustomed to rock concerts than civic-minded rallies—Legal Aid's second mistake. Their first was to hold the rally. Why go on the defensive quite so publicly? Why not take out a series of ads instead, spelling out some of their accomplishments to offset some of the glaring failures?

They had bought themselves a lot of sunshine, at least, and one of those cloudless true-blue skies that make even your confirmed Manhattanite long for a day in the country instead of an afternoon in the park. As the crowd thickened, I felt out of sync: lady in black linen suit and snappy red blouse, headed for an onstage reserved seat. My natural inclination, these days, was to lose myself in anonymity.

Allan waved. He looked like he needed moral support.

What I gave him and his colleagues was polite chatter while I wrestled with a reckless impatience. When someone complained about "the damn crime statistics costing us public support," I allowed myself a mild reproof. "Statistics?" I chided. "Those are people out there getting mugged by your five-time losers."

No comment. A few people looked surprised.

Not Allan. He had heard me sound off more than once since our daughter's murder. "Looks like we have a semi-full house," he observed, staring into the bleachers. About eight hundred people."

With five hundred lawyers and twice as many employees, I figured they'd probably papered the house. But not completely, not with Kagan in the wings. From my corner seat, I took in a deceptive sight: people relaxed in jeans and shorts and bright cotton shirts; a lot of smiling faces turned to the sun. The calm before the storm? This was to be Legal Aid's version of a Rouser, after all. Whatever Kagan had planned, it would be disruptive.

The first few rows had been reserved for Legal Aiders of high standing who preferred the bleachers to the stage. Stan's wife, Jan, her dark eyes snapping enthusiasm and quick intelligence, was among them. I caught her eye and we exchanged nods and smiles.

I hadn't really expected to see Stan—not his kind of show. But there he was, milling around the outskirts. On duty or off?

"Well, what do you know," Allan said when I pointed him out. "Jan never told me."

On duty. Puzzling; an experienced detective relegated to crowd control in Central Park? . . . Or was Stan here in his capacity as head of New York's vigilante-investigating task force?

I shifted my attention to the podium—they hadn't bothered with a dais. "Too formal," Allan had told me. The executive director, who looked like everybody's vision of Santa Claus, had left his center-stage folding chair. He peered for a moment into the crowd while he fingered his beard, then took firm hold of the microphone. Everyone stayed polite all through the obligatory introductions and public acknowledgments. As he launched into a bit of Legal Aid history spiced with self-laudatory statistics—old history to me—I tuned out and searched the crowd for Stan.

I found him. The watcher being watched. I tried not to wonder whether he was here on a guess or a tip. The police have informants, too.

A mellifluous voice demanded attention and got mine as soon as he replaced the director at the mike. Allan was sitting back with a this-ought-to-be-good expression.

And this speaker *was* good—the "opening act" at your typical Legal Aid fund-raiser; I'd watched him sway audiences maybe half a dozen times. Only today wasn't a fund-raiser, exactly, and the man sounded a touch defensive as, mike in hand, he moved his imposing Lincolnesque figure across the stage and swung into a string of or-else exhortations.

"—must rid ourselves of a primitive idea—retribution," he was saying, "or else lose our grip on civilization.

"We must balance toughness with compassion. Or else see that which we hold most sacred—our Bill of Rights—ripped apart piece by piece.

"We must stop balancing the budget on the backs of the poor! Or else see them rise up in rebellion and—"

"Thirty million bucks of our tax money ain't enough for Legal Aid?"

I saw Stan's head snap around—too late. Just an angry voice in the crowd. One of Kagan's?

The speaker ran a hand through dark, shaggy hair. "Or else," he continued calmly, "see the poverty-stricken of this city rise up in terrible rebellion. If we wish to avoid the backlash of increasing crime, ladies and gentlemen, we must come to grips—"

"The poor my ass!" Another voice, another part of the crowd.

And another. "The working-class poor? Don't you bums go using the workers as your excuse."

"They're not the criminals!" someone else yelled.

"Don't lose sight of the Bill of Rights!" the speaker yelled back. "If you're saying that an accused has no rights—"

"What about the rights of the victim, you mealymouthed bastard?" This voice was harsher. The crowd cheered.

The speaker was too experienced not to know when he'd lost his audience. He mock-bowed to it and yielded the floor.

My eyes found Stan again. I saw nods and unobtrusive hand signals that meant "stakeout." How many plainclothes police were out there—and for what? No way Stan's men could identify every heckler. A quick shout, a snarling comment, then shut up fast— like a telephone caller who hangs up too quickly to be traced.

The next speaker up at bat was a syndicated columnist of my acquaintance, a self-proclaimed expert on juvenile delinquency. A woman of strong conviction who'd come all the way from Boston. I expected her to come out swinging.

She came out smiling, looking girlishly young in a full-skirted linen suit as pale a yellow as her hair, which she wore Peter Pan style.

I figured she'd lambaste the hecklers with horror stories about crowded prison cells, homosexual rape, the inefficiency of a court system that deprived the accused of a speedy trial.

Wrong again. She began spoon-feeding a volatile crowd with the usual pap she dished out weekly to a loyal following. Talk about misjudging your audience! Prisons degrade kids, she said to an increasingly restless assembly. Let's not warehouse our children. Let us work together, shoulder to shoulder, to help our "seriously disruptive teens"—to focus our energies on "more positive" solutions to crime. "I vote for fewer working moms!" she said with what I'm sure she thought was infectious enthusiasm. "I vote for less TV violence and more federal subsidies to help our kids—"

In time with her gasp, an apple core struck her cheek and rolled, staining her pale yellow suit.

Allan was chewing his lip. "Here comes Matt to the rescue."

"Matt" unfolded from his chair like a giant accordian and strode to the podium, a majestic figure well over six feet with a shock of white hair and the kind of blunt features that remind you of Mount Rushmore. His huge arms shot out, waving the unruly crowd into silence; I thought of a spreading fir tree.

"Impressive performance," I told Allan. "Who is he?"

"Not one of my favorite people," Allan whispered back.

"You folks got gripes?" the big man thundered like Moses from the mountaintop. "Fine with me. We want to hear them. We hope to answer them. But, by God, we'll do it like reasonable men and women. I'll take one question at a time."

You have to admire a man for throwing down the gauntlet.

Some punk-rocker with half a shaved head picked it up. "I got mugged in the fuckin' park on my way home from a concert. Motherfuckers had on fuckin' Calvin Klein jeans. And gold neck chains," he said, his own collection of chains glinting in the sun.

"What's your question, fella?"

"You turned 'em loose on me, man. That's your job, ain't it?"

A hardhat, sleeves rolled up to reveal muscular arms, was on his feet like an exclamation point. "I read where you people defend seventy, seventy-five percent of this city's criminals and get fifty percent of them off. True or false?"

True-blue VA figures. The guy at the podium rumbled into the microphone, slipping into part explanation, part excuse, as the questioner resumed his seat. Down the same aisle, an old lady rose and waved her cane. She kept waving until the speaker noticed and motioned her forward. The crowd murmured approval.

Points for fair-mindedness, Matt, but a strategic mistake. The audience is with the old lady now, every faltering step of the way. Look how long it's taking her to get where she's going. . . .

She was handed the mike with deference. She gripped it with determination. Her hair was grey and her free hand shook. But not her voice. I listened to her tell an old story. . . .

Easy prey, our senior citizens. And not just to the mugging community. To lawyers who've made an art out of cashing in on vulnerability. Old people who wear glasses and can't remember details make lousy witnesses on cross-examination.

She was too good to be true, this old lady. I was close enough to look for the subtle signs of premature aging. To see a first-class makeup job and a pair of familiar eyes. One of us.

It made me mad; I had wanted her to be real. Victimized old ladies and a sympathetic crowd—this was a genuine constituency. Why did it have to be staged?

The man called Matt was all diplomat as he tried to close Pandora's box by moving the "old lady" out of the spotlight. But another old lady in a yellow print dress had sprung up in her place—a brassy, big-bellied black woman with steel-grey hair. The complaints she was making from fourth row center came gushing out as if she'd been damming them up for years.

"That girl confused me!" she wailed, jabbing an irate finger in the direction of the reserved section. "No way I'm not gonna know who cut me up. I got eyes, don't I? I got the scars! She tripped me up with her fancy words, that young snip of a black girl." The old lady spun around to a collective gasp. "You heard right! One of my own done it to me!"

More than a few Legal Aid lawyers were young black women, but only one of them was prominently featured in the front row. It was a moment of acute embarrassment for Jan.

In the next moment, epithets were zipping like well-aimed arrows toward the stage.

Allan gripped my arm as if he'd been hit. "It's getting out of hand," he mumbled.

But big Matt glowered and waved his arms, and the crowd—it was not yet a mob—settled down to let the verbal sparring match go on. It was going to be all right. The speaker may have played into Kagan's hands, at first, but his approach—an air of no-nonsense bordering on the impatient—was as effective a crowd-control measure as I'd ever seen. Insults and smart retorts petered out in favor of tough questions and thoughtful answers.

I asked Allan why this Matt wasn't one of his favorite people.

"Too volatile," he said as Matt turned the mike over to a colleague, a man with a reasonable face.

He turned out to be an articulate lawyer. He was followed by a succession of articulate lawyers.

Matt sat, arms at his sides, long legs stretched out—but not as relaxed as he seemed. His eyes radiated tension.

A woman in the audience—a striking redhead—stood up. "I was wondering how you people feel after springing a rapist," she said, "or some pervert who goes after kids. Would you comment?"

The question may have been politely asked, but it sounded like a plant to me.

Volatile Matt was up out of his chair like a shot. He seized the microphone like a man who'd exhausted his patience. "You want to know how I sleep nights?" he growled. "Just fine. That's my job, lady. Defend the accused no matter what he—"

A piece of fruit smashed against the podium, then a bottle. A whole series of bottles. There was a mad scramble as curse words gave way to screams and screams competed with the eruption of fistfights and the sound of breaking glass. The bleachers were emptying fast, people clutching each other and rushing off in every direction. The people around me seemed frozen in disbelief.

I tugged at Allan's arm. "We have to get out of here."

. . . I have to find Stan, find out what's happening.

Allan looked at me in a daze. "Back way," he said, pointing.

I left the stage and ran toward the sound of shouted orders.

I found Stan. He was holding a gun and shouting at other men, other guns. Without their weapons, I'd have figured them for part of the crowd. I counted ten of them—no, twelve.

Stan didn't notice me, too busy rounding up hecklers and askers of questions. Smart. Maybe the foulmouthed kid with the half-shaved head and the black lady in yellow print were legit. Maybe the hardhat and the old lady with the cane weren't. He would sort it all out at the station house.

If he got there. A tight little crowd—a mob?—was moving in on him and his men with "barricade" written all over their grim faces. I fell back as a black arm thrust a papier-mâché symbol in the air, as a white arm raised a fist and voices rose in a chant. *Fox, fox, don't let them take the fox. Fox, fox*—

An anonymous voice shouted, "Victims Anonymous!"

The barricade expanded into a large ring—maybe seventy, eighty people.

"Break it up!" Stan was shouting.

His men were shouting, spreading out, using their weapons like cattle prods. Trying to cave a circle in on itself. The hecklers who'd been rounded up moved within the circle like the tail end of a restless herd bumping against the gate.

One of them, the brassy old black lady, edged away from the others—and bolted.

I gasped as the mob made a hole and she dove into it with the agility of a young woman or an athlete. She would have made it if some hardhat hadn't deliberately stuck out his foot to send her sprawling. I wouldn't have given the man a second glance—too intent on the woman—if something about his lean figure and the angle of his neck hadn't jumped out at me as he hurried off. . . .

Kagan?

The black woman was up and running.

But so was Stan. He made a grab for a long yellow sleeve even as I cried out to stop him from bringing her down again—

To stop him from seeing, as her right hand shot out to break her fall, the sensuous entwining of jade and gold on her finger.

". . . Claudia?" he said with soft bewilderment.

She wrenched away like a wild creature tearing at the net and raced through the center of the chanting, touching off chaos.

Fists, screams, bottles and bats. The hecklers following Claudia's desperate burst for freedom by scattering in all directions. A sympathetic crowd merging, blocking, falling back—

Kagan had created a diversion.

A glint of sunlight on metal caught my eye. Mine and Stan's. A man positioned on a boulder just above the rim of the mob. He was slim and fair-haired and he looked like a cattle ranger as he brandished his gun, as he took aim—

Stan and I must have had the same frantic thought.

Claudia, in the line of fire?

Stan shouted. Smashed his way through the mob. I saw him pull her down. Behind me, more shouting, the sound of gunfire—

Chaos.

The bullets fly. Too fast to see. Too deadly. It's easy to shoot. So easy to die.

A detective, aiming for a killer as a killer aimed for him, had spun sideways, his aim spoiled by a bullet in the shoulder.

Stan lay dead from a policeman's bullet in the back.

Claudia had disappeared.

Kagan had won the match without losing a player.

I stopped weeping long enough to do what he'd taught me so well. I vowed revenge.

Chapter 31

"Coffee's cold, doughnuts are warm." Angela offered me one.

I shook my head.

"Try her again," Zack told me.

I dialed the wall phone in Angela's pint-sized office to the din of martial arts. "She's been gone all night," I said, hanging up. "Where can she be?"

"When did you start calling?" Angela asked me.

"When did I stop? I gave up at midnight and took a cab over to wait. She never came home. We've been calling since what?"

"Eight this morning," Zack said. "At least the police aren't looking for her."

The police were looking for a big-bellied old black lady.

"I wish I'd been there." Zack, sounding like a cop.

"Praise be to God you weren't," Angela said. "Stan Cole wasn't tipped off—I found out that much. He went with the odds."

"So did Kagan." Zack crushed a Styrofoam cup, leaking what was left of his coffee onto the table. "Kagan was hoping the cops would show so he could treat them to a slam-bang display of public support for Victims Anonymous. Did Claudia see who tripped her?"

"Not from where I was standing. What if Stan hadn't been killed? Once he'd spotted Claudia's ring . . . she'd have had to disappear," I said, answering my own question. "Kagan used her, damn him! And now she *has* disappeared. What's he done with her?"

"I think she's off somewhere on her own," Angela said. "I think we have to get out."

"No." Zack pushed his chair back. "It's Kagan who has to get out. He and his new pals are psychos. Damn it, Angie, we cut and run now and we throw it all away."

"The body count's starting to climb," I said. "That was a cop out there who was killed."

"Low blow, Karen." He walked over to a window too grimy to see much out of. "Cops like Stan don't grow on trees."

"Cops like Stan?" I said when he didn't turn.

"He was committed. I liked him," Zack said softly. "Under other circumstances . . ."

"We won't just lose friends," Angela told him. "Civilians will die. The violence is bound to get random." She was fingering Joe's shield, her rabbit's foot, in the pocket of her slacks.

"Zack," I said, "I've been doing a lot of thinking ever since my Judge Younger Mission. You know what Victims Anonymous cashes in on? Weakness. People who've turned bitter when the system lets them down. People vulnerable to flattery. Sickos out for kicks. Even the best of us lose our perspective. I used to root for the jury to come down hard on the muggers and rapists I read about—a guilty verdict, a stiff sentence, maybe next time a stiffer one. No more. It's quicker and easier—and much more satisfying—to break some arms and legs. That's not just scary, it's . . . unholy."

Zack came back to the table.

"Damn," Angela said, "I'm out of cigarillos." She made a clean basketball shot with the empty wrapper.

I offered cigarettes all around—solemnly—as if I were passing a peace pipe. Angela grinned. Zack took one with a guilty expression and said, "I have to quit."

"That, too."

"All right," he said, "what makes sense here? Do we pick up our marbles and go home? Does Karen resign from the double-agent business without giving McCann so much as a fare-thee-well and two weeks notice? Do we stand by while VA rolls merrily along?"

"Or do we stick around," Angela said, following his train of thought, "long enough to help McCann bring it down?"

"Do we have a consensus?" I said cautiously.

"Not so fast. You have a meeting coming up," Zack reminded me. "Let's see what's on Kagan's agenda, what he wants you to take back to McCann. Between now and then I'll . . . think about things."

"While you're at it, think about how we get out of this in one piece. Karen, especially," Angela said, eyeing me as if she could already see my head on the block. "Up on your SIS training, kiddo?"

"Are you suggesting I fend off Kagan with a karate chop?"

"Funny. I'm suggesting something more reliable."

"Yeah, I been thinking the same thing," Zack said. "I'll get her an unmarked weapon just to increase the safety margin."

"You cops are all alike," I groused. "Have you got some big gun barrel down at the precinct you can just dip into? Every time I read in the papers—Oh dear God," I said, bringing a chill to the room and memory to Zack's face. . . .

"My 'just-in-case' piece. Don't worry. It's an unmarked gun, courtesy of my ex."

Zack beat me to the phone. He got the super, this time. We counted the minutes, Zack with the receiver against his ear, Angela and I letting the ash grow on our cigarettes. Zack held up his hand and we breathed again because he was smiling.

Claudia had been spotted at the elevators.

We gave her five minutes for three floors. Five more to open Stan's formidable battery of locks and bolts. Zack dialed and handed me the phone. I steeled myself for the change in her voice.

But not for silence.

"Let's go," Zack said—to me, not to Angela. "No point risking Angie being identified in case of trouble," he said.

We went over our cover story in the car . . . just in case. I was the semihysterical friend who'd been trying to reach Claudia since the tragic death of her ex-husband last night. Zack was a cop who happened to be passing by when I ran, screaming, into the street. Zack told me I was admirably calm. I told him that hysteria lay close to the surface.

"Just so you're aware of it," he said.

I was off and running almost before Zack killed the engine, hitting a buzzer seconds after the unlocked door to Claudia's apartment building flew open in my hand. *Claudia, pick up the—*

"She won't answer."

I whirled around just as Zack rushed into the vestibule.

Tony, backed into a corner and looking scared.

He had followed her home on one of Kagan's motorbikes, he told us, just to keep an eye out—his own idea. Kagan had brought her in after the rally.

Tony's eyes were wide. "He chloroformed her, Jamie said."

Jamie had stayed up all night with her. He had been with her all morning.

"She's okay, then." Zack was breathing for all of us. "Jamie would never have let her go if she weren't stable."

"But she won't answer," Tony reminded him.

I held the buzzer down.

"This is no good." Zack was at the vestibule door with a credit card. The door swung open.

I went for the elevator but reversed course. Zack and Tony were already racing up the stairs.

They were waiting for me outside Claudia's door.

I called out to her. I rang her doorbell. I rang it again.

On the third ring, I screamed her name.

Zack cut me off with a look. He made a calming gesture with both hands. "It's Zack, Claudia."

Something in his tone . . . I had heard it before. I had seen it on television. Cops trying to cajole you back to safety. *Don't jump off the ledge, lady. . . .*

"Tony is with me, Claudia. And Karen, of course. Let us in, please. Claudia?"

Footsteps. Then, "Go away!"

Not her voice at all. Not Claudia. Pure anguish.

The look on Zack's face was more frightening than the silence. He was staring at the locks on her door in an agony of frustration. He started at the top and worked his way down, testing, probing, makeshift tools useless in his hands. He went back to the top one.

"Barricade lock," he whispered. "Damn thing is anchored." He waved us back and took out his gun.

Tony covered his ears. I closed my eyes, bracing myself for a loud crack.

I heard a muffled one.

I heard Zack sigh.

"What?" I whispered, eyes flashing open to look for a lock hanging loose, a bullet hole in the door, smoke coming out of the gun hanging loose in Zack's hand—anything. "Claudia?" I said cautiously. "Claudia, please Claudia!"

When we found her, Zack let me go on screaming.

Chapter 32

I took one last look in the mirror. A composed woman stared back. I'd had a week and a half to work on her. A week and a half since Claudia had killed herself.

I left the apartment and got a cab right away. I told the cabbie where to go—an address new to me—and ran through my "emotional checklist."

Pain. Jammed into nerve endings. Carefully hidden behind my dark glasses. But so palpable—like an aura—that it was impossible to hide.

The rage was invisible. Packed away for another day. "Don't let them win," Zack had urged after the first wave of hysteria had subsided and the rage had set in. "Don't let Kagan know we know. Don't let him sense what we're up to. You want to avenge Claudia? Start with this meeting. Stay in control." Put the rage on hold.

Guilt. The hardest to bear.

"This outfit of Kagan's, it's bad news. And you know it."

"Bad news for whom?"

For all of us, CC, but most of all for you. . . .

Fear. None for myself. Guilt has its compensations.

Horror. Receding but not gone. Would it ever be?

A sense of loss. Piercing. A word—a name—not to be pronounced in the next hour—Claudia!—or everything will come undone.

I sat back and concentrated on the hard one, on rage.

The building I entered was what I'd expected: innocuous. A man I didn't know in an office I'd never seen showed me to a room.

Come with me . . . into an interrogation chamber.

It was dark. At the end of a long table was a single chair. I took it. Bright light in my eyes when I took off my dark glasses. Shadows with no faces at the outer edges of the room.

An overhead light snapped on. Kagan stood by the door. I looked around at the others: O'Neal, Bart, Lee—Jamie, in his Blackbeard attire. I said, "What's this supposed to be?"

Kagan stepped forward. "A reminder, in case you've lost the flavor of Christmas Eve. Figured it would be easier for you to reconstruct it for McCann. Jamie's the only one you'll describe."

"Reconstruct what?"

"The exact conditions under which we meet with strangers or unreliables."

I thought he'd sit down with me, but he stepped back with the others. I said, "So which am I?"

"Unreliable," O'Neal said. "The FBI's section chief in criminal investigations is getting impatient. McCann had two months to get results. Time's almost up."

"If Rees doesn't get a bead on our leadership soon, he'll be forced to consider alternative action," Kagan pointed out.

"We've decided to oblige him," Lee said. "Tonight we expand Operation Feeder. You'll be given new information for Mr. McCann, just enough to keep him in the game. But the rules have changed."

They were taking turns just like that first time. "I get the point," I snapped. "I'm not seeing faces, just hearing voices."

But they persisted. Bart's turn . . .

"You'll tell McCann your cover's blown," he said. "If he should ask, you don't know how we got onto you, but we figure you for an FBI stoolie. So instead of a roundtable discussion on PR tactics, we're turning you into a go-between."

"No more double-agent business," Jamie said. "I've come up with a proposal."

He sounded pleased with himself. Kagan's expression was deferential. Jamie, back in favor? *Where did that leave me?*

"The FBI has vastly underrated the size and scope of Victims Anonymous," Jamie said. "You're about to educate them so they have a better idea of just how national our 'national conspiracy' is."

"How?" I asked.

"Using my updated figures," Lee said. "You'll give Mr. McCann hard evidence of VA cell activity all across the country—in small towns, suburbs, and what I call our big-city cells. I've included a very rough approximation of our total membership, as well as the number of people who run things locally. Since the FBI only wants national leaders, we can afford to be vague about it."

"Lee's data will reveal our organizational clout," Jamie said. Once Max knows there are vast numbers out there and that we in New York control them, both he and Rees will realize they have only two options—and one of them is unworkable. Either the FBI stems the tide of vengeance in this country by filling up the county jails, or they do business with us. With the leaders."

"We can pull the plug, nobody else," Kagan said. "Tell McCann we're ready to strike a deal."

Even out of his treacherous mouth, the words touched off hope.

"Our proposal has two parts," Jamie said. "Tell Max—"

I wanted to tell him to stop saying "Max" in this room.

"—and foremost, our people won't cease and desist until our list of demands has been met. Strike that. Our list of proposed reforms. Think Max will agree that our criminal-justice system needs reforming?"

A private joke. He grinned right through his bushy black beard. I remembered what he'd said once about glasses creating a barrier between people. I put my dark glasses on.

He looked as if I had slapped his face. "Second," he said, all business now, "the matter of incentive. No deal without complete immunity for the deal-makers."

I couldn't help myself. I said, "You're crazy."

"It's McCann who's crazy if he doesn't go for it," Bart said with conviction. "He's the one keeps talking about wanting to wrap things up in a hurry."

True, I thought as Lee came forward to hand me a folder.

"The figures," she said. "There's nothing in here that will compromise anyone." Her succinctness was out of character.

"You're a pro, Karen," Kagan said as Lee stepped away. "We appreciate what you're going through."

. . . Don't, Kagan. Don't say her—

"What happened to Claudia was more than a tragedy. It was something none of us can avoid. Our fate."

For the second time in my life, I was grateful for dark glasses. And for not having a gun in my hand.

"Like you, Claudia was a pro. We'll miss her."

I picked up the folder and walked out.

I held onto my stomach, barely making it to the ladies' room.

When I came out, Jamie was waiting by the elevator.

I hadn't seen him since before the rally. Hadn't heard from the bastard even after Claudia . . . died. I'd have brushed past him if I could.

I couldn't because he was crying. We clung to each other.

As we rode down together, he looked at me with a flagellant's eyes. "I misread the signs, God help me," he said. "I let her go too soon. What kind of psychiatrist am I?"

"The only kind there is," I said. "Fallible."

"It was a hellish night," he said. "Claudia was inconsolable. But by morning I saw a surge of defiance—of strength—when I insisted that she stay. I thought it was the strength to go on."

I could see in precise detail what he had misread, Claudia's typical stance: defiantly straight and poised for flight; tough and tender as a young birch. Impossible to know the breaking point . . .

"You did the best you could," I told him.

You never had a chance.

"I misread the signs," he repeated, a man in a trance. "What she revealed to me was a greater strength. So few of us have it." He spoke with slow reflection. "The strength to die."

I entered my apartment pressing hope, in the form of a manila folder—contents unread—to my chest. Max wasn't due for an hour. I sat down to look through Lee's figures, then read Jamie's list of "proposed reforms"—or, more precisely, Kagan's demands.

I saw at once why everyone thought Max would be impressed with us as a national organization. The number of cells had increased tenfold, mostly in the suburbs and the small towns.

Lee's "big-city cells" had only gone up by less than fifty but every one of the existing units had expanded in size.

And I saw what everyone was hoping for: The FBI couldn't begin to nip this thing in the bud, let alone follow Rees's scheme of doing it in a hurry—our cellular structure was much too diffuse and widespread for that—unless they "came to terms" with the leaders in New York.

I turned to Jamie's list. Immunity for the leaders was the first item. I knew Max wouldn't go for it and I doubted that Rees would, either—not *complete* immunity, not for everyone. I scanned the other items and had to stop myself from rolling my eyes. Everything that was wrong with our criminal-justice system was on it, complex problems that were swelling the ranks of Victims Anonymous because even the well-meaning people in law enforcement hadn't been able to solve them. It wasn't that the demands were outlandish. It was the notion that the FBI, even in the person of a sympathetic Max McCann or a Bernard Rees, could meet them.

I picked a proposal at random: eliminate parole. Great idea. A few states already had, and it looked as if more were ready to follow suit. But how was a federal agency supposed to eliminate it en masse? To be realistic, a proposal for reform should match up with a proper remedy—in the case of parole, state-by-state legislation—or else it's doomed from the start.

I picked another. Prosecute violent juveniles as adults. Be nice if more states would follow New York's lead, but not many are that enlightened.

I sighed and went on down the list. They were all pie-in-the-sky as far as getting the FBI to do something about them. Overhaul "the obscene pragmatism of plea bargaining." Clean up the bail situation. Standardize federal sentencing.

Jamie, Jamie, so what if Max has genuine compassion for the crime victim. So what if he thinks parole boards like to play God at the public's expense. What can he do about it?

I tossed the list aside and went to make coffee.

When Max arrived, I handed the list over without a word and followed him into my den, giving him ten minutes.

He took five.

"You've read it?" I nodded. "This list of theirs—their de-mands," he said, calling them by their rightful name, "Karen, they can't be serious about getting an answer to this nonsense in a week. Can they? Unless we're dealing with a pack of fools." He pondered the possibility. "It's not how I read them."

I knew what he was thinking: It's not how Jamie had described them. . . .

"I need time," Max said, reaching for his coffee. "If you can convince them that I'm open to a deal, I'll put this package"— smart slap to the folder—"through our computers in Washington. With these new details . . ."

Smart slap to my heart. The National Crime Information Center joins the fray.

I listened to Max rummage through Lee's updated figures and some details about our cellular structure, his voice low and slow, like a man sifting through gold dust. . . .

"This stuff spells widespread cell activity, all right. And big-city strength. Won't Bernie be surprised by the extent of it?"

"I'll leave you alone so you can call him," I said, noting that Jamie's formidable list of "proposed reforms" lay, forgotten, on the arm of his chair.

I left him alone so I could think. How could Jamie and the others have thought Max would go for any part of their so-called reforms? How could Jamie go from being such a perceptive person to a man detached from reality?

He could if he saw himself as Dr. Frankenstein. This was his chance—his only hope—to destroy the monster.

Kagan's lapse of judgment was something else again. "We're ready to strike a deal," he'd told me, sounding like he meant it. What was I missing? I could almost hear a voice saying, It's not as farfetched as it sounds. The FBI can back us up—give our reform measures real public support by pushing for appropriate legislation that would bind the states. But that was Jamie's voice of rationalization I was hearing, not Kagan's.

I thought about Max McCann, pushing for a federal solution to local crime. Hadn't I laid that one to rest a long time ago, right down to a verbatim quote? *They won't be happy until they've turned the FBI into a national police force.* Kagan would remember. Kagan was nobody's fool.

So who was he trying to make a fool out of now?

It came to me, the idea of shooting down before you get shot. I waited for Max to call me into the den. He would be eager for me to describe the meeting. In detail.

Max came out and headed for the kitchen to make fresh coffee. "Ready to re-create the scene of the crime?" he said lightly.

"Ready, willing and able," I said, matching his tone. "But I think you'll be disappointed by what they didn't let me see."

After I set it up for him the way Kagan wanted me to, Max said, as I knew he would, "We have to keep them talking, convince them we're open to some sort of deal."

I came right back with "People convince more easily if you tell them what they want to hear, Max."

He got the point even before I had finished making it: how they'd expect the bargaining to take a certain turn. . . .

Kagan had set the timetable: One week from tonight, I was to report back on which of VA's proposals Max and his boss were considering, along with a couple of counterproposals. All that remained was to settle on the approach.

And to wait for Max to press me again for more "details" on the people I had heard but not seen. To savor the moment when, picturing Kagan's probing glance and knowing smile, I sent him a silent message: *Meet Karen Newman, triple agent, you bastard.*

Max pressed, of course.

"I have an idea," I said, and went to unlock my desk drawer, only to remember that I'd transferred my sketch pad to the wall safe where Kemp & Carusone projects were now sharing space with my various endeavors for Victims Anonymous. I retrieved the pad and went to work.

"I'm no artist," I told him, sketching away, "but I do a fair imitation of a caricature when the mood is right. It wasn't as dark in that so-called interrogation chamber as they thought."

I started with my sketch of Kagan. "Not much to go by," I apologized, handing it to him. "The angle of the neck rings true, I think. The chauffeur at my daughter's funeral?"

"Could be," he said, studying it while I went on sketching.

"This bozo," I said as Max leaned over me to look at the more detailed sketch of Bart, "had the bad judgment to hit the men's room just as I was leaving the women's."

"Might be an innocent bystander," Max said.

"In case he's not, he was wearing a friendship ring," I said, and described the one Lee had given him.

I told Max I'd caught a fleeting glimpse of "a very distinctive battering-ram shape." And turned in O'Neal.

Not Lee, though. Not Jamie.

I tossed the sketch pad aside, feeling good.

Max pushed my coffee mug away and gave me the pad back. "Do one of the guy you saw, for a moment, in a spotlight," he urged.

I took back my mug.

"Go ahead. While the image is still fresh. Blackbeard, you called him?"

"Why bother?" I stalled. "It was such an obvious disguise."

"Maybe it was a lousy disguise. Give it a try."

"One black beard," I said, making it come out neat. Jamie's had been thick and bushy. "Black hair . . ." I said, making it sleek and straight, ". . . and blue eyes." I drew buttons within buttons and filled in the irises with blue ink.

Max studied all four sketches before stowing them, carefully, in his briefcase. "It's a start," he said, looking as if he wished I could do four more.

Not four, I thought. One. "Open your briefcase, Max. I forgot about the guy who handed me the folder," I said. "It was only a split second, but I got a sense of the bastard's shape and the way he moved. Wait." *Just you wait . . .*

A full figure, like O'Neal, only this one stood poised in space (this one had stood on a boulder), one hand brandishing a manila folder instead of a gun. I worked at it. Crumpled it up. Started over. Got it right in the end.

Max stared. "Looks like a rodeo star," he said.

. . . Looks like Kagan's protégé.

"Hey, watch it, cat!"

Pola had landed on the sketch. She was sniffing it with a touch of disdain.

"Apologies are in order, Pola," Max said, grinning, as he eased the sketch out from under her. "I know the difference between a name and a species—Uh oh, apology not accepted," he said as Pola jumped down and started dashing in and out of corners—she has a real sense of drama. Her brother Marco launched into his repertoire of late-night yodeling.

Nothing eases tension better than tuning in to a cat.

"Time for a drink." Max led the way to the living-room bar and poured me a brandy. "To be followed," he said, "by one of your hot baths—bubbles, perfume, the works. I'll run the water."

I made a frown. "Don't get domestic on me, Max. I don't think I could bear it."

"Can you bear to lie in my arms for what's left of the night?"

. . . Without wishing it would last forever? I don't think so, Max darling, I don't—

He took my untasted drink away.

I led him into the bedroom.

I loved him with a ferocity that rocked us both.

Chapter 33

Max played mock interrogator while I worked at my lines and smoked too many cigarettes (I was supposed to be nervous). I kept asking what he was worried about. Either the vigilantes bought it or they didn't.

"I must be crazy letting you go off tonight without a backup."

He picked Pola up. I watched him stroke away his own nervousness.

"Rees is right," I said. "You can't afford to risk severing the lines of communication with these people. They're too good at picking up tails."

"Sorry, baby," he said as Pola decided she'd had enough of him and darted from his lap, heading for her favorite spot: the windowsill. "Helluva place to do your toilette." He frowned as she slipped into a languorous stretch, one grey-orange leg extended for grooming. "She really safe up there?" he asked me.

"You really *are* in a worrying mood."

"You're not?"

"Tonight's showdown bothers me less than stopping off, first, at Claudia's place. She'd jammed so much color and life into three and a half rooms, you forgot how small it was. Seeing it empty . . . It feels claustrophobic. Too many ghosts," I whispered.

He reached for my hand. "Must you go there?"

. . . Kagan says I must. *"Let McCann know where the pickup is—outside Claudia's place is as good as any. Use some excuse for going there first. If he double-crosses us, we'll spot the tail."*

"Just one last time," I told him. "That sketch of Claudia the cousin promised me—it's my favorite."

"Not one of yours, you said?"

"I'm not that good. Some offbeat friend of hers managed the impossible in a caricature. Grace, not distortion, is the theme. Those cheekbones," I said, remembering. "That face, growing out of a tiger lily . . ."

And that was how we said good-bye; Max kissing away my tears.

The sketch may have been an excuse, but Claudia's cousin Karla really was waiting to hand it over. I slipped it into my briefcase, wondering if I'd ever be able to look at it without crying.

I stood, dry-eyed and depressed, in front of Claudia's brownstone, vowing never to set foot in the building, the street—

A car pulled up. The two men inside were strangers, but they said the magic words. I got in.

I was taken for a ride, blindfold and all. Security, again. Wherever we were going, I figured it took us roughly forty minutes to get there, and another five to walk me inside.

They took the blindfold off and left.

I was in a two-room cottage, a real charmer in tasteful French Provincial. I wondered if the view was charming, too. No way to tell with the windows boarded up. I took inventory. Plenty of logs for a ceramic tile fireplace. Soap and guest towels in the bathroom.

Tiny kitchen but with a well-stocked pantry. Plenty of my favorite brand of mineral water in the fridge.

My brand of cigarettes on the living-room coffee table?

What the hell was going on?

I had just noticed the absence of a telephone when the only door in the place opened. Enter Kagan, O'Neal, and Bart. Not a friend in court.

"Like it?" Kagan asked me with an expansive gesture. "Our hideaway away from home. On loan from a fellow traveler."

"We use it when security is top priority," Bart explained, as if that explained anything.

O'Neal pulled out a cigar and then put it back in his pocket.

Kagan gestured me to a chair. "Well? Did McCann go for it?"

"Any part of it, you mean?"

I laid it all out: Max's and my compromise, hoping they'd believe it was real. Bart looked confused, O'Neal skeptical.

Kagan was typically inscrutable.

He leaned forward. "McCann is willing to go this far?"

I shrugged. "He seemed eager to 'strike a deal.'"

"He's faking. His type doesn't deal, he stalls. McCann's all wrong for this. Wrong man, wrong FBI faction. I tried to tell Jamie but he insisted we give McCann a shot."

"Why didn't Max level with me?" I said, pretending annoyance.

"So you'd be more persuasive with us."

I tried to look like I believed him.

"McCann's usefulness is over." Kagan's words had an ominous ring. "He has to be discredited with his own people."

"That way, we knock the ball into another court," Bart said.

O'Neal pulled out his fat Havana. "We'll find us some feds who'll go for our national-offensive-against-crime pitch. Get the picture?" He stuck the cigar in his mouth. He didn't light up.

Why not? My aversion to his cigar smoke had never stopped him before. I reached for the cigarettes on the table, letting them see how calm I was as I lit one and blew smoke in their direction.

"I thought we wanted Max McCann as a way of stopping his publicity-hungry colleagues from putting out a dragnet?" I said in a tone so reasonable even Kagan wouldn't sense my rising panic. I was remembering what Bernard Rees had told me about "certain factions" in the Bureau and what they were after. . . .

"If we bring down this Victims Anonymous with a series of big splashes, it could spawn that national police force we have every reason to be afraid of."

When Kagan didn't answer, I said, "What if the feds you have in mind won't follow Max's scenario? He and his boss have said all along that they wanted to stop Victims Anonymous by stopping the leaders, not the little guy running a five-man cell from Peoria."

Kagan saw through my facade. "What are you afraid of, Karen?"

I answered with part of the truth. "That some new faction won't stop with—with us. That they'll drag things out for their own personal glory and go after everyone in sight."

"Not if they're willing to deal. Unlike McCann, the idea of a federal solution might appeal to them."

"Max won't give up," I said. "If he gets pulled off the case, he'll continue on his own."

"M. McCann, the company man, who suffers through lousy assignments in loyal silence like a good boy eating his spinach? I don't think so. No, what I see," Kagan said, "is one over-the-hill agent who lets his snitch get bagged."

"He'll look like a schmuck," O'Neal said through the cigar in his teeth.

"In other words," Bart said with a grin, "you get kidnapped."

"Forget it," I said, getting up fast.

"Sit down," Kagan ordered.

"How long would I be here?" I stalled, not sitting.

"Couple of weeks at the outside. Don't force the issue," he warned as my eyes roamed to the door. "All the comforts of home," he said with a last look around. "We'll keep you informed."

By the time I'd found something to throw, the three of them were gone, the cigarette box cracking open on the thick-paneled oak of a door closing in my face.

Closing and locking.

I sat on the carpet cursing my dimwittedness and putting cigarettes back into the broken bottom of a box. O'Neal's unlit Havana should have tipped me off. The bastard must have been forewarned not to foul my new living quarters with cigar smoke.

A flame shot up, hissing. Died. No contest against wet wood. Just my luck to pull five days of rain out of six on my mock vacation. At least it took the sting out of being locked indoors. I looked around at what I'd dubbed my "enforced coziness." One more day of staring at cornices and a ceiling that looked like a giant upside-down tray and I'd burn the place down. I glared at the built-in bookshelves that lined the octagonal room; as well stocked as the pantry. Words on a printed page. Try concentrating when all there is to do is read. And think.

About crime victims. Decent people. A lot of them seething,

these days, with a survivor's inner rage and the sense of being betrayed by their "civilized" society. I knew the feeling.

About solutions to insoluble problems. I felt stranded between Max's "I don't have the answers" and "Neither do they."

About my conviction, now, that giving in to the rage was primitive.

Most of all, about division of labor. It really is civilized. Policemen with discipline and skill—professionals—the best of them restrained by the rule of law.

But when the professionals can't cope, when a cop is hamstrung by the wrong rules and regulations and a dedicated FBI agent admits he doesn't have the answers, what does the victim do with his rage? Drive it inward and self-destruct? Turn it over to vigilantes? Join a convent? What are the options? Eleven months ago, what were mine?

Support groups, I thought. The how-to-cope clinics. Cope with what, the trauma? An insensitive cop? Help pay the medical bills or the cost of a new lock on your front door? But if you got lucky—if there was a trial in your future—what you could expect from a support group's emergency hotline would be one piece of sound advice: "Don't expect too much in court."

God forbid you should expect justice.

Join your neighborhood watch group? Go on patrol, armed with a walkie-talkie? Not much of an outlet for widows and rape victims.

Protest groups? They tended to fade in and out of the boldest headlines, the latest murder in the park.

Networking. I'd read about a senior citizens group that regularly monitored the courts. About private crime commissions in big cities that compiled statistics and recommended more cops on the beat. Good as far as it went, but local. Hit-and-miss.

Not like Victims Anonymous. We were big, national in scope. An organization run by thinkers and planners. We were organized. I hadn't grasped the principle, Jamie told me.

I grasped it now.

The door opened, catching me off guard. I hadn't heard a car. Tony came in, looking glad to see me. Twice in the past six days he'd been admitted into my cottage-prison. Kagan's messenger boy. My sole contact with the outside world.

"They treating you right?" he asked.

"Got everything but fresh air and freedom."

"Need anything? Kagan wants to know."

"Your visits," I said—lightly, so he wouldn't know how much I meant it. "But don't tell Kagan."

Big grin. "Yeah. He'd stop sending me."

He loved talking about it: how he would "bad-mouth" me every chance he got; how Jamie, the house shrink, always backed him, saying Tony had a "problem" with me because of his sister, Maria. I smiled. That Tony could put even this much of his conflict into words told me he'd stopped blaming me and, more important, himself.

"You going to ask me about your FBI man?"

"I've been afraid to."

"Nobody told him about any kidnapping. Jamie wants to, but he can't. Jamie says he thinks you're dead."

"Damn you, Kagan!" I had to turn away. "I'd rather Max know the truth, damn it! I've got to get out of here—"

"I'll get you out, Karen."

I'll protect you, he was saying. I blinked back tears.

"I will," he promised. "I'll think of something."

"Sure," I said, letting him see I was all right again. "Any other news from the front?"

"I heard something about a Mission. They're getting ready to go after some judge."

They, not we. Hallelujah. "Who is Kagan out to reeducate?"

Small shrug. "Didn't hear the name. It's not what you think," he said, voice tinged with awe. "They're gonna kill him."

Two words jumped out: felony murder. Angela, telling me how you don't have to pull the trigger to be part of the conspiracy.

I cross-examined him like a trial lawyer, looking for signs of a thirteen-year-old's imagination and love of melodrama, a hint of unreliability in his usually reliable eavesdropping.

He stuck to his story. A Mission to kill a federal judge had been in the planning stages for at least a week.

I looked at four-feet-ten-inches of stubborn determination in patched denims and a jacket one size too large and felt like an enlistment officer sending a child off to war. I talked to him.

Eyes solemn, he repeated his assignment: Get the name of the Target. Nail down the Mission: date, time, place.

After he left, I filled the silence with the innocuous chatter of television, voices drifting in and out of my consciousness. I barely tasted a listlessly prepared meal. Half-listened as a popular talk show wound down the hour with the usual cheerfully brisk announcement of tomorrow's guest lineup.

I went to bed missing more than the comfort of Max's arms. Just as Angela was never without Joe's shield, I always carried the memory-scent of my Sarah: her perfume. It had faded by the end of the first day here, one more outrage of my confinement. Now the night table mocked me with its ashtray and its unread magazine. I missed my photograph. I went to sleep and dreamed of Sarah—but not with Susie clasped in her arms; with Tony.

I didn't come fully awake until I was en route to the kitchen to make breakfast. My morning paper lay by the door.

Suddenly I was on the floor flipping pages, then scanning television listings.

A list of scheduled guests for "Dan Brudnik's Headliners" read like a Who's Who in criminal-justice circles. Our outspoken DA from the Bronx. The head of a prestigious, privately funded fact-finding commission. An American Civil Liberties lawyer. National headliner Judge Kevin Reilly. Live at eight.

Reilly.

I turned back to the entertainment section. Stared at a candid shot. A man out of central casting. The thick white hair that strikes envy in the heart of middle-aged males. The puckish smile that slips easily into an off-color joke or a sly invitation to "meet me at the corner pub for a beer in, say, fifteen minutes?"

The copy under the photo wasn't as entertaining. Judge Kevin Reilly had a reputation for flexing his judicial muscles in the federal district court where he was king. The bigger the clamor set off by his questionable—some said outrageous—edicts, the better he liked it. A month ago he had heroically—some said sanctimoniously—"struck a blow for overcrowded jails" by ordering a mass release of hundreds of felons awaiting trial in New York City. The reporter gave estimates on the ones who'd already jumped bail or been rearrested for new crimes of violence.

The last two lines read like a death sentence. "Since early last week, pickets have been protesting Judge Reilly's scheduled network appearance. More are expected tonight."

The last two lines sent me flying to my boarded-up windows, as if I hadn't gotten enough splinters going over every inch of them. I didn't bother with another pantry search; Kagan hadn't left me so much as a sharp knife.

That left pacing and three cups of black coffee while I filled in the blanks of Tony's assignment. Name of Target: Judge Kevin Reilly. Date: September the fifteenth. Time: eight o'clock. (Tonight!) Place: an office building, home of a television studio in midtown West Side Manhattan.

I heard the car, this time, but knew that it couldn't be Tony. Not two days in a row. It wasn't necessarily for me, either.

The outside bolt slid back and Tony came in.

With Rosa? Rosa, who bounced through life like a windup toy. Walking, now, with a cleaning lady's tired shuffle, an apologetic don't-pay-me-no-mind slope to her narrow shoulders. She wore a baggy, threadbare coat, dark glasses, and a scarf. "Babushka style," she was fond of calling it.

We waited until the door closed before we flew at each other, Tony looking faintly disgusted at this display of female silliness.

"I told the guy outside you were complaining yesterday," he said. "I told him Kagan sent me back with a cleaning lady."

"Ingenious," I said, meaning it.

Rosa and I measured each other in silence. Like me, she was short, dark-haired and small-boned. Also heavier and big-busted, but nothing the coat wouldn't hide. I was thinking our skin tones would present a problem when she pulled out a bottle of tanning lotion. I laughed, delighted with the irony.

You could be Puerto Rican. Yes indeed, Kagan. . . .

"Target," Tony said, "Judge—"

"Kevin Reilly, I know. Tonight. We don't have much time."

"How 'bout this lady, Antonio? She knows the answers almost before she asks the questions. Karen," Rosa said, the good humor draining from her face, "I thought I hated this judge. But what they're planning puts us one rung lower in hell than him. I don't want to be part of killing the man. You got to *do* something!"

I knew what I had to do. What I had to become. In World War II, they were called kamikaze pilots. I said, "Max McCann—"

"Knows something's up," Rosa said. "He's been alerted."

"Diverted," Tony corrected her. "He's expecting 'big trouble' tonight—outside the Brooklyn House of Detention."

"Not in midtown Manhattan," I said, dumping the contents of my purse, reaching for Rosa's. "Kagan thinks of everything."

Rosa shed her baggy coat and went poking around in the closet. She emerged with a vacuum cleaner. "Got to keep up appearances," she said with a nod at the door, and turned it on.

The noise clung to my nerve endings as I spread tanning lotion with nervous fingers. As I buttoned Rosa's coat over my too-bulky sweater. Tony moved through the octagonal room snapping pictures.

"What's the point?" I asked him.

"You'll see. I told the guy outside Kagan wanted photographs."

The guy outside wouldn't win any prizes for inquisitiveness. Our luck was turning. We'd need it all, I thought: luck, good timing, cool heads.

Zero hour. We held a whispered consultation. Tony knocked on the door—yelled—took a step back.

When the outside man stuck his head in, a flashbulb went off in his face. Momentary blindness, while Tony mumbled an apology and a "cleaning lady" shuffled out the door. From the kitchen, a new complaint issued forth over the sound of the five o'clock news: "Tell that bastard Kagan if I'm not out of here in two days, I want a cook as well as a cleaning lady! You hear me, Tony?"

A cab would pick us up outside the gate in a few minutes, Tony told a male figure—faceless as far as I was concerned; I kept my own face averted.

"Outside the gate" meant walking at a reasonable pace down a steep hill bordered by trees that were just starting to turn color. Prison grounds I'd had no chance to see, and no time, now, to admire.

"Nearest phone's ten minutes away by bike," Tony announced, parting some bushes.

I stared, openmouthed, at a couple of motorbikes.

"But I heard a car before!" I protested.

A cab that had happened by empty, Tony told me, as he and Rosa were concealing the bikes. Ten bucks will take you a short way (like up a steep hill) if that's your pleasure.

Motorbikes. We were forty minutes from civilization.

"We have to get back before Kagan misses them from the bike pool," Tony said. "Do you ride? It's not hard. Ask Rosa."

Rosa, favorably disposed by her son's passion for bicycles, had caught on fast. To me, motorbikes were old hat. "Bermuda vacations," I told him so he shouldn't be too impressed.

End-of-the-day Westchester traffic heading for points south cost us an extra ten minutes, so it was five-thirty by the time we got to a phone. I rang Max's Manhattan office. He wasn't there. He wasn't in his hotel room, either. I shook my head at Tony, who watched from the light and warmth of an adjacent booth.

I dialed again and got Jamie at home.

I gave myself five minutes to bring him up to date (five and a half; he was in shock). Three to hear what was happening on his end. One to plan future strategy, which consisted of: We'll catch up with each other outside the TV station. When? Before eight.

Jamie took fifteen seconds vowing to find Max and head off another wild-goose chase to Brooklyn. I took two more to wish him Godspeed.

Tony waved me over to his booth. He was dialing. "You the FBI man?" I heard him say, and, wordlessly, he slipped something into a numb appendage doubling as my hand.

It didn't stay numb. The phone shook as I brought it up to my mouth. ". . . Max?"

Have you ever heard silence? There's one kind that I don't recommend. Once you hear it, you never want to hear it again.

"Max," I said again, "I'm all right. Dearest, I'm not hurt. But someone else is about to be. Listen. Listen to me, please."

"Oh God, Karen."

After that he listened. The next time I heard his voice, the professional was back.

Then it was my turn to listen. With gratitude. Events were taken out of an amateur's hands.

"Figured he'd be at your place," Tony said when I hung up.

I hugged him.

We returned to our motorbikes, neither of us looking forward to the long ride home.

"It'll take hours," Tony grumbled. "We'll miss the action."

He could afford to miss it. I couldn't.

An alternative bore down on us: a flatbed truck. Room for us, plenty of room for the motorbikes.

"Wave," Tony urged. "Pull up your skirt!"

He looked sheepish as I displayed a corduroy-trousered leg.

The truck stopped anyway.

Chapter 34

It was seven o'clock when I let myself into the apartment. Max would be long gone. Tony would have returned the motorbikes. And kept his promise by going straight home from there? Sure he would. Like I'd keep mine to Max.

My bedroom door was rattling off its hinges. That would be Marco. Pola's protest took the more delicate form of chicken-scratches. With a release-the-prisoners flourish, I opened the door and almost cried to see them race out full of pent-up energy and looking none the worse for Max's devoted care and feeding. "Ten minutes for the run of the house," I warned them.

Ten minutes to get my house in order. To empty my safe of incriminating papers and emergency cash. To fill a hefty shoulder bag with essentials. To catch the cats and put them back.

I went out the door in tight jeans, pea jacket, dark glasses, and navy watch cap. Add Rosa's tanning lotion and all that was missing from an old nightmare, I thought ruefully, was chewing gum and a "ghetto blaster."

I hit the street and got lucky: a cabdriver who tackled the traffic like an inspired Grand Prix contender. I arrived early.

Only a handful of pickets? They paraded back and forth in the disorganized fashion of a New York labor dispute that's gone on too long. The object of their attention, a ten-story office building, was as far west as you could go in Manhattan without falling into the Hudson River. Behind revolving glass doors, a bored-looking guard presided over his round glass booth, the better to direct in-house traffic (not much at this hour). I took in the neighborhood.

It was mixed. A cluster of automobile dealerships, deserted now. Office skyscrapers competing with small brick buildings, their ground floors given over to a cleaning establishment, a bar, a coffee shop. Construction everywhere, promising an edge in the distant future to the skyscrapers but filling the present with the usual dust and debris. Adding drama to a darkening sky: eerie silhouettes of naked beams and cranes and what I've always called, for want of a better name, "those steel ball-and-chain affairs."

I looked around for a friendly face. A recognizable enemy. A sign of foul play. Kagan moved in mysterious ways but, so far, he was invisible. The only thing that beckoned was your friendly neighborhood bar. On closer examination it proved old and full of character. It was on the main drag: a wide avenue bordering the river. It was where Jamie would think to look for me.

The bar crowd was watching television. A couple of big guys with shoulders that made you think "longshoreman" made room for me with more surprise than discourtesy, then forgot me. I ordered a beer and had to stop myself from exploring the woodwork, a mahogany bar so lovingly carved it demanded to be touched.

Two things made me look up: a noticeable dip in barroom banter and the familiar theme music of "Dan Brudnik's Headliners."

Dan Brudnik, whose blond crew cut was as dated as his trademark bow ties, and whose sardonic smile said he took pride in the title of "gadfly." Not for him the seamless delivery of the broadcast superstar; Brudnik served up controversy, red-hot and abrasive. Starting with his format. A brief intro all around. Camera lingering on the guest star of the evening—on Judge Kevin Reilly. A quick snap of a question to set the theme and tone of the show.

"Prisoners' rights versus the public's right to be safe. Isn't that what your 'outrageous' court order is all about, Judge?"

"It's about an outrage called prison overcrowding."

Brudnik's camera strayed from the judge's bland expression to the flushed face of the Bronx DA.

"What about the outrage being perpetrated on innocent—"

"Innocent my foot," the ACLU lawyer cut in, adjusting his glasses; interruptions were encouraged on Dan Brudnik's show.

"We're talking gross constitutional violations here," he said, thin mouth twisting. "We're talking about the humane act of a judge releasing—"

"Hard-core criminals," said the silver-haired spokesman for the fact-finding crime commission, his razor-thin smile aimed first at the lawyer and then at the judge. "If I have my facts straight, Norman—and I do—most of these 'solid citizens' didn't take a deep breath of free air before committing some new crime."

The bar crowd applauded, drowning out the opposition. So did Brudnik's studio audience. The noise subsided.

"Hard-core, Tom?" Brudnik said. "I hear talk about a lot of welfare cheats being turned loose, petty thieves, people of that ilk. . . ."

"What about the felons with conviction records as long as Judge Reilly's arm?" the DA said hotly. "The public has a right—"

"Not to inflict cruel and unusual punishment on its prison population!" snapped Reilly, anger reddening his already ruddy complexion.

The crowd reacted with bottle-smashing rage.

I was spun around on my barstool.

"You shouldn't be here, love," Jamie chided, leading me out. "This bar is one of Kagan's powder kegs."

"We never said where we'd meet. I figured you'd find me here. Why the costume?" I asked. He was dashing in his black buccaneer mode, complete with bushy beard and blue contact lenses.

"Good question," he said, but didn't bother to answer it.

"Where's the action? That picket line looks anemic."

There were more of them now—men in windbreakers, women in thick sweaters and jeans—still parading in front of the brightly lit building entrance, still moving with a trace of lethargy. That would change, I thought, when Brudnik's show broke—I checked my watch—in three-quarters of an hour. At the moment, the only lively thing about them were their IMPEACH JUDGE REILLY! signs.

"The 'action' is on the way," Jamie said, indicating the river. "Boat trip around Manhattan, sponsored by the Victims Rehabilitation League—remember them from Christmas Eve? They'll be making an unscheduled stop. See that pier?"

"They're joining the picket line?"

"With their friends, their relatives, anybody they can get to join the fray. Look for Passives and Actives on this one. Kagan wanted big numbers. Our New York City cells—ten at last count—will be out in force. The fun begins when Brudnik's ends. Look!"

A dark structure loomed, heading into shore. It was crisscrossed with lights; a contradictory omen.

"What do all these people think—that they're here just to protest Judge Reilly's mass-release order?" I said, frowning.

"Exactly. They have no inkling of Kagan's real intention."

"Assassination," I said, still not able to make it real.

"Kagan fed me the same story. Our purpose is to create the impression of a spontaneous uprising, with nary a fox symbol in sight. Judge Reilly was targeted so we could tap into his national television coverage. It makes sense," he mused, looking out over the river. "A big turnout. Crowds objecting to a bunch of felons being released in the middle of a crime wave. With VA keeping a low profile, tonight's well-orchestrated anger will be seen as a People's Protest—a call to arms for reform legislation."

"For national solutions. Grist for the anti-Max FBI faction," I said gloomily.

"What puzzles me," Jamie said, arms outspread as he examined himself, "is why Kagan insisted on disguise. Lee and I are both card-carrying members of the Victims Rehab League. Yet she's to address them as her own sweet self while I . . ."

"Come to the party as a buccaneer. Maybe Kagan doesn't want Dr. James Coyne anywhere near an assassination attempt?"

"What about Lee? We'll *both* be center stage."

"Maybe Lee is . . . expendable? I'm thinking about her exposure on those out-of-town Missions, especially Atlanta. Kagan's attitude was too damn—"

"Cavalier," Jamie said, looking troubled.

"Now that we've warned Max off Brooklyn," I said, frowning with worry, "he'll be here, seeing to the protection of a federal judge. What if he spots Lee and makes a connection to the 'mysterious blonde' he's heard about? What if he connects her to *you?* I had to draw him a picture, for God's sake—Blackbeard, the dashing vigilante! If I were you, I wouldn't set foot on the same stage with Lee."

I might have been talking to the moon. Jamie just smiled, pulling at his fake beard. "The big question," he said, "is what Kagan is really after. This People's Protest of his is a smart way to cash in on some national publicity. Why take out the judge?"

"The boat's pulling in," I said. I dug in my purse. "I brought you some papers—incriminating stuff. Mind stashing them with your tapes?"

"I've destroyed them. Give Tony your secrets, love. He's holding some of mine." He threw his head back and laughed. "Will you look at this magnificent sky?" he said, grabbing my hand. "To see the moon and the stars in Manhattan! To smell a river in the dark!"

"Let the night be magnificent, Jamie. You be careful."

"Wonderful, witty and wise." He was looking at me, now. "I knew that about you from the beginning. I knew so much . . . and so little. Do you know that I love you?" he said with quiet pride. "That much I've managed to achieve. Don't worry," he said quickly to the tears in my eyes, "the only role I want is guardian angel. Yours," he said, touching my face, "and Max's."

I lost sight of him in a mad vortex of bodies. People pushed past and around me, practically through me. Angular patches of white filled the air: anti–Judge Reilly picket signs, held high. Behind me a door flew open; a bar emptied. The wide avenue filled up with a rush. I looked at the river running parallel to it. Moonlight glinted off the water. And off metal: the hardhats in the crowd. A slow wind tugged at overhead clouds, teasing them into sensuous shapes. Like Jamie said, a magnificent sky.

A good omen? So it would seem. The mob, settling down. A hot-dog cart, open for business. Good crowd control . . . to keep the police off base? They came on horseback: two helmeted boys in blue, youthful and fit, riding with the easy confidence of men who don't expect trouble but can handle it if it comes. I smiled to see them living Max's childhood dream.

I abandoned them for the men and women still massing on the avenue. They'd begun to march, people with angry signs and protest banners: MUGGERS AND MURDERERS BELONG BEHIND BARS— DON'T TURN OUR STREETS INTO BATTLE ZONES—LET'S JAIL ALL THE JUDGES!

The marchers walked ten abreast past tall buildings and gaps between buildings that were construction sites, moving inexorably toward the entrance of the building that housed the television station. I fell into step.

And got caught up in a vortex of SOUND—MOTION— MILITANCY. It reached out and pulled me inside—made me part of a strength of purpose infinitely more powerful than my own! I saw strangers who seemed familiar, familiar faces that blended into one another.

I caught sight of a friend. From this distance and out of uniform, he was barely recognizable. *Look beyond the anger of the marchers. Can you sense the hope? Do you see what I see, Zack? The opposite of a lynch mob. We don't have to give it up—not all of it. I've thought of a way. . . .*

We halted before a wooden platform in front of an open construction pit, adjacent to the targeted building. I cut around a tight concentration of bodies to move back for a longer view. A couple of portable floodlights appeared. A microphone.

And Lee, being helped onto the platform. Lee, in a white leather trench coat, her burgundy scarf caught in the wind, her hair a golden halo under the coveted spotlight. *A real showstopper, Lee. You're a damn fool, Lee. . . .*

The black woman who joined her was holding on to a sign, but I couldn't read the words. Lee turned, distracted. Looking for her cospeaker? She would be on first. She had probably arranged it; Jamie was a hard act to follow.

People pushed closer—an orderly crowd. Couple of hundred strong, now. They were staying clear of the front of the building, a stone's throw from the platform to its right. One of the cops urged his horse to the left of the entrance; good visibility of the scene but practically on top of whoever would be coming out of the building. His partner, looking much too complacent, was closer to me, hugging the rim of the crowd; good visibility of the platform. TV coverage had arrived in the form of a three-man crew: cameraman, reporter and a guy fooling with lights he'd never need—not when Kagan had anticipated the occasion with floodlights.

Lee took the mike and introduced herself in dulcet tones. She introduced the black woman—"a victim like so many of you," she said to an audience straining to hear every word. "For the past hour, ladies and gentlemen, a federal district judge—a man who has climbed to notoriety on the backs of victims like this poor woman—has been trying to justify himself on national television. He has unleashed countless muggers, rapists, and, yes, murderers, on the streets of our city. He has called it *justice.*"

Sound and fury. For just a moment, the crucial moment, I relaxed my tense vigil over the building's entrance so that I heard a collective gasp before I grasped the reason—before I saw Judge Kevin Reilly come spinning toward us through revolving glass doors, preceded by one man, followed by another.

The first man out . . . was it Max? Wasn't it? No signal was needed for the black limousine parked across the street. It roared to life, negotiated a deft U-turn, and pulled up to the entrance.

Just as deftly, Lee, jabbing a savagely accusing finger toward the adversary, boomed out his name: *"Judge Kevin Reilly!"*

She didn't give the mike away; it was taken from her. The black woman howled into it like a wounded animal. "You killed my husband! You turned his killer loose, Judge Reilly. *You* did it!" A hush as she stopped brandishing the sign in her hands to hold it high, to hold it still as a cross. *In nomine patri et filii . . .*

JUDGE REILLY MADE ME A WIDOW, said the sign.

Impatient hands were edging Judge Reilly toward the limo. He brushed them away, brushed thick white hair off his forehead as he turned to his accuser. Could his anger match her rage?

Max kept us from learning the answer, unceremoniously depriving us of the star of the show. He spun Reilly around like a top and shoved him into the waiting arms of a man who had leaped from the limo. It was over with the sound of a door slamming.

The judge was safe.

In the moment when I realized he needn't have been, that he'd been vulnerable to a sharpshooter's bullet, I spotted Kagan in his hard hat. What chilled me was his expression as soon as he spotted me. It wasn't just indifference; I saw no sign of surprise.

"We came here to protest and protest we shall!" Lee was playing, now, to television, demanding attention from her audience.

She got Max's. I couldn't see his features clearly, but I knew what he had to be thinking as he turned away from her voice to speak to the nearest cop, as he turned back and moved rapidly toward a woman who fit an FBI description.

The cop bellowed into his bullhorn: "Let's break it up and go home, folks!" Behind me, his partner took up the cry.

I wanted to seize the thing and bellow a warning to poor Lee. I wanted to run away and hide.

I let out a cry as someone—Jamie!—seized my arm. "Look," I said, pointing, "Lee's drawn Max to the platform like a magnet!"

"But why *me?*" Jamie's face was an agony of frustration. "Why did Kagan want *me* up there?"

My eyes went back to the platform: Max in profile, a restraining hand on Lee's arm as she bent to him, gravely attentive. Max in a khaki raincoat, Lee in white leather, the two of them freeze-framed in floodlit relief against the yawning blackness of a pit and the deeper black of cranes and construction beams, barely visible, eerily still.

Not quite still. "Jamie, is something moving behind them?"

He had seen it, too. "A revolutionary must have his martyrs," he said softly. "Kagan, you unmitigated bastard. BAS-TARD!"

Heads whipped around. People backed away. Jamie's cry had carved out a corridor. He dashed through it, running straight to the cop on horseback.

"Look!" he yelled, pointing at nothing. One minute the cop was looking, the next he was falling out of the saddle. Jamie was astride, maneuvering the animal to create a new corridor, riding hard toward the platform as people scattered out of the way of his piercing cry: "Hi-jahhhh, hijahhhhhh!"

He reined in to avoid a collision. The horse reared—

Moonlight caught the moment: head thrown back, magnificent torso taut with the strain and exhilaration of his effort, one arm raised—you could almost see the sword in it, or the banner—

Moonlight had also made Jamie a target. I whirled at the sounds of a scuffle in time to see an unhorsed cop, who had gone for his gun, hit the ground a second time. Tackled by a black man.

"Zack?" the cop said, his anger becoming a question mark.

I ran through Jamie's corridor, my view of the platform spoiled by too many picket signs. I ran until I heard a gasp that rolled all the way back through the scattered remnants of the crowd, until I drew abreast of a hot-dog cart and, desperate to see one platform, clambered on top of another.

I saw death hurtling through the air. I saw a giant ball slice through the sky, dangling a murderous hook.

In the moment when I thought it would strike two spotlighted figures, like pins in a bowling alley, a figure on horseback swept them out of its path and sent them sprawling to the sidewalk.

In the moment when I thought I had lived through a surrealistic dream, I heard a sickening crunch, saw the side of a building take the punishment intended for human beings—and recognized the stuff, not of dreams, but of murder plots: a steel wrecking ball.

A revolutionary needs his martyrs . . . and his Judas goat.

You didn't get yours, Kagan. Lee is up, she's on her feet. Jamie saved her. And Max. I fell for your phony assassination plot but, thanks to a guardian angel, I didn't lead the man I love to his death. Max is—

I heard a crack, heard it repeat itself. It didn't penetrate.

What did was a splotch of red spreading across white leather and Lee, reeling like a drunk, while a horse reared up in fright, throwing Jamie.

I leaped down from my perch and ran.

To find bodies bending over bodies.

Lee, dead from a sniper's bullet.

Jamie, dead from a broken neck.

He didn't look dead as, eyes closed, he lay on his back. Just deeply asleep. Tousle-haired . . . arms and legs askew. A boy who had kicked off his bedcovers. I wanted to rock him in my arms.

I would have, but for Max.

Max bent over him. Max's fingers explored more than Jamie's poor broken neck; they were touching a beard. Black. Peculiarly off center. They moved on, Max's fingers, to a spot of blue crystal that lay on Jamie's cheek like a counterfeit tear.

When Max reached for a silver fox medallion on a chain, I knew I had been robbed of my chance to say good-bye.

I stood in the shadows only long enough for a final tribute. . . .

You had it after all, Jamie dear. The strength to die.

Chapter 35

My change purse was full of quarters. Making calls from a pay phone without a credit card was habit by now.

"How's it going?" Angela said, recognizing my voice.

"It's over. One wrap-up session and I'm out of here."

"Two days early." Her voice had a fill-me-in sound.

I filled her in on ten days of carrot-and-stick activity, good news, mostly. Thanks to Lee's off-the-record list of "real administrative talent," culled from her trip to the provinces and liberated from my safe, I had tracked people down fast. Met with them.

The "chic blonde" who ran our Baltimore cell. Some "plucky" housewives from Atlanta and Detroit. A gingham-curtains-and-apple-pie lady from Houston who was a "crack shot" with a pistol. The "savvy" black woman from Charlotte.

I had spelled out their options. One by one, they had come aboard—and not reluctantly.

"Five cities—tip of the iceberg," I told Angela. "That's the bad news. But if we could get our hands on Lee's administrative records—the ones she compiled just before I took over—if I could feed all those names into a computer, *then* I could go to Max."

"Hold on," Angela said. "Someone wants to file a report."

"They get fresh water every day. Their teeth look great—People Crackers twice a week," Tony said proudly. "Pola never finishes her supper but she looks okay. Marco killed a mouse."

Ugh. "Giving them plenty of hugs and kisses?"

"Yeah, sure. You coming home? Where are you?"

Home. To whom and for what? "Yeah, sure," I said. "I'm in the airport bar in Charlotte, North Carolina. You be good."

I hung up just as she came in . . . the woman who bore an unsettling resemblance to Claudia. It wasn't just the "onyx" eyes. There was a touch of the exotic in her bone structure (not to mention her name—Sulette) and a hint of vulnerability in the mouth. But she moved with the confidence of the tough-minded.

She had been my first ally.

We took a booth and waited for our drinks before she gave me a report. Her experience with VA's Charlotte contingent had been almost identical with mine in other cities. Initial shock. A show of resistance, a touch of false bravado. The slow realization that it was the only way to go.

What invariably followed was a resolve to make it work in their own territory—with hard evidence of new commitments.

Giving me the bargaining power I needed.

Sulette had made an identical discovery: To most people, the FBI was a mythic organization, either dismissed out of hand as so much TV melodrama, or the source of instant fear. Like me, she had tried to flesh out the myth, to make the threat overhanging every one of us personal—real. But not overwhelming; not yet.

"We're batting a thousand in Charlotte," she said cheerfully. "Sensible people don't need much persuading if they're looking a jail cell in the face—or a tiger eating its own tail. Seen this?"

"In Houston," I said, fingering a dog-eared press release that had—in tone, at least—the earmarks of a Karen Newman knockoff. It was a call to arms, rushed to every VA cell in the country, from the sound of it. Kagan's version of the Big Lie—a doubleheader.

Dr. James Coyne, unmasked as the martyred Leader . . . prominent psychiatrist lays down his life for the Cause.

Lee Emerson, glamorous heroine of the hour who'd managed to stay one step ahead of the FBI, only to die from a madman's bullet.

See for yourself. It's on national TV!

"It arrived an hour before I did. Gave us something special to talk about in Houston," I told Sulette, smiling at an old memory and a new friend. . . . *"Victims Anonymous in the murder-for-martyrs business? A scenario for losers, honey. You got a better one?"*

"We're going to make this work." Sulette gripped my hand.

She saw me off at the gate. Looking at her, I couldn't help thinking it. Saying it. "You make me think we have a future."

"We're even. You make me less ashamed of the past."

I walked away wondering if someone could do the same for me.

Good to be back? Not when it means a hair shirt . . . the death throes of a best-loved friend. Back to Claudia's place, not mine. Three and a half claustrophobic rooms. . . . Ghosts, I had told Max. Everyone agreed it was the last place he'd think to look for me.

"The lease is in my name?" I asked.

"We thought better of it after you left." Angela handed me half a driver's license, a supermarket charge card—and a lease.

"Mrs. Rosa Ramirez." I shook my head, smiling. "So now Rosa's generous impulses extend to sharing her identity. What's left?"

"Her furniture." Angela gestured at a couple of chairs.

I stared at the daybed couch.

"For Tony," she said. "The kid he's been bunking in with drove him to the Bronx for his gear."

"His idea," Zack said, offering me a cigarette. "Take a closer look at that lease."

October one, it said—ten days ago. Mrs. Rosa Ramirez and son, it said. You're not too late, Jamie had assured me. Too early.

"Using Rosa was quicker and safer than manufacturing a new ID," Zack said, pretending not to see the tears. "We have more pressing matters to risk our necks over."

"Such as Zack being spotted by an unhorsed cop."

"Come on, Angie, I'm in no immediate danger. That kid's naive where I'm concerned. It wouldn't occur to him that I was lying."

"What did you tell him?" I asked.

"That I was working undercover for Stan Cole. After Cole bought it at the Legal Aid rally, we wanted . . . live witnesses."

"You did save Jamie's life," I reminded him softly.

His mouth twisted. "For about five minutes."

"Were we right about O'Neal?"

"Figuratively," Angela said. "Our very own construction mogul was the brains behind the steel wrecking ball."

"No trouble with my boss Larry?"

"Not once your letter arrived. He's on hold. Your computer is in the bedroom. The desk is Zack's contribution."

On hold while I "recuperated." Not from one week of kidnapping and two more on the road. From a new strain of the flu.

"You up for a small piece of good news?" Zack said. "A fence sitter by the name of Hugh has yielded to his better instincts. He's with us—at the moment, in spirit. It's safer."

"A businessman with a penchant for fund-raising is *big* news," I said, sinking into the couch. "We're going to need him."

The sound of the buzzer lit up smiles all around. "One orphan coming in out of the storm," Angela quipped.

Tony came in with a load of camera equipment and a noisy carrying case: Marco and Pola, protesting their confinement. Zack went for the suitcases. Angela tousled Tony's hair. I was content with his solemn watchfulness whenever he looked at me; Jamie said he had looked at his sister Maria that way.

We helped him unpack, exchanging high-spirited "Mrs. Ramirez and son" one-liners, climaxed by an ID card Tony produced from his pocket: TONY RAMIREZ. "I forged it," he said the way a kid would say, "I got an A on my math exam."

"You dropped something, Antonio." Zack picked up a folded envelope that had fallen out of Tony's pocket.

Tony colored. "I forgot." He handed it to me. "From Kagan, I'll bet," he said.

He had found it under his door, addressed to me but with a definite Kaganesque touch: *For Your Eyes Only.* I opened it the way you'd approach an unfriendly dog: with extreme caution.

Sure enough, Kagan bit me. "Better read this," I said, handing it to Zack with a steady hand while my stomach did a nosedive. We crowded around. I read it again over Zack's shoulder.

Give it up. Too late for second thoughts or a bad conscience. Scotch takeover plans. Any further action by you or yours will be met by the truth that hurts.

Five items messengered to an FBI man—picture them.

One: a photograph. A woman shooting her daughter's murderer to death.

Two: a bullet. It's from the same gun.

Three: the gun. Her prints are still there.

Four: yet another bullet. This one belongs to a rifle with a telescopic sight—the one fired at poor Lee.

Five: one last photograph. What have we here? Short, dark-skinned person in navy cap and pea jacket, high above the melee, kneeling on top of a panel truck. Taking aim with a rifle?

Get the picture, if you'll pardon the pun? The FBI was tipped to a mysterious blonde—a leader? In the very act of confronting her, the FBI man loses the lady to a bullet. Very convenient if the real *administrative head of Victims Anonymous wanted to deflect suspicion from herself.*

So harness your friends—I won't bother to name them. Just tell one of them that revenge delayed tastes the sweetest of all. Cop killers can't stay hidden forever. I know the whereabouts of two. Stay loyal, A.

What makes a cover story stick? Why, the finest corroborating evidence that money can buy—and it's all yours, Z. Stand down or I'll see you consign your beloved uniform to the garbage heap.

I'll wait for your answer, K. But not too long.

Zack spoke for us all. "Son of a bitch."

Angela, her face averted, slipped one hand in her pocket. Fingering Joe's shield?

"I saw you up on the panel truck," Tony said to me, dropping his

little bombshell like it was yesterday's lunch. "I almost went up
there only I thought you'd be mad at me because I hadn't gone
home. But then I—"

"It wasn't me," I said faintly.

"I knew that." He looked impatient. "You can't fire a rifle."

"Thanks for the vote of confidence." I turned to Angela and
Zack. "Kagan is waiting, folks. Want to hear my answer—the part
that's not unprintable? I won't quit. But you two must."

"Pretend to quit—that what you mean?" Zack said.

"He can take his 'sweet revenge,'" Angela hissed, "and—"

"Stop it," I snapped, wanting to hug them both. "Kagan is
uncanny. He'll smell pretense—"

"He's got us by the balls. *That's* what he'll smell."

"Maybe. I just don't want your names messengered to the FBI."
Angela was giving me that head-on-the-block look. "I'm not being
noble," I told her with a wan smile. "After Operation Trojan
Horse, who better to blow the whistle on the bad guys while I burn
our bridges? The interesting question is whether we can build
anything on the ashes. The problem," I said, sinking into melancholy, "is that I can't go to Max, not yet. Now Kagan will get to
him first."

"Maybe not," Zack said. "His blackmail sounds better than it
plays. Eyewitness testimony would slap a 'self-defense' label on
Indio's death. Kagan knows I'd testify if he forced my hand. As for
firing at Lee, you can't be in two places at once. Somewhere out
there is a hot-dog vendor who spotted you on top of his cart."

"We'll find him," Angela promised. "What's your timetable?"

"Depends on whether I can pry Lee's records out of Bart."

"A hard call," Zack mused. "We have to assume he's swallowed
some cock-and-bull story about Lee's murder."

"He's in mourning," Tony announced solemnly. "I saw him
cry."

I pictured myself, rifle in hand, blasting away at Kagan's face.

"Before you go looking for hot-dog vendors," I said, "how about
some evidence which places that protégé of Kagan's on top of a
panel truck? I can personally vouch for his marksmanship."

"Too tall and blond for the job," Angela said. "But he has a
sidekick who just happens to be short, dark and trigger-happy."

She and Zack exchanged looks that said: His days are numbered.

"Let's get started," Zack said to Angela. To Tony, "I hear a Mrs.
Ramirez is in the market for a combination bodyguard, gofer and
good pal. You applying for the job?"

"Yeah, sure," he said, trying not to smile, looking delighted with
the job description.

"Stay one step ahead of Kagan, will you?" I said to Angela.

"Hell, we've been in this business longer than he has—I think. What we all need right now is something to replace Operation Trojan Horse—a cleaner symbol for what we're trying to pull off. Give something a name," she smiled, "and you give it a future."

"Operation Lazarus," I whispered.

Zack had to explain it to Tony.

We clasped hands on it.

Chapter 36

"I was *not* followed. I gave him the slip!"

"Tell me again. Slowly, Tony."

But I already knew. I was beginning to develop a sixth sense on how Kagan operated—a little late in the game, I thought ruefully. An alarm had gone off in Tony's head two days ago when he'd discovered Kagan's envelope under the door. On his way to me, he had known enough to look for a tail, had even spotted one—a tan Peugeot—and "given him the slip."

But if there had been *two* tails—one to drive off in the wrong direction, the other to follow you home?

It would explain Bart showing up at our brownstone just now with an ultimatum that almost made Tony drop his bag of groceries.

Kagan wanted a truce. Now, he wanted it. "Zack and Angie had convinced him." Together we could accomplish what I had already set in motion: transform the organization. No need for anyone to take a fall.

Kagan without fall guys? It didn't ring true.

Until I realized he already had them: Lee and Jamie. The FBI wanted leaders? VA had two dead ones to trade with. Was that it?

The carrot, maybe. The stick, I explained to Tony, was the prospect of a messenger knocking on Max's door.

I had thirty minutes to decide. Either Bart delivered me to the truce table, or we would all be "plunged into full-scale war."

I was not without advice and counsel. "It's a trap! Zack's on duty so he sent Bart? You believe that?"

"Tony, I need those records. Even if Kagan is playing some new game, I'd have a chance to work on Bart. It's worth the risk."

He regarded me with one of his "she's hopeless" looks and promptly dipped into the oversized flowerpot by the door. "Better take this, then."

Up came Zack's "house gift," dropped off last night—my trusty .38-caliber revolver.

"Unmarked," Zack had said.

I couldn't bring myself to touch the damn thing. "Bart will search my purse," I said hopefully.

"Wear boots. Angie showed me how she straps it to her ankle."

I sighed and went for my boots.

I let Tony strap a revolver to my ankle. "You stay put," I ordered, and reached for him, knowing he'd go along with a hug; he was so used to hugging Marco and Pola.

I walked to the elevator feeling like a human time bomb even though Tony had assured me the gun couldn't go off without my help. I rode down, wishing a survivor's instinct could be shared, like handing someone a good-luck charm. I walked out the door with a show of confidence that was all sham and pure self-defense. *If the animals in the jungle catch the slightest scent of fear—*

Bart was a looming presence by the side of a tan Peugeot. He gave me a hard-edged nod (I gave it right back) and held open the passenger door; real polite. So far so good. But my stomach lurched when I noticed how he held it: like it was hot metal. Like he was a hairbreadth from slamming it against my body!

I recovered in silence while he drove east through Central Park and pulled onto the drive heading uptown. He's in mourning, I reminded myself. "Bart," I said, "I want you to know how sorry I am, how appalled by what happened to Lee."

Two automatic reactions. My hand touching his arm in genuine sympathy. His arm flashing off the wheel in violent recoil.

That's when I knew what cock-and-bull story Bart had been fed. Me, taking aim from a panel truck.

"You're crazy," I whispered. "I had nothing to do with it."

Silence. Not so much as a sideways glance while I told him my own theory about Kagan's sharpshooter protégé and his short, dark, trigger-happy sidekick. "Damn it, Bart, I've never even fired a rifle! I don't know how."

"You could have learned. Kagan says you're one smart lady."

"Not so smart," I said faintly into the raised collar of my camel-hair coat. I had just noticed where we were. Crumbling buildings and vacant lots. Back to the Bronx.

Murky twilight descended. Traffic was thinning out, cabs mostly. They'd be running a race with their meters: drop off the fare, get the hell out before dark. Unless the Bronx was home; I saw one off-duty light that had been with us since the East River drive in Manhattan. I lost it when Bart turned into a side street.

When Bart pulled over, I reached for my purse. He got to it first.

"Waste of time," I said, as he reached inside. "It's too small for a rifle."

He handed my purse back. "Time to go."

This time he let me open my own door.

"If I'm on my way to a truce negotiation," I said, walking over to his side of the car, "then Kagan sent the wrong messenger."

"You think so?" he said, grabbing hold of my arm. "Maybe there is no truce. Maybe you're here to take a fall."

I would have laughed at his Dashiell Hammett dialogue if he hadn't pressed a gun against my side. It looked to be the same size as the one strapped to my ankle, but Bart's grip was so tight I couldn't get anywhere near my boot.

"Lucky I don't kill you first," he said.

First? Before Kagan?

I made myself go limp while I mentally reviewed Angela's basic strikes, kicks, and escapes—*how,* when Bart had grabbed both my hands in his huge paw and started to drag me forward? Past hollow-eyed buildings. Through empty lots. Around dark corners—

A flash in my eyes blinded me. Bart, too; he had dropped my hands, and his gun.

I went for mine.

"Don't do it, Bart! She's got you covered!" said the voice behind the flash. Said the boy behind the camera.

Bart had stopped short, one hand extended toward the gun at his feet, his face in shadow. What would it show right now? Fear? Wounded pride?

He went for his gun.

I fired.

"Jesus!" Bart's face came, sweating, out of the shadows.

I gaped at the hole I'd torn in his shirt just under his shooting arm. I had aimed for his thigh.

"Try that again, I'll aim for the arm, not under it," I said.

"Never even fired a rifle, huh?"

Swell. "Tony," I said, "his gun—"

Tony already had it.

"Where were you taking me, Bart?"

"Gang headquarters of a creep named Indio."

No wonder it had seemed familiar! "Why there?" I pressed.

"The guilt-ridden lady returns to the scene of the crime," he said. "You pumped three bullets into the creep when his back was turned, remember?"

"That was self-defense. What's it to do with a truce? What is Kagan up to?"

He let me see a grin. Its lack of humor was chilling. It wasn't enough of an answer—close, but not enough. I figured if I pressed a gun to his ribs and said "Talk or die," he'd call my bluff. He stood there like a dark, lethal weapon.

That's when I remembered who I was dealing with: man with a glass of whiskey shaking in his hand.

Tony and I held a whispered consultation. I sent him on a foraging expedition. He found the first item in a pile of debris.

He put it to immediate good use. While sharpshooter Karen kept the enemy in her sights, Tony tied Bart's hands with a strand of wire, then, from a sitting position, his ankles ("loose enough so he can walk, sort of," Tony explained).

It took no time at all to find item number two: a discarded city vacate notice—very large with lots of writing space on the back. I pulled out the last item, a lipstick, and went to work, grinning in the dark.

The look on Bart's face when I brandished my homemade sign in front of him was worth every moment of painstaking effort. Two-inch-high letters in red spelled out—no, screamed—their message:

I AM A STATEN ISLAND PK (CORRECTIONS OFFICER). COME AND GET ME, YOU BASTARDS!

Silence while the three of us tuned in to unmistakable sounds in the night. "Hear that?" I asked, striving for a menacing tone. "It's a jungle out there," I said, feeling like a character out of a Mickey Spillane novel. "I swear to God, Bart, if you don't give me some answers right now, I'll leave you to the animals."

A crack in the facade—hesitation pulling at the corners of his mouth. I bent down to him, motioning Tony out of hearing.

"You won't let me walk away, leave you like this," I told him softly. "I know where you're coming from, Bart. I know what you are."

Coward.

The unspoken word hung in the night air. A wild look came into his eyes.

I asked him again what he knew. He told me.

We used his own handkerchief as a gag. As the three of us made our way to the abandoned building (slowly; Bart didn't walk, he hobbled), I longed for the reassuring sounds of conversation, words to blot out what I'd just been told. Bart wasn't the only coward in the group.

Tony obliged with a lively account of Operation Save Karen From Herself. He had bolted down the stairs as soon I hit the elevator, gone through the basement, and beat me to the street. When he got a cab, he made it wait until a tan Peugeot went by. He had taken an old piece of friendly advice; thank you, Zack. . . .

"Next time, get the cabbie to light up his off-duty sign in case the guy you're following should look back."

We had to untie Bart's ankles in order to sneak up six flights of stairs. Tony rewired him in the stairwell. And stayed put, Bart in tow, while I went looking for the right door.

I remembered it well.

I didn't have to pretend to put strain and tension, a touch of uncertainty, in my voice as I knocked and called Kagan's name. As I told him Bart had a problem with the car but would be along any minute now.

The door opened. Kagan greeted me with his sloping half-smile.

How many times had I vowed to wipe it off his face?

Chapter 37

Tall, rail-thin and laconic. But with a difference; I knew how to read tension in those smoke-grey eyes. With a half-turn of his angular neck, he gestured me inside, invited me to look around.

Instead of fur-draped beds and piles of stolen appliances, I saw desks, file cabinets, charts on the walls—even drapes across the windows. The only reminder of "gang headquarters" was a rusty generator and a safe. The den of thieves had become an office.

"Every secret organization needs a secret operational heart. I never trusted you," he said. "You see things too quickly."

"And put a name to them. Jamie called you a revolutionary. I say you're a murderer twice over. Can we build a truce on that?"

He watched me carefully as I tossed my coat on a chair, my purse on top. "Help yourself," I told him. "Bart already did."

He laughed and went to sit behind the farthest desk. With the drapes as backdrop, he looked like a businessman about to conduct a meeting.

"Why not admit it? This truce talk is an excuse for both of us," he said with disarming candor. "How could we resist a final confrontation, you and I?"

"About what?" I challenged. "You must know Victims Anonymous is through. You've manufactured a couple of martyrs for nothing."

"I never do anything for nothing. Don't you know that about me? It's true I have my share of failures. McCann, for instance."

"The Judas goat that leads the lamb to slaughter," I said. "I have to hand it to you, Kagan. It almost worked."

"Which is easier, a fatal accident with a wrecking ball?" he asked with chilling matter-of-factness. "Or discrediting a man with McCann's record—my alternative plan? I didn't figure on Jamie's last-minute heroics. Which, unfortunately for you, pushed me back to square one." He smiled. "Back to you, Karen."

My answering smile was parchment-thin. "What do you have in mind, this time?" (Bart had told me what he had in mind.) "You really think Max will fall for that sharpshooter nonsense?"

"Do I think he's in the same league with Bart? We both know better. No, the only photograph earmarked for your friend McCann is a candid shot of what happened in this room on New Year's Eve."

I closed my eyes and relived what had happened in this room.

"Why gild the lily?" he said softly. "It's proof enough of what he has good reason to suspect after Jamie's melodramatic unmasking. Your undeniable talents as double agent and Mata Hari."

I considered ending the cat-and-mouse scenario; I considered going for the gun in my boot. No way he was concealing a weapon, not with the tight fit of his jeans. But the cat was still in a playful mood, talkative, and the mouse had more to learn. I *had* to know if he'd already poisoned the well with Max.

"You pride yourself on being practical, not vindictive," I told him. "What's the point?"

"I thought you'd never ask," he said cheerfully.

He took some chalk from his pocket and started to draw on the floor; mesmerizing. An ersatz cop outlining the body of a corpse.

"Step one." He looked up. "Have I got it right?"

He'd got it right. I looked down at more than a flat chalk figure; I saw . . . Indio. One arm outstretched. Body propelled forward by three bullets in the back.

I hadn't realized how cold the room was even with a thick sweater and wool slacks. I needed my coat. I also needed complete freedom of movement. I restrained a shiver.

Kagan picked up on it anyway. "Shall I turn on the portable heater? I have one by the desk."

The genial host. No way I'd give him the satisfaction. I shook my head.

"Step two, then," he said, walking to the safe. Removing a strongbox. "My little black box, I think you called it. Apt as always." He reached inside for a pair of gloves. Then a gun.

I had waited too long to go for mine.

"The pistol that I used on Indio," I said, letting him hear hardness, not sinking despair.

"The very same. Shall we keep count together? Three for the departed. Two for his hated memory—"

He blasted away at his chalk outline!

"That leaves one for the suicide victim—you." He pulled on the gloves and wiped the gun, then the piece of chalk. "Look!"

What do you do when someone throws something at you? If you have good reflexes, you catch it. I caught the chalk.

And damned my reflexes as Kagan snatched it back. He had my fingerprints.

He pocketed the gun and removed his gloves. "I'll add it up for you," he said. "An FBI agent named Max McCann is about to look the classic fool: man sacrifices judgment to passion. In his hunt for vigilante leaders, he unwittingly enlists their administrative head —that's you. The day you caught me in Jamie's office—"

"You were taking inventory, you said."

"I was doctoring tapes and making my own copies. Jamie never could keep himself from running off at the mouth. It made my job easier: implicating people, naming names. Jamie, elevating *you* to leadership level. Care to guess how McCann will view this mea culpa of yours? Conscience-stricken, torn by conflicting loyalties, Karen Newman arranges for the revealing tapes and the incriminating photograph to be delivered to her lover. But not before she vents her rage one last time"—his gesture took in the chalk figure—"then . . . takes her own life."

Kagan means to kill you and make it look like suicide.

"So Max still doesn't know. You haven't contacted him?"

"Soon. Have I overlooked anything?" His soft intonations made my skin crawl with more than fear. He moved to the door, the only way out other than through the windows and a six-story drop.

"When I told you once no sacrifice was too great for the Cause, I didn't expect you to take me literally," I said. And saw that Kagan still liked his humor dry. I reached down to smooth a crease in my slacks. "You *have* overlooked something. I've been in contact with VA cells in five cities. They know about your murder-for-martyrs scheme—in detail. They'll guess what happpened to me."

"What's happened to Bart? Did you charm or disarm—"

"Forget Bart." I played with a lock of hair. "How will you explain it?"

"I won't even try." He was leaning against the door, enjoying my nervousness. "Victims Anonymous will have a titular head shortly after I appear to disappear, the victim of stepped-up FBI activity. Democratic of me, don't you think, becoming one of my own fall guys?"

"Imaginative, as always." Back to smoothing the slacks and playing with the hair, letting him enjoy the spectacle: nervous Karen and her pretense at being in control. "The law closes in, you cover your tracks with fall guys. You're not out to make a deal with the FBI, you never were," I said slowly as reality hit home.

"Sounded good though, didn't it?"

"To whom?" I said, moving down. Coming right back up with a .38 that no longer felt like a stranger in my hand.

I could see it took him by surprise. That didn't stop me from doing it right; I'd seen it a hundred times on TV. I pointed the gun at his chest and I used both hands.

He laughed at me.

With good reason. In the time it took me to grasp his intention—for the light switch by the door to register—his arm shot out and plunged us into darkness. My shot rang out in the night.

This time his laughter came from behind. I turned on a dime and fired again—to the sound of breaking glass. The silence afterward was as mocking as a Kagan smile. Frightened amateur pitted against professional killer? I backed up, moving toward the door.

I backed right into him. All I had going for me was a hand that had petrified, one immovable finger locked onto a trigger.

He pulled me into a bear hug. "Have you counted your bullets like a good girl should?" he teased in my ear.

Three. Counting Bart, I had fired three.

"How many left, Karen?" His hand squeezed mine.

Two? Three? I wasn't sure. I couldn't remember!

We squeezed off two more shots, Kagan and I. The "click" afterward told me I could stop counting.

It told him he could let me go. He flicked the light back on. All smiles. "I never trusted you because I sensed what I would be up against in a showdown. A formidable adversary."

A dubious tribute. At least it kept me from sagging. What kept me from screaming my head off was the neighborhood; the lack of one. All I knew to do now was keep it going as long as I could, talk until I could think of something. Or until I couldn't think.

"Kagan, the man with the soul of a revolutionary," I said, putting the useless gun aside. "What did Jamie mean by it?"

The question seemed to startle him, but only slightly, as if he'd heard it before but never tried to answer it for himself. "I think of myself," he said finally, "as a professional soldier."

"A mercenary? You have all the earmarks. Join the Cause, insinuate yourself with its leader, work tirelessly until you're indispensable. But a mercenary is a man with a price, Kagan.

What's yours? What are you greedy for? If we rule out the obvious—money and macho—what are we left with? What do you get out of life?" I said slowly, wanting to know.

I'd done that much, at least; wiped the smile off his face.

He shrugged. "Like you, animals give me pleasure."

"You're no animal lover," I said, sure of my ground. "It's not the same thing, being comfortable with them. I wonder about a man without friends, without a home or a woman—no ties of any kind. Does such a man find the human animal threatening in some way? Does he even take pleasure from his Cause? Victims Anonymous was full of worthy goals and good intentions. You saw how contagious Jamie's sense of justice could be. Did you care, Kagan, one way or the other? Do you give a damn even now, with everything you helped to build on the verge of collapse and—"

"I care about the fight, you little fool! I *am* a revolutionary."

"Any revolution?"

"As long as it's in ferment." His eyes flattened as he considered his own statement. "And against established order," he added with the slow reflection of a man in the process of discovering and enjoying a personal revelation.

"What if your revolution succeeds?" I pressed, feeling close to a discovery of my own.

"You mean, what if Victims Anonymous had turned respectable and ushered in a New Order?" He shrugged. "How long before the whole thing turned sour?"

"Before what turned sour? What are you saying?"

"Look, no revolution ever succeeds—not for long. There's always something new to rebel against. That's where people like me come in. We go to ground, organize the opposition—"

"You rebel . . . for the sake of rebelling?"

We stared at each other. I was thinking of a man who lacked the antennae to tune in to people except for his own limited purpose, a man whose sole interest was in how they functioned. A man who only came alive when *he* was functioning in a certain way.

"I'm what society spits up after a gluttonous meal," he said, still thinking about rebellion. "The indigestible man."

"But you're invisible," I said, groping to understand. "Don't you have any desire to take credit, to seek notoriety for—"

"You do things wholesale and in the dark. *That's* the secret formula. Shoot a subway mugger, take out the neighborhood bully, and what have you got? A feeble, isolated 'protest.' But take your time—organize the shooters—and you can pull it all down. . . ."

I knew him then. No goals but one: tear down what others build. His is a darker need. . . .

But I still didn't know why. "You were born into the wrong century," I told him. "The pillaging hordes that destroyed entire civilizations would have suited your purpose far better than a sorry mix of misguided crime victims and assorted neurotics. The breakdown of a criminal-justice system—"

"Is as good a cause as any." He looked amused.

". . . You're in no danger of running out of causes, are you?"

"Or out of steam."

What do you know about a person who repeats a process over and over? He's out to prove something, isn't he—over and over because it can't be proved? Out to destroy the worthwhile—the positive—in an obsessive need to disprove a negative? What if this man, who has no discernible values, derives his sense of identity, not from anything he is or wants, but from what he does to other people's values?

I didn't dare say it aloud, afraid he'd kill me on the spot. A man without a value to his soul is scarcely human. A man terrified of his own verdict may spend his life trying to disprove it. *I am not a worthless human being, I am not a worthless—*

"So," I said—daring—because I had run out of options, "Victims Anonymous never stood a chance, did it? The good guys can never do business with the bad and come out ahead. People like you contaminate everything you touch. You're worthless, Kagan. You lack even the nobility of the animals you pretend to love. People like you," I said slowly, "aren't even human."

The back of his hand across my cheek sent me reeling across the room to crash-land against the door.

I slid to the floor, not as dazed as I looked, and told myself he wouldn't shoot from this distance, not with only one bullet left—not if he wanted to pull off a "suicide." I turned my back on a loaded pistol long enough to yank the door open and make a dash for the stairwell, wondering for the first time why Tony hadn't come running when he'd heard the shots.

He was in no position to. Bart, still bound and gagged, held a silent, squirming Tony in what looked like an iron grip. The gun we'd taken away from him lay a good yard away.

Classic mistake, not tying a man's hands behind him. And not tying them tight enough. At least Tony had managed to kick the gun out of reach.

Their reach, not mine.

Kagan's expression, when he came into view, was comical. The man who spent his life posting guards had been taken by surprise.

I had to hand it to him. Unlike Bart, he didn't underestimate me. He slid his gun right over. Bart got religion and released his grip. Tony scrambled for Kagan's gun.

"Back inside, everybody." I motioned for Tony to untie Bart's feet while I tried to remember if I'd seen a telephone inside.

No phone. "No way to call the police," I said.

"Sure there is," Tony said. "We start a fire. Maybe the cops come with the firemen."

"The streetwise kid. Makes you wonder about his past." Kagan, softly insinuating, was looking at Bart when he said it, not Tony. "Doesn't it make you wonder, Karen?" he said as Bart grinned.

"Bart should be wondering about yours," I snapped. "Tell him about Lee, Kagan. Tell him," I said, remembering Lee's records, "or else I take aim at the heart you haven't got. At this distance, even a lousy shot like me can't miss."

"You really want me to tell him? From here?"

They were standing right next to each other; within strangling distance. Kagan moved cautious steps away. Hands raised above his head, he went behind his desk and sat in his chair. "*Now* I'll tell him," he said, wisely keeping his hands where I could see them.

Bart really would have strangled him.

"Nervous, Tadpole?" said Kagan, the picture of calm. The drapes behind him added a bizarre touch. The ones to his left were stirring in the breeze—from the bullet hole I'd put in the window.

Tony was fingering the camera strap around his neck.

"Very nervous," Kagan observed, acting nervous himself; he was fidgeting with the portable heater by his chair. "The streetwise kid who never goes anywhere without a camera," he said, "is a boy with a guilty secret. May I tell Karen your secret?"

Kagan's gun shook a little in Tony's hand. He didn't see me open my mouth to yell; he lowered the gun on his own.

I couldn't believe what he did next: put it down on the floor beside him. Hands free, he took Kagan's picture.

Kagan's laughter had a false ring. I knew, suddenly, that if the gun weren't back in Tony's hand, Kagan would have ripped the camera off Tony's neck and smashed it.

"Tony, our pint-sized cooptee," he drawled, looking at me, now. "How grateful you were to the boy who'd risked his life and helped identify your daughter's killers. Devastating photographs. They distracted you," he said thoughtfully, swinging around in his chair, swinging slowly back, one hand dropping below the desk. "You never asked yourself a key question, Karen. Where did Tony get them? *How* did he get them . . . without being Johnny-on-the-spot?"

"Kagan!" Tony's scream mingled with Kagan's laughter.

"Young Tony, alias the Tadpole," Kagan said. "He got all dressed up in his Halloween Muppet costume—Kermit the Frog, wasn't it?—and took those photographs himself."

"Would you believe old-fashioned ghosts outside my door? . . . One modern touch. An adorable little Muppet frog."

A boy had turned into a statue.

So had I.

I don't know how long I stared at him—screamed at him—or when I realized I was staring into a conflagration . . . fire to bring the firemen. Flames to consume a chamber of horrors and everything in it—

The drapes were in flames. From the portable heater Kagan had been fiddling with?

I yelled Tony's name—too late to warn him, to stop Kagan from tearing the gun out of his hand.

I could have stopped Kagan from shooting out the light, I could have shot him in the heart he didn't have, if it hadn't happened again. Petrified hand. Finger immovable on the trigger.

I might have shot him in the back as he went out the window, if I hadn't thought he was a sure suicide. If I had remembered what he'd told me the night we waited outside gang headquarters . . .

"Everyone's left by the fire escape. The punks back to whatever gutter they crawled out of."

Bart didn't follow him down the fire escape; too busy putting out the fire.

Afterward, I confirmed what had ignited it: Kagan's portable heater. He'd flipped it on, edging it up against the drapes, while dropping the bombshell about Tony. The ice-cold room and the air leaking through the window with the bullet hole had done the rest.

I went to the window, not knowing what I'd find.

Kagan stood looking up, as if waiting for me to show my face. One hand rested on the wrought iron of the fire escape—the bottom rung. It was too dark to see the smile, but I felt it as he shouted his farewell.

"There will always be a Victims Anonymous!"

There will always be a Kagan.

When I turned around, Tony was gone.

Chapter 38

"Nobody home." Zack sounded grim. "Tony hasn't been back."

I followed him inside. "Good. Tomorrow I change the locks. When can you get his stuff out of here?"

"Karen, Karen, can't you at least—"

"Not another word. I need a clear head to deal with this." I went into the bedroom to slap "this" onto the desk next to my computer: Bart's protection copy of Lee's coveted membership lists.

Zack followed me in. "What did it, finally?"

"Bart's change of heart? Certainly not my threat to file kidnapping and aggravated-assault charges."

"He must know you can't protect his ass with the FBI."

"But I *can* protect a lot of other people with the lists. I can maybe salvage something out of the mess. Bart wants that, I think. Something to do with poor Lee not dying in vain."

"How long before we lay it on the line with McCann?"

I looked closer and saw the strain. Of waiting? Of the inevitable aftermath? I said, "A week at the outside. I don't dare stretch it beyond that. We have one clear-cut adversary, now. We have cards. Maybe it will be all right."

We looked at each other, both of us pretending to believe it.

We hugged at the door. "It's after midnight," Zack said, noticing. "Happy Friday the thirteenth."

"Can't be much worse than Thursday the twelfth."

Not true, I admitted after he'd gone. I was examining the bruise on my face. I could be lying right now in a cold room, I thought. Max could be racing up to the Bronx to recover a body. My new lucky day, the twelfth.

Unlike Friday the thirteenth, which rang a melancholy bell. The night Tony's sister was murdered. The day I sat in on his recurring nightmare . . . thanks to Jamie. Jamie, who had known all along. Who had let me get close to Tony—encouraged it.

I mashed out my cigarette. The quicker I got Tony's stuff ready, the sooner Zack could dispose of it. I found some cartons and went at it. The drawers in a dining-room cabinet served as Tony's bureau, the first one filled with T-shirts. The second was a tangle of socks, underwear, whatever else could be jammed in.

The bottom drawer was a surprise. Among his sweaters, neatly folded, was a small recorder and some tapes. A tape with an envelope rubber-banded around it was addressed to me.

Give Tony your secrets. He's holding some of mine.

I had to light another cigarette before I opened the secret meant for me. Before I read Jamie's note . . .

I was hoping this wouldn't be necessary, though I knew, some day, it would. Forgive me my half-truths and the method I've chosen to see you through the bitterness and pain.

I put out my cigarette so I wouldn't start a fire; one a night was plenty. When the brandy didn't help, I ran out of excuses. I watched my hand shake as I put on the tape. . . .

Tuesday, the third. The day after Labor Day.

The day Claudia killed herself. In this room, Jamie . . .

So much left undone. After what's happened, I dare not put it off any longer. This tape is for you, Karen, in the hope that Tony listens to me one last time and gives it to you. Now, you listen. Tony was not *one of the Savages who raped your Sarah.*

The question eating away like acid. How well you know me.

He was not even there to vandalize and rob. Do you hear me?

I don't want to hear you. I don't want to hope.

Remember New Year's Eve and why you didn't give yourself up? I talked you out of it.

Take a life to protect a life. I remember.

The law is just as savvy when it comes to something called duress. The books define it as unlawful constraint. Forcing someone to do something he wouldn't do of his own free will. Are you with me? Do you see what I see? A boy short on stature but long on smarts, trapped in a nightmare not of his making.

Now let me correct some half-truths in the nightmare he's been living with, the one you sat in on. Remember where it begins? With crashing cymbals, screeching violins, people in uniform—street violence, I told you. In fact, Tony was reliving a terrifying threat: Indio's gang had cornered him, tapped him for their Halloween robbery binge. If—

But why Tony?

—asking why Tony, remember the "drowning" incident that follows? He's surrounded by wormlike fish—tadpoles. Indio, who had his own brand of street smarts, had gone looking for a little runt of a fellow to wear a disarming costume, a real door-opener: Kermit the—

An adorable little Muppet frog, Sarah said . . .

—tadpoles, in aquatic terms, being the larval stage of the frog. That night, Tony was christened with a hated nickname.

Tadpole. But then, how could you keep teasing him—

The boy floundering in the river hears howling. A combination of dream elements into a single impression: Indio and the others, carrying on like macho wolves. And later, Sarah—

Sarah, screaming when they cut off her finger.

In self-defense, Tony's subconscious absorbed the shock and horror of mutilation by shifting scenes. He's at the circus, his subconscious combining elements again. Maria, part Madonna, part whore, the sister he adores and is ashamed of, is the sideshow dancer who rips her own blouse open to expose her breasts. But she's also—hang in there—she is also your Sarah in the first stages of her defilement. I'm sorry to have to—

Hang in there? I'm hanging by a thread, Jamie.

—sideshow is suddenly off limits. His sister, dragging him away, is really Tony turning away from a scene he can't bear to witness but has no power to stop: gang rape.

I couldn't stop it either, Jamie, I can't bear to keep hearing it! Howling . . . whooping . . .

—recall the juggler who kept pelting Tony with wooden balls that metamorphosed into apples? Tony's psyche was re-creating an earlier scene: Sarah, opening the door, a platter of candied apples in her hand. Events spinning out of control as the fruit goes flying. Fast forward, now, to a shout: Watch out for the umbrella! And Tony, racing toward a bonfire. Translation: Watch out for the iron tongs! And Tony, running to the aid of a little girl by the fireplace—to Susie, wearing a Muppet costume of her own.

I know. I heard . . . "Hey, anybody want some roast piggy?"

The climax upset you . . . remember? Tony, growing smaller by the minute, running and shrinking. From what? you wanted to know. From helplessness and fear, Karen. From guilt. Because— and this is the worst of his living nightmare—Tony blames himself for being on the other side of the room when it happened: the fatal stabbing. Somehow, he could have prevented it. Once you two had met, once he'd come to love you, that unearned guilt became close to unbearable. The conflict over you and his sister wasn't the true source of his terror. It was the prospect of you discovering how he came by those photographs. Karen, I'm—

Are you asking me—

—not to forgive him. That's like asking the widow of a man clubbed to death with his tire iron to forgive him because he forgot to lock the trunk. Tony is a child. He has an excuse for confusing cause and effect with moral responsibility. You don't. A recurring nightmare can be repressed—or it can be exorcised. Tony will survive without you, Karen, but he won't be whole. He's too young to know

how to forgive himself—do you hear me? You must show him how.

It was an effort to stand, to reach for the tape—

Wait. I've left for last the reason I took refuge in a tape recorder. . . . To confront the look in your eyes when I can barely confront myself? Unbearable. I made Tony my responsibility, I've helped him. God knows, I've tried. But I used him, too. The photographs he gave me led straight to you. Oh, he was willing enough to cooperate in return for the sanctuary Victims Anonymous offered him. But with Indio out of the picture, he became the boy who knew too much. I . . . capitalized on his growing attachment to you. Calling him Tadpole in your presence. Letting him know we had mutual secrets to guard, he and I. It kept him in line and . . . it was blackmail, God help me. He didn't hold it against me. Even before I apologized. So you see, my moral responsibility, not Tony's, is on the line. What I did was . . .

Unforgivable.

—givable. Still, I had the wits to recognize a mutual need, to sense what you two could mean to each other. I nurtured that; an achievement of sorts. Each of us has our nightmare. This ends mine. You helped end Tony's by sitting in with us that day while we played a trick on his psyche—giving him the illusion that you had learned his secret but had not rejected him.

The improvement is temporary. Make it permanent. Get him to describe what went through his mind as he sped toward Westchester, wedged between the bodies of those young predators. How he would turn the camera he'd been forced to bring into a tool—a distraction. How it became just that when he used it to help Sarah. How he blames himself for not resisting harder. Sooner. For not running away before Sarah opened her front door. Convince him that it wasn't his fault. Unless you really believe that a terrified boy, utterly alone with his camera and his protests, could have stopped the carnage.

"Leave them alone! Don't hurt them!"

Karen, Karen, what Tony needs so desperately—I need it, too. Can you forgive me?

"For everything but dying on me," I told him out loud.

The tape ran out.

"Sorry I'm late," Angela said.

"No problem. Dinner's in the oven, not on the table. Zack is making drinks."

"You set a nice table. How about laying on another plate?"

"Tony?" I whispered.

There'd been no word for almost a week.

"Showed up this afternoon," Angela said. "Right in the middle of a martial-arts session. What happened to those cartons you packed?" she asked with a casual look around.

"Still in the closet. Angela, I don't know if—"

"Tony Montes, alias Ramirez." She took a chair, as if she were conscious of towering over me. "Runaway kid, waiting to be found," she said. "Have we found him?"

I closed my eyes. "Where is he?"

"In the hall. Maybe you can make him come in."

In the hall.

I went out, apron and all. Behind me, the door clicked shut.

He was all eyes: big, black, solemn as a boy-priest.

I was hollow, as empty as the hallway.

But only for a moment.

When I opened my arms, he walked into them.

Chapter 39

I walked through the rooms of my Central Park West apartment, not like someone who's been away for a month. Like someone who didn't live here anymore. For Marco and Pola, it was a homecoming; more space to run around in, more places to hide.

For me, the hiding was over. Max was due in twenty minutes.

I checked the mirror. Big mistake. He had liked my hair long. A week ago I'd chopped away at it, an unflattering cut. My makeup job was wasted effort; the eye cream hasn't been invented yet that can disguise that sunken look. I wore the lavender dress of our first dinner date. You grasp at straws when you're scared.

You grab hold of a cat and make him purr when you want to bring your blood pressure down. Marco obliged. Pola slipped into her languid windowsill stretch, becoming part of my soothing park view. Peace before the storm.

When Marco bolted out of my arms, it occurred to me that a doorbell is its own kind of mirror. It can be cheerful, annoying, tense, exciting. This one struck me as violent. That's how I went to the door: prepared for the violence of stormy emotions.

What greeted me was flat, empty, a face devoid of everything but recognition.

I said his name. He nodded. I said, "Let's go into the living room." He followed at a polite distance. I gestured at the couch.

He sat on the arm of a chair and unbuttoned his raincoat, as if to say, I'll give you the courtesy of an explanation, lady, but make it brief, will you? I'm a busy man. No surprises when I offered him a drink. He turned it down.

I took the couch he'd rejected and refused myself the false security of a cigarette. "I'm sorry," I said. "Max, I'm so sorry." Empty words under the circumstances, but I had a year's worth of explanation behind them.

And maybe ten, fifteen minutes to pull it all together. There was so much to be sorry for where he was concerned. I started with that. He had a right to be angry, hurt, a lot of things. I spoke slowly so part of me could watch for a hint of anything behind the thinking machine in the khaki raincoat.

After a while, I forgot to watch. That's what can happen when you plunge into an inferno. At some point you stop explaining the events that have consumed your life; you start to relive them.

I came back to earth. To the sound of contempt in his voice.

"Dr. James Coyne," Max said. "My good friend, Jamie."

"He *was* your friend. What I'm trying to say—"

"You had a few laughs at my expense, did you? You and your vigilante lover?"

Guilt puts you on the defensive. But anger takes you off. I reached for an envelope on the coffee table (one more secret fished out of Tony's bottom drawer) and tossed it at him. "Choke on this, McCann," I said. "Go ahead, open it. It's for you."

"From whom?" he asked. Suspicion is his forté.

"The man who died saving your life."

I went back to watching him. Poor Max. It was a losing battle. Even from the other side of heaven or hell, Jamie could work his magic. Not with charm, this time; with a passionately truthful account of our relationship, from his Svengali efforts to recruit me to my actual role in Victims Anonymous and my "valiant" attempts of late to thwart Kagan and his minions.

True to form, Jamie rose to a dramatic climax—I knew the lines by heart: *Max, I never slept with her, she never loved me. But we both love you.*

Pola chose that inopportune moment to break off her toilette. Jumping down from the windowsill, she ambled over for a greeting. Max never could resist her any more than he could Jamie. As she brushed against his legs, defrosting that rigid countenance, as he bent to stroke her, I knew she'd accomplished what I never could.

When Marco, prowling my bookcase, knocked over a bright yellow plastic bird, I held my breath, tempted to wind it—to watch it dart all over the floor until it keeled over. *Something to keep you smiling.* I looked at Max. "Keep it with you at all times, you told me." He shrugged.

I gave it up. "Vigilantism is loose in the land," I said, a flat quotation from a recent headline. "You wanted to wrap this up fast?"

"Ah yes, the deal." He deserted the arm for the chair.

"Ignore the little people. Take out the leaders. If Rees meant what he said, tell him I can deliver—that I've cut off the head of the snake. You need visible leaders? Lee Emerson is one."

"Dr. James Coyne is another."

"Yes," I said, "Jamie."

"Any live ones?"

"Francis Xavier O'Neal, construction business. Earl 'Black Bart' Bartholemew, corrections officer. Kagan—no known first name. Ringleader," I said, and handed him Tony's handiwork: the only known photograph in existence. Everyman, captured, finally, by a camera.

"Proof?" he asked.

"Of Bartholemew and O'Neal. Also, the guy you said looked like a rodeo star—the man who turned that Legal Aid rally into a shooting gallery. Some others. In here," I said, handing him the proof right out of Kagan's little black box.

"And all the rest? Just little people?" Skepticism in those true-blue eyes.

"Not quite. It's all you're going to get, Max."

"Right," he said, pulling out a notebook. "Something for us, something for you." He made a note of it. "It's not enough."

"I know. I'm in a position to identify every VA cell in the country. A complete membership list." I took my time lighting a cigarette. "Since we don't really expect the FBI to trust the word of a bunch of lawbreakers and coconspirators, I'm authorized to offer you the list."

I saw a flicker in his eyes—the equivalent of, Now you're talking! "Since it's nowhere in evidence," he said, "I assume we're getting to the heart of the matter. The list, in return for what?"

"Complete immunity from prosecution for every member— every decent person—who wants out. Their numbers are considerable."

He wrote in his notebook. "How considerable?"

"Every cell leader has been contacted, some in person, the rest by phone. A solid majority, maybe as high as eighty, ninety percent, are ready to renounce their vigilante activities in favor of operating within the law. There are bound to be some holdouts, especially with Kagan still in circulation. Not many."

"But the list—"

"Would enable you to keep tabs on whoever has not gone to ground, make sure they live up to their end of the deal. Nobody likes living under glass, but I reminded them that far-flung surveillance costs money and manpower. The FBI can't keep it up forever."

"That it?"

"Not quite. Before you huddle with Rees, you should know I've stacked the deck against you. Every cell has—let's call it a blackmail box. Incriminating photographs of members 'making their bones.' " He nodded, familiar with the Mafia expression. "By now, every cell leader has destroyed that particular source of evidence. You won't be able to prove a thing against the 'little people.' "

"And without your list, we won't even be able to keep tabs." More notes. "If I were to tell you it's no deal—"

"I would have to tell you, when you asked, 'What list?' "

"Someone has been talking to a smart lawyer."

Someone named Zack.

He put his notebook away. "The little people," he said. "The good vigilante versus the bad. Nice euphemism."

"It happens to be true. Only a small percentage of the people I've met revel in the violence. The rest are victims . . . in more ways than one. It can permeate your life, vengeance. It can push the human qualities aside.". . . *Starting with me, Max.*

"Brings out the worst in you?" he said, making it sound like the cliché it was.

"Destroys the best. Wipe the blood of a killer off your hands and then go home and try to bake a cake, tuck in the kids—"

"Water the plants."

A meeting of the minds, of sorts. Was he good for another?

"There's something else Rees should know. Ninety percent of crime is handled locally, he said. But with every major failure on the part of the cops, every breakdown in the system, we hear cries for national solutions. Maybe the way to respond is through a national organization that works to keep things local—you know, arm people with facts and figures, offer them the strategy and skills they need to fight parole boards and politicians." I leaned forward, warming to the subject. "We could channel all those fragmented, disorganized efforts into a unified whole—the structure's already in place. We could build on the ruins of Victims Anonymous, with cells—let's call them chapters—in every major city. We could—"

"We?"

So there it was. Max, the company man, who would never cut corners. Not even for me, Jamie said. Especially not for me.

"A figure of speech," I said slowly. "The foundation exists. Any number of people can build on it. You want one more head on the block, Max? Will it cinch the deal if I cut myself out of it? Is that what you're waiting to hear?"

It was what he was waiting to hear. I saw it in his eyes.

"You'll hear from me." He stood up.

"How soon?"

"A week."

I went with him to the door. I saw the knob turn in his hand.

I saw it stop. That should have been signal enough, giving me plenty of time to close my eyes or turn away—flee into the next room. Jump out the window.

Rather than see what was happening to his face: a ghastly jigsaw puzzle, every feature cracking to pieces.

"Don't you know what it means—your 'deal'? What an agony of indecision? I loved you!"

I was glad I hadn't turned away, after all. Glad he had let me see what I had done to him.

It made the rest of what I had to do a little easier.

Chapter 40

I've never quite approved of Halloween. A morbid holiday under the best of circumstances. Under the worst . . . a recurring nightmare.

Still, it's a good excuse for a party or a celebration. Some of us had a lot to celebrate.

It had taken a week, just as Max promised. The message delivered to my apartment five days ago had said, "Offer accepted."

That wasn't all it said. Whether Karen Newman was or wasn't part of the deal was still "under consideration."

It went on, the agony of indecision.

For Max, not me.

"He hates you that much?" Zack had wondered aloud when the message arrived.

I looked at Angela. She knew better. "Max loves me that much," I'd told him. "Had I meant less to him—"

"I don't understand."

"It would be like letting himself off the hook. Now do you understand?"

We had falsely reassured the others. Tony, especially. So that tonight, people could drink their champagne with undiminished joy and heap extravagant praise on the chef and pass hugs and kisses around the table like party favors.

Only Zack was privy beforehand to my carefully constructed toast. Like the other toasts, it was unabashedly emotional, in keeping with the occasion. Unlike them, it singled out friends, one by one. The dead as well as the living.

Only in retrospect would it sound less like tribute and more like farewell.

Certainly Angela didn't tumble, happy to have Tony and the cats bunk in with her while I "got my act together."

Zack had insisted on taking me home. One look at the sky and I had insisted on walking.

We talked about Claudia. And Jamie . . . about the magnificent sky on the night he died. We talked about what might have been.

"I'm under investigation," he blurted out.

"Zack, I'm sorry. That young mounted policeman . . . ?"

"Not so naive as I thought. Don't worry. When the time comes, the department will look the other way. They could do without the publicity."

"When the time comes for what?"

"My resignation. It only feels like a death sentence."

I knew he didn't want me to look at him just then. I couldn't help it. I couldn't help thinking how well he wore his uniform.

"Sorry," he said for the tears he couldn't hide. "I didn't mean to lay it on you. You've paid the biggest price of all."

"Not from this. From last Halloween."

"The one thing I admire more than brains," he said softly, "is courage."

I shrugged. "The courage of my convictions?"

"Hell, no. You expect that of decent people. But the courage to change them? That's harder to come by."

He deposited me at my door with a single word. "Courage."

Had he sensed how much I needed to hear it?

I felt Jamie's presence in my apartment. I'd felt it all evening. Not surprising; Jamie was big on symbolism. "It's Halloween. I've come full circle, Jamie dear," I said softly.

I took him with me through my last-minute check of the living room . . . the bedroom . . . the den.

I lost him when I sat down at my desk to write my "Dear Max" letter. It began with "Forgive me." It ended with a poem.

In between, I released him from an awesome responsibility—a terrible choice—that should have been mine, not his, to bear. I asked him not to grieve, not to blame himself for the . . . consequences of my actions. I told him why.

*I think I knew all along that I would never make it past another
Halloween. That I found you in that year of borrowed time, that
we found each other, is more than I deserved. Think of me,
dearest, when you read these lines, as I will think of you. . . .*

> *Before our lives divide for ever,*
> *While time is with us and hands are free,*
> *(Time swift to fasten and swift to sever*
> *Hand from hand, as we stand by the sea)*
> *I will say no word that a man might say*
> *Whose whole life's love goes down in a day;*
> *For this could never have been; and never,*
> *Though the gods and the years relent,*
> *Shall be.*

Jamie was gone for me now. But Max . . . Max, I had to put
away. No room, now, for anything but the little things.

Swift, sure—precise. Time to take your medicine, Karen . . .
and go out on a pun.

Done. The empty bottle goes—where? In plain sight on my
night table, where a doctor would be sure to see it.

Forgive me, Roger, but an offer's an offer. I'm taking you up on
it. Will Max remember you, I wonder? A man he met, once, at a
funeral? The doctor who belonged to a gun club?

Susie's funeral, not Sarah's. Not mine.

Too many funerals.

Time to lie down.

Is it? Not quite. Not until the wallpaper starts to swim.

It's swimming.

Don't wait too long. Pick up the phone and—dial. If you
should . . . need me, call. I'm calling you, Roger, I'm calling—

"Roger? Quickly! I . . . need you. Oh God, I—I need Max."

It was slipping away . . . phone . . . wallpaper . . .

Me.

6

CATHARSIS

Purge me with hyssop and I
shall be clean; wash me, and I
shall be whiter than snow.

—Psalm
51:7

Epilogue

National Victims Rights Week dawned on a ho-hum Monday in mid-April. Insiders were saying it promised to be even better than last year. Of the many and diverse groups that took to the podium this day at the behest of some obliging governor or besieged mayor confronting high crime statistics, only one organization sent the hot-copy boys all across the country scrambling for ringside seats.

The Houston chapter created the biggest stir. A convention-sized gathering sat before a giant television monitoring screen, a sense of expectancy mingling with the air-conditioning. Cameras flashed as a pert woman walked with brisk authority to the podium.

"Some folks launch missiles, not advertisin' campaigns," she began without ceremony. "But like our good neighbors in Pennsylvania, we Texans are partial to the notion that self-defense begins at home." The lights dimmed to thunderous applause. "We thank the Pennsylvania legislature for its good example," her voice went on. "We thank every one of you whose private contributions paid for what you're about to see. Let's keep it comin' in, folks. This is just the beginnin' for get-tough laws in Texas!"

The screen filled up with the silhouette of an armed thug, caught off guard by a warning voice. *"Go ahead. Blow away five years of your life—five years! Commit your next crime with a gun."*

The beautiful blonde from Baltimore, they called her. For the second year in a row, she presided over Operation Swampum.

She was quick to remind reporters that an annual dose of national consciousness-raising was a fine idea, but they should note that this sort of thing went on all year long. Duly noted. "Our job," she told them, a touch of mischief in her smile, "is to swamp 'em even more than last year. Your job is to keep tabs."

The press kept tabs as best they could. Radio call-in shows throughout the state of Maryland. Petitions that landed simultaneously on the desks of mayors, legislators, district attorneys, a first-term governor. Solidarity marches and candlelight vigils. "Get the message across, please," she'd urged.

The message was the same everywhere: Fight crime.

"And don't leave out the particulars."

The list of particulars was long. Give victims and their families a right to be heard at sentencing and parole hearings. Give violent juveniles fixed detention periods in locked facilities. Keep computerized conviction records for repeat offenders. Keep rearrested felons off our streets by removing the authority of judges to set low bail. Make the neighborhood cop a routine presence, using police cadets and specially trained civilians.

Pennsylvania drew a crowd second only to Houston; no refreshments were being served after the show. "Electioneering in April, for Chrissake?" sniffed a cub crime reporter for the *Philadelphia Inquirer.* But his skepticism was not shared by his more experienced colleagues, who knew a good political ploy when they saw one. "One spring preview coming up," someone quipped. True, only a handful of judges were into the last year of their terms, with reelection campaigns looming in the fall. But every one of their colleagues, who had reelection in their future, could read the writing on the wall, and the Philadelphia chapter had writ large.

Legislators already were being lobbied on determinate sentencing. Judges partial to lenient sentences for heinous crimes could look forward to the intense scrutiny of Operation Spotlight. "If Americans for Democratic Action rate congressmen on the environment," a pug-faced hardhat put it to the cub reporter, "why can't we rate judges on crime, can you tell me?" He couldn't tell him.

Lobbying the legislature in Lansing brought out more scandal sheets than skeptics—not surprising if you'd followed the morning headlines. MICHIGAN'S FIRST LADY TO DEFY GUV ON DEATH PENALTY!

Predictably, the press turned into paparazzi as the speaker mounted the steps of the capitol: a cool-looking, tough-minded redhead who had sworn allegiance to a national victims-rights organization as well as her own conscience even as her husband, in the name of his, had year after year defied the voice of the people and his own legislature. Her statement, brief but delivered with passion, had a single theme: Override the veto.

In North Carolina, people were talking excitedly about "a first" for their state. People were crowding around a tall black woman with a striking figure and onyx eyes.

"See that guy?" she was saying. "There, the one with the beard." She pointed out one of her colleagues. "He'll give you the details. I've got a plane to catch."

But the press dogged her all the way to the airport. With twenty minutes to spare before boarding, she relented long enough to sum up Operation Watchdog.

"The idea is to fill our courtrooms and legislative chambers with monitors—crime victims, most of them, though that's changing fast. More people are volunteering because they don't want to *become* a victim. We'll be checking out every stage of the criminal-justice process throughout the state. . . . A parting shot? Plea bargaining is top priority. . . . Why? Because the other side of that coin is accountability—the lawyer's as much as the criminal's. And you can go tell *that* to the judge."

Sulette's plane was on time. It was the usual New York traffic (a nasty tie-up at the Queens-Midtown Tunnel) that made her late for her midafternoon meeting in Manhattan.

She shook her head over the modest West Thirties brownstone, where so much was being done for so many. Not that the organization lacked funds for classier headquarters and a fancy address. They had better use for their money, or so Hugh kept telling her.

The real class act, she thought, going inside, was the board of directors—the four that were permanent. Rotating chapter heads (of which, happily, she was one) made up the others; a real nice bunch.

"—response exceeded my projections. Hell, my wildest expectations," Hugh was saying. "It means no money problems next year."

"Thanks be to you. Coffee's still hot, Sulette."

She acknowledged the Chair with a smile.

"Recruitment is next on the agenda. Lydia?"

"The revised training kit is in the mail. We could use some solid activists in the Southwest chapters. New membership is way up in the big cities—some of it high visibility. Say, how *about* that lady from Lansing!"

"A toast to the wives of politicians who rise above politics!"

"The coffee is *not* still hot," Sulette announced.

Rosa Ramirez offered to make a fresh pot.

"Report on the career criminal. Any encouraging words, Zack?"

"The pilot programs in New York and Boston are showing good results. Speedy trials. Harsh penalties for the hard cores."

"How can we bring in more states?" Angela said, frowning.

"Hit them over the head with a statistic," Zack said dryly. "Seven percent of our criminals commit one-fourth of our crime."

"Statistic, hell," said the Chair. "It will make a great slogan. We'll use it. Anyone object if I leapfrog to next year's agenda? I'm out of here in ten minutes. I have a train to meet before I take off for the Denver rally."

"Determinate sentencing," Zack said.

"What about it?"

"Put it at the top of the agenda. A dozen states have some form of it. Only a dozen. I say we go the Pennsylvania route and push Operation Spotlight for all it's worth."

"Sentencing isn't our biggest problem," Angela said. "Let's say the judges get religion and clean up their act. What then?"

"Jail space . . . the toughest nut to crack," Zack muttered, acknowledging her point.

"Private enterprise is part of the answer," Sulette said. "They're shaving costs like you wouldn't believe."

"And they're not the only game in town. You put army authorization on the agenda," Zack told the Chair, "and I'll work overtime on that baby. Think of the jail cells you can fashion out of surplus military installations."

"Hasn't some government commission just proposed that scores of military bases be closed?" Rosa asked. "Wouldn't the corrections people in this country go bananas over all those empty barracks!"

"Okay, sentencing and prison space go on the list. Anything else?"

"How about a toast before you go—this one with brandy." Zack smiled. "It's been a good year and a half. It's going to get better."

Sulette went for the brandy.

Angela poured.

"To Victims Watch!"

Voices raised in unison. Good brandy.

It called for another toast. "To a really dedicated board of directors," Sulette said. "So dedicated you guys are practically invisible. Isn't it time to drop the low profile and become prominent national leaders?"

"I hope it will never be time for that," said the Chair.

"Why? Leaders inspire. Good ones, anyway."

"Strong ones can inspire weakness. Remind me to introduce you to one of my all-time favorite movies next time you're in town. Oppressed Mexican villagers, liberated by their charismatic leader. Only after he's killed by the enemy do they learn how to fight for themselves. It's the only lasting strength."

"I stand corrected, Mrs. Ramirez, but only if I can revise my toast. Here's to the mind, heart and soul of this organization. Here's to you, my friend."

"Here, here!"

Eleven glasses raised high. Eleven people on their feet.

"Damn," said the Chair. "There goes the eye makeup."

Sulette laughed. "Good thing you're partial to dark glasses."

She left Zack in charge, Sulette second-in-command, and race-walked to her apartment—her only form of exercise, these days. She gave herself five minutes to pack; under real pressure, she could do it in three. On the way out, she remembered to hit her answering machine for messages.

There was no denying the urgency in the cryptic message of the last caller. *Come to the office. Right away.*

She checked her watch and made a mental calculation. "Right away" would have to be right after Penn Station.

She got there just as his train pulled in. This was the way they liked to meet each other. On the platform of a train station. At the airport gate.

He had done the expected adolescent thing, she thought, letting the sight of him warm her even as it brought tears to her eyes. He had shot up like Jack's beanstalk in the last six months. *Don't grow up too fast, please. . . .*

They moved toward each other.

"Mrs. Ramirez." The ritual greeting. Big grin.

"And son."

They walked arm in arm, indifferent to the ebb and flow of the crowd.

"How was Washington?"

"Full of fascinating things to do and no time to do them."

"Are you sorry about using up vacation time on VW business?"

"No way. It's not every day you get to be a star."

She laughed. "I take it things went well. Give me a play-by-play. Come on, Tony, you promised."

He described his testimony before a congressional committee. The press conference afterward. The kids he'd met, some from chapters as far away as Portland and San Diego. "Subchapters," he corrected himself, beaming with the pride befitting the president of the newly formed Juvenile Division of Victims Watch.

"Want company to the airport?" he asked as she hailed a cab.

"Don't bother. I have a stop to make first. I'll be back—"

"Karen, I saw him. He was at the press conference."

She closed her eyes fast. Saw what she always saw—the color of his: cornflower blue. And the shape, the narrowed squint.

She said, "He looks the same? Older?" she pressed when Tony hesitated.

"Tired. He asked me about VW. I gave him some stuff."

Tony opened the door of the cab, making it easier for her to move, to get in. "I'll call you from Denver," she said and blew him a kiss.

She gave the driver Roger's address. And kept her eyes closed all the way downtown.

The urgency in Roger's voice came back to her in a rush when his nurse, ignoring the frowns and murmurs of a full waiting room, ushered her right in.

Roger dispensed with his usual greeting—a bear hug—in favor of runaway questions.

"Why would he call me? Why, after—what, almost two years? Why, all of a sudden, is he coming here to talk? About what?"

"Who?" she gasped. "When?" Panic can be contagious.

"Max McCann, who else? This afternoon, he's coming! Karen, I signed your death certificate. What if you bump into each other on the street?"

"Not today we won't," she said, sinking into a chair. "I'm on my way to Denver."

"What do we do now? What are you thinking?"

She was thinking that Zack and Angela were wrong; it got harder, not easier. To think of him in Washington was one thing. To think of him here, sitting in this chair . . .

She said, "Don't panic, Rog. He doesn't suspect anything—he can't."

"Can we go over it again? Just in case?"

He sat tugging at his beard while they went over it, the ruse that had worked on a Halloween night . . .

A call (prearranged) to a doctor friend—a panicky change of heart. *I swallowed sleeping pills, a whole bottle. Help me! Call my love, call Max!*

Dr. Roger Stern rushing to the scene. Checking things out. Beating Max McCann to her place by a safe margin.

Gently escorting Max to the bedroom to see for himself. Empty pill bottle on the night table (contents flushed down the toilet).

To feel for himself. No pulse, no respiration. Inject yourself with "naloxone"—morphine—and sleep the sleep of the dead.

A suicide note, read with a steady hand and a rigid countenance. Then useless words; impossible to comfort a man in shock.

An "official" call by one Zachary Gray, cop still in uniform.

A death certificate, prelude to a funeral.

A weighted coffin ringed with genuine mourners—a doctor and a policeman friend excepted. The FBI in attendance.

From that day forward, it had meant the underground life. A permanent hair shirt.

With two consolations. Tony, and work.

Roger interrupted her reverie; he said, "I was so afraid you wouldn't come out of it."

"Risky business, injecting yourself with—how many milligrams of morphine?"

"Twenty. Even with the best antidote to narcotic overdose burning a hole in my pocket, I was afraid," he said, remembering.

"With at least two hours to counteract the morphine?"

"What can I tell you? I'm a worrier."

"At this point, so am I. Roger, I *have* to stay dead for him."

"Go to Denver," he told her, patting her hand, calm descending on them both. "I'll take care of our FBI friend."

She rode to the airport on memory lane, putting it behind her in the usual way. . . .

> For this could never have been; and never,
> Though the gods and the years relent,
> Shall be.

"Drink up, McCann! When the Bureau springs for Dom Perignon, it's an occasion."

"Even when the occasion is the birthday of an over-the-hill agent, right Moxie Maxie?"

Even a drunken sod could hit the nail on the head, McCann thought. He put in his time, feeling nothing except the need, like a knot in his stomach, to get out.

To get to New York.

He tuned out shop talk and inane chatter with thoughts of a press conference. He had gone less out of curiosity than of pain and a dim sense of loyalty. Victims Watch was an idea whose time had come . . . and the idea had been Karen's. But seeing that boy with the big, dark eyes had been a shocker. Would he ever blot out the funeral? Would he ever forget a single grieving face?

He had approached the boy with curiosity, nothing more. And sensed more than politeness on his part—and less than a hard sell, when the kid had loaded him down with literature.

He knew, now, that what he'd sensed was purpose. He knew it as soon as he had started to leaf through the material.

Leaf through? He had read every word. Read and reread until his eyes burned from the effort and the small print.

She was alive.

There it was on every page, every line: her mind at work, her way of putting things, her inimitable—

There it was in his hand: hard evidence of his insanity.

But how could he deny what every fiber in his being told him was true?

He went through the motions—meaningless good-byes, most of them. Most, not all. Bernie Rees waited by the door.

"Leaving us, are you? About time, don't you think?"

"Is that your way of saying birthday boys should be the last to go home?"

"It's my way of saying that I see another party in your future, one I'd be proud to host."

"My retirement," he said with a rueful smile. "Saw it coming, did you?"

"That press conference yesterday. Can you guess what I saw when you walked into my office afterward? Hope, Max. Maybe even deliverance. I just wanted you to know, before you go off on your . . . minivacation to Manhattan, that I wish you well."

He had to look away.

"Go and retire in peace, my good friend," he said, a priest giving his blessing. "Whatever you do, whoever you decide to do it with—" A small shrug. "It's your own affair, isn't it?"

He thought about that on the plane. Bernard Rees, the man who never missed a trick. He should have known the old beagle would sniff the truth out of his whitewash report. . . . And then bury all of his unasked questions like discarded bones.

In the cab taking him to the office of Dr. Roger Stern, he thought about Jamie. About time he retired, Rees had said.

. . . *About time I found myself another home,* he told the man who had saved his life, the friend who had left him with an emptiness he had no way of filling.

He found Dr. Stern less edgy than when they'd talked on the phone. But much too pat in his answers to careful questions.

In the end, he had spotted cracks in the veneer; the man was too nervous to be telling the truth. Wasn't he?

The boy was the living truth, he told himself. Tony Ramirez had dropped more than an armful of victims'-rights literature on him. He dug in his pocket for the kid's address.

And brought out more than a piece of paper. One stale People Cracker. . . . *Washington's stray-cat population owes you a debt,* he told her, the sense of her physical presence growing with every measured step.

He studied the brownstone's shabby facade. The puny excuse for a tree, with a few pathetic buds. The stoop that people sat on when the sticky heat of summer drove them out of their rooms.

He rang the bell. With every passing second he felt her presence slipping away from him.

In desperation he rang another bell. Apartment three-A, facing front, the super told him. Kid's out. So's the mother. Puerto Rican lady. Travels a lot.

The mother.

He turned away, numbed by the death knell of a hopeless dream, fumbling for his handkerchief.

Something made him turn. The poem in his heart? A last look at what might have been?

Three-A, facing front. *Think of me, dearest, when you read these lines, as I will think of you.* As . . . I . . . will . . . think?

He saw her then, stretched out on a windowsill that warmed to the rays of an afternoon sun, one grey-orange leg languorously extended for grooming.

He saw everything.

He sat down on the stoop to wait.

About the Author

Erika Holzer is a novelist, journalist and lawyer, whose first novel was the human-rights espionage drama, *Double Crossing*. A New Yorker for most of her life, she has just moved, with her lawyer husband, to Santa Fe, New Mexico.